Praise for Charl

From the W[...]

"[N]onstop action and vivid depictions of the wilderness keeps the pages turning...[A] satisfying diversion."—*Publishers Weekly*

"I enjoyed this one very much. I thought the cast of characters were really interesting. Anything queer, supernatural, and survival horror is going to catch my attention 100%. This kept it throughout...Action packed. Queer. Survivalist horror. It hit a lot of my marks."—*Raychel Bennet, Librarian (Bullitt County Public Library)*

"Greene is an accomplished writer and she's able to ratchet up the suspense extremely well—whether it's a slow mounting sense of danger as the heroines find more and more things 'off' or the race through the forest with god knows who or what chasing them down. This is a book that will grab you and drag you along. It was hard to put it down (at 1am) but I didn't want to continue reading when I was tired and miss stuff."—*To Be Read Reviews*

Legacy

"Greene does a good job of building suspense as the story unfolds. Strange things happen one by one in increasingly spooky fashion. Background information is revealed a little bit at a time and makes you want to try and solve the mystery...I recommend this to those who like to read about hauntings, nature, history, DIY home maintenance, violent husbands, scary things in the woods, and water."—*Bookvark*

"The characters are well developed, and Greene hit just the right amount of tension between them...I rarely like every character in a book, but I loved the whole group. The creepiness never let up, the tension built steadily, and...things escalated rapidly. The ending was very satisfying! Horror is definitely Greene's forte."—*Bookish Sort*

"This is a wonderfully scary paranormal novel. The setting is perfect and well described. The characters are well-drawn and likable. The romance between Jo and Andy is especially charming and fits perfectly into the tale. This is just a wonderful story, and I'm so glad I read it, even in the middle of the night. If you love a good scary story, I believe you will love it too."—*Rainbow Reflections*

"Greene likes to take her time to work up the suspense, starting with smaller and seemingly inconsequential things that build up a suitably creepy atmosphere. Placing the characters in an isolated setting ratchets things up. This isn't a gore-fest nor is it relying on jump-scares to set the atmosphere—instead it's a well paced ghost story with strongly developed characters."—*C-Spot Reviews*

"Greene does a great job of establishing a creepy atmosphere by setting a rather slow (but not overly so) pace, taking the necessary time to describe the woods, the uncared-for cabin, the ominous well from the cover, the sounds, the smells, the weather and temperatures."—*Jude in the Stars*

"Very fun horror story that just touches on the creep factor without going full blown scary. There's a lot of really good elements to the book, from the menacing spook, to the mystery, and even the relationship…Great work!"—*Colleen Corgel, Librarian, Queens Public Library*

Gnarled Hollow

"Greene has done an outstanding job of weaving in all sorts of layers; mysterious patterns in the gardens, missing rooms, odd disappearances, blandly boring journals, unknown artwork, and each mystery is eventually revealed as part of the horrific whole. Combined with intensely emotional descriptions of the fear the characters experience as they are targeted by the tortured spirit and this book is genuinely a page turner…not only could I not sleep after reading it, I didn't want to put it down."—*Lesbian Reading Room*

"*Gnarled Hollow* by Charlotte Greene is an awesome supernatural thriller that will terrify and entertain you for hours on end."—*The Lesbian Review*

"*Gnarled Hollow* is a creepy mystery story that had me gripped from the start. There was layer upon layer of mystery and plenty that I didn't see coming at all."—*Kitty Kat's Book Review Blog*

"Scared myself to death, but hauntingly beautiful! Had my heart beating at rapid speeds and my mind working overtime with this thought-provoking story. Piecing together the mystery of *Gnarled Hollow* was both fascinating and scary as hell. It takes talent to put that much suspense and thrill into words that build the picture so vividly, painting descriptions that you can imagine perfectly and see as you read."
—*LESBIreviewed*

"I really enjoyed this. This is the fifth book I have read by Greene and by far my favorite. It had some good twists and kept me in suspense until the end. In fact, I was a little sad when it ended. This would be a perfect book to read around Halloween time…I would absolutely recommend this to paranormal-crime/mystery fans. I really hope Greene takes the opportunity to write more books in similar genres. I would love to read them if she does. 5 stars."—*Lez Review Books*

A Palette for Love

"The relationship really works between the main characters, and the sex is steamy but not over the top."—*Amanda's Reviews*

Pride and Porters

"Have you ever wondered how *Pride and Prejudice* would work if it were two women falling in love with a brewery as a backdrop? Well, wonder no more!…All in all, I would say this is up near the top on my list of favorite *Pride and Prejudice* adaptations."—*Amanda Brill, Librarian, Rowan Public Library (North Carolina)*

"Greene's charming retelling of *Pride and Prejudice* transplants the Bennets into the world of Colorado craft beer…The story beats are comfortingly familiar, with the unusual backdrop of brewing and beer competitions, modern setting, and twists on the characters providing enough divergence to keep the reader engaged…Feminism, lesbianism, and class are all touched on in this refreshing update on a classic. (Starred review)"—*Publishers Weekly*

"*Pride and Porters* by Charlotte Greene is a contemporary take on the classic romance novel *Pride and Prejudice*, by Jane Austen. Greene works within the framework of Austen's novel and owns it with her particular blend of attraction, money, and intrigue as the women journey towards Happily-Ever-After. While the original focused on the struggles of English women to attain financial and social security through marriage, Greene shows women for whom love and partner compatibility aren't simply happy bonuses. Readers will appreciate the ratcheting drama, character chemistry, and thawing emotions in this modern-day retelling."—*Omnivore Bibliosaur*

By the Author

A Palette for Love

Love in Disaster

Canvas for Love

Pride and Porters

Gnarled Hollow

Legacy

On the Run

From the Woods

The Wedding Setup

Visit us at www.boldstrokesbooks.com

THE
WEDDING SETUP

by

Charlotte Greene

2022

THE WEDDING SETUP

ISBN 13: 978-1-63679-033-6

This Trade Paperback Original Is Published By
Bold Strokes Books, Inc.
P.O. Box 249
Valley Falls, NY 12185

First Edition: January 2022

CREDITS
EDITOR: SHELLEY THRASHER
PRODUCTION DESIGN: STACIA SEAMAN
COVER DESIGN BY TAMMY SEIDICK

Acknowledgments

Because I grew up in Loveland, Colorado, I grew up thinking Valentine's Day was a much bigger deal than it is in other places. Imagine my surprise and dismay when it occurred to me that the holiday celebrations, at least at the scale I knew, were very localized.

While the giant wooden hearts are a real deal, and the remailing program is world-famous, and the beautiful sculpture foundries are real, and Loveland has seen a number of Valentine's Day festivals come and go, much of what you'll read here is an exaggeration, or, possibly, a fantasy. I think Loveland could be the major Valentine's Day destination in the U.S. with someone like Maddie to shepherd the city into a unified effort.

That said, it's absolutely worthwhile visiting around Valentine's Day (or any other time of year). If you like beer, Loveland Aleworks has some of the best in the world.

For my one and only valentine. I love you, honey.

CHAPTER ONE

R yann threw the doors to the boardroom open, one of them swinging so hard and wide it slammed into the wall. Normally she'd let one of her assistants open them for her, but she was on such a high after that meeting, she didn't think of it. And anyway, opening her own doors had a dramatic effect. She couldn't be sure without turning around, but she thought her board members watched her leave, mouths hanging stupidly open.

Her assistants were scrambling to catch up, Ted scurrying to her left, clutching her coffee and leather portfolio, Gloria to her right, trying to manage a pile of papers she carried despite their speed.

The three of them turned from the hall into the bullpen, the large central room with open cubicles most of her employees shared. They almost instantly hushed at the sight of her. Several of them blanched and sat down at their desks, whatever they'd been talking about or doing forgotten. She couldn't help but smile. Her triumph from the meeting was too perfect, too glorious to dim. She acknowledged a few with a quick tilt of her head, their surprise evident as they stood there gaping.

"Open," she told Ted, indicating her office doors with her chin. He ran to get there before her, throwing them wide just in time for her to waltz through. Gloria slammed the door behind the three of them, sending the papers in her hands sailing everywhere. Her face drained of color, but Ryann was too happy to chastise her.

"Oh my *God*," Ted said, positively beaming. "That was the most impressive thing I've ever seen."

"Wasn't it?"

He set her coffee and portfolio down on her desk and held out his hands, as if in defeat. "You absolutely *killed* them."

Ryann pretended to polish her fingernails on her blazer, blowing on them before giving him her biggest grin. "I did, didn't I? I fucking nailed them."

They looked at Gloria for confirmation, but she was still collecting the papers she'd dropped, scatterbrained and out of it, as always. Some of her hair had come loose from her bun, and her clothes were wrinkled and sweaty. Ryann frowned slightly, but Ted caught her attention again.

"You reamed them, Ryann."

He was the only employee allowed to call her by her first name. They were relatively friendly, or at least he was—she didn't like talking about herself at work or with colleagues, but she liked hearing about his life, which was far more colorful than her own. She opened her arms, surprising him, and after hesitating, he launched himself into the hug. They jumped up and down a few times, giggling and clutching each other before she remembered where and who she was and stopped.

Gloria had finally finished gathering what she'd dropped and deposited the messy, uneven pile on Ryann's desk. Her annoyance at the unseemly sight must have shown, as Gloria paled again.

"You can leave now," Ryann said, only just managing not to snap at her. "Please check with the girl in reception…" She didn't remember her name. "Anyway, see if she has any messages for me."

"Jessica," Ted offered.

"Yes. Check with Jessica."

Gloria dropped briefly into what seemed remarkably like a curtsey, before leaving them alone, closing the door much too loudly in her wake.

Ryann rolled her eyes. "I don't know about her, Ted. She's really not fitting in here."

"Who, Gloria? She's great! And I don't just say that because I hired her. She's efficient, a hard worker, and smart. You just don't see her at her best."

"Hmm." Ryann walked over to her coffee and took a careful sip. "And why is that?"

Ted laughed. "You scare her."

Ryann laughed. "I scare her? So I should want to keep her on?"

Ted shrugged. "Everyone here is scared of you, Ryann, even me, sometimes. Don't pretend you don't love it."

Ryann lifted a shoulder, turning back to her desk. Behind it, the city shone in the morning light, surprisingly bright despite the thick cloud cover. She'd chosen this office suite entirely because of the view from this room. Ten years ago, she'd used her start-up money to rent this office and part of what was now the bullpen. As her business grew, it had taken up first this entire floor, then the next, then most of the next three floors. Over the years, various business partners and her board had suggested that she move her office to a bigger, more impressive room upstairs. She'd declined, happy to see this sight out her floor-to-ceiling windows for the rest of her career, however much she'd outgrown this space.

She walked closer to the windows, staring down the many stories to the busy road below, following the line of cars and cabs to a slivered glimpse of Central Park to her right. It had snowed last night, leaving a long expanse of white and frost-crusted trees dappled with early morning light. She imagined she could smell the candied nuts from a stand there at that corner, the owner probably just setting up for the day. She pictured herself there, buying a sleeve of honeyed pecans and a cup of bad coffee and then walking until she was either too cold or too tired to keep going. She hadn't been to the park in weeks, maybe even months. It was her favorite place in the entire world, yet she couldn't remember the last time she'd been, despite how close it was to work and her apartment. Assembling today's proposal had eaten her whole life.

When she turned around, Ted was biting his lip. She had to fight to remember what they'd been talking about.

"You think I love having people scared of me?" she asked him.

He laughed, clearly relieved. "Of course you do."

Actually, she didn't care one way or another. She didn't try to intimidate people, and she certainly wasn't as cruel as some of the other CEOs she knew. Still, it never hurt to have a distinct line between herself and her employees, and she didn't allow familiarities from anyone on her staff except Ted. Even he didn't cross that line too far, always waiting for her lead. He also didn't ask personal questions, despite the leeway she gave him.

"Let's talk about the timeline on the proposal again." She gestured at a chair behind him.

He sat, pulling out his tablet and flipping open the cover. She leaned back onto the front of her desk, half sitting, tapping her teeth with a polished nail.

"Okay, so Hong Kong and Tokyo are ready right now, Dubai will be available at the end of February, and San Francisco, Sydney, and LA should be set by then, too. What about London?"

Ted scrolled a little. "Not until the middle of March."

Ryann cursed. "Unacceptable. We need them to move that up. See if we can get them to agree to February—even late that month would be better than March. Tell them everyone else is ready or has agreed to February. That might put some fire under their ass."

Ted made a note and nodded.

"Do we have any other outliers?" she asked.

He scrolled and then shook his head. "No. It's only London. Everyone else is on board for now or some time in February."

The slightest delay for some of these companies could make the whole deal collapse. When she'd sprung this massive partnership agreement on her board today, she realized if she couldn't pull the whole thing together quickly, they would force her to back out or let one of the bigger companies take over. She'd surprised and totally flummoxed them with the amount of money their company stood to make. The returns would be astronomical for everyone involved, but especially for a relatively smaller firm like theirs—ten to twenty times their usual profit on a marketing deal. Still, what she'd proposed would tie up most of the assets of her company to pull off. But it was worth the risk.

She could probably lose almost any other city, but London was too important to cut out. She *had* to have them on board and soon.

"Okay. That's your job. I want pressure on London nonstop. Get as many people as you can on this. Get LA involved if you have to. I want London falling over themselves to make this work for us. Do whatever you can to get them to agree to February."

"Even if it means a trip over there?"

She grimaced. London in January—yuck. "If I have to, yes. But maybe we can send some of the old men over there instead." She meant her board. "London might find them more impressive."

"Than the CEO?"

She sighed. "Okay. If it means sealing the deal, I'll go. Use the old men first. Set up a meeting in London for them as soon as possible."

"Yes, ma'am." He leapt to his feet.

"And Ted?"

"What?"

"Thank you. I couldn't have done this without you."

He blushed to the tips of his ears, almost grinning. "Thanks. I won't let you down."

As he left, Gloria returned with a clutch of wrinkled message slips.

"Took you long enough," Ryann said, taking them from her.

Gloria paled. "I'm sorry, Ms. Sands. John from—"

"I don't need excuses. Be quicker next time."

She visibly relaxed. However, she continued to stand there, lips working on themselves nervously as she tried to speak.

"Yes? What is it?" Ryann asked.

"Y-you told Jessica to tell you anytime your friend Stuart called. Jessica wanted me to tell you that he did this morning. More than once."

Ryann's chest squeezed, and she waved at the door. "Yes, Gloria. Thanks for letting me know. You can leave now."

She almost ran from the room, and Ryann riffled through the pile of messages she held. Stuart's name appeared once, twice, three, four times. It was only nine in the morning here, and his calls had started coming almost an hour ago. That meant he'd called at what, six or six thirty his time?

She picked up her desk phone, her fingers hovering over the keys, and then set it back in its cradle. Her hand was starting to shake, and she balled it into a fist, turning to the window and crossing her arms tight across her chest.

A little over two years ago, her friend Stuart had moved to Colorado. Despite the distance, their friendship hadn't stumbled at all the first six months he'd lived there. They'd split the costs of his flights to New York once or twice a month, and he usually stayed with her for the whole weekend. They'd go dancing on Friday, have a long, gossipy, all-day mimosa brunch and a boozy dinner together on Saturday, and he'd fly home again on Sunday. In fact, they saw each other more during his first months in Colorado than they ever had when he'd lived here.

At the beginning of his time there, Stuart had been something of a wreck, terrified he'd made a big mistake moving, missing his friends and the nightlife in New York. She'd had to hold back an "I told you so" every time she saw him. Then, almost overnight, he'd started getting caught up in his new life. His career had taken off, and he was busier than ever. And not just busy—happy, excited even.

At first, the changes had been subtle. One weekend trip was switched for a later one—no big deal. Then the trips became less frequent—once a month, then every other month, then every third. Then, late last spring, they stopped altogether. The weekly phone calls had also gotten less frequent, until sometimes a whole month would pass without them catching up one way or another. Still, they'd managed to keep their friendship on life support through social media, and he'd met her in San Francisco for the Fourth of July weekend a little over six months ago. That, however, had been the last time they'd talked in depth. Ever since, they'd been missing each other altogether when they did try, or managing, at best, a five-minute chat here and there.

This wasn't entirely his fault. She'd been incredibly busy all autumn and early winter, and without him around, pestering her to leave the office, she'd allowed herself to overwork. She'd occasionally seen his calls and tried to return them, but with the different times zones and her extremely late hours, they simply hadn't managed to sync up for a long conversation, and they hadn't talked at all in over two months.

Still, she'd tried harder than he had. He hadn't even attempted to contact her for a few weeks now. She'd managed to suppress her disappointment with her busyness, but his behavior still hurt and, she realized now, angered her. He'd basically abandoned her.

Someone knocked on the door, and she spun, startled.

"Come!" she shouted.

Gloria and Jessica entered, followed by several more administrative assistants and interns, all of them carrying vases of flowers. People behind them continued to stream through the door, dropping off vases before rushing out again, seeming terrified of her reaction. She, however, watched this parade happen in stunned silence. Gloria held back, her eyes dark and worried, until the two of them were alone.

The vases were enormous, all tied with large, silk ribbons. Each was filled with different arrangements of roses and hydrangeas, all red, all gaudy. Altogether, the flowers covered nearly every surface of her office, their scent heavy and heady in this small room.

"This card came with the flowers," Gloria said, handing it to her.

"Thank you. You can leave now."

Gloria practically fled again, slamming the door.

The card was in a thick, creamy envelope lined with velum— heavy, substantial, and soft. She tended to choose exactly this kind of paper—impressive without being tacky, solid, dignified, but also beautiful. She didn't even have to open it to know who'd sent it.

Inside was a simple card with bold, thick script.

Please Forgive Me.

Love Stuart

Tears sprang to her eyes, and she shook her head, dismissing them, trying to retain her earlier anger. The flowers were ridiculous. He knew her tastes ran to the simple and elegant, not the ostentatious, and this display was exactly that.

Her hands were shaking again when she picked up her office phone, and she struggled to remember how to use it. She needed to push a number for an outside line and couldn't recall what it was. Normally, she connected through the front desk, but this was a personal call, and that would be unprofessional.

"Shit, shit, shit," she said, her hands shaking even harder. She slammed the phone down and jumped up, breathing hard. This emotion was strange, overwhelming. The rage was there again, but it was at war with something else now—sadness, happiness? She couldn't explain it to herself.

Her personal cell phone was somewhere in this room, and she couldn't remember the last time she'd even used it.

Suddenly her office phone rang. She squared her shoulders, took a deep breath, and picked it up.

"Yes?" She tried to convey every bit of her anger in that one word.

"There's my beautiful lady," Stuart replied.

She sighed, sitting down in her chair hard, almost collapsing. She could stay angry at the idea of him, but hearing his voice was something else. Still, that hurt was there.

"You can't buy me off, Stuart."

He laughed. "You don't like the flowers?"

"You know I don't. You did this to piss me off even more. It worked."

He laughed again, braying nearly, and she couldn't help her own amusement. But she wouldn't let him win—not yet, anyway.

Stuart, as if sensing her train of thought, sounded a little chastised when he spoke again. "Can we be serious?"

"Please." Her anger was rising again.

"I've been a complete ass. I know I have, and you don't even need to make me feel bad, since I already do. I was checking my phone yesterday when I was going to call you and realized that you'd tried to get in touch six times last month. You even called me on Christmas, which is the saddest thing ever, by the way. I'm a shit for missing that. Anyway, guess how many times I called you back?"

"Not once," Ryann said.

"Exactly. I'm sorry, Ryann. I really am. What I did was inexcusable. The flowers might be kind of a joke, but I did want to show you how sorry I am for what I did—well, didn't do."

She was quiet again, suddenly overwhelmed and almost choking on sorrow and rage. Christmas had been a low point. It was a terrible day for her every year, and she'd wanted to hear at least one friendly voice. When he'd lived in town, the two of them got drunk together and watched bad musicals all day, singing along and making fun of each other, screaming and laughing to the point of hoarseness. The year before last, they'd been apart but had managed a version of their ritual via videoconference. This year, she'd been entirely alone. She'd gotten very, very drunk and cried herself to sleep. That had been almost four weeks ago, and she hadn't tried to call him since.

Again, as if sensing her train of thought, he didn't make her respond. "But hey, listen," he said. "I hope what I tell you next will go a little way toward explaining what happened."

"Uh-huh," she managed, blinking rapidly. The last thing she needed to do was cry at work, and she'd almost done that twice now.

"Okay, hon—you better be sitting down." There was a long, dramatic pause. "I'm getting married."

She jumped up, her wheeled desk chair flying into the windows behind her. "You're what?!"

He laughed. "I'm getting married, you old fag hag, and I want you to be my maid of honor!"

"Hold the fuck on—to whom? Who the hell would marry you?"

He laughed again. "Do you remember me mentioning this guy I met last year about this time—Jai?"

She tried to recall. He dated so many men, it was hard to keep up. Still, she had a vague memory of this one. Jai worked for the city Stuart lived in now, if she remembered correctly, which was unlike Stuart's usual beaus. He normally refused to date anyone who wasn't an artist, like him, or something similar. There'd been actors, musicians, professions of that nature, but nothing so workaday as a city employee. He had been upset about Jai last summer—she remembered that much, anyway, and she recalled him making fun of his job, but he hadn't really wanted to talk about him much after that first day together.

"You two were on the outs last time we discussed him," she said.

"Well, yes, but not exactly. I was scared, I guess, and causing drama, like I do, pushing him away."

"Oh?"

"Well, anyway, after I saw you last summer, I spent another couple of months being a dickhead, trying to convince myself I was over him, or that he wasn't what I really wanted—all the crap I usually tell myself when I meet someone I like. But it was just that—crap. I realized I was in love with him and knew I was jeopardizing the best thing that ever happened to me. But I was still too scared to do anything about it. I didn't call him. I avoided him—the whole nine yards. I was making myself sick with it.

"Then, one night, right before Halloween, after stewing in stupidity for all that time, I basically forced him to meet up with me, and I apologized. I begged him to take me back, Ryann."

"You did what?"

He chuckled. "I know. It was totally out of character for me. Anyway, I apologized, we made up, and we've spent practically every second together for the last three months. Now we're getting married."

She was still dazed. "Wow. WOW. I'm so, so happy for you, Stuart. I hope this guy is good enough for you."

"It's the other way around, honey. He's the best man—no, best person I've ever known. He's *my* person. I can't wait to spend the rest of my life with him."

She was still too surprised to reply. People changed, everyone changed, but Stuart had always been a playboy, a browser. She couldn't even remember the last time he'd had a boyfriend for more than a couple of months. College maybe? The idea of him settling down was almost too much to take in.

"He must be great if a wedding is on the way. Congratulations. Really. I'm so happy for you. I can't wait to meet him."

"Thanks, hon."

They were quiet for a while, Ryann still trying to absorb this news. The emotions of the morning were warring with each other, but one was winning out—happiness. The resentment, the anger, the loneliness—all of it was drifting away. Her best friend was getting married.

"Anyway," Stuart said, clearing his throat, "will you?"

"Will I what?"

"Will you be my maid of honor?"

She laughed. "Of course! What kind of jerk would I have to be to turn that down? And anyway, I think I still have your wedding dream book around somewhere."

"You what?" Stuart laughed. "I can't believe you kept that."

"It's only twenty years old," she said, smiling. "And I keep everything—you know that."

"You *have* to bring that when you come here."

"I will."

He was quiet again, and she thought she heard a soft sob.

"So you'll really do this?" he asked, voice breaking. "Even after I treated you so poorly?"

"Of course, you old queen! You can't get rid of me that easy."

"Thank you. I've missed you so much."

"Me, too."

They were quiet again, and she had to brush away a few loose tears. She was relieved, happy, and somehow sad—relieved to hear from him again, happy for his news, but sad that he seemed to have moved on without her. The two of them had been closer than siblings since the day they met—closer than any friend she'd ever had before or since. Losing him these last months had been like losing part of herself.

"So how quickly can you get here?" he asked.

She flinched. "What? What do you mean?"

"How soon can we expect you in town? I'd say you could stay with us, but Jai has about a thousand cats, and I know you're not a fan. There's a pretty cute B&B in town, though, or I could see if one of Jai's sisters could put you up—whatever you're more comfortable with. I know you have the money, but a couple weeks in a hotel is a lot to ask."

Ryann paused. Had she missed something?

"Wait a minute," she said. "When are you guys getting married?"

"Oh! I didn't mention it, did I? In a little over three weeks. On Valentine's Day."

CHAPTER TWO

Ryann had never been more uncomfortable or worn out. No, scratch that—she had, once, after taking the cheap bus between Puerto Vallarta and Mexico City in her early twenties. She and Stuart had thought it might be fun to travel like the locals. It hadn't. That said, this trip to Colorado was almost as bad, and it hadn't been some naive, youthful, classist whim. Instead, every part of her journey had conspired against her to put her right here.

It took several days to even consider leaving New York, and then she'd been delayed further. Her board members were flying to London this week in the private jet, so she'd been forced to fly commercial. It had snowed Sunday, the first time she'd tried to leave New York, and after several canceled flights, she'd accepted an economy-class ticket to Salt Lake City Monday afternoon to get closer, at least. After an incredibly uncomfortable and long, hot flight squashed between two corpulent chatterboxes—really, how did people travel like this?—she'd landed in Utah in the middle of a blizzard well after midnight her second full day of trying to get to Colorado. Her luggage had somehow been routed through to Denver after all, and she was stuck in a city in the middle of nowhere, still hours from her destination, with nothing but her purse and a dead cell phone. The car-rental agencies were snowed in or closed entirely, and all the nearby hotels were booked. She'd spent the rest of that night freezing and dozing on an airport bench with only her light blazer to use as a pillow.

The storm continued overnight, and by morning she was marooned in a mountain of snow outside the airport. She'd planned to drive from here, but with the roads clogged, and the snow still falling, driving and flying were a no-go. Everything was grounded. After another screaming match with another incompetent ticket agent, some jerk employee had suggested taking the bus, and, basically to spite them, she had done just that.

Which is where she found herself now—in the last seat at the back of a bus many, many hours later—Wednesday, now, actually—overheated and sweating despite her light clothing. The bathroom, if it could be called that, was right next to her, and even without someone using it, the odor leaking from the door was nauseating. That smell wasn't as bad as the stench of spoiled and sour milk that drifted from somewhere, everywhere here in the cabin—a stink she was pretty sure could be traced to a child some three seats ahead who had been trying to make eye contact with her the last several hours. Fucking kids.

They'd crossed the Colorado border from Wyoming over an hour ago as the sun was rising. They'd stopped three times already since the border, all in towns she'd never heard of before. She'd asked the driver to warn her when they were close to Loveland, where she was headed, but she needn't have bothered. Once they'd crossed into Colorado, the billboards practically screamed it at her, letting her know almost in real time that Loveland was coming their way. Every single sign she saw announced some kind of major Valentine's Day festival—Fire and Ice, it was called. She had to hand it to the town—it was smart marketing. She couldn't imagine they had much else going for them to bring in tourists, so banking on Valentine's Day and dropping the name Loveland every five miles on the interstate was pretty clever.

The bus finally made it to the Loveland exit, pulling in next to a dirty, gray slush pile that had been cleared to the side to make room for vehicles. She was the only person to stand up. The kid who had been eyeing her most of the ride here stuck his tongue out at her, and it took everything in her power not to flip him off. She made eye contact briefly with the mother, glared at her, and stumbled the rest of the way to the front, tripping and nearly going down on the wet rubber steps.

The bus driver closed the door so quickly behind her she was worried her blazer would be caught. She jumped forward, right into the slush, the icy mixture instantly saturating her favorite heels.

"Great," she said, shaking some of it off her foot. "Just fucking great."

The driver didn't seem to notice her obscene gesture at him, so she made her way slowly toward the depot, stumbling on her sodden feet through the ice and snow and almost falling inside after wrestling with the door and wind.

Unlike the other depots she'd explored—mainly to get off the bus and use the toilet—this one had been jauntily decorated. Nearly every inch of the place was covered in either a heart or a cupid cutout, with white and pink heart streamers crisscrossing the room above her head. An enormous red mailbox stood in one corner, above which a sign read "Loveland Remailing Program," which was also festooned with little silhouettes of cupids and hearts. Someone was kneeling in front of the mailbox, fiddling with the locked door, their back to Ryann.

She stamped her feet a couple of times on the sodden floor mat, splashing more wet water on herself. Disgusted and enraged, she marched directly to the front desk and the only other person in the room besides the postal worker.

The young man behind the counter seemed as disgusted with the situation as she was. Someone had apparently made him wear a jaunty red forage cap and vest, which had metal conversation-hearts buttons in bright pastels pinned to them. "Be Mine" said one, and "UR A QT" said another. His hair, however, was dyed black, and he was wearing heavy black eyeliner. He had been reading—Nietzsche, of course—and did little but look up at her, one hand firmly under his chin.

"Yes?" he said, his tone entirely devoid of interest.

"Do you have a pay phone somewhere? My phone's dead."

He pointed with a black-nail-polished finger rather than say anything, and she had to fight the urge to reach out and shake him into some semblance of life.

The phone, she realized, was old school. It was even in a little booth—something she'd seen only in movies. The phone itself was low, attached to the wall on a kind of desk, with a little leather seat cracked with age. There were absolutely no instructions for using a credit card, and she had no change.

"Christ Almighty," she said, sitting down heavily. She was close to tears or screaming—one of the two. If one more thing went wrong, she was fairly certain she would either explode with rage or have a complete breakdown. It was now days since she'd tried to leave New York the first time. She'd barely eaten or slept since, and she was still wearing the same clothes she'd put on forty-eight hours ago between canceled flights. She couldn't even imagine what she must look like and didn't really want to know.

She stood up, straightened her blazer as best as she could, and ran her fingers under her eyes, wiping away what was likely the last of her smeary mascara. She stepped out of the phone booth and started walking back to the disaffected goth, trying to give him her warmest smile.

The postal worker finished with the mailbox and stood up, turning just as she walked by. Ryann couldn't help a little shock of surprised delight at the sight of a handsome butch woman, here in the middle of practically nowhere. She, like the young man at the desk, was wearing a Valentine-themed uniform, so gaudy and over the top she might have been wearing a costume. The woman smirked at her and winked, then walked past her toward the door, close enough for her to detect a whiff of vanilla. She couldn't help but turn to watch her leave, and, as if sensing her interest, the woman glanced back at her, her smirk widening. She touched the brim of her silly hat and winked again before leaving, the bells over the door jingling merrily. Ryann watched her walk across the parking lot and then approached the front desk.

Once again, the young goth barely acknowledged her, and she had to bite down another urge to strangle him. She read his nametag.

"Cliff? The phone in the booth won't take my credit card. Do you think I could ask you to make a call for me? I need a ride."

"Okay. Who do you want me to call?"

She opened her mouth, ready to recite Stuart's number, but then closed it. She was a complete mess, and the last thing she wanted to do was to meet his fiancé looking like this. She could ask Stuart to come alone, but she didn't really want him to see her like this, either.

"I guess I need a cab," she said.

"You can just go outside. You should find at least one if you follow the building around the side to the left." Again, he pointed, his book still open, his hand still propping up his head. She had a wild thought then, picturing his head simply rolling off if he moved his hand from his chin, and she had to bite back a braying laugh. Something in her expression must have given this thought away, as he frowned slightly.

"Thanks," she managed, and marched back outside into the freezing morning air. The wind tried to ruffle her skin-tight skirt and shirt, and she pulled her blazer ineffectively closer around her, now shuddering with cold.

She rounded the building, and a single, late-model cab was sitting next to a TAXI stand sign. The cab, like everything she'd seen so far in this town, was festooned in Valentine's decorations, whether permanent or temporary—red and white hearts and cupids over a bright-pink body. Sweetheart Rides, the company was called. She waved at the driver, who popped out, opening the back door for her. She dropped inside a blissfully warm, cozy back seat. The space smelled strangely of vanilla and cinnamon, and she inhaled deeply, the last of the spoiled milk from the bus leaving her sinuses. There was a white fleece blanket with red hearts back here, which she gratefully draped over her nylon-clad legs.

The driver climbed in front and slammed the door, then turned to make eye contact with her.

"You must be freezing in those clothes!"

Captain Obvious, she thought. "Luggage was lost."

"On the bus?" he asked.

She sighed. "It's a long story."

"Seems like you've had a rough time of it. Sorry if this is your first time in Loveland. Hopefully things start turning around for ya."

"Thanks. They couldn't get worse, I suppose."

"Where we headed?"

Her mind was completely blank. Stuart had made the reservation for her and had given her all the information in her phone, but that was days ago now, and she hadn't really been paying attention. Still, she remembered that the place had a funny, kitschy name in keeping with all the other Valentine's-themed things she'd already seen here.

"Love Lodge? Lover's Hideaway? Something like that? I'm sorry. I can't quite remember the name. I know it's downtown, anyway."

"You probably mean the Love Inn."

She snapped her fingers. "That's it—yes, the Love Inn. You guys really go all in for this Valentine's stuff, huh?"

He laughed. "Heck yes, we do. It's our busiest time of year." He winked and turned forward, slowly easing the cab onto the icy, snowy road that led out of the depot.

All of the light and telephone poles were festooned in twinkle lights and red garland, and every pole they passed had at least one enormously large wooden heart attached to it with names and messages from people, conversation-heart style. They were soon driving a little too fast to read most of them, but she saw messages of love and friendship, clearly personalized. "Ken Loves Jo." "Alice Loves Her Kitty." "Carl + Rhonda 4EVR."

"Looking at the hearts?" the driver said, pointing. "Anyone can have one of those commissioned in December or January, and they're different every year. It used to just be a local thing, but now we get people from all over the world asking for them. Then they can show pictures of their heart to their sweetie, or they can bring their loved one here and show it to them on Valentine's Day. Lots of engagements begin in front of those hearts, I can tell ya."

"It's a really cute idea," she said, smiling with something like genuine warmth for the first time in days. "Someone must make a fortune."

"It's a charity that does it, actually, but yeah, they really sweep up this time of year."

The drive wasn't long—some ten minutes, give or take. Once they passed the usual stretch of strip malls and car dealerships near the highway, the town was revealed, cute and unassuming, a charming mix of small, local businesses and early twentieth-century Craftsman homes with an occasional Victorian here and there for flavor. The entire town was done up for the upcoming holiday in varying levels of success—tacky here, cute there. Still, with the snow, the red-and-white decorations stood out in pretty contrast.

Downtown was clearly a relic of nineteenth-century railroad buildup, with the flat, two-story wood and brick facades she recognized from various Westerns she'd seen. Here the lights and hearts simply exploded, covering every surface she could see. Today was the first day of February. Was all this year-round or temporary? Still, the town officials, or whoever ran all this, could easily make a year-round thing of it for the tourists. It was a little overdone, but that was almost always the case with places that banked on tourist money around a holiday. She'd been to Salem, Massachusetts a week or so before Halloween once, and it was similar there most of October. The whole thing was a smart marketing move by whoever had drummed it up. It was unique and specific, and something she hadn't seen before. Valentine's Day was almost two weeks out, but they probably made money on it even now.

The Love Inn was a tacky monstrosity, even from the outside. From the name, she'd expected a kind of late-'60s throwback, with psychedelic tie dye and flower power, but she realized she should have adjusted her expectations once she saw the rest of the town. It was a small, two-story mid-century painted a hideous Pepto-Bismol pink with white, lacy trim, doors, and shutters. It was a nightmare directly from the Barbie Dream House style of architecture.

"Here we are," the driver said, pulling into the loading area.

"I can't stay here," Ryann said, shaking her head.

"What? Why not?"

Ryann shook her head. "I'm not going in there."

The driver's eyes turned from her out the front window and back several times, clearly trying to understand her aversion. Finally, he met her eyes.

"I don't know what to tell ya, except that you'll have a hell of a time getting another room anywhere this time of year. I mean, there's probably something in the bigger chains out by the highway, but nothing downtown—not if you don't have a reservation. Stay out there, and you'll need a car, and a lot of the car places are all booked up, and—"

She held up a hand, shutting her eyes. The migraine she'd managed to suppress with gallons of coffee the last few days was trying to take over, and she rubbed her temples with her fingertips. Stuart had mentioned something like this, she now remembered. There were only a few places to stay downtown, and with all the wedding activities located here, it wouldn't make any sense to stay farther away. He'd told her the place she was staying was a charming piece of Americana.

"You're right," she said, opening her eyes. "I'm sorry. It's been a long trip. How much do I owe you?"

As she paid, she reflected on her earlier feelings about Stuart. When he'd called, she'd eventually been willing to let bygones be bygones. He was, or had been, her oldest and dearest friend. Now, as she climbed out of the cab and into the frigid morning air, she wondered if she shouldn't have simply turned him down. She would have shown up for the wedding, of course. She didn't hate him, after all, but she didn't need to be here, of all places, for two weeks. It was asking too much of her. The fact that he didn't realize that this was the last place she would ever stay spoke volumes about how distant they'd become.

The cabbie gave her a little toot of his horn, and she jumped, her nerves frayed nearly to breaking. She waved at him, squared her shoulders once more, and marched into the Love Inn.

The scent that greeted her upon opening the door sent a wave of nostalgic longing crashing through her. She couldn't immediately identify the scent, but she was suddenly reminded of getaways to New Hampshire when she was a kid, skiing and sledding and spending more family time together than they did the rest of the year. Between her parents' busy schedules and her brother's boarding school, those annual trips had been their only extended moments together as a family.

Some sleigh bells had jangled as she entered, and a small, graying woman appeared from the back, waving her inside.

"Come in, come in! You must be absolutely frozen to death!"

The woman was wearing a long-sleeved white cotton shirt decorated with pink and red hearts; an apron made of two felt hearts lined with frilly, white lace; and bright-red penny loafers. Her hair had been set, blue-rinsed a little too brightly to a near-platinum, and her blush and lipstick were almost garish. Still, her smile was wide and warm, and she looked invitingly friendly.

Ryann, still shaken by her childhood memories, didn't immediately respond. She stood, still motionless, frozen in fact, in the doorway, the cold wind blowing her from behind.

The woman blanched and rushed over, grabbing her hand and pulling her inside.

"Oh, you poor thing," the woman said. "It's going to be okay. Let me get you something warm to drink."

The woman led her into a small dining room and directed her into a heart-backed chair festooned with white lace. The seat was also heart-shaped, and this, alone, was enough to finally break through Ryann's strange fugue. As she came back to herself, tears were coursing down her cheeks, and she wiped them away hurriedly, shocked and embarrassed.

The woman returned a moment later, a steaming red mug in her hands, and handed it to her. The scent that had struck her immobile was coming from the mug—hot chocolate with vanilla. Her mother made it this way.

The woman sat down in a similar chair next to her and patted her knee. "There, there, honey. You drink that up. You must be absolutely frozen to the bone."

"I-I'm sorry," she managed, suddenly fighting tears again. "I don't know what's come over me."

"We all have days like that," the woman said, still smiling, eyes kind and warm. "Is there someone I can call for you? Someone that can come get you?"

She frowned, not following. She realized that this woman must think she'd simply wandered in off the street. "Oh, no. I'm sorry. I didn't mention it, did I? I need to check in. I'm staying here."

"Oh, you are! You must be Ryann. Stuart told me to watch out for you. Let me go get your paperwork and the key. You just sit there, honey, and drink up. A nice warm bath should help you feel better."

She was angry with herself. She couldn't understand these feelings. Why was she reacting this way to a mug of hot chocolate? She took a long, deep whiff of it and set it down, tears rising to her eyes again.

"Get ahold of yourself, lady," she whispered, wiping her eyes. "You're just tired."

The woman was back again, her expression still warm and friendly, and Ryann began to thaw in response. Normally this kind of person came across to her as phony, at best, or outright manipulative at worst. Instead, she was struck with the deepest conviction that this woman was genuinely nice—all within a few minutes of meeting her.

"The bill has already been covered for you," the woman said, handing her the key.

"It has?"

"Yes. By Stuart. What a lovely young man he is! And so talented!"

"Mmm," she said, taking the key. It was an actual key, not a card, something she hadn't seen in years. The keychain was, of course, a red plastic heart.

"That's our best room," the woman said, smiling even wider. "I'd ask one of the boys to carry your luggage up for you, but I didn't see any outside."

"It's coming later," she said, standing up. Her legs felt weak, nearly loose beneath her, and a wave of fatigue made her almost swoon. The woman grabbed her elbow and started walking her toward the main entry room. This space was, like the rest of the town, absolutely plastered in Valentine's decorations, with another enormous red mailbox, that same sign above it: "Loveland Remailing Program."

She was too baffled to ask about this now and let the woman lead her up the flight of stairs. Even the carpet was decorated in stylized golden hearts stitched into the fabric. They reached the next floor, and she let herself be led to the door at the end of the hallway.

"Here we are," the woman said, "the Honeymoon Suite!"

"The what?" Some of her fatigue retreated at the words.

"It's the best room, really," the woman said. "Stuart even paid for the Honeymoon Package, so you'll find some goodies in there waiting for you—all on the house. My name is Ethel, so if you need something, you call the front desk, day or night, and me or one of the boys will bring it to you. Breakfast is from seven to nine. Tomorrow and Friday you'll have your pick of several options, but things will change to family style on Saturday. You're the only guest right now, but we're booked solid through Valentine's starting this weekend, so you're going to see a lot of friendly faces in the hall here pretty soon." She paused, smiling again. "Can I get you anything now? More hot cocoa?"

"No," she said, almost snapping.

Ethel's expression faltered for the first time.

Ryann adjusted her tone, trying to give her a real smile. "Sorry. I mean I'm fine for now. I just need to lie down for a while. Take a long bath, like you said."

Ethel patted her arm. "Of course, honey. And if you need someone to run and get you some clothes, you call me. I have a friend with a little boutique here in town that would be happy to send some things over for you at a discount."

She had to suppress a shudder of revulsion, but she managed to keep her expression neutral. "Thank you. I'm going to try to get my things delivered, but I might have to take you up on that. I'll call down later."

Ethel excused herself, and Ryann watched her go, shaking her head. As if she'd ever allow herself to be dressed in something like that.

The room was as tacky as she'd predicted, which meant Stuart was messing with her. Like the ridiculous flowers he'd sent her in New York, he was purposefully annoying her. It was a relief, really, to realize this ploy, as it meant her friend hadn't changed as much as she'd thought. The fact that he had found this awful place for her was a testament to how well he knew her. He must know how completely and utterly she would hate everything here. It was the only explanation.

The bed was heart-shaped, and after she examined it, she saw that it was also motorized. It could spin in a slow circle, like a merry-go-round, or gyrate, or both. It had a grandiose, flamboyant lacy canopy overhead. White doilies covered every surface of the room—over the back of the red loveseat, under the old TV, over the back of the armchair, and in the middle of the desk. Cloth rose petals had been strewn all over the room, and several bundles of balloons floated in different parts of the room—Mylar hearts, and standard red, white, and pink. She counted three vases of actual roses—perhaps the only classy thing in here, but their heady aroma was almost sickening in this close, hot space. Heart-shaped streamers were draped from corner to corner, and cutout cupids and hearts had been pasted to the walls. In the little fridge, she found a bowl of berries, several different types of cheeses, water crackers, a local yogurt, of all things, some chocolates, and a chilled bottle of champagne.

The bathroom had been decorated as well, with cutout hearts, streamers, and another vase of roses. The bath had several bath-bombs near it, all in rose scent.

She walked back into the bedroom, looked around again, and laughed—real laughter this time. Finally, she grabbed the champagne from the fridge and took it into the bathroom with her.

She'd get Stuart back for this. That was for sure.

CHAPTER THREE

D espite the cold weather, or perhaps because of it, the brewery was packed. Ryann paused on the small patio outside to collect herself before going in. She'd managed to delay this moment all afternoon, but this was finally it. Stuart and Jai were waiting for her, and if she tried to put off seeing them again, Stuart, at least, would come looking for her. She wasn't entirely sure why she was so hesitant, but she was.

This morning in the hotel—was it only this morning?—she'd taken a long bath, called the airline, spent the extra money to have her found luggage expedited to her here, and then napped until it showed up in the late afternoon. Of course, only one of her suitcases had made it to Denver, but at least she had some more clothes, her chargers, her makeup, and her heavier coat. She'd slept some more, and then she'd finally called Stuart, arranging to meet him in the early evening rather than in her room right then and there. She tried to sleep a little longer, gave up, watched the market on TV for a while, and then got ready, putting herself into meticulous order before walking down the street to the brewery, some twenty minutes late now.

And still, she hesitated.

It was so packed inside, Stuart wasn't likely to spot her lollygagging out here, so she backed away from the door and sat down on an empty bench. A straight couple sat nearby under a heat lamp, snuggled together and completely oblivious of her presence. She watched them, amused at how wrapped up they were in each other. The man's expression was dopey, almost drunk, and it had nothing to do with his beer. The woman was clearly enjoying his attention—her cheeks rosy, smile wide. Ryann rubbed her leather gloves over her tired face, trying to whip up some courage, enthusiasm, or both, before going in.

"Hey, stranger," Stuart said, making her jump.

She peered up at him and then froze, stunned. He'd grown a beard. It was nicely trimmed but full. He'd been entirely clean-shaven the whole time she'd known him, even in the goatee heyday of the late nineties. The beard had a slight reddish tinge, unlike his naturally near-black, curly hair. He was wearing dark, thick-framed glasses, which was also unusual—he'd worn contacts their entire friendship. Unlike his former hipster-wear, his clothes, too, were very different. He was wearing a Sherpa-lined green flannel coat, blue jeans, heavy tan snow boots, and a gray wool-knit cap. He couldn't have looked less like himself if he'd been wearing a costume.

"Hey, yourself," she finally managed.

He held out a hand and helped her to her feet, pulling her into a long, fierce hug.

"Oh my God, is it good to see you," he said, drawing back. He kept his hands on her shoulders.

"You, too."

"You've lost some weight, honey. Taking care of yourself?"

He'd always been the one to bring or send her lunch when he'd lived in the city, and sometimes even after he'd moved. She forgot to eat most of the time at work, which could be a major problem when she had long days. Gloria had taken on that task as part of her daily rota, but she wasn't as persuasive as Stuart, who knew her tastes and how to guilt her into taking breaks.

"I'm fine," she said. "And anyway, it's not like I'm the one who's changed around here."

He laughed and gestured at his beard. "Like it?"

She considered him closely for a minute, long enough for him to shift from foot to foot, clearly uncomfortable.

"You know what?" he said. "Forget I asked."

She laughed. "No, no, I'm sorry. I do like it. It's just…really different."

He laughed. "I've gone native, Ryann. Jai and I even have the same jacket."

She pretended to gag, and he play-punched her arm.

"Anyway," he said, "what are you doing out here? It's freezing! I told you to come inside when you got here. We have a table. Come on in and meet everyone."

"Everyone?" she asked.

Stuart ignored her, pulling her after him and inside the crowded room. Everyone there was in high spirits, jolly and loud, and she had to fight the urge to turn around and go back to her quiet hotel room, ugly as it was.

She saw Jai before he spotted them. Like Stuart, he was bearded, with thick-framed glasses, and as Stuart mentioned, he was wearing exactly the same outfit as her friend. The resemblance ended there, however, as Jai was much taller, much broader than Stuart—she could tell this even with him seated. Stuart was relatively tall, slightly over six feet, but quite slim. Jai was also fairer—blond hair and pale skin and eyes in contrast to Stuart's darker coloring.

Jai seemed to sense her watching him, and as he turned their way, he broke into a wide smile. He stood, his height greater even than she'd expected, and lumbered their way, arms wide open. She let herself be engulfed in his enormity, the light suddenly disappearing as he pulled her into his broad chest. Moments later, he was pumping her hand up and down in his enormous paws.

"It's so nice to finally meet you, Ryann," he said, his voice surprisingly soft and high.

"Same here. And thanks so much for letting me be part of this. I'm really excited to be here."

She realized as she spoke that she meant it. Most of her reluctance and hesitation had been an outcome of her exhaustion, but part of it had been her own cowardice. She hated meeting new people. While she could command a board meeting or a business proposal with complete strangers, she'd almost always struggled with personal situations like this. And Stuart meant a lot to her, and Jai meant a lot to him, which meant he was going to be a part of her life now, too. It was a lot of pressure. But seconds with him had erased all of that. This was a kind, warm man.

"Come! Sit! Stuart told me all about your awful ordeal getting here. Let me buy you a beer to make up for it."

She followed him back to a little table in the corner of the room. Two women were sitting there—one a cute, androgynous elf of a person, the other a formidable, stunning, icy blonde. Ryann, Stuart, and Jai sat across from them, and she shook the women's hands as Stuart made introductions.

"This cool drink of water is Darcy," the blonde, "and Erin is the owner and master brewer here and Darcy's wife. We hired Erin to help us arrange the alcohol for the wedding, including, of course, the beer brewed here. This is the best beer around."

"Oh, I see," Erin said, sneering dramatically. "That's all I am to you, then? A beer monger?"

Stuart laughed. "They're also our friends," he told Ryann. "We just started talking details before you got here."

"Nice to meet you," Ryann said.

"You, too," Erin said. "I have to say, Stuart didn't do you justice."

Darcy's lips twisted in a smirk. "Agreed. Not at all."

"He said you were beautiful, but I never expected—" Erin gestured at her vaguely.

Ryann looked down at herself, wondering what they meant, and everyone laughed.

"Hey!" Stuart said, slapping the table. "You're embarrassing my maid of honor, Erin. Can you wait five seconds before you flirt with her? You're a married woman now, for God's sake, and she's had a rough couple of days."

Erin laughed. "Okay, okay. I'll hold back on my charm while you get yourself together, Ryann." She slapped her forehead. "Oh, shit, that's right. I forgot. I meant to get you a drink before you got here. Hang on a sec." She shot to her feet and disappeared into the crowd, the four of them left watching after her.

"Please don't mind my wife," Darcy said.

"And don't mind them," Stuart said, rolling his eyes. "They got married on New Year's, and they keep dropping the 'wife' word every chance they get."

Erin appeared soon after, carrying two flights of beers. She set them down in front of Ryann and started talking.

"This is our current lineup," she explained, gesturing. Each flight held six two-ounce pours, the beers gradually getting darker from the beginning of one board to the end of the next. A little descriptive card was tucked into each of the flights that named and described each of the beers.

"This last one," Erin continued, pointing at the final and darkest beer, "won't be released until Friday, but since you're a friend of the family, you get to try it early. We're calling it Cupid's Kiss."

"This is a lot of beer," Ryann said weakly. "Do I drink it all? Or is it like wine tasting?"

Everyone laughed.

"Whatever you like," Erin said. "You can taste them or drink it all. There's a lot of them, but altogether, they're less than two pints. Stuart said you can hold your own, so you should be okay. Let me know if you want a full pour of any of them, or if you have any questions."

"Please, please, don't ask her any questions," Stuart said. "She'll talk your ear off about beer if you let her, and we'll never make it to dinner."

Ryann started drinking a moment later, letting the others talk around her. They were laughing and discussing the details for the beer, wine, and liquor for the wedding, and she should probably be paying attention since she was going to be a part of this thing, but her attention was centered on the little glasses in front of her. She'd taken a hesitant sip of the first—not sure what to expect—and had been pleasantly surprised. It was a honey lager, but unlike any she'd had before. It was refreshing, light, and almost sweet for a time before the slight bite of light hops took over her palate.

Stuart had mentioned that the beer in Colorado was the best he'd ever had, but she hadn't really expected that he meant the beer here in this little town, too. She'd thought most of the best places were in the bigger cities. She was no connoisseur, and she'd never really been in a brewery before, but this might be the best lager she'd ever had. She continued down the line, mostly just tasting, and each beer was surprisingly good and refreshingly different from the one before it. She especially enjoyed the two sours at the end of the first flight board, but her favorite was the last beer—the darkest. It was sweet and bitter, with the slightest hint of cherry on the back of her tongue.

She could tell Erin had been trying not to watch her this entire time, but when Ryann put the final glass down, Erin turned in her stool toward her, smiling.

"Did you like any of them?" Erin asked, clearly excited.

"I loved them. I mean, really loved them. I didn't know what to expect, but they're all great."

Erin's grin became wider, and she heard Stuart sigh next to her.

"You're going to give her an even bigger ego than she already has," he said.

"You like them?" Erin said, ignoring him. "Really?"

Ryann nodded. "I really did. I'm blown away. I'm more of a wine person. I've never enjoyed any beer this much. I mean it."

Erin blushed prettily, and Ryann was pleased she'd managed to convey what she actually thought. She liked these nice people and was always glad to give a compliment when it was deserved. The beer was helping with her nerves, too.

"Which one is your favorite?" Erin asked, almost babbling in her glee and standing up. "Can I get you a glass of something?"

"Hey, hey," Stuart said, gesturing in a calming motion. "Sit down, lady. Give her a second to breathe. She just got here. Remember she still has her sea legs."

"What's that supposed to mean?" Ryann asked.

Stuart touched the back of her hand. "It's not personal, hon. You came from sea level to elevation. Beer and alcohol will hit a little harder for the next day or two—that's all. Let your body adapt a bit before going all out."

"Okay, okay," Erin said, holding her hands up in defeat. "I won't get her drunk...yet. Still, which one was your favorite?"

Ryann didn't hesitate, pointing at the last glass—the Cupid's Kiss. "It was delicious."

"I knew it!" Erin said, high-fiving Jai.

"What kind is it?" Ryann asked.

"A chocolate-cherry stout," Erin said. "There's a Valentine's contest between brewers around here at the festival, and lots of us submit a beer for it. I think this is our best one yet."

"It's delicious," Ryann said.

Erin's face went red again, and she turned to her wife, fanning herself with a hand. Darcy laughed and kissed her lightly, slinking an arm around her shoulders. Ryann had to admit she was a little surprised by this, too. She hadn't expected them to be so open in public—not in this small town. She realized then that Stuart and Jai were holding hands, and not a single person in the rest of this crowded room seemed to care.

The beer had warmed her, and she started removing her outer layers and hat. Jai stood up, taking the clothes from her and hanging them on a coatrack a few feet away. Erin and Darcy were staring at her again, eyes wide.

"What?" she asked.

"It's just—" Erin began.

"Your hair," Darcy finished. "It's glorious."

"Amazing," Erin added.

Ryann touched it self-consciously, pulling one of her red curls straight for a second. "Oh yeah?"

"I haven't seen it natural in years—not since we were kids," Stuart said to the others. "She normally straightens it."

"What a tragedy that would be," Darcy said. Her icy blue eyes were locked on Ryann's, and Ryann heated even further under that cool gaze.

She looked at Stuart, desperate to detract attention from herself. "I haven't had time to go to a salon in a while."

"It's really long, too," Stuart said, pulling one of her curls lightly. "I don't remember seeing it this long before. It's gorgeous."

All four of the others were staring at her, and her cheeks warmed even more. "Thanks," she managed.

"Okay!" Jai said, clapping his hands. "We've embarrassed her enough. We'll save the rest of the wedding details for another day, if you don't mind, Erin. I want to get to know my fiancé's friend a little, and then we need to get something to eat."

"All right," Erin said, standing up. "I know when to leave a party."

Darcy stood with her, taking her arm. "A lady always does."

"I wouldn't call myself a lady."

Darcy kissed her cheek. "I wasn't talking about you, hon."

Ryann laughed, shaking their hands again, tuning out a little as Stuart and Jai made plans for another get-together with them later this week. Between the beer, the embarrassing compliments, and her general exhaustion, she was starting to lose the ability to keep up with everyone. Her eyes were still sandy, and the dry air was making her skin and nose tickle. Jai and Stuart stood talking to their friends, and she took the opportunity to slide around to Darcy's vacated chair in the farthest corner, which gave her a view of the entire room.

It was strangely busy in here for a Wednesday evening, especially this early in the evening, but the excellent beer likely explained the crowd. The room was wide and airy, with exposed brick walls, soft yellow light, and light pine floors. The tables and chairs were also pine and dark metal, the whole place sophisticated and almost urban. Valentine's decorations were in here, too, though somewhat more subtle than she was used to seeing here in town—a few of those enormous wooden conversation hearts on the walls and some heart-shaped streamers hanging from the rafters.

A pint of dark beer was set in front of her, startling her back into reality, and she smiled up at Erin.

"Nice meeting you, Ryann," she said. "I'm sure we'll see more of you soon."

She started reaching into her purse, but Erin held up a hand. "No charge, of course. You get the friends-and-family discount."

"Thanks."

After Erin and Darcy left, the men sat down in their chairs again across from her. Now, seeing them side by side, she couldn't stop the stab of happy melancholy piercing her heart. Watching Stuart was enough to tell her everything. He was wholeheartedly, gloriously happy—more so than she'd seen him in the entire twenty-plus years she'd known him. And he'd changed so tremendously—not just the clothes and the beard, but everything about him. It was almost like meeting someone new, someone better, as if this person had emerged from inside her old friend.

"Do I have something in my teeth?" he asked, scrubbing at them with a finger.

"No," she said, smiling. "No—I'm getting used to you again."

He took her hand in his. "God, I missed you."

"Me, too."

"So, Ryann," Jai said. "Tell me all about yourself."

"What do you want to know?"

"Well, Stuart told me some of the details, but I want to hear them from you, too. I know you two grew up in Cold Spring and moved to the city together for college. And now you're in marketing, and you own your own business."

Ryann laughed. "That's me in a nutshell. Not much more to tell, really."

Jai rolled his eyes. "Yes, yes—but I want the rest of it. Family? Girlfriend?"

Ryann couldn't help her reaction, her spine stiffening. "No," was all she managed to say, looking away and at Stuart. His eyes softened, and he squeezed her hand, still in his.

"Ryann doesn't talk to her family anymore," he explained.

"Oh, God," Jai said. "I'm sorry. Stuart mentioned that before, and I forgot."

She rotated her shoulders, trying to relax. "No. Please don't apologize. I'm not usually so touchy about it. I'm just tired." She took a moment to sip her beer, tasting, this time, a hint of chocolate under the cherry overtones.

"My family and I stopped talking after I came out," she explained.

"Christ," Jai said. "I'm so sorry."

She lifted a shoulder. "It's fine. It was a long time ago now. And I got a parting gift—a college degree and enough money to start my own business. Could be worse."

They all sipped their beers in awkward silence, and she wondered, once again, why she'd bothered coming here. The fact that Stuart hadn't reminded Jai about her past before she came actually hurt more than anything. It suggested a lot, foremost of which was that he barely talked about her. Both men were staring at their hands, and if she didn't say something to change the subject, the tension would get even worse.

She plastered on her most executive smile. "Tell me about the wedding party, fellas. There's me and who else?"

Jai seemed grateful for the chance to move on. "Uh, well, we're still deciding."

She laughed. "So close to the wedding?"

"We still have thirteen days," Stuart said.

She rolled her eyes. "Okay, but really? You guys don't know yet?"

"Well, we only got engaged last week—the night before I called you," Stuart said.

Jai glanced over at him. "And it's not that we don't know. We just can't agree on who to include."

Stuart nodded. "Jai has sisters, but you're all I've got on my side. I told him he could have as many people as he wanted in his party, but he doesn't want it to be uneven."

"Couldn't you have some of his family on your side?" she asked.

"See!" Jai said, triumphant. "I told you that's what we should do."

Stuart lifted his shoulders. "I guess so. But who goes where? I'm worried some of your sisters won't see it like you do, Jai. If they end up on my side, won't that seem like, I don't know, they're not as important?"

Jai put his giant arm around Stuart's shoulders, squeezing him. "You know that's not true, sweetie. All my sisters adore you. I actually think some of them like you more than me. You're like another little brother they never had."

"Really?"

"Of course!"

Stuart's smile was broad and happy, and Jai kissed him, long and deep. Once again, Ryann glanced around the room, wondering if anyone would notice or care, but everyone here was in their own world. She wasn't sure she'd ever seen two men kiss in public outside of a gay bar or at Pride.

"So tell me about your sisters," she said when they broke apart. "I'd like some idea what to expect. Which one is your maid of honor?"

"Well, actually," Jai said, "my maid of honor is my best friend, Maddie. She's supposed to be here in a few minutes."

"Maddie's actually how we met," Stuart explained. "She's an artist, too, a sculptor, like me. She and I met at the foundry here in town, and she introduced me to Jai last year."

"Almost a year to the day," Jai said, staring at Stuart.

They were lost in each other's eyes long enough that Ryann wondered if she should remind them that she was here with them.

Stuart shook his head as if to clear it, his expression a little sheepish when he turned to her. "Sorry about that."

"It's fine. You two are really adorable."

"We try."

"So, sisters?" she said, turning back to Jai. "How many are we talking?"

"Four."

She whistled. "Wow. Older, I think you said?"

"Yes—I'm the baby. My eldest, Jos, is ten years older, and then it's one about every two years on down to me."

"They all have 'J' names," Stuart said, rolling his eyes.

"So do my parents and the aunts, uncles, and grandparents on my dad's side," Jai said. "And when my parents got to me, they just spelled the letter."

"Wow. Four sisters," she said, shaking her head. "Must have been a lot of baby-dress-up parties when you were little."

"You better believe it. And tea parties, and slumber parties, and makeovers, and everything else. It was a blast."

"They're all nearby?"

"Yes. Jos is the farthest—she lives in Denver. Joan is just outside of Berthoud—a few miles south of here—and Janet and Julia are here in Loveland, still, like me."

"You grew up here?"

"Born and raised! A little like you two—small-town gay. Stuart and I have joked about it before. Difference is, I never went to the big city."

The men were staring fondly at each other again, and Ryann took a moment to sip her beer and check her phone. Ted was supposed to call her with an update today, but so far she'd heard nothing from him or anyone else. She'd have to excuse herself to check in some time soon.

"I hope you two hit it off," Jai said.

"I'm sorry, what?" she asked. He'd said something before she caught this.

"You and Maddie—my best friend. You'll be working a lot with her the next couple of weeks, so I hope you hit it off."

"Oh, yes, of course. Me, too."

She saw Stuart beaming next to him and narrowed her eyes.

"Excuse me a sec, guys," Jai said, standing up. "I'm going to go in back and call her to see if she's on her way. It might make more sense to have her meet us at the restaurant."

He stood and fought his way through the crowded room toward the back hall. Once out of sight, Ryann leaned forward, motioning Stuart to do the same.

"You two better not be doing what I think you're doing," she said.

"And what would that be?" he replied, one eyebrow raised.

"Setting me up with Maddie."

"Who said anything about setting you up?"

"I see some wild scheme in your eyes, Stuart. I swear to God, if you planned this whole thing—"

He laughed. "Sure, Ryann. We planned an entire wedding so we could set you up with our friend."

Her blood pressure lowered, and she leaned back, drinking her beer. Of course Stuart would never do something like that to her. He couldn't possibly think she'd sunk so far or become so desperate. She smiled weakly at him, trying to apologize with her gaze, and he lifted his glass in a mock salute, draining it before setting it down.

"You're right. I'm sorry. I'm being stupid."

"Still…" Stuart said.

"What?"

"She *is* your type."

She launched to her feet and slammed her hands on the table. "Goddamn it, Stuart—"

"Whoa! I'm sorry," a woman's voice said next to them. "Am I interrupting something?"

She glared over at the woman, ready to snap at the interruption, but her voice caught in her throat. It was the same handsome butch she'd seen this morning at the bus station, collecting letters. The one who winked at her twice.

"Hi," the woman said, holding out her hand. "I'm Maddie."

CHAPTER FOUR

R yann's mouth snapped shut, and she stared at Maddie for an awkward length of time, long enough for Maddie's happy expression to falter with uncertainty. Finally, Ryann's brain kicked in, and she held her hand out to the other woman, adding her usual boardroom smile.

"I'm Ryann. Nice to meet you."

Maddie's grin broadened, and the grip with her gloved hand was solid, almost hard. "You, too. If I'd known who you were, I would have given you a ride this morning. I almost offered anyway. You seemed a little...lost."

Ryann sat back down. Maddie, strangely, sat next to her rather than on Stuart's side. Stuart was peering back and forth at them, obviously confused.

"We saw each other in passing this morning," Ryann explained. "At the bus station."

"I was doing a letter pickup," Maddie added.

"Ah!" Stuart smiled. "That makes more sense. For a second there, I thought you two knew each other, and I couldn't figure out how. I don't know why you didn't call me when you were there, Ryann. I would have come and gotten you."

She didn't know how to explain herself without coming across as pathetic, so she sipped her beer, hoping the topic would change. She was strangely unsettled by the woman and the situation, and she was still pissed at Stuart. Her hand was shaking slightly, and she had to concentrate to bring her glass to her lips without spilling it.

"Is that the Valentine's beer?" Maddie asked.

"Yes," Ryann said. "It's delicious. They're calling it Cupid's Kiss."

"Can I try it?"

Ryann was surprised, but after a moment's hesitation she held it out to her. Maddie took a long swallow, her eyes closed, and Ryann's breath caught in her throat at the sight. Maddie opened her eyes and handed back her glass, smiling.

"That's so good. Erin's really outdone herself." She stood up. "I'm going to go get one. Do you need a refill?"

She hesitated, wanting another, but shook her head. Maddie gave her a quick wink, and Ryann watched the woman walk away, weaving through the crowd. She and Jai ran into each other in the crowd, and they embraced, Jai enveloping her.

"See something you like?" Stuart asked, startling her.

She jumped. "What do you mean?"

"Oh, come on," he said, laughing. "You can hardly tear your eyes off her."

Her anger was returning, and she leaned toward him, lowering her voice. "Stuart—I'm warning you. Don't start this shit."

He held his hands up. "Okay, okay! I'll drop it. You two can work it out for yourselves. You'll be spending enough time together the next two, well, almost two, weeks. I'm sure things will develop on their own."

She couldn't help but laugh. "You're an asshole. You know that?"

He winked, and then his attention moved away to Jai and Maddie, who were coming back, both holding two beers.

"I got you one anyway," Maddie said, sitting down next to her again. "You looked like you wanted another. But I'll drink it if you really don't."

She was surprised again. Maddie was right.

"Thanks."

"You're welcome. I actually lucked out with you being here. The beer hasn't been released to the public, so Erin wasn't going to give me one until I told her this one was for you. She gave us both of these for free. You charmed her, I think."

She started taking off her outer layers of clothing then, and Ryann made herself move her eyes away. She was starting to feel the effects of the beer now, and that, coupled with her fatigue, had lessened her self-control. The urge to watch the other woman was tugging at the edges of her willpower, and she made herself concentrate on the men, who were staring at each other, moony and starry-eyed, Jai playing with a curl of Stuart's hair.

"Don't mind them," Maddie said. "They're always like that."

Ryann had to look up to meet her eyes since Maddie was a little taller than her. She was also little broader overall, with wide, strong shoulders and obvious muscles under the sleeves of her flannel shirt. She had light, sandy hair cut in a short pomp fade, dark-blue eyes, and a light scar that cut through one dark eyebrow. She was dressed very much like Stuart and Jai—in a thick blue flannel shirt and dark jeans with heavy snow boots. She was striking, with a sharp jawline and high cheekbones, her features overall somewhat aquiline and altogether appealing. Stuart was right—she was very much Ryann's type.

She blinked rapidly, realizing a second too late that she'd been staring at her again.

"I don't mind," she said. "I'm just so glad they found each other."

"Me, too," Maddie said. "I've never seen Jai so happy."

"Me, either, with Stuart, I mean," Ryann said.

Stuart broke in. "You two getting acquainted now?"

"A little," Maddie said, flashing those bright teeth and dimples at her again. "Though I don't know much about you, Ryann, other than you being Stuart's friend from New York. He said you're in marketing?"

"Yes—that's right."

She glanced at Stuart, who was watching them intently. He was grinning at her, knowingly, but she couldn't work up to her previous anger.

"That's partly why I wanted her here," Stuart said. "She's really, really good at event planning. You should see the galas her company puts on. Incredible."

"Have you done weddings before?" Jai asked.

"No," she said, "and Stuart's overselling it. I've planned some big work events is all."

"Hey, that's great!" Jai said. "Maddie has some experience, too. You guys should be perfect together."

"Oh?" she asked, looking at Maddie. "You've done events, too?"

"She's basically the whole reason Loveland's even on the map," Jai explained. "She's involved in all of the Valentine's Day stuff here in town."

"He's exaggerating," Maddie said. "I do some volunteer work—that's all."

"And she's understating it," Jai said. "All those decorations out there in town—that's her doing."

"He's really embellishing now." Maddie rolled her eyes. "I helped design some of the lights and decoration displays—that's all."

"And she volunteers for the Rotary Club, and the Lion's Club, the Elks, the Loveland Chamber of Commerce, and everything else. She knows about everyone in town."

Maddie's cheeks had reddened slightly, and Ryann couldn't help but think about how cute she was slightly embarrassed like this.

"And this morning?" Ryann asked. "When I saw you in the bus station getting letters? Is that one of your jobs?"

Maddie smiled. "No. It's another thing I help out with. We have a remailing program here."

"What's that?" Ryann asked.

"People from all over the world send their valentines here, inside a second, bigger envelope. Volunteers take the valentine out of the larger envelope and stamp it with special Valentine's Day stamps. I help pick up the local letters and stamp them a couple of days a week."

For Ryann, it was hard to gauge the vast resources of time and money all of this must take—the remailing program, the decorations, the advertising, all the various endeavors she'd seen devoted to the holiday here in town. She'd been here less than a day, and she could tell how well it had been done. And it was run by volunteers? For no compensation? It was hard to fathom.

"She's our resident do-gooder," Jai said.

Maddie's cheeks and ears reddened further, and she ignored him. "This is the city's busiest time, so of course the guys decide to get married now. I'll help where I can, though."

"Of course," Ryann said.

"I'm usually free most of the day on Tuesdays, Thursdays, and the weekends. I have class on Mondays and Wednesdays, and studio time on Fridays and a few other afternoons."

"Class?"

"She also teaches at the community college," Jai explained.

"I'm an art professor," Maddie said.

Ryann returned her attention to her beer, sipping it again to give herself a moment to compose herself. Her heart was racing a little. Damn it, Stuart, she thought. She hated when he was right. Maddie was exactly her type. Her volunteering was a little hard to understand, the scale of it anyway, but it was commendable, and of course the results were impressive even from what little Ryann had seen. Plus, she'd always had a thing for professors.

"So," said Stuart, clapping his hands. "We have a full list of tasks for you to take care of for the wedding, and we agreed: a lot of it will be up to you two. Neither one of us wants to step on your toes. You're the experts."

"Exactly," Jai said. "We want you to have full control. You don't even have to ask our opinion—we trust you completely."

"And what will you two be doing while we do all the work?" Ryann asked.

"Getting my beauty sleep," Stuart said, fluttering his eyelashes.

Jai rolled his eyes. "We're doing some of the other tasks ourselves, but we're mostly working on Stuart's show."

"Your what?"

"I have an art show in May."

She leaned forward, taking one of Stuart's hands. "Really? You didn't mention it."

He squeezed hers back, now appearing excited. "I wanted it to be a surprise. But of course a bunch of things are due soon, and I'm in the middle of all the planning stuff with the people at the museum."

"So you decide to get married in the middle of a major project," she said, laughing.

"Exactly! I can't make things easy on myself, can I?"

"You never have."

"Anyway—you're better at all that planning stuff than I am. You know how I am about making decisions."

"You're terrible. It took you two hours to choose a scarf that one time in Venice."

Everyone laughed.

"That sounds like Stuart," Jai said.

"Exactly," Stuart said. "And you know me better than anyone, Ryann. You'll know what I like. Again—I place my whole faith in you and Maddie here."

"What are we in charge of?" Maddie asked.

Jai and Stuart shared a quick, almost guilty glance, before Stuart said, "Let's talk about that later. We should move to the restaurant first. It's down the street a bit. I don't know about you guys, but I'm famished."

"Sure," Maddie said, standing up. "I could eat."

"You can always eat," Jai said, and she smacked his arm.

As they all gathered and donned their winter wear again, Ryann fought against a rising resentment. She didn't like that silent exchange she'd witnessed between Jai and Stuart. She could read her friend entirely, and that flash of guilt meant that they'd given her and Maddie the bulk of the work. While she'd never been in a wedding before or planned one, she'd had friends get married in the past and understood how much effort it took to line things up. And last-minute like this was bound to make everything harder. While she'd been excited to join him here, and help where she could, she resented the idea that she'd likely be busy the whole time on the wedding and what she could do for the office from here.

Maddie whistled, her eyes roaming up and down Ryann's body once she was dressed.

Ryann glanced down at her outfit. "What?"

"That coat is incredible. Is that cashmere?"

She fingered the lapel briefly and nodded.

Maddie whistled again, shaking her head.

"What?" she asked again.

"Nothing. I just don't think I've ever seen one outside of a movie."

She frowned, not sure what she implied. Despite the "incredible" comment, Maddie didn't seem impressed per se. In fact, if Ryann had to guess, she almost seemed put off. Resentful? Jealous? Not quite, but something similar.

"Cashmere's the best," Ryann said.

"I'm sure it is," Maddie said, and winked.

She was about to reply, but the men started walking away, and Maddie followed. She had to hurry to catch up with them, still miffed. Who the hell was Maddie to question her wardrobe? Especially dressed the way she was now. Maddie wouldn't look out of place in a lumber mill.

The last of the day's warmth had faded from the air outside, and the chill was biting. Some of the melted snow had also frozen on the sidewalk, so it was slick with ice. The brewery was a little removed from the center of downtown, but from here she could see the stunning light display that crisscrossed over the streets. The ones above the street had been set up a little like the ceiling of a circus tent, rising to a point in the middle of the street. All the light poles were festooned in lights as well, sparkling under the garland, everything in reds and bright whites. It was pretty and impressive, altogether an effort that bespoke a great deal of effort and money.

She bundled herself a little tighter, letting the others get far ahead, wondering, then, how long it would be before they noticed her absence.

Maddie turned back for her, shoulders hunched up a little against the cold, hands stuffed in her coat pockets. She jerked her head toward the guys, and Ryann moved to join her. She almost slipped, and Maddie was there in an instant, catching her elbow in a strong, steady hand.

"Whoops," she said. "Careful. Those aren't the best shoes for winter weather."

Ryann stopped still, glaring at her. "So now there's something wrong with my shoes, too?"

Maddie shrugged. "Just telling it like it is."

"Stop flirting back there, you two!" Stuart called. "I want to eat sometime this century, thank you very much!"

"Shall we?" Maddie asked, offering an elbow.

She ignored it and hurried to catch up with her friend. The last thing she wanted was gallantry from the woman after she'd insulted her. Twice.

"Wait up, Ryann!" Maddie called. She heard her jogging to catch up, and a moment later, her hand was on her arm again.

"Look. I'm sorry. I didn't mean to piss you off."

She stopped and turned toward her. She glared and yanked her arm free. "It's fine. Let's drop it."

Maddie's eyebrows popped up. "Jeez. Touchy much? I guess what they say about redheads is true."

"And what's that?" she asked, voice rising despite herself.

"Hot tempers," Maddie said, smirking.

She let her mouth drop open, almost unable to believe what she'd heard.

"Are you fucking—" she said.

"Hey! Ladies!" Stuart called again. "I'm starving here! Come on, already."

Maddie smirked again and left her there, nearly breathless with rage. It took every ounce of her willpower to make herself keep walking. She caught up to the three of them outside a busy place called Henry's and managed to catch Stuart before he went inside.

"Can I talk to you for a sec?" she asked him.

"Sure," he said, clearly confused. He turned to Jai. "Go ahead and get a table. We'll be in soon."

Jai raised his eyebrows briefly, but he and Maddie disappeared inside.

"What's up?" Stuart asked.

She opened her mouth, almost ready to tell him about her recent exchanges with Maddie, but his happy, excited expression stopped her. The last thing he needed was some weird drama, not when he was so clearly thrilled with everything. She didn't need to bring him down.

"It's nothing. I'm not feeling well. I'm tired, and I shouldn't have had all those beers." She paused. "Do you mind if we pick up again tomorrow? I'm not up for any of this right now."

Stuart squinted at her. "Are you sure something else isn't going on? What were you and Maddie talking about?"

She shook her head. "Nothing. I'm just tired."

He squeezed her shoulder. "Okay, Ryann. You're right. This is a lot to handle after the trip you had. I'm sorry. We should have saved the introductions for tomorrow."

"No. It's fine. You couldn't have known. And I'm so glad to meet Jai. He's really incredible."

"He is, isn't he?"

"Yes. He really is. Give them my apologies?"

"Sure. If you want, I can even order some food sent over for you. You have to eat something."

"Thanks, but it's fine. I can ask Ethel for a sandwich or something."

He raised an eyebrow at her, clearly not buying it. She laughed.

"Okay. I'd love it if you sent something over. Something light, please. A salad."

"Are you sure? They have a really great steak sandwich here."

She gave him a quick hug. "Salad's good. So I'll see you tomorrow?"

"Yes—first thing in the morning. Nine a.m. I'll give you and Maddie the lowdown so you can get started. You have an appointment at ten and one at two, so dress for a whole day out."

She sighed again, suddenly as tired as she'd claimed to be. "Okay. But you better bring coffee."

She spent the walk back to the hotel going over her interactions with Maddie. What on earth had made her behave that way and say what she'd said? Finally back in her room and lying on the ridiculous bed, she was too tired to wait up for the food to arrive. She started to drift off, fully clothed, long before someone knocked on her door. She didn't get up.

CHAPTER FIVE

Ryann was up before dawn and showered and dressed long before sunup. The time difference worked in her favor, as she was able to call into the office and check in with Ted the moment he was there.

"Tell me how it's going," she said.

"It's dominoes, Ryann," he said. "Everything is getting set up, but at the same time, everything could fall down at the slightest screwup. I can't think of a single moment since I started when things seemed so exciting or precarious."

She laughed. Only Ted could or would be this honest with her. "You didn't seem to have any of these misgivings when I was still there."

"Well, that's just it—you're not here."

She had to bite back a hot reply. She hated the idea that the company would fall apart the moment she wasn't there. Still, this deal was her baby, so she could appreciate how delicate the situation could seem with her gone and not assuaging anyone's nerves.

"What's happening on the London front?" she asked.

Ted sighed, obviously stalling for time, rustling papers.

"It's not good. The board went back and forth with them all day yesterday, and they're doing the same today. So far, they're not budging. London can't commit to anything sooner than the first week in March."

"Which means we'll lose Tokyo and Sydney." She squeezed the bridge of her nose, eyes pinched tight. It was much too early in the day for a migraine.

"Have you done the numbers yet?" she asked him.

"Yes. It's not an easy choice. Sydney is pretty small potatoes— even smaller than our firm. But Tokyo is a giant. Together, they're basically the same as London, so even if we can get the others to agree to wait, it's basically the same one way or another in terms of shared costs."

"What about the possible projections? How would they be affected?"

"Okay—so here's where it gets really complicated."

"The fast version, please."

"In a nutshell, we'll make more money if we have London than if we have the other two. But either way, if we lose anyone, it really, really hurts the numbers."

"Damn it."

"Exactly. I don't see the board taking the risk if we can't increase those profit margins with a loss of one or more of those cities." He paused, and she knew without seeing him that he was reluctant to keep talking. Finally, he took a deep breath. "I hate to say this, Ryann, but the board will force you to pull out whether we lose London *or* Tokyo *or* Sydney, or any combination of those three. The numbers don't justify the possible losses otherwise."

"Well then, we're back to square one. We have to get everyone on board." She rubbed her eyes again. "What time is it in London right now?"

"Almost three."

"So the board will probably be negotiating for another three hours, maybe longer if they have drinks at the pub and the cigar club after."

"A given," Ted said.

"How long are they in town?"

"Today and then a half day tomorrow before they fly home."

She calculated. "Okay—here's what I want you to do. First, call me the minute you hear anything today from London—good or bad. Do you have someone on the inside?"

"Bill's there. He's the new CFO's assistant. He's been texting me on and off."

"Good. Let me know when you hear from him. The board won't bother contacting me until Monday if it's bad news. And start working on Tokyo and Sydney. Get those exact figures to me, and set up a phone meeting for some time tomorrow."

"Not possible. Our tomorrow is their Saturday."

Ryann sighed. "Right—I always screw that up. Okay then—their tomorrow afternoon or early evening, whatever time that is here."

"Might be close to midnight for you. Is that okay?"

"Sure. Just get me an hour with the CEO of each, and let me know the time here."

"Consider it done."

"Keep brainstorming about London in the meantime. Maybe we'll luck out, and the board will come back with good news later today or tomorrow, but we can't bank on it. We have to know someone over there who can put some pressure on them from the inside."

"I'll start combing the files again." He cleared his throat. "What about you, Ryann? Are you still willing to fly to London if they won't budge? I still think that's the best way to persuade them."

She rolled her shoulders a little, the strain now causing her entire body to ache. "Yes. I could get away next week for a couple of days, maybe, if I did a red-eye and came back as soon as possible. But let's hold off on booking until we know the outcome of the board's trip."

"Sounds good." She could hear him typing and waited for him to speak again.

"So how is it going out there?" he finally asked.

"I'm calling you from a heart-shaped, rotating bed, to give you a mental image."

He laughed. "Listen. I don't want to be the jerk here, and I know Stuart's a major part of your life, but maybe this isn't the time to disappear for two weeks? Any other time, perhaps, but even then, it seems like a lot to ask."

She frowned. He was right, especially after last night. Juggling a multi-million-dollar deal and a wedding was not going to be pleasant, or maybe even possible. Still, it wasn't her assistant's place to say it.

"I'll be the judge of that. Get those meetings set up."

"Yes, ma'am."

She hung up, tossing her phone aside and lying back, her head pounding. She'd kept the heavy blinds down, the room illuminated by the only lamp with tolerable light in the whole place. Still, the sunlight was peeking in from outside now. Glancing at the clock, she realized she would need to rush downstairs if she wanted something to eat before Stuart showed up in a little less than an hour. It all seemed far too complicated and annoying, and she closed her eyes. She would take a short nap.

Startled awake by loud knocking, she sat up almost screaming, clutching her chest. Her mouth was dry, and she was disoriented. It took her several seconds to remember where she was. She spied the clock then. It was after nine. It must be Stuart.

She climbed unsteadily to her feet, stretched briefly, and then walked over to open the door.

"Taking a nap, were we?" Stuart said.

She let him come inside without a word. He handed her a wrapped muffin and a large mug of steaming coffee.

"These are from downstairs," he explained. "Ethel was worried that you didn't come down for breakfast, so she sent this mug and a German muffin."

"What's a German muffin?"

He laughed. "You got me." He stood still, taking in the decorations, and then turned back to her, suppressing laughter. "So how do you like the room?"

"You're an asshole."

He laughed again and steered her back to the bed, the two of them sitting down at the foot.

She took a sip of her coffee and wrinkled her nose. "You were supposed to bring me coffee. Real coffee."

"And you'll have it. Maddie is coming with your double espresso."

She couldn't help but pout a little, but she unwrapped the muffin and sniffed before nibbling at it, grimacing when she finally recognized the ham.

"Do you want this?" she asked.

"Still off the swine?"

"They're intelligent animals."

He laughed. "You don't give a shit about animals, and you know it." He started eating it, cramming in large bites. He'd always been a voracious, messy eater, but she'd forgotten. She couldn't help but smile as she watched him shovel the rest of it in, and when his cheeks were totally stuffed, he asked, "What?" mouth still full, crumbs flying out.

"Nasty!" She pushed his shoulder. "Swallow first."

He did, with some difficulty, looking like he might choke. He finally managed to get it down, clearly trying not to laugh.

"That's what he said."

"Did you seriously almost choke to death so you could make that joke?"

He snorted, and she pushed him again. He retaliated, and before long they had devolved into a wrestling match, which then turned into a pillow fight. Neither of them heard the knock at the door, so when Maddie came in, they were still distracted and engaged.

"You cheater!" Ryann said. "You can't use a throw pillow."

"Oh, yeah?" he said. "Why not?"

"Because they're harder. They hurt more."

"Like you can feel it through your thick head," he shouted back.

"Children, children," Maddie said. "Do I have to separate you two, or can you play nicely?"

"She started it," Stuart said, pointing.

Ryann flushed with embarrassment and dropped the pillow. She tried to smooth her messy hair, which was surely sticking out in all directions from the static in here and the pillows that had been pummeling her the last few minutes. She could hardly stand the idea that this stranger had seen them playing like—well, as she put it— children.

Maddie, however, was smiling, her hair today more sophisticated and styled than it had been last night. She was once again in a version of lumber-wear, but those burgundy workpants hugged her shapely legs so well, and that nice gray-flannel shirt brought out the rich blue of her eyes.

"Excuse me for a moment, please," Ryann said, heading toward the bathroom.

"You embarrassed her," Stuart said behind her.

Ryann didn't hear Maddie's reply, closing and locking the door. Her forehead pressed into the wood, she waited for her face and body to cool a little before turning to the mirror.

The color was still high in her cheeks, and her hair was, as expected, a complete mess. She'd planned to have it straightened sometime this week, but after Erin and Darcy's compliment last night, she wasn't so sure. Her curls had always been a source of frustration and anguish. She'd been straightening her hair since elementary—first at her mother's insistence, then her own. Then, when everything had picked up at work last autumn, she'd missed one appointment with her stylist, then another, until now she could hardly remember the last time she'd had her hair done. It was, in fact, longer and curlier than she could remember it being, even as a child. It brushed the middle of her back. The color was a fiery red, one shade darker than orange, another source of displeasure most of her life. Still, as she regarded herself now, she recognized how striking and wild it was. It was entirely different than her usual style, but maybe she'd leave it alone. She liked the change. She used some mousse to tame the flyaways and tied it back in a loose, thick bundle at the base of her neck, too tired to try anything more elaborate.

Her eyes, a pale green, were bloodshot and red-rimmed, propped up by dark, almost purple circles. With her pale complexion, it was always obvious when she was even the slightest bit tired, and she was exhausted. She dabbed some more concealer on the darkness, swiped on a little more mascara, and then straightened her shirt. Did she have time to change it?

When she came out of the bathroom, Maddie was laughing, leaning against the room's doily-covered desk, and Stuart was back at the foot of the bed, chuckling at whatever they'd been talking about. They looked her way, and she gave them her best boardroom smile. Stuart, clearly recognizing its phoniness, stood, arms out, and pulled her into a crushing hug.

"Maddie's sorry and so am I. I didn't mean to reveal our antics to an outsider. I forgot you two don't know each other yet."

He pulled back a little, surveying her up and down. "You're a little skinny, sugar, but you look really good in this outfit." He fingered the edge of her blouse. "Lovely. I can't remember the last time I felt silk like that."

She swatted him once and stepped away. "Maybe you should get out of town more. I can't help it if apparently the only thing you can buy in this town is flannel."

"Hey!" Maddie said. "I resemble that remark."

She glanced Maddie's way, meeting her eyes for the first time this morning. Maddie winked, which immediately caused her face to heat again, and she looked away, embarrassed once more to be so transparent.

Stuart had apparently seen this exchange, and his head turned back and forth between them, eyes narrow.

"What is it with you two?" he asked. "Did something happen last night that I need to know about?"

"Nope," Maddie said, emphasizing this "p" sound by popping it.

"Not a thing," Ryann said.

Stuart didn't seem convinced, but he eventually sighed. "Okay, fine. Be mysterious. Anyway, you guys have two tasks to take care of today." He reached into his pocket, pulling out a folded sheet of paper. He handed it to Ryann, gesturing for Maddie to join them. Maddie stood up from her perch on the desk, walking closer, and Ryann once again caught a strong whiff of vanilla when she neared. The scent reminded her of the mini-breakdown she'd had yesterday in the lobby—the friendly mug of hot chocolate that had thrown her for a loop. She opened her mouth slightly to avoid inhaling the scent.

"First up is flowers," he said, pointing at the top of the list. "Those are our colors—red, pink, and white. You two have an appointment for ten, so you're going to have to leave in like fifteen to make it on time. Then you have a break until two, which is the first of the bakeries."

"There's more than one?" Ryann asked.

Stuart stared at her, putting one hand to his chest, aghast. "You know how I feel about cake, girlfriend. It has to be exactly right."

"Shouldn't you choose it, then?"

"No time today," he said. "I'll try to make it to the next one. Just choose the best-tasting one. We'll take care of the design."

"How many bakeries are there?"

He had the wherewithal to look ashamed and mumbled something under his breath.

"What was that?" she asked, cupping an ear.

"Five. But they're spread out."

"We're going to only one florist, but we're checking out five bakers. Am I hearing you right?"

He nodded, grinning now.

"Okay. What else are we doing?"

"That's all the planning stuff for today. Jai's still setting up some of the rest. We're doing the ceremony outside at the festival, but the reception venue is still in the air. He's getting all of those appointments lined up for tomorrow and Saturday."

"I have studio time tomorrow," Maddie said.

"He's working around your schedule," he said. "Don't worry."

"What about next week?" Ryann asked.

Stuart started ticking off his fingers. "There's the photographer, the caterer, and maybe the linen and equipment rentals for the venue, depending on which place you two book for the reception." He smiled at Maddie. "And, of course, the decorations."

"All of this with less than two weeks before the wedding?" Ryann asked.

He shrugged. "Jai said it shouldn't be a problem. This isn't New York, or even Denver."

"And the budget?"

"He's not booking appointments anywhere we can't afford."

Ryann was suspicious. Stuart had a small trust fund, but it was just that—small. He got some kind of stipend with his grant here, but even that was likely miniscule. She couldn't imagine that Jai made a lot of money working for the city, either. If this was as last-minute as they claimed, they weren't going to be able to afford much of anything at all. She shouldn't feel disappointed—after all, it wasn't her wedding. But she'd known Stuart almost all of their lives. He'd outlined exactly the kind of wedding he'd wanted countless times. The two of them had talked about it in detail over the years, and that kind of event wouldn't be done on the cheap. How on earth could she get him what he wanted on his budget?

He squeezed her arm. "Don't worry about it. Jai has a really big family. They're helping out."

She relaxed a little. "Okay."

"In fact, tonight we're having a sort of informal gathering at Jai's parents'. All his sisters and their families will be there, too. I wanted them to meet you before the hordes show up next week. They're really great people."

She had a slight flicker of panic at the thought but managed to give him a weak smile. "Wouldn't miss it."

"Okay!" He clapped. "You two better be off, but I'll see you out."

As she grabbed her things, she couldn't help but watch Stuart and Maddie joking around as they waited for her. They were very easy together, much like she'd always thought of herself with him. Seeing that gave her a kind of pang. Here was his new friend, one he obviously saw a lot of, and they were clearly close and had a lot in common. Maddie was an artist, like him, after all. While she and Stuart had fun this morning before Maddie showed up, and she was incredibly glad to see him here, happy and healthy, she couldn't quite shake the idea that she'd been replaced.

"Ready?" Maddie asked, her gaze sweeping up and down Ryann.

She fought an urge to ask her about her appraisal.

"Yes. Let's go."

CHAPTER SIX

They parted from Stuart outside, and Maddie led her to her beat-up classic red Bronco, apologizing in advance for the over- or under-enthusiastic heater.

"It's either the Sahara or the arctic—your pick."

"The Sahara, please," Ryann said, smiling.

Maddie started taking off her outer layers again, smiling when she saw Ryann watching her.

"I'm not kidding. It's like a thousand degrees in here when the heat's on. Sometimes I roll down the window to try to regulate it, but then my nose gets cold."

Ryann unbuttoned her coat slightly, not sure if she should completely disrobe, and sipped the rest of her espresso. She glanced around the cabin as they started driving. The car was old but clean. She saw no coffee cups or food wrappers, and the worn carpet was freshly vacuumed. The back seat had been laid flat, and plastic sheeting covered the entirety of the carpet back there. Having been Stuart's friend as long as she had, she recognized the dried, red streaks on the plastic for what it was—leftover clay.

"I'm not a serial killer, if that's what you're worried about," Maddie said.

"Isn't that exactly what a serial killer would say?" she asked.

Maddie chuckled, and they drove in semi-awkward silence for a while, the radio playing soft classical music, the town unrolling in the piercing brightness of the winter sunshine reflecting off the snow. The care that had gone into the decorations was a little more obvious than what Ryann had noticed in the taxi yesterday, when it had seemed overdone and over-the-top. Now she recognized a coordinated theme and the professional quality of the lighting displays. She'd seen some of this lighted last night between the brewery and the restaurant, but here in the daylight, it looked festive, fun.

Remembering that Maddie had a hand in creating these displays, she glanced over at her, curious once again about this woman. She was an artist, a sculptor, like Stuart, and, like them, had grown up in a small town. Maddie bobbed her head along with the Mozart, and the morning sunshine lit up her sandy, wavy hair like a halo. She was, in a word, compelling. But she'd been confusing last night—those digs about Ryann's clothes had been weird to the point of rudeness.

"Like what you see?" Maddie asked, glancing her way and then back at the road.

"Yes," she said, then froze, realizing the implication.

Maddie laughed.

"I meant the town," Ryann said, a little too late.

"Sure you did."

"No, really! It's very…cute."

"Cute, huh?" Maddie asked, squinting at her before winking. "Okay. I'll take it."

She knew her face had colored again and wondered how this woman could get under her skin so quickly and thoroughly. Ryann didn't know how to respond to the flirtation. Erin and Darcy flirting had seemed safe—but they were married. Maddie was something else.

Their car crested a hill, and suddenly snow-capped mountains appeared in the distance before them. A wide space opened on the right as the road curved around what Ryann soon realized was a lake covered in a sheen of white, crystalline snow and ice. All the light posts along the lake were festooned in red and silver garland, lights, and those oversized conversation hearts she'd seen everywhere in town.

"This is really gorgeous," she said.

"It is, isn't it? It's my favorite view in town. I actually took a slight detour so you could see it."

"Worth it," Ryann said.

"If you keep heading this way into the mountains, you end up in Estes Park. Ever been?"

"No. I've actually never made it to Colorado before."

Maddie turned her way with her eyebrows up. "Really? Never? Not once since Stuart moved here?"

"Never had the chance until now."

Maddie returned her attention to the road, her lips turned down a little at the corners. She could explain, but excuses would likely sound pathetic, even to her. Initially, when Stuart had moved here, his visits to New York were his escape. He'd soak up everything he missed about the city in his weekend getaways and then come back here, reluctantly, to live out his time until his next trip. Then, last year, when things had so abruptly changed, and he'd stopped coming to New York, they'd played around with the idea of her coming to Colorado, but in fact, it had never occurred to either of them for her to come here to Loveland. They'd discussed Denver or Aspen.

All of this, if she said it, would sound like she was blaming him, which was only half the truth. They'd sneered at this town when he first moved here. Stuart might have had a change of heart, but he'd never invited her here, and she would never have known how nice it was until she came.

Maddie, however, had seemed to take her justification as an almost personal affront. She still seemed a little upset, still frowning slightly, eyebrows low, their earlier banter apparently forgotten. They pulled into a strip mall with the flower shop, Blooms and Grooms, and Maddie parked the Bronco, turning it off and simply sitting there, hands still on the wheel. The car rattled a little as it settled down, the heat wheezing to a stop several seconds later.

"He was really lonely, you know," Maddie suddenly said, turning her way. "When I first met him, he didn't know anyone here. He would come into the studio, work, and leave. I never saw him around town, never knew anything about him. Then we had a little job to work on together—we consulted on a public piece for the city—and I realized what a nice guy he was. I invited him out with me, introduced him around." She paused, still looking put out. "It was like he didn't have a friend in the world. In fact, I never even heard your name until last week."

Anger and sorrow rose in Ryann. "And what do you think happened to me? I was alone too, you know. I missed, no, miss him more than I've ever missed anyone in my entire life. We tried, goddamn it. When he first moved here, we tried. Then, all of a sudden, he stopped calling, stopped visiting. We've barely spoken in the last year." Tears rose in her eyes, and she blinked them away. "I lost my best friend, my only family. And yes—I should have come out here. I'll admit that. But he shouldn't have cut me out of his life like that, either."

They were quiet for a while, Maddie apparently giving her a moment to collect herself as she dabbed at her eyes. When Ryann was brave enough to glance over at her, Maddie was staring at her evenly, brows still furrowed. She seemed to be considering what Ryann had said. Finally, her expression cleared, and she gave a weak smile.

"Long distance, huh? What a bitch."

Ryann couldn't help but laugh, and Maddie laughed with her, the tension immediately lifting.

Maddie touched her gloved hand. "Look. I'm sorry. I made some assumptions, and I shouldn't have. It sounds super complicated, and it's not my place to judge what happened. He probably didn't bring you up because he missed you. Really. I'm sorry."

"Thanks. It's okay. You couldn't know."

"And I'm glad you're here now. When the guys told me they were getting married, I was afraid they'd end up making me do everything on my own."

Ryann narrowed her eyes. "Oh, I see. You just want me for my labor."

Maddie shrugged. "What else?"

She turned away to hide her disappointed shame. She'd thought they were back to flirting. She cleared her throat. "You know," she said, "we could probably split up some of this work. We don't both have to go to these appointments. I could borrow a car from someone, or maybe rent one."

Maddie stared at her strangely, one eyebrow raised. "If that's what you'd prefer, sure. I'll let the guys know they can make some appointments when I'm busy."

Maddie got out of the car, walking quickly to the door without waiting for her. She couldn't help but think she'd made some kind of blunder—insulted her somehow. But how and why, she couldn't imagine.

Despite its modest appearance outside, the flower shop was nicely appointed inside. There were various types of pretty, loose flowers in black buckets for sale, as well as premade bouquets, large and small. The air in here was humid, though cool, and everything seemed fresh and clean despite the somewhat-crowded aisles.

A middle-aged woman with long, graying, black hair appeared from the back, drying her hands with a towel. She wore a flowered apron over denim overalls and sandals with socks.

"Welcome to Blooms and Grooms, ladies. Are you my ten o'clock?" she asked.

"That's us," Maddie said. She grabbed Ryann's hand, pulling her closer. "We're so excited."

The woman beamed. "I'm so happy you've chosen my shop for your wedding. My name is Brenda. Please," she gestured, "follow me to the back. I'll get you some cocoa and show you some samples to review."

Brenda turned to lead them, and Maddie started to follow. Ryann pulled her back, whispering as loud as she dared.

"What are you doing?"

Maddie grinned. "Come on. It'll be fun."

"But why?"

Maddie winked. "No reason. It's just pretend."

She let herself be led to the back office, still holding Maddie's hand. Brenda gave them a warm, almost goofy smile, and she felt compelled to give her one in return, though still confused.

Maddie was giving her emotional whiplash. She had no idea what this was about, or why she was suddenly in the mood to play make-believe, when not five minutes before she'd basically shot Ryann down. Where was this coming from?

They were led to a windowless room with a small table and three chairs. Several binders lay on the table, along with some color swatches, each in various hues of the same relative color, a little like paint samples.

"Please, sit," Brenda said. "I'll be right back with some cocoa."

Once she was out of sight, Ryann pulled her hand from Maddie's and sat down, taking a moment to remove her outer garments and her gloves. She was rattled, both from the conversation in the car and Maddie's behavior here in the shop.

Maddie rolled her eyes and sat down next to her. "Boy, oh, boyo. You sure know how to have a good time."

Ryann glared at her. "I don't understand the point. And the 'pretend' isn't even a good idea. I mean, at the very least, Brenda will figure it out once we pay for everything. And if not then, she will once she delivers the flowers to Jai and Stuart's venues."

"And? So we'll get caught. Who cares?"

"I do!"

"Clearly."

They lapsed into a tense silence again, Ryann almost fuming. Something about this entire situation with Maddie was tearing at every defense she had. Normally cool and collected, she'd been angrier with this perfect stranger than she had with almost anyone, and it had happened several times in less than twenty-four hours.

Still, she thought, risking a quick glance at her, they had to work together. She might be able to lessen their contact with some careful dodges over the next week or so, but she couldn't completely avoid her, either. She was going to have to make the best of this weirdness between them.

"Listen," she said, touching Maddie's sleeve. "I'm sorry. You're right. It doesn't matter at all. We can pretend, if that's what you want."

Maddie perked up at once, her face lighting up. "Really? You don't mind?"

She still didn't see the purpose of the make-believe, but Maddie seemed really happy with the idea. It didn't seem to have any malice behind it, anyway. And really, what difference did it make?

"No. I guess not. It could be fun."

If Maddie detected the lie or her reluctance, she didn't let on.

"Great!" Maddie said. "I have this theory that we'll be treated better if people think we're a couple. Let's see if I'm right."

"Really? Even though we're…" She gestured between them.

"What?"

"Two women?"

Maddie's brows lowered. "What do you mean?"

She laughed. "I mean, don't you think some people might treat us *worse* if they think we're a couple? A lesbian couple, I mean?"

Maddie was about to reply, but they heard Brenda coming their way again and froze. Ryann took Maddie's hand almost unconsciously, and Maddie squeezed her fingers just as Brenda walked into the room holding two steaming mugs. She smiled at the sight of them and set the drinks down before sitting across the table from them.

"Did you get a chance to look at any of this?" Brenda asked, indicating the swatches and the binders.

"No," Maddie said. "We weren't sure if we should wait for you."

"That's fine. Let's start with colors."

"Red, white, and pink," Ryann said.

Brenda chuckled. "Makes sense for Valentine's Day. Let's see what we have here in those shades." She riffled through the swatches, pulling two for each of the colors. She slid one of each to them. Each swatch had about thirty different squares on it, all variations of the same color.

"Wow," Ryann said. "I didn't realize so many different reds existed. Or pinks or whites, for that matter."

"Actually," Brenda said, "there are far more than you see there. If you don't see the exact color you want on one of those, I can show you more."

Ryann and Maddie made eye contact, and Ryann raised an eyebrow. She was totally lost, with no idea which of these Jai and Stuart would like.

"Any ideas?" she asked. "You're the artist, so that makes you the expert."

They were still holding hands, and Maddie squeezed hers again, lightly, almost as if for reassurance.

"Let's aim for the classic Valentine's hues," Maddie said. "What do you think of this one?" She pointed.

While Ryann could clearly see the difference between most of the reds (some were very subtle), she couldn't really see why one might be better than the other. That said, the one Maddie indicated did in fact seem very "Valentiney"—a bold, bright red that reminded her of the various paper cutouts and streamers she'd seen around town.

"Looks good to me."

Brenda made a note. "Okay—Candy Red. The next two are a little harder."

"Why don't you pick the pink, hon?" Maddie asked.

She couldn't help but glare at this endearment, and Maddie smirked in response. She focused on the color swatch to avoid saying something but immediately felt out of her element. It was true—there were a lot of pinks in the world. Some seemed closer to red, some to white, obviously, but a whole swath in the middle were something else—maybe a little blue or purple? She couldn't tell. She'd seen greater variations in the pink decorations around town, as well. She couldn't determine a correct choice here.

"Boy, I don't know," she finally said. She glanced at Maddie. "They're all so different."

"Which one do you think would go best with our red?" Maddie asked, holding out the swatch to her.

Why was Maddie making her do this? She'd meant what she'd said before—she trusted Maddie's eyes more than her own. Still, she could see that Maddie wanted her to choose, and it wasn't as if she'd never selected colors for an event before. She started dragging the swatch of Candy Red near each of the pinks, finally stopping next to two that stood out to her.

"One of these?" she asked, uncertain.

Maddie bent closer and nodded. "Good choice. I like them both. You decide."

She was strangely pleased with herself and Maddie's trust in her. She studied them for a few more seconds before pointing at one. "This. Carnation Pink."

"Nice," Brenda said, making a note. "Okay, and finally the hardest of all—the white."

"This one's on you, sweetie," Ryann said, smirking at Maddie.

Maddie laughed and pulled the swatch close to her face, brows furrowed. "Gosh. I don't know. I think as bright and as vivid as we can with those other colors, but our red and pink have a little blue in them too, so I guess that means this one." She pointed.

"Great! Chantilly will go nicely with your other colors," Brenda said, once again making a note. "That was very quick, ladies. I have to say, I'm impressed with both of you. Most couples are in here choosing colors the entire first session. Five minutes has to be a record."

She couldn't help but meet Maddie's smile with her own. This was all pretend, but it was hard not to feel a little proud.

"Thanks," Maddie said. "We like to think we agree on a lot of things."

"That's lovely," Brenda said. "I always say I'm lucky to work in this field, and it's because of nice people like the two of you. You're adorable, by the way."

She thought Brenda was laying it on a little thick at this point, but she didn't really care. She was actually starting to enjoy this little fairy tale. Now a little emboldened, she decided to push things a little farther.

"Thank you," she said. "That's partly why I couldn't wait any longer to marry her. Because she's so dang cute."

Maddie's eyebrows lifted in clear surprise, and Ryann couldn't help but smirk at her. Two can play this game, she thought.

Brenda chuckled. "Well, you two made it just under the wire, I'd say. Yours is the last wedding I can squeeze in. Busy time of year."

Ryann thought it was basically a miracle that she'd had any openings, but as Stuart had mentioned, this wasn't New York.

"All right then, let's talk flowers and arrangements. This can be even harder than colors, but I can certainly narrow it down for you based on your color choices. Let's discuss arrangements, first, and then we can think about what kinds of blooms you like. These three binders should get you started. This one is bouquets, boutonnieres, and corsages. This one is centerpieces and other decor. And this is for everything else. I'll be back in a few to give you some more guidance."

She closed the door after herself, and they exhaled audibly, suppressing giggles. Ryann remembered then that they were still holding hands and let go, picking up her lukewarm cocoa and taking a sip.

"You're enjoying this now, aren't you?" Maddie asked, smiling.

She pretended to consider. "Yes. You should have seen your face."

Maddie laughed. "Yours, too, 'hon.'"

They laughed again, and she turned her attention to the first binder. "I hadn't thought about this part. Now she'll know it's not us getting married."

"Why?"

"Because there won't be any bouquets."

Maddie snorted. "Of course there will. Jai specifically asked for them."

"He did?"

"Yes. And boutonnieres. And corsages. And flower crowns. He basically wants a million flowers on everyone."

"Do you have a list of how many we'll need?"

"Not yet. But I think we can choose the arrangements now and tell her numbers once we have them."

"Okay. Which one do you want to look at?"

"We should do it together," Maddie said, pulling the wearable binder toward them. She scooted her chair closer, her shoulder brushing Ryann's now, their knees touching. Ryann didn't know if she should pull away or stay where she was, but since Maddie didn't seem to notice how close they were, she stayed put. She had to turn the pages as they opened from her side, and Maddie leant forward, examining every page closely. Ryann wanted to get closer herself, but that would put her farther inside Maddie's personal space, and she wasn't sure if she should do that. It was all fine pretending when Brenda was in the room, but alone was different.

"I like the bouquets on this page the most," Maddie said after flipping back and forth a few times. "What do you think?" She leaned back, and her eyes met Ryann's, their faces very close now. Ryann didn't look down at the binder, her gaze still locked in those blue pools of light.

"Beautiful," she said, almost whispering.

One of Maddie's eyebrows rose, and she leaned forward slightly, amusement tugging up one corner of her mouth. Ryann inched forward, her eyes fluttering closed, and then the door opened, startling them away from each other.

"Oh, gosh. I'm sorry," Brenda said. "I didn't mean to interrupt."

"You didn't—"

"It's fine," Maddie said. "We can always kiss later."

Ryann flushed with heat, suddenly mortified. What on earth had almost happened? What had she almost done? She didn't know Maddie at all. It wasn't like her to kiss some stranger on a whim. Even someone so cute.

Damn it, she thought. She really is cute.

As Brenda and Maddie discussed the bouquets and matching boutonnieres, Ryann let herself drift, still wrestling with what had almost happened. It was entirely out of character for her. She'd let herself get carried away in their little playact.

She managed to smile along as they moved on to the other arrangements, letting Maddie take the lead for all the specifics. Maddie threw her a few confused, concerned glances, so Ryann squeezed her hand a couple of times in reassurance. However, Ryann remained in a tumult. By the end of the session, she almost ran for the door.

CHAPTER SEVEN

Outside, the air was still piercing, but as Ryann stood there nearly panting, the sun was warm on her skin. She closed her eyes, tilting her face toward the light, breathing deeply to calm down. Stuart had mentioned the elevation when he first moved here, but until she'd been here herself, she hadn't realized how much it would affect her. The air seemed thin, insufficient somehow as she took it in.

"You okay?" Maddie asked, startling her.

She managed a weak smile. "Sure. I was getting a headache in there with all those flowers."

Maddie narrowed her eyes. "Are you sure that's all? You got kind of funny after we almost—"

"I'm fine."

Maddie continued to squint at her before finally lifting one shoulder, dismissing the issue. She checked her watch.

"We've got almost two hours before the next appointment. Anything you need to do in the meantime?"

"I should probably check in with the office."

"Do you need to go back to the hotel?"

Ryann paused. "No. I can do everything on my phone and tablet. I just need somewhere quiet to work for an hour or two. I have a phone call and some email to catch up on."

"Great. I was gonna drop in on the remailing program, see if I can help for a bit. It's not my shift, but they always need extra hands. It's on the way to the bakery, so it will save us a trip back downtown if we go there from here. They have a little table in the break room you could use while I'm busy. Would that work?"

"As long as I won't be in the way, that'll be fine for me."

They made their way back to the Bronco. It was colder inside than out, and Maddie glanced her way.

"Still want the heat?"

"Please."

They drove in relative silence, Maddie pointing out her old high school and a few other landmarks, classical music playing softly all the while. Verdi, this time. A few minutes into the drive, Ryann started to relax again. She'd been afraid Maddie would bring up the not-quite kiss, and she didn't want to talk about it. The less said about that near disaster, the better. In fact, if they never talked about it at all, she'd be much happier about the whole situation. She'd blame the elevation.

"What are you smiling about over there?" Maddie asked.

"Inside joke."

Maddie was still glancing at her every few seconds, clearly waiting for an explanation, and Ryann scrambled for a new topic.

"So, you like classical music?"

Maddie squinted, looking suspicious, then turned her eyes back to the road. "When I'm driving. Keeps me calm. How 'bout you? You want to listen to something else?"

"No. Classical is nice. I used to play, you know, in high school. So did Stuart."

"Oh yeah? How funny. So did me and Jai. Wait! Let me guess. You played…viola. And he played cello."

Ryann laughed. "Close. *He* played viola, and I played cello."

"Really? That's…" Maddie gave her a wry smile.

"What?"

She turned her way, lips curled impishly. "Hot. I've always thought lady cellists were sexy."

Ryann looked away, cheeks warm. Maddie laughed. They drove in silence another minute or two, Ryann desperate for a comeback but not thinking of one. She was usually smooth, a flirt, at least when she wanted to be, but the whole situation had thrown her off. Further, she didn't know if she wanted to be flirting. Was this Maddie's usual banter, or did she mean something by it?

"We were bass and piano," Maddie suddenly said. "I played the bass, Jai the piano. We were in the full band and in the orchestra pit for musicals, too."

Ryann was relieved to be back on safer ground, and she tried to make herself relax. "Wow. The bass is really heavy. Did you have one at home so you didn't have to lug it back and forth?"

"Unfortunately, no—my parents couldn't afford it. But I had the Bronco then, too, and a special dolly. It wasn't too bad if I got places on time. Jai helped a lot."

Ryann glanced in the back of the cabin again, picturing it. She could see a young Jai and Maddie stuffing the big instrument back there together, both in bad late-nineties fashion with terrible teenage haircuts. Maybe they shared a cigarette or two before heading home, like she had with Stuart.

She and Stuart would sit on the hood of her car blowing smoke rings, trying to outdo each other before she drove him home. Sometimes she'd stay over at his place for a night or two. Neither set of their parents had cared. In fact, she was pretty sure Stuart's parents had been hoping the two of them were up to something together in his bedroom those first couple of times she met them at breakfast. The less-than-subtle winks and smiles were a dead giveaway. His parents must have known he was gay long before he came out, but they seemed to have hoped for other news. And her parents had simply never kept track of where she was, even before she came out.

Maddie pulled into the parking lot in front of a small building with a canvas *Loveland Chamber of Commerce Volunteers* sign above the door.

"You wanna stay out here for your phone call, or come in now?" Maddie asked.

"Where would I go if I come in later?"

"We're all right there right inside the door, and don't worry. I'll see you. Or you can follow me in and meet the ladies now, and I can show you that quiet area to work."

She was already getting chilly, so she indicated that she'd follow her inside. They climbed out, leaving their heavier coats and outerwear in the Bronco. Ryann brought her phone and tablet in her purse.

Inside was a whirlwind of activity and decorations. Several long picnic tables had been set end-to-end in three rows, all covered with red plastic tablecloths with white hearts. More of the usual cutouts and streamers hung on the walls and from the ceiling.

Seated at the tables were some forty or fifty seniors, mostly women, all with various boxes of letters next to them, all wearing a red volunteer T-shirt. One woman removed a large manila envelope, opened it with a knife, and then stamped the smaller letter inside with a red inkpad. Laughter and high, excited voices, hammering stamps, and a radio blaring Perry Como nearly pierced her ears.

"Oh, good, you're here," an older woman said, bustling toward them. "And you brought a friend. That's great. We're actually short two people today, so we could use the extra bodies." She was wearing a bright-red shirt with white hearts, nearly identical to the tablecloths. Her hair was a bouffant of gray, almost bluish tight curls, her eyes twinkling behind her glasses.

"Doris, this is Ryann," Maddie said. "Doris is the volunteer coordinator here."

"Pleased to meet you," Ryann said, shaking her hand.

"And you, dear," Doris said, grasping Ryann's with her warm, soft ones.

"Unfortunately, Ryann has to make some phone calls and things for work," Maddie explained. "She was just with me in the car."

"Oh, well. That's too bad," Doris said, patting her hand a couple of times before letting it go. "We'll make do, I guess. I can always call someone on the waiting list if it looks like we won't have time."

"Waiting list?" Ryann asked.

"There's a long list of volunteers. We can pick only about fifty a year, though we're hoping to move to a bigger space next year. It's the most popular gig in town."

"A waiting list for volunteers?" Ryann repeated.

Maddie laughed, steering her away. "We might have broken her, Doris. Let me show you to that quiet space I was talking about, Ryann."

Maddie led her across the room to a door, greeting several people along the way. Behind the door was a small breakroom that had a tiny kitchen with a fridge, kettle, and microwave. The far corner had a little table and chairs, and Maddie indicated that she should sit there.

A couple of older women were in here, waiting on their tea, and Maddie greeted them warmly. Everyone here seemed to know Maddie. Of course, as the only butch lesbian and one of the only people under forty in the building, Maddie stood out a bit. Still, neither of these differences explained everyone's warmth toward her. She was obviously well known and liked. Ryann remembered then that Jai had called Maddie the town do-gooder, and he clearly hadn't exaggerated. Everyone seemed excited to see her, some of the volunteers even coming into the break room to greet her.

Ryann tried to tune them out while she made herself comfortable at the little Formica table. She got her tablet up and running and took off her cardigan. It was incredibly hot in here, but seeing the way all the volunteers were bundled up likely explained the heat.

Maddie walked over to the table. "You'll be okay in here, then?"

"Fine, thanks. I'll try to join you out there if I have some extra time. When do we need to leave for the bakery?"

"About 1:40, 1:45—so you have about an hour and twenty."

"Great. That should be plenty."

Maddie rejoined some of the volunteers, all of whom were throwing not-so-subtle glances her way and tittering, one of them whispering in Maddie's ear. Maddie laughed, blushing, her gaze meeting Ryann's for a brief moment, a little guilty. Maddie moved to leave, and the others all scurried out after her, talking and chatting at full volume. Ryann was left entirely alone.

After reading a few panicky emails from some of her own board members as well as some of the CEOs from the other companies hers was working with, Ryann spent the next hour on several frustrating phone calls, the process a little like trying to hold people's hands. She had to remind all of them in detail of what they stood to gain if they saw this deal through, although they had those numbers in front of them. Her board she could understand, but somehow, several of the other companies had heard rumors that London might be backing out. She had to try to assuage her board members who were on the ground in London telling her that London was about to back out, while also assuring the CEOs of the other companies that they weren't. It was a nightmare.

Meanwhile, as she made these phone calls, an occasional looky-loo came into the breakroom to gawk at her. It was obvious this was what they were doing, as none of them did much beyond glance not so subtly her way, pretend to search for something in a cupboard or in the fridge, and then leave empty-handed. She would wonder about them, then, pulled back into whatever conversation she was having, be forced to dismiss them.

When she was on her last call with Ted, an elderly man came in, nearly sneaking and hunched over, his glances at her verging on staring.

"Can you hang on a sec, Ted?" she asked.

"Sure."

"Can I help you with something?" Ryann asked the man in the room.

He froze, clearly startled, expression nearly panicked. "Uh, no! I just, uh…" He raised his hands in defeat. "All right. I don't have an excuse. I heard there was a real looker in here, and I wanted to see what all the fuss was about."

Ryann laughed. "And?"

He smiled back. "Now I understand."

She laughed again and held up a finger to the man before speaking in the phone again. "Hey, Ted? I'm going to have to call you back later tonight."

"That's fine," he said. "We're basically in a holding pattern until we know what's going on in London. I'll forward you the details about your Skype meetings tonight. Do you want to check in beforehand?" She was talking with the CEOs of Sydney and Tokyo starting at midnight.

"Let's play it by ear, if that's okay. I'll text you."

They hung up, and she gathered her things, the elderly man she'd been talking to still watching her every move.

"Shall we?" she asked, indicating the main room.

The man held out an elbow, and she let him lead her back into the chaos. If anything, things seemed even busier than before, with more volunteers at the tables and more overall activity as Doris and a few others bustled around helping people. The radio was still blaring (Rosemary Clooney now), and many people were shouting to project over the din of the music and the other people yelling at each other.

She spotted Maddie right away, there in the center of the room, laughing in the middle of a group of older women.

"You've got a real keeper there," the man said, lifting his chin in Maddie's direction.

"What do you mean?"

"She's a real peach. Probably one of the nicest people I've ever known."

She opened her mouth to explain their connection, but Maddie, spotting them, waved her over.

"Thanks for the escort," she said.

He tipped an invisible hat. "Any time."

She maneuvered her way across the room, dodging around the various people moving from station to station, as well as boxes of materials and letters stacked all over the room. Maddie indicated a spot on her left that was open.

"Have a seat," Maddie said.

It was hard to climb into the picnic-style seat gracefully. She had to basically step into it, and the fit was a little tight, her legs and elbows once again flush with Maddie's.

"I have a few letters left," Maddie said, pointing at a small pile, "and then we can leave. Do you want to do one?"

She hesitated, uncertain. "I guess. If you show me what to do."

Maddie grinned at her. "It's easy. You have to get the stamp placed in the right spot. But no one's a perfectionist here, so don't worry if it's a little wonky."

She gave the other women watching them a quick smile, and they all beamed at her. Two women across from them whispered together before snickering at her and Maddie, but before she could ask them about it, Maddie was already putting a stamped envelope in front of her.

"Here's a model." Maddie held up a laminated example that showed the Loveland stamps. A black one next to the postage stamp was made of two intertwining hearts, and another red one on the left side of the mailing address featured a baby cowboy and a poem.

"You can't always fit this one on the back of the envelope," Maddie said, pointing to the one with the cowboy. "But it should work on this card. Just go slow. Get it lined up before stamping down."

Ryann stood up so she could look straight down at the envelope, took the first stamp from the inkpad, and pressed it down. She picked it up, suddenly nervous, but it was aligned nicely.

"That's wonderful!" one of the women nearby said.

"Great work, young lady," another said.

She was strangely pleased by the praise, and when she happened to glance at Maddie, she, too, was beaming at her. She forced herself to turn her attention back to the second stamp and managed to press it cleanly in line as well.

"Nice," Maddie said. "Do you want to do the rest of these?"

She hesitated and then nodded. As Maddie set them up for her, she reflected on her own pleasure and excitement here. It was silly, really, to enjoy something like this. But on the other hand, everyone around her was excited, so maybe it was rubbing off on her. And having Maddie look at her like that—pleased, amused—certainly added a little something, too. She was embarrassed with herself. She was letting this whole thing go to her head.

The remaining envelopes stamped, Maddie helped her out of the picnic table, waving at Doris and pointing at their station, apparently so she could replace them. Doris gave her a big thumbs-up and turned to the senior next to her, gesturing wildly in her enthusiasm.

"You're leaving already?" the woman next to Maddie asked.

Maddie squeezed the woman's shoulder. "Yes. I'm sorry. I'm just second-string today, I'm afraid. Ryann and I are off to sample wedding cake."

At this, a wave of oooing and ahhing came from people near and far around the room. Then, it seemed, everyone spoke at once.

"You're getting married?"

"When did this happen?"

"How long have you been engaged?"

"Lucky girl!"

"Who's getting married?"

"To her?"

"When's the wedding?"

"Whoa, whoa," Maddie said, making a dampening gesture with her hands. "The wedding is Valentine's Day, everyone."

Another round of oohs and ahhs as well as a flurry of questions followed this announcement. Ryann was watching Maddie closely, wondering if she'd say something to explain, but when Maddie finally met her eyes, she was beaming, seemingly expectant.

Ryann leaned closer to her, whispering through a tight, forced smile. "Are you serious right now? Don't you actually know some of these people?"

Maddie rolled her eyes. "Okay, okay," she whispered back. "Do you want to tell them now?"

She recoiled, glancing around at the smiling faces turned their way. Everyone watching them seemed excited, happy. The two women who had been across from them at the table seemed particularly pleased with the situation. One had tears in her eyes.

Ryann sighed. "No. It's fine."

Maddie beamed at her and took her hand. "Thanks, everyone! We have to head out now. I'll be back this weekend."

A chorus of disappointed groans and good-byes followed them all the way outside.

She let go of Maddie's hand the moment the doors closed behind them.

"What the hell, Maddie?"

"Don't pretend you didn't like it."

"What? Of course I didn't. Now you've got half the town thinking we're getting married."

"Hardly," Maddie said, smirking. Then her brow lowered, and she touched her lip thoughtfully. "Though some of the biggest town gossips were in there, so you're probably more right than you know."

Ryann frowned at her, still confused. "So why didn't you let them know?"

Maddie paused and then shrugged. "A few reasons, chief of which is that they already thought we were a couple. You should have heard some of the things they asked me about you when you were working. Very…personal, let's say."

"And you didn't correct them?"

"No."

Ryann stared at her, completely confused. "Why on earth not?"

Maddie was quiet for a long pause. "To tell you the truth, I don't really know. They were so happy. I guess I didn't want to burst their bubble. Didn't you feel that way when they heard we were getting married?"

"Well, yes, but—"

"Exactly!"

Ryann took a step closer to her. "No, not exactly. You know these people. I don't. You live here. I don't. What will they think if they find out?"

"They'll think we broke up. Really, it's no big deal." She glanced at her watch. "And now we need to get going, or we'll be late."

She walked away and toward the Bronco, and Ryann stared after her, still rooted in place. For some reason, the idea that these people, these complete strangers, would think that she and Maddie broke up, despite the fact that their relationship was entirely fantasy, bothered her quite a lot. They all apparently adored Maddie, so what would she tell them when Ryann was no longer around? That Ryann had left her? She didn't like that idea one bit.

Sighing, she hurried to catch up, looking forward, at the very least, to the warmth of the car.

CHAPTER EIGHT

The drive to the bakery took them outside of town a bit—south, according to the little ball compass on the Bronco's dashboard. The houses dropped away behind them, and wide, expansive, and seemingly empty snow-filled plains opened on both sides. The snowcapped mountains to their right were crystal clear in the afternoon sun, the snowy expanses between them and the road so white they almost blinded her. The mesmerizing sight was startling in a way. Ryann couldn't tear her eyes away.

Maddie seemed happy to drive in silence, and she didn't protest. For once it didn't need to be filled. The unimaginably beautiful scene gave her enough to reflect on.

When she did finally look Maddie's way, her gaze rested on the road in front of them, her light, untroubled expression making her appear content. She glanced her way when Ryann kept watching her.

"Yes?" Maddie asked.

"It's really lovely out here. I guess I never realized how close the Rockies were to town."

"Ever been to the Rockies? In another state?"

"Never. I've seen the Cascades, and the Sierras, and the Appalachians, of course, but never the Rockies. I always..."

"What?"

She hesitated. "I don't want to insult you."

"Now you really have to tell me."

She still paused before replying. "Okay. I guess I always thought of this part of the states as fly-over country. I'm sorry. Obviously I didn't know what I was missing."

"How could you have known?"

She gave Maddie a grateful smile. "That's nice of you to say. But

I hate it when people make assumptions about things, and people, and places, really, and I guess I'm as guilty as anyone else."

"Well, now you know better. And you can go back to New York and tell all your friends about it." Maddie paused. "But not too many of them. We don't need *that* many tourists."

Maddie slowed, her directional on for a dirt road.

"There's a bakery out here?" Ryann asked.

"Yep. One of the best, I'd argue."

She saw the sign then, so small she would have missed it if they'd been driving faster.

"I know what you're thinking," Maddie said. "But I've been here before—that's how I knew to watch for the turn. They don't have a commercial storefront. They do baking for restaurants, catering companies, events—that kind of thing."

"Ah. That makes more sense."

She glanced over at Maddie again, wondering if she should ask. They were having a nice time now, the tension low. She didn't want to make things weird again. Still, she had to know.

"So…are we going to be pretending again?" As the words left her mouth, she suddenly dreaded the answer.

Maddie laughed. "No. Can't get away with it this time. The owner is one of Jai's sisters, Joan."

"Ah," she said, suddenly nervous. Jai had been wonderfully welcoming and warm last night, but that didn't necessarily mean his sister would be the same. She'd already been dreading the family get-together later tonight, but she would at least have a chance to look her best in front of them. Now, in her casual wear and with very little makeup, she was worried about first impressions. In a family as close as his, word would no doubt spread about her before she met the rest of them.

She flipped down the sun visor, hoping for a mirror, but of course a car this old didn't have one. She dug around in her purse, finding her compact, and checked her makeup, rubbing the smudges away from the corners of her eyes and lips.

Maddie drove past a surprisingly large farm-style house, circling to the back. Here Ryann saw a separate building, its design something between a barn and a warehouse, long and white with a peaked metal roof. Another small sign for the bakery hung above the single door, and someone came out as the car turned off. The woman who appeared was blond and small, a red apron tied around her middle.

"That's Joan now," Maddie said, climbing out of the cab.

She followed, more nervous than before, hanging back a little as the two greeted each other.

"Joan, this is Ryann, Stuart's maid of honor," Maddie said, waving her forward.

"Ah! I see," Joan said, holding out a hand. "Jai wasn't exaggerating."

"About what?" she asked, shaking her hand.

Joan and Maddie shared a sly glance, and then Joan shook her head. "Nothing, nothing. Come on in, ladies. It's plenty warm inside, and you have a lot of cake to try."

Maddie followed her at once, but Ryann held back, wondering what that exchange had been about. What had Jai told her?

As she walked inside, she was blasted with the mouthwatering aroma of baking bread. Most of the room was taken up by large-scale, industrial-sized ovens, but a small area had been set up here near the door with a table with chairs and a glass display case, in which several model wedding cakes sat under bright lights. Joan indicated the chairs, and she and Maddie sat down.

"I'll be back in a minute with the first round," Joan said, then disappeared in the back.

"I have a question," she said once they were alone.

Maddie laughed. "I thought you might. But don't worry—it was all good gossip."

"What?"

Maddie's brow furrowed. "You weren't asking about what she said outside?"

"No, actually, but now that you mention it—"

"Forget I brought it up!" Maddie said, holding up her hands.

She laughed. "Okay. Fine. Keep your secrets. Anyway, I was wondering why Stuart has so many bakeries lined up for us to try. You would think Joan's would be a given."

Maddie leaned onto her elbows. "You *would* think that, wouldn't you? Actually, Jai insisted we try more. He didn't want there to be any favoritism or nepotism."

"Does he think there will be an audit later?"

Maddie barked a laugh. "Right? That's what I said. But anyway, you know how Stuart is with sweets, so he didn't really argue with him. I think Stuart just wanted to go to a bunch of bakeries to try all the samples, but now it looks like that will be our job, not his."

She couldn't help a slight stab of something like jealousy. Clearly Maddie knew her friend well, which meant he'd spent a lot of time with her. She made herself shake it off.

"That sounds about right. And yet—here we are, and he's missing out."

"True. Hopefully he'll get to at least try some of the others with us."

Joan reappeared then, carrying two plates. She set one down in front of each of them before sitting next to Maddie. Each plate had a ring of tiny slices of cake, about a quarter inch a piece, eight total.

"You said this was the first round?" Ryann was a little apprehensive now.

Joan laughed. "I have another plate with just as many."

"Wow," Maddie said.

"I'll walk you through each slice. If you like a frosting or a cake or a filling, it can be combined with another cake or filling if you like one better."

"Gosh," Ryann said.

"The first," Joan said, pointing at a tiny slice on each of their plates, "is lemon cake with raspberry filling and lemon-cream-cheese frosting."

Ryann took the smallest bite possible, but the lemon flavor burst across her tongue, making her mouth water and pucker. Then the sweet raspberry filling caught up, mellowing it slightly. Maddie had taken a bigger bite and was still chewing, her eyes closed.

"What do you think?" Joan asked when she was done.

"Too sour," Ryann said. "But I like the raspberry."

"Same," Maddie said. "But it's really good, too."

"Okay. The next is a vanilla cake with strawberry filling and champagne frosting."

Once again, Ryann took the smallest bite she could that included all three parts of the cake. In this case, the strawberry was mellow, the frosting light and sweet on her palate.

"Mmmm," she said. "I like this one a lot. But it's a little plain for Stuart's tastes."

Maddie finished her bite and nodded. "Totally agree. I love it, but it's not for him."

This went on for each of the eight pieces. The next was chocolate cake with hazelnut filling and vanilla frosting; then yellow vanilla with chocolate filling and frosting; then a dark chocolate with cherry filling and whipped frosting, Black Forest style; and on and on. By the end of the first plate, Ryann's mouth was grainy with sugar, and she was having a hard time tasting any differences—it all seemed much too sweet.

"Wow," Maddie said. "This is really hard. I had no idea I could get tired of cake."

"Ideally, you'd try two or three kinds at a time and come back another day," Joan said. "But I understand you two are under a bit of pressure with that silly brother of mine. Why he couldn't wait for next year, like a normal person, is anyone's guess."

"He's just excited," Maddie said, waving a hand dismissively. "You know how he is."

Joan grabbed Maddie's hand, squeezing it. "Of course. They're so damn cute together I can't even be mad at them." She looked at Ryann. "We're all so crazy about Stuart. You must be really happy, too."

Ryann smiled. "I am. And Jai seems like a real sweetheart."

"He's the best," Joan said, and stood up. "How about I make us some coffee? That way the two of you can have a little break between the sweet stuff."

"That'd be a lifesaver," Maddie said.

Joan squeezed her shoulder and disappeared in the back somewhere again.

"So?" Maddie said. "Did you like any of them besides the plain one?"

Ryann stared at the leftover bits of cake. "I mean, they're all really good. I'm sure Stuart would like almost all of them except my favorite. But he's a chocoholic, so I think we should go with a chocolate cake, at the very least. Maybe this dark-chocolate hazelnut, or the Black Forest?"

"Agreed. Should we try them again?"

Ryann nodded, but before she could get a new bite, Maddie had already speared a little sliver of one and was offering it to her. She hesitated and then leaned forward, taking the morsel in her mouth, Maddie all the while watching her eat. Maddie's eyes darkened slightly, her lids somewhat hooded. Ryann looked away first, and Maddie seemed to shake herself awake, stirring next to her before taking her own bite. Ryann was drawn her way again a few seconds later, and she liked the way Maddie's forehead wrinkled slightly, obviously deep in thought as she revisited the cake.

Finished, she looked satisfied. "I'm in complete agreement. It comes down to that one or the Black Forest."

"Should we try the Black Forest again?" she asked.

One corner of Maddie's mouth lifted, wryly, and before she could chicken out, Ryann cut a little piece for her from her own plate, offering it to her somewhat boldly.

Joan appeared then, and Ryann dropped the forkful in her lap, startled.

"Whoops!" Joan said. "I'm sorry. Was I interrupting…you know what? Never mind. Let me get you a wet rag, Ryann."

"Actually," she said, standing up, "do you have a restroom I could use?"

Joan waved, indicating for her to follow, and she was led through the warehouse, past several of the hot ovens, the scent of bread heady. In the very back corner of the building were a small office and a tiny restroom, and Joan left her there to rejoin Maddie.

She closed and locked the flimsy door behind her, letting out a breath of relief. She turned to the sink, glad to see a pile of cloth hand towels, and wet one before patting off the frosting and cake from her thigh. Clean enough for now, she checked her face in the mirror.

"What the hell are you doing?" she whispered. In the space of— she checked her watch—less than six hours, she'd gone from annoyed with Maddie, to flirting with her, to almost kissing, and then flirting again with the cake. What was this? Was she really this starved for affection? True, Maddie was attractive. She didn't normally go for the whole woodsy, outdoorsy type—couldn't actually remember meeting a woodsy, outdoorsy type in New York—but she'd certainly always had a thing for confident butch women. And Maddie's confidence didn't come with some dark, self-centered arrogance, either, like so many of her exes. No, Maddie was simply a nice person. People were drawn to that. She was a good person who did good deeds and volunteered and helped friends plan weddings with no ulterior motive but to help people.

And she was really hot.

She gripped the edges of the sink harder, still staring at her reflection. After all, what difference did it make how hot Maddie was? Ryann had been acting like an idiot. She might see this woman a few more times between now and the wedding, and then what? It wasn't as if it would go farther than this week. Maddie would never come to

New York, and she wasn't likely to see Stuart more than once or twice a year. So, yes, they would probably run into each other when she visited sometime in the future, but thinking of that made all the flirting potentially more embarrassing. Imagine if they slept together and then had to pretend, over the next however long, that it didn't happen every time they saw each other? Mortifying.

No, she needed to stop now. No more flirting, no more leaning in to meet her lips, no more casual touches. They were simply acquaintances helping their friends get married. Nothing else. She could be cordial, but at the slightest hint of a flirtation, she needed to change the topic. And she had to put her foot down about the whole pretending thing, too. All of it had to stop and stop now.

She took a deep breath and studied her reflection, collecting herself. She reapplied some of her makeup and swished her mouth out with cold water, proud of herself for making the right choice.

Outside of the bathroom, the bakery seemed even hotter than before, and it took her a couple of minutes to wind her way back to the front of the building. She could hear merriment, and when she rounded the final corner, Maddie's head was thrown back, laughing, and Joan was wiping at her eyes, face red. They spotted her at the same time, still chuckling, and she blushed. Had they been talking about her?

"Have a seat, and I'll pour you some coffee," Joan said. "Didn't want it to get cold."

She hesitated. Which chair should she sit in? But she decided, as she moved forward, that sitting down next to Joan would be stranger than taking her previous seat next to Maddie. Maddie watched her the whole way, still smiling. Joan pointed at the cream and sugar on the table, and she shook her head, taking a long sip of the hot, bitter brew, smiling at Joan in thanks.

Maddie's humor had died a little, and, seeing her notice, she looked away, her cheeks slightly red.

What the hell was that? Ryann wondered.

"Okay—round two," Joan said, pushing another plate of cake in front of them.

She and Maddie groaned at the same time and shared a quick laugh before starting in. Again, Joan explained each of the cakes, but even with the coffee to sip between bites, it was hard going. She saw Maddie grimace before a bite and couldn't help but giggle. Maddie grinned more broadly at her before shoving it into her mouth, appearing determined, chewing quickly and swallowing before chugging her coffee again. Ryann laughed out loud.

"You would think you guys were being force-fed," Joan said.

"I'm sorry, Joan," Maddie said, touching her arm. "Like I said earlier, I never knew I could get tired of cake."

"Which is exactly why this is such a terrible way to do this," Joan explained. "Still, you've only got a couple more to try."

Ryann and Maddie made eye contact, and Ryann nodded reassuringly. They could get through this.

She set her fork down after the last bite, trying to catch something in this one beyond the overwhelming sweetness. She couldn't. She grabbed her mug, drinking the rest of the contents, fighting the urge to swish the bitter flavor around in her mouth. She shuddered slightly and then realized the others were watching her.

"I'm so sorry, Joan," she said. "It was just too much."

"I understand. Well, hopefully this doesn't turn you completely off whatever cake the two of you decide on."

"Oh, no! Not at all," she said. "I'm just not much of a sweets person. I'm not even sure…" They stared at her, seeming expectant. "Never mind."

"What?" Maddie asked.

She laughed nervously, fidgeting. "I was going to say, if *I* were getting married, I'm not even sure I'd have a cake."

"Oh?" Maddie asked, leaning forward. "What would you have instead?"

She gazed at Maddie's eyes, struck at once by the sensation of sinking into those blue depths. Her breath caught, and she made herself swallow against a strange tightness in her throat.

"Sushi," she managed to say.

Maddie's lips curled slightly. "Really? I'll have to keep that in mind."

Joan was looking back and forth between them, her eyebrows up in her hairline. She cleared her throat. "Uh, so, despite the overabundance, did either of you try something you liked, or think the guys would like? Well, Stuart, really. Jai likes anything."

"Black Forest," they both said and shared an amused smile.

"Okay!" Joan stood up. "Sounds like a consensus. I'll need to know whether you choose my bakery no later than this Wednesday. Does that work for you two?"

"Yes," Maddie said, also standing. "We're trying the last bakery Tuesday, so we should be able choose fairly by then." She paused. "When are you getting there tonight?"

"Mom said no later than seven, so probably about six thirty. You?"

"About then. I have to take care of some stuff first, but I should be done by then."

Joan turned to her. "It's been a pleasure meeting you, Ryann, and I assume I'll see you tonight?"

She stood and took her offered hand. "I'll be there."

"Great. But be forewarned. My family is a little crazy, and it's always a madhouse over at my parents' when we're all there."

She saluted with two fingers. "Noted."

"Don't worry," Maddie said. "People will be there to watch out for you. Me and Stuart, I mean."

"Thanks," she said, a little confused. Joan was surely exaggerating, but Maddie sounded serious. What on earth could they be so worried about?

CHAPTER NINE

Maddie dropped her off at the hotel, and she spent the next two hours on the phone and her computer, calling and videoconferencing with various people to discuss her meetings with Sydney and Tokyo later tonight. Ted had set them back-to-back: one at midnight and the other at one in the morning Colorado time. Ted and some of the other numbers people went over and over the details with her to get her up to date and ready to twist some arms to make sure the two companies stayed in this deal. They still had no clear word on London, either, which didn't help. Her board simply shared that things were still under negotiation. She'd wanted firm dates from London, but she would have to go into tonight's meetings without those specifics.

At 6:20, she finally closed her laptop, now running behind. Stuart was swinging by at 6:45 to pick her up, which didn't leave her a lot of time to do much of anything with herself. Her second suitcase was still MIA, which limited her clothing choices, but she had a couple of nice pieces in the bag that had been delivered. She debated for as long as she dared, finally settling on a casual outfit of a silky-soft gray sweater and navy slacks. She took a quick shower, and when she got out, she wasn't surprised that her eyes appeared even more sunken and tired than this morning. She didn't even want to consider how she'd ever get through a big family get-together and two tense meetings before being allowed to sleep.

She was finishing her makeup when Stuart knocked on the outside door, letting himself in, as usual.

"You really should lock this door," he called from the bedroom.

"I left it open for you," she yelled back. "Just let yourself in! You always do."

"Are you decent?" he asked, coming into the bathroom before she answered.

She grinned at him in the mirror, capping her mascara. "Would you care?"

He paused, tilted his head back and forth as he thought, and then shrugged. "No. I've seen you naked."

"Lucky you," she said, staring at her reflection again. Her pallor was less apparent with some makeup, but she still wasn't sure what to do with her hair like this besides tying it back as she had before. No time for a braid. She turned around to face him.

"How do I look?"

He surveyed her up and down and then stepped forward and held out his arms. They embraced and he kissed her cheek. She'd missed the scent of his cologne, and she pulled him closer for a deep nose full and another quick squeeze before letting him go.

He swept his gaze over her again. "You look like a million bucks, as always. Jai's family won't know what hit 'em."

"Are they nice?" Her nerves were rising again.

"They're super nice. They're like a damn Hallmark Channel family. But honey, they're a lot."

"So Maddie said."

Stuart's eyebrows shot up. "Oh? And what else did the two of you talk about?"

She rolled her eyes at him, walking out into the bedroom to get her coat and scarf. "I'm not doing this, Stuart."

"What?"

She laughed. "You know what. I'm not talking about her when I know your motives. She and I are not interested in each other like that."

"Oh, really? Cause that's not what Jai said."

Her temper flared, and she squared her shoulders, hands on her hips. "What's that supposed to mean? How would he know? Did Maddie say something?"

Stuart was clearly trying not to laugh, his lips twisting. "Nope. Jai said Joan told him the two of you were very lovey-dovey at the bakery today—feeding each other, staring longingly in each other's eyes—the whole nine yards."

"Well, Jai—no, Joan is absolutely—" She held up her hands. "Damn it! I'm not getting into this with you. You're goading me, and I won't fall for it."

Stuart sighed dramatically. "Okay. Have it your way. I won't say another word."

"That's what you said last time," Ryann said, amused despite herself.

"I'll try harder. It's just that the two of you—" He shook his head. "Sorry. Never mind."

She wanted him to finish his sentence, but he was trying to pull her in again, so she fought the urge to ask him.

"Shall we?" she asked, indicating the door.

He seemed a little put off by her lack of follow-up, but he led her outside and down the stairs to his car. His car and driving together was also a new thing for them.

"I didn't even know you could drive," she said, getting in.

"I couldn't! Maddie taught me, actually, in that big-ass truck of hers. Before that, I was using Uber and the bus. But Uber was getting expensive, and the busses don't run very often."

"A car is cheaper?"

"It's actually one of Jai's cars—well, one of his sisters' husband's, to be exact. He wasn't using it, so he gave it to me. I just have to pay insurance, which is next to nothing on this old heap."

"He gave you a car."

"Exactly. That's the kind of people you're about to meet. I'm telling you, be ready for anything. They are seriously extra. Oh, and expect animals. His parents have like I don't even know how many cats, and one of his sisters takes her dogs with her everywhere. Oh, and there's like a million kids, too."

Jai's parents lived fairly close to the hotel, the drive perhaps five minutes through the neighborhood connected to the downtown area. The house itself was a smaller, late-Victorian two-story, nestled in the middle of similarly older homes from the late nineteenth and early twentieth centuries. Several cars and trucks were parked in front, and it appeared that every light in the house was on. The Beatles were blaring, and raucous laughter was coming from inside. Despite the cold and the hour, a few children stood outside on the front lawn around a fire pit roasting marshmallows. Several of the kids called out to Stuart, and he waved before setting a hand on her lower back and leading her up the front steps and inside.

They entered a warm, crowded living room and encountered a moving mass of people and several barking dogs, two of which immediately jumped all over them before two large men led them away.

Jai suddenly appeared, dragging her through the crowd. She lost her grip on Stuart's hand, and he waved after her as if lost at sea. She kept following Jai, who paused and shouted names occasionally, all of which she missed, but her hand was thoroughly shaken several times. She met Joan again, and another sister whose name she missed, as well as a handful of cousins and uncles and family friends. She got some full body hugs here and there and cheery pats on the back, the entire experience loud and hot.

Finally, Jai led her into the kitchen through a pair of swinging doors. The room was very bright and open compared to the living room. An older couple were the only people here, and Jai introduced her to his parents, Jackie and Jim.

"Oh, we've heard so much about you!" Jackie said, squeezing her before shaking her hand vigorously and soundly with both of hers.

"Such a pleasure to finally meet you," Jim said, his frame and body, like Jai's, enormous as he wrapped her in his arms.

"Thank you," she managed. All three of them—Jai and his parents—were smiling at her as if expecting something more. She widened her smile, and they returned it before turning to each other and chatting about one of the sisters, Janet.

His parents seemed a little older than her own—late sixties, perhaps. Jai was the youngest, so this made sense, assuming he was close to her age. Jackie, like her daughters, was small, slight, and had clearly contributed her light hair and overall coloring to her children. Jim was darker and very tall—towering at least a few inches above his huge son. Both parents were very casually dressed—he in flannels, she in a red, heart-embossed sweater like Ryann had seen on so many various older women the last two days. Did a store in town sell them?

A cat started weaving between her legs, and she had to fight an urge to jump away.

"Get away from there, Fido," Jackie said, swatting at the animal. "Oh, gosh, look at your legs!" she cried. "You have fur and dog prints all over you. Let me get you a rag."

"That'll be Onion and Rags," Jim said, brow furrowed. "Jos's dogs. She didn't train them very well."

"Oh, hush," Jackie said, flicking him with the rag. "She doesn't need all the dirty family details."

Ryann took the rag and dabbed at her legs, grateful for the moment to herself. Stuart hadn't joined them yet, and she had no idea what to talk to these people about.

After the last muddy paw print was wiped away, she realized the three of them were watching her and couldn't help the slight blush that warmed her cheeks.

"Thanks for this," she said, handing Jackie the dirty rag.

"Of course. I'm so sorry about that. And you have such nice clothes."

"Thanks." She stuttered. "And you have such a lovely home."

Jackie waved at her, dismissively. "Oh, gosh, this old shack? Well, thank you for saying so. It's hard to see anything with half the city of Loveland in here. It was supposed to be just family, but word got out, as it always does."

She threw her husband a suspicious glare, which he pretended not to see, peering up at the ceiling and whistling. Jackie laughed and pulled him closer with one arm.

"This guy," Jackie said. "He can't help but invite everyone he knows if there's even the slightest bit of good news."

"Well, this is good news and big news, honey," Jim said. "Not every day my only son gets married."

"Oh, Dad. Gosh," Jai said, color staining his cheeks.

Stuart was right. It was like the damned Hallmark Channel in here. She smiled back at them, still awkward with their jolliness, and, if only to have something to take attention off her, she had knelt down to pet the cat—a different one this time, she suddenly realized—when the back door opened directly off the kitchen. Maddie came in, carrying various grocery bags, and Jai and his parents greeted her and divested her of the bags.

After they finished fussing with her, Maddie spotted her and approached, smiling broadly and giving her a quick hug. The scent of vanilla filled her nose, and she leaned into it this time, inhaling deeply and with something like relief. Maddie pulled back, her eyes filled with concern.

"You okay?" she whispered. "You seem a little...overwhelmed."

Ryann laughed, weakly. "Is it that obvious?"

Maddie snorted. "Maybe, but don't worry about it. I know these people, and it's always a lot. You need a drink. Let me show you."

Maddie grabbed her hand, and she didn't fight it, letting her lead her back into the chaos outside the kitchen. Things were, if anything, much louder than before, and judging from the state of several of the groups, the booze was really flowing. A whiff of pot came from somewhere to her right, and she turned that way, surprised, but whoever was smoking was out of sight, possibly in a back room. It was too crowded to spot Stuart, despite the close confines, and they basically had to brush and push through the crowd.

"The fire marshal would have a field day with this," Maddie said to her, volume just shy of a shout.

"Do I smell pot?" she asked.

Maddie grinned back. "It's legal. There's an enclosed porch on the side of the house if you want to go join them—some of the cousins and their friends, probably. Jai's uncle Jake is undoubtedly out there, too. He's the real family pothead."

So not quite the Hallmark Channel after all.

"No. That's okay," she said. "Just a drink is fine."

"Maddie!" A woman suddenly shouted to their left. "Get over here. I haven't seen you in ages."

Maddie changed directions, still pulling her along.

"Jos!" Maddie said. Ryann hadn't met this sister yet, who seemed older than the others. Dressed in professional attire—a skirt suit and heels—she also had her hair and makeup more carefully styled and done.

"Oh my God, Maddie," Jos said. "It's been like a thousand years."

"Something like that," Maddie said. "Almost two months, anyway. I saw you at Christmas."

"That was ages ago."

Jos's voice was louder than necessary, and her eyes were slightly watery. The empty glass in her hand probably wasn't her first.

Jos noticed her then, her eyes going wide as she stared at her. "Wow, Maddie. Who's this?"

"This is Ryann," Maddie said. "She's—"

"Holy shit," Jos said. "She's gorgeous. I mean, you're gorgeous, Ryann, really. Wow. Maddie always has the prettiest girlfriends. She must be dynamite in bed."

Maddie laughed, opening her mouth to say something, but Jos was dragged away a moment later by a woman that looked suspiciously similar to her—one of the other sisters Ryann had briefly met.

"I'm sorry," Maddie said.

She waved a hand dismissively. "Don't worry about it. You tried.

She was…well, anyway, she probably won't remember meeting me next time I see her."

Maddie was clearly grateful. "I don't know about that. You're pretty memorable."

She had no immediate reply, and as she tried to think of something, someone jostled her from behind, making her stumble into Maddie, who steadied her, hands on her forearms strong and sure.

"Sorry!" someone shouted.

She took a small step away from Maddie—as far as she could in this press of people—but their faces were still very close, their bodies nearly flush. A tried New Yorker, she didn't have a problem with crowds, but this proximity was testing her in other ways. She was close enough to see little flecks of steely gray in Maddie's blue eyes and a smattering of pale freckles on her nose.

"It's getting crazy in here," Maddie said, sounding quiet and calm. "Let's get you that drink and out of this hubbub. There's a little TV room upstairs where we can escape. I bet you anything Stuart's already up there."

"Lead the way," she said, still flustered.

Once again, Maddie took her hand, and as they wove through the rest of the room, several people called out. Maddie didn't stop this time, only lifting her free hand and waving them off. She held up their linked hands a couple of times to show someone that she was busy.

They finally made it across the room and through another doorway, which led to a blissfully empty hallway, at the end of which was a steep set of stairs.

"We should find something to drink upstairs," Maddie explained as they climbed. "I didn't want to have to face the craziness of the bar down there."

They were still holding hands, and Ryann didn't fight it, a small part of her giving up. She was tired, overwhelmed, and didn't want to make any kind of deal out of it. So they were holding hands. *Who cares?*

Apparently someone.

When they walked into the TV room, Stuart's eyes flared wide, and he stood up, gaping at them.

"What the hell?" he said, pointing.

"What?" Maddie asked. Then following his finger and seeing their linked hands, she said, "Oh. Well, Ryann was about to get swallowed by the crowd. She needed—"

"She needed a strong woman to rescue her," Stuart said.

"Can it, Stuart," she said, letting go of Maddie. "She said there was alcohol up here?"

"Some beer, but it's good—local," Stuart said. "In that little fridge in the corner."

"Do you want one, too?" she asked Maddie.

"No—better not. I have to get up really early. Unless you'd be willing to share?"

"Sure. What kind?"

"Whatever you like."

She ignored Stuart's giggles, her attention on the many different cans in the fridge. A toilet flushed nearby, a sink was running, and then a door opened somewhere behind her. She stood, turning with a can of coconut porter, and recognized what had to be one of Jai's sisters as she emerged from the small powder room in the corner.

"Hi, Ryann," the woman said. "We met downstairs, but I'm sure you were overwhelmed with that crowd. Jai is terrible at introducing people. Anyway, I'm Janet."

"Nice to meet you properly," she said, shaking Janet's hand.

"My sisters are still downstairs, but Jai's supposed to bring them up soon for a little family time alone."

"And he's bringing food," Stuart said.

"Thank God," Maddie said. "I'm starving."

The four of them sat down on an overstuffed sectional couch, worn and frayed with age and use. It was arranged in a U-shape around an enormous television and coffee table. Stuart sat next to her on her right, slinging an arm around her shoulders and squeezing her. Maddie sat on her left despite the many other seats. She'd grabbed two glasses and now divided the can between them before handing her a glass of dark beer.

"Sorry about that down there," Stuart said. "I should have warned you."

"You did," she said. "I didn't know it would be quite so crazy."

Janet laughed. "My parents always go all out. It was only supposed to be the ten of us tonight—the siblings, my parents, you, Stuart, and Maddie. Even the kids and husbands were supposed to stay home, but things got out of hand, as usual."

A cat plopped on to Ryann's lap, seemingly out of nowhere, and she flinched away. The cat, clearly oblivious to her discomfort, circled a few times before making itself into a ball of orange fluff on her lap.

"You can push him off," Janet said.

"It's okay."

She pet it—once, twice—awkward and unsure. The cat, however, purred loudly, so she figured she was okay.

"Not a cat person?" Maddie asked her, smirking.

"No. I mean, I'm not used to them. I didn't grow up with pets."

"You should see Jai's place," Stuart said. "He has like a million."

They sat in relatively comfortable silence. Janet's eyes were on her, but every time Ryann looked her way, she would avert her gaze, seemingly just as awkward and shy as she was. This sister seemed younger than the others she'd met—closer to Jai's age, if she had to guess. All four women were very similar to their mother—slight, short blondes. Janet's hair was very long, tied up in an elaborate style of several braids that wrapped around her head in something like a crown.

"How were your students this week, Janet?" Maddie asked.

"I'm a teacher. Third grade," Janet said to Ryann. Then to Maddie, "Uh, okay, I guess. They're getting a little crazy with the holiday coming, but that's to be expected."

"The holiday?" Ryann asked.

"Valentine's Day," Janet said.

"Really?"

Janet laughed. "Oh, sorry, yes—it's a big deal. Parties, assemblies, choral concerts. I forget sometimes that it's such a local thing."

"Oh, yes, of course."

As Janet launched into a story about her students to Maddie, Ryann let herself relax a little, sipping her beer. She was still wearing her heavy coat, but she was cozy here on the couch. Her left leg was brushing Maddie's, and the cat was warm and calming.

She'd never really seen the point of a cat. They seemed somewhat useless, really. You had to clean a nasty box, and they got fur all over everything. But having one warming your lap on a cold winter night had its appeal. She stroked its back, and it opened one green eye at her, its purring increasing, before closing it again, obviously at peace.

She let her own eyes drift closed, leaning back into the seat behind her, her exhaustion suddenly catching up to her.

"You look worn out," Stuart whispered near her ear.

She opened her eyes. "I am. I actually have two meetings later tonight, if you can believe it."

He squeezed her hand. "I'm sorry, honey. You're such a peach for coming. I know you're busy at work this time of year. And I'm sorry we haven't had a chance to get caught up. But I promise we will this weekend. I'll show you my place, and we can have a whole evening together—just the two of us."

"That sounds really nice."

They were speaking quietly, and Janet and Maddie were wrapped up enough in their own conversation that it was almost as if they were already alone. She was surprised to tear up, and Stuart squeezed her shoulders with one arm, his eyes sparkling, too. The cat stood up, disturbed, but quickly settled again when Stuart let go of her.

"So, Ryann," Janet said. "Are you ready for tomorrow?"

"What's tomorrow?"

Janet grimaced. "Stuart didn't tell you yet?"

Ryann stared at him, and he refused to make eye contact, staring down at his beer.

"What's tomorrow?" she repeated.

After a long moment of hesitation, he met her eyes. "The dresses."

"What dresses?"

"You, me, and my sisters are all getting our bridesmaid dresses fitted tomorrow," Janet said. "It's my half day, and that's why Jos came up from Denver. Then, once she told Mom and Dad she was coming, they decided to throw this whole soiree."

"A dress? Really?" Ryann asked Stuart.

"Or you can do a suit, instead," Stuart said, wincing slightly.

"Are you kidding me right now?" she asked.

Stuart opened his mouth, but the door opened, and Jai, Joan, and another sister came in—not Jos—all three carrying trays of food and paper plates.

"We come bearing sustenance!" Jai shouted, triumphant.

"Jos is passed out already," Joan explained.

"I'm Julia, by the way," the other woman said to Ryann. "We met downstairs, but it was really loud. You must be Ryann."

"Yes, thanks. Nice to meet you."

Everyone stood up to gather food, Stuart almost running away from her. Exhaustion was weighing on her, but her temper died down once she got in line for a plate. She decided to let it drop. After all, she was in it this far. What difference did it make what she wore to the wedding?

Stuart, as if sensing her thoughts, glanced back at her, a plate piled high. He had a carrot hanging out of his mouth, a dollop of ranch staining his lips, and she gave him a wide smile and a wink. He wiped his forehead dramatically with his free hand before taking the carrot out to speak.

"Don't worry, Ryann. The dressmaker is really good."

Julia laughed. "Thanks, Stuart." Julia turned to her. "It's my shop, actually."

"You and your sister are both in the wedding industry?" she asked.

Julia laughed. "No. Actually, a lot of my work is for theater companies, though I also do a lot of cosplay costumes now, too."

"And you get to sleep in," Stuart told Ryann, cutting off further questions with something like panic. "The fitting isn't until noon."

"All right, all right," she said, waving a hand dismissively. "I trust your taste. It's fine. I was just surprised. I guess I thought I was wearing something of my own."

She waited her turn for the food behind Maddie, who helped her load her paper plate with a sandwich and a pastry. She'd stupidly carried her beer with her.

"Thanks," she said.

"No problem."

"Will you be there tomorrow?" she asked, unable to keep a hint of hope out of her voice.

"I might drop by, but I have studio time most of the day," Maddie said. "My fitting was a few days ago. But we'll see each other at one of the venues later in the afternoon."

"Ah, okay," she said. She felt slightly disappointed, maybe because she wouldn't have a friend there, but she was probably fooling herself. If she was being honest, she was disappointed because she wanted to see her, and whatever that meant, it wasn't good.

CHAPTER TEN

The virtual meetings with the CEOs in Sydney and Tokyo went as well as they could, considering Ryann was nearly stammering with fatigue by the end of the second. She'd always done well in one-on-ones with powerful people. Ted told her she could charm them better in person (by which he meant flirt with them), but she got the job done. By the end of both calls, she'd gotten both companies to confirm a start the last week of February—almost two weeks later than their original agreement. She sent a quick email to her board with the new dates and a longer one to Ted with more details before dropping, deathlike, on her heart-shaped bed, still fully dressed in her work clothes.

She woke the next morning with a stiff neck, the room blazing with sunlight. She'd forgotten to close the blinds. She sat up, a crust of drool at the corner of her mouth, her eyes still sandy. She rotated her neck a couple of times, wincing, and made herself crawl over to the edge of her bed. She got up, staggering slightly before stumbling into the bathroom. It was blessedly dark in here with only one window, and she kept the lights off while she showered with water as hot as she could get it, her skin lobstering in the heat.

She spent the next hour in her bathrobe, checking in with a couple of her board members over the phone before they flew home. Things seemed better on the London end now, too. They had agreed to the first week of March, but her CFO thought they might be able to bump that back to the last week of February with a little more needling.

Nothing more could be done over the weekend, though she wanted to run the numbers one more time and set up a conference call with London. She got Ted and his team on it before wrapping up her morning.

She still had an hour before she was supposed to be at the dress shop, and she had no idea who was taking her there, or if she was supposed to get there herself. No one had texted her all morning, and Stuart didn't pick up when she called. Still, she needed to be dressed at least, and she started rooting through her only suitcase for something easy to take on and off.

A knock at the door startled her. She walked closer.

"Yes?"

"Hi, honey. It's Ethel," she said from the other side of the door.

"The hotel manager?"

"Hi, Ethel. What can I do for you?"

"I wanted to make sure you were okay. You weren't down for breakfast again, so I'm checking to see if you'd like another German muffin."

She closed her eyes. Clearly the woman was trying to be nice, but she also didn't like people keeping tabs on her, especially strangers.

"No, thank you!" she said. "I appreciate it, but I'm going out for lunch soon."

"Okay, dear. I'll let you get ready, then."

She spent the next thirty minutes dressing and doing her makeup and hair. She checked her phone several times, tried calling Stuart twice more, but at 11:45, she still hadn't heard from anyone. She did an internet search for costume shops in town, but as far as she could tell, none of them were associated with Jai's sister Julia.

Frustrated with waiting, she got her laptop up and running again, trying to catch up with some of her email. As she was finishing the first one, someone was knocking on her door again.

"Yes?" she called.

"Ryann? It's me, Janet. I'm so sorry I'm late."

She opened the door, and Janet came in at once, enveloping her before stepping away, her face red with embarrassment.

"Oh, gosh," Janet said. "I don't know why I did that. You must think I'm a fruitcake. I'm so, so sorry. This is exactly why Jai didn't ask me to help with anything. I always get things mixed up."

"It's no problem," she said. "Really. Let me grab my coat."

"You're so nice," Janet said.

As she donned her coat and checked her hair and makeup again, she watched Janet in the mirror. She was still standing inside the doorway, wringing her hands, clearly worried.

"Is the shop far away?" she asked, indicating the door.

"No, thank God," Janet said, leading them out. "It's like ten minutes. But we're still going to be late."

"I'm sure it's fine, Janet." She put a hand on her shoulder. "You can always blame me."

Janet laughed, and she was relieved to see her relax a little, some of that pent-up tension loosening her shoulders.

"You'd do that for me?" Janet asked.

"Of course! Stuart's like a brother to me, so that makes you my new sister-in-law, too. Okay?"

Janet beamed. "You're the best. Thank you. Just remind me of that when Jos gives me a hard time."

"Jos is the oldest, I take it?"

Janet sighed. "Yes. And she never lets anyone forget she's in charge. You'd think, now that we're all adults, all that crap would be over with, but it's not. It was kind of a relief when she moved to Denver. We only see her for holidays and things now." She winced. "I'm sorry. I shouldn't be airing the family laundry. I have a bad habit of saying everything that's on my mind. I blame it on spending all my time with children."

"It's fine—I promise."

They were outside now, and Janet pointed at a bright-red classic VW Beetle. They both climbed in, Ryann tickled by the idea of being in one of these things. She'd seen them around, of course, but didn't think people actually drove them as their primary car. It was loud when it started, but it seemed to run well, and they tore out of the downtown area, tires squealing on the corners.

"Sorry," Janet said, when she had to brace herself from sliding out of her seat. "I drive like shit, too. It's because I'm always late, I guess."

She wasn't used to this kind of woman—the self-deprecating kind. Was she supposed to reassure her, even if what she'd said was true? She settled on a weak smile, which Janet returned tenfold.

"We're going to be great friends," Janet said, squeezing her hand. The motion made the car swerve wildly, and she was forced to grab the dashboard and her seat again.

The brick building they pulled up to ten minutes later didn't seem like a dress shop, or a business of any kind, really—a little like Joan's bakery yesterday. Both businesses seemed to be for people in the know. A small sign was affixed above the door, but as this entrance was in the back of the building, it hadn't been redone in a while, and the lettering was faded to the point of illegibility.

Janet dragged her inside by one hand. It was even stranger inside than the out, the two of them walking into a lowly lit room packed with garment racks and clotheslines stuffed with dresses and suits.

"We're back here," a woman called from somewhere in the distance.

Janet led her through tight rows of clothing to a back area. Here was a small office and some brighter lighting. They also found the other sisters, all of whom were seated on a couple of old couches, drinking champagne.

"You're late," Jos said.

Janet said, "It's not my fault—"

"It's not, really. It was mine," Ryann said. "I got the times mixed up."

Jos narrowed her eyes. "Okay. We'll blame the new girl this time."

Julia stood up, holding two champagne flutes.

"There are some sandwiches, if you want anything to eat," she said, pointing.

She grabbed a plate before taking a seat on the only empty couch. Janet joined her a moment later. Ryann smiled at her, sipping the surprisingly good wine.

The other three sisters were watching them, Jos's eyes still narrowed, assessing, the others smiling lightly, like Janet.

"So…" Jos finally said. "Maddie's new piece is in the wedding for some reason."

"What?" Janet said.

Joan said, "She's not—"

"I mean, I get it," Jos went on. "You're hot. You'll be great in the photos."

"Jos," Julia said. "You are way off base, here."

Jos glared at her. "Let me finish. *Anyway,* it seems a little premature for you to be actually *in* the wedding. I can see you coming and being there for Maddie, but in the actual party? I mean, how long have you two been together? She didn't even mention you at Christmas."

"Jos, you're completely wrong about her," Janet said, holding back laughter.

Ryann held up a hand and gave Janet a quick wink. "It's okay, Janet." She turned to Jos. "I guess it does seem really fast. But we're just really in love, and I think Stuart and Jai recognize that it's for keeps."

Joan and Julia laughed, and Jos threw them a confused look. Janet's eyes were bulging, and she slapped her hands over her mouth to keep from laughing.

Jos, still oblivious, went on. "I mean, okay, yes—who wouldn't be in love with Maddie?"

"Aren't you married?" Janet asked, giggling a little.

"Aren't you straight?" Julia added.

Jos tutted. "Oh, come on, you guys. We *all* have a crush on Maddie—we have since we were kids. What's not to like?" She narrowed her eyes at Ryann. "You better not be fucking around on her."

"Oh, no. I would never," Ryann said. "In fact, I don't, uh, fuck around at all. Even with Maddie."

"What?" Jos said, slamming her glass down on the table. "You mean to say—"

"We're waiting for marriage."

Jos's mouth opened and closed several times, fish-like, before everyone else burst out laughing. Ryann managed to keep a straight face for a few seconds before she, too, cracked, chuckling a little at the way the other sisters carried on. Julia stood up to clap her on the back, and Janet squeezed her arm, still giggling.

"What's going on?" Jos said. "Why are you all laughing like that?"

"Oh, man, did she ever get you!" Janet said between giggles.

"Ryann is Stuart's friend, you ass, not Maddie's girlfriend," Joan said, pushing Jos's arm.

"Wait, what?"

"We were trying to tell you," Julia said. "But you steamrolled over us. As usual. Ryann was playing along."

"Really?" Jos said. "But last night—"

"You didn't let Maddie explain then, either," Ryann said.

"But the two of you were holding hands," Jos said. "What was that about?"

Ryann laughed. "Have you seen her? You'd hold hands with her, too."

Jos laughed at that and stood up to give her a high five. "All right. You got me. Jesus. Once you said you hadn't slept with her yet, I should have known—"

"Okay, okay!" Julia said, standing up. "Enough about Ryann's sex life, or lack of a sex life—whatever. We need to start on the measurements."

"Does that mean I get to see this one naked?" Jos said, winking at Ryann.

Ryann laughed. "In your dreams."

"But you are a lesbian, at least, right?" Jos asked.

She shook her head, amazed at this woman. "Yes. What's that have to do with anything?"

"I'm making sure my gaydar still works."

"That's not a thing," Janet said. "Straight women don't get gaydar."

"Uh, they do, too!"

As they continued to argue, a little lift of something like hope rose in Ryann's chest. She'd been dreading this more than she'd realized. Not this moment, specifically, since she hadn't known about it until last night, but dreading moments like it, personal moments with people she didn't know. But she found, as they laughed and joked and teased each other, that she didn't feel left out or awkward. They'd made her part of it.

Once they'd finished their lunch and drinks, Joan led her into a small dressing room near the office. She was asked to step onto a small circular dais on the floor, and then Joan began taking measurements.

"What kind of dress am I going to be wearing?"

"It's a nice red and white in Regency style."

"Excuse me?"

Joan laughed. "That's why the guys asked me to do this—not just because I can squeeze you in before the wedding, but because I do this style all the time. I already have the dresses made for a show from last summer, so it'll only take some alterations for everyone's measurements. You're in red, Maddie's in red, the guys are in white, and the rest of us ladies are in pink."

"But why Regency?"

"Oh, gosh, of course you don't know. My brother has like a real thing for Jane Austen—the books, the adaptations. He's been nuts about her since he was a kid. He and Stuart are going to England for their honeymoon to see her house and her grave, places where the movies were shot—that kind of thing."

She hadn't thought to ask about the honeymoon and could hardly believe her ears. It was the very last thing she could imagine Stuart agreeing to go along with.

"Really?"

"Yep," Joan said, jotting something down. "And don't worry—the dress is really nice. It won't seem like a costume at all. And you have the figure for it. You'll look great."

She let her mind wander as Joan continued to take measurements, writing things down in a little spiral notebook. Stuart had described exactly the kind of wedding he'd envisioned—she had the dream book in her suitcase to prove it—and it didn't include anything like this.

"What are they wearing—the guys?"

"Same era, only in men's styles. Jackets, waistcoats, white leggings, buckle shoes, the whole shebang. Maddie, too."

This gave her pause, and a slight blush rose to her cheeks at the idea. She too had liked and read most of Austen's books in school, and she'd seen the odd adaptation here and there over the years. Kiera Knightly and Rosamund Pike had been really hot in that one movie. She could picture more or less what those suits and dresses looked like, and imagining Maddie dressed like Mr. Darcy wasn't exactly a terrible fantasy. Still, the whole thing was a little strange. She was going to have to grill Stuart when they finally had a moment alone. This seemed like an awfully big concession.

She rejoined the other sisters when Joan finished with her, Janet heading back for her measurements. Jos called her over to try on shoes, and the two of them ended up laughing about it quite a lot when they wanted the same pair. They eventually decided to flip for it, though it took a while to find a coin to use. Ryann won the toss, and Jos tried to wrestle the quarter out of her hands to flip again. Ryann squealed and pushed at her, nearly doubled up with laughter.

"Ha!" Ryann said, finally holding up the coin clutched in one fist. "No cheating, Jos. I won fair and square."

"What did you win?" Maddie asked from behind them.

She spun, her face flashing with heat at the sight. Maddie was smirking lightly, clearly recognizing the effect of her entrance, as everyone fell silent at the sight of her.

"We were just talking about you," Jos said, giving Ryann a side eye. "Ryann was saying—"

"Never mind, Jos!" Ryann glared at her. "What are you doing here? I thought you had studio time today."

"I did. I knocked off a little early because Julia asked me to come over for my final fitting, and I'm supposed to take you to one of the venues after this."

"Ah."

They were quiet, staring at each other for a long beat. Finally, Jos cleared her throat.

"Um, okay, as much as I like watching you two make heart eyes at each other, we were in the middle of a major debate."

"The shoes are mine, Jos," Ryann said, without breaking eye contact with Maddie.

Jos sighed dramatically. "Fine."

Janet came out from the back, squealed at the sight of Maddie, and rushed her, throwing herself into her arms.

"Isn't this fun? I can barely stand the excitement."

Maddie laughed. "Me, either."

"I can't wait to see what you're wearing," Janet said.

Julia came from the dressing room. "Oh, good—you're here. Come on back, Maddie. Let's see how it fits."

Maddie followed her to the rear, and Ryann sat down with the sisters again, Jos shoving another flute of champagne into her hands and sitting next to her, uncomfortably close.

"Are you trying to get me drunk?" Ryann asked.

"Is it working?"

Joan swatted her sister's knee. "Give it a break, Jos."

"For real," Janet said. "Be nice."

"I am nice. I'm trying to get to know her a little, loosen her up a bit," Jos said, smiling slyly.

Ryann took a long pull on her drink for courage. "What do you want to know?"

"Stuart told Joan, who just told me, that you're a big-time hotshot in New York. Judging by those clothes of yours, I don't doubt it."

"Thanks?"

"What's your love life like out there?"

"Jesus, Jos," Janet said.

Ryann met her eyes, unwavering. "I do just fine, thank you."

"Hmm…I bet you do. You are really attractive. I don't usually go for a femme type—"

"Or any lady at all," Janet broke in.

"But you're really something," Jos continued. "Still, you could do a lot better right here, you know. Maddie likes you, and you like her. I can tell."

Jos's expression was a little too sincere for her liking. They'd been joking around before, but she was clearly at least half-serious now.

She tried to think of some cutting comeback, something lighthearted enough to come off as a joke, but stern enough to get Jos to drop this line of questioning, but she didn't get the chance. Maddie came out in her wedding outfit then, and Ryann's mouth snapped shut audibly.

Imagining her dressed like this and seeing her dressed like this were entirely different. The jacket was a lovely dark red, inlaid with braided silver thread and buttoned at the top across her chest. Part of the waistcoat showed on her stomach, an off-white with silver braiding, the knee-length pants a bright, floral, decorated silver, the stockings a blinding white. She had an old-timey, scarf-like white necktie (cravat, some deep part of her brain tossed in) and black buckle shoes. With her messy short, blond waves completing the style, she was, in a word, gorgeous.

"So how do I look?" Maddie finally asked, her eyes meeting Ryann's, specifically.

"Check out Ryann's face for an answer," Jos said.

She elbowed Jos hard, and everyone laughed, finally breaking the tension.

"Is it totally silly?" Maddie asked, clearly uncomfortable. She plucked at the buttoned lapels a little, rocking back and forth on her heels.

"You're hot as hell," Jos said. "Isn't she, Ryann?"

She had to shake herself into reality. She cleared her throat. "It's really…nice."

"High praise," Maddie said. "Oh, well. I guess it's what the guys want, so it'll be fine for a day. At least it's more comfortable than I thought it would be. Let me change, and we can get out of here, Ryann."

Maddie disappeared in the back, Joan following for some further measurements. Ryann took a moment to gather her wits, finishing her champagne and desperate for another.

"You've got it bad, girlfriend," Jos told her.

Ryann didn't argue.

Chapter Eleven

Once in the Bronco with Maddie, Ryann found herself struggling to make conversation. Maddie didn't seem to mind her silence, humming along with the radio (Bach) and watching the road. On Ryann's end, however, it was a nightmare. More than wanting to make an effort at being polite and friendly, she had a desperate need to get her mind off what she'd been thinking about earlier. She absolutely did not need to encourage herself in any more lustful thoughts about this woman. It was ridiculous. Every time her mind wandered back to the memory of Maddie in that suit, she became hot, uncomfortable, and her stomach and guts twisted with something like excited dread. Each time this happened, the words she was reaching for died in her throat, until they'd been driving in complete silence for several minutes.

"How was the studio today?" she finally managed to ask.

"Great. I've been doing the fur for the last two weeks and am finally in the last stretch."

"Fur?"

Maddie laughed. "Oh, right. You've never seen my work. I do animals, mostly. I'm on a commission right now for the City of Longmont, which is south of here. The piece is two dogs—a kind of fuzzy mutt and a Lab-mix. They're actually based on real shelter dogs. I even got to meet them. Anyway, they'll be outside the new dog park that's opening this spring."

She was surprised. Stuart's work was more conceptual and abstract. He'd done some public commissions, too, but all had been in his usual vein. She'd assumed, for some reason, that Maddie did something similar.

"I'd love to see your work some time," she said.

"And I'd love to show you." Maddie paused, looking around.

"Actually—I can show you one right now. It's a public piece. We'll have to drive by, since we're short on time."

She signaled at the next block, and they turned, coming up on a traffic circle a couple of blocks later. There, in the center of the circle, was an enormous sculpture of several geese bursting into flight. They were connected in a way that made it appear as if some of them were actually in the air, while others were merely getting ready to jump off the ground. Even from here on the road, she could see individual feathers on each of the birds and their beady, eager eyes as they reached for the sky. She craned her head around as they drove the full circle before heading back the way they came.

"It's incredible," she finally said. "Really beautiful."

Maddie glanced at her, slight color in her cheeks. "You like it?"

"I do. It's amazing. Why do you sound so nervous?"

Maddie chuckled weakly, her eyes rooted on the road. "Well, it's just…I mean, Stuart's art is nothing like mine. His work is so, you know…well, he's been compared to Calder and Picasso, for God's sake. His art is…well, anyway, different from mine. I guess I thought you preferred his more abstract style."

This was the first time she had heard Maddie sound anything but sure of herself. Stuart was like this about his work, too, she remembered. No matter how many people told him how great his pieces were, he always doubted himself and needed constant reassurance. Maybe all artists are like that, she thought.

She put a gloved hand on Maddie's arm, and Maddie glanced over at her and away again, still appearing uncertain, nervous.

"I really love it, Maddie," she said. "Honestly—it's gorgeous. I want to see more of your work."

Maddie beamed at her this time. They were waiting at a red light, and Maddie grabbed her hand. She squeezed it back, returning the smile as warmly as she could.

Maddie wiped her brow, dramatically. "Whew! I was really nervous about showing you."

"You shouldn't be. You're incredibly talented."

Maddie kept smiling, her face very red now, and someone honked behind them. The light had turned green.

"Whoops," Maddie said, and returned her attention to driving.

"Are your other pieces like that?" she asked.

Maddie shrugged. "Most aren't that big, but yes, like I said, I do a lot of animals. All my public pieces are animals, anyway. I have a family of deer here in the Benson Sculpture Garden, a big grizzly bear in downtown Denver, an elk in Aspen, some otters in Anchorage, some quail in Cheyenne, and now there will be the dogs in Longmont. I can usually do a commission once a year or so."

She took a moment to absorb this information. She'd learned the sculpture foundries here in town were famous and that Stuart had been very excited to be selected to work here, but she hadn't given much thought to the other artists. Of course they, too, would be as talented as he was, and of course they would likely have different styles. Not everyone could or wanted to do the same kind of art. When Stuart had started working in bronze and other metals about a decade ago, it had been such a big production to get his works cast. Here, apparently, artists had space for both the molding and the casting.

"I'd love to see the studio sometime," she said. "If I'm allowed to visit."

"You certainly are. One of us can take you over there while you're in town."

"Or both of you?"

"Sure. We can ask Stuart about it when we get there."

"What? Where? I thought we were going to a venue."

"We are. He's joining us. There was some kind of delay on something he's working on, so he has the afternoon free."

She was glad she would be seeing him, but she also couldn't help a slight stab of disappointment that only she and Maddie weren't doing this. She didn't exactly know why, or, to be more precise, she didn't want to examine why she felt this way, and she suppressed the thought.

They had been driving away from the mountains this time—east, according to the compass, and were far out of town now. They'd turned off the bigger highway they were on and onto a small frontage road, well in the country again, with few houses or buildings visible. The sun was so blindingly bright off the snowy expanses, she was squinting even with her sunglasses, but it was incredibly pretty nonetheless. She saw some hopping animals in the distance—deer-like, but not quite—but before she could point them out to Maddie, they'd disappeared.

"Pronghorn, probably," Maddie said after she'd described them. "Some people call them antelope, though that's not technically correct. Like how some people call bison buffalo."

"Antelope," she said. She was still peering that direction, hoping to see them again. "I've never seen them before. Or bison, for that matter."

"All sorts of interesting animals out here on the plains," Maddie said, smiling slightly. "It seems empty, but it's teeming with life."

Maddie would know all about this, being interested in animals, and Ryann liked it when people shared their enthusiasms. She had so few interests herself outside of work, it was refreshing to hear someone talk about something else that mattered to them. She continued to stare into the snow, hoping to see something new.

A building finally appeared in the distance, sitting atop a slight bluff. Raised above the plains, it stood out in sharp contrast with the snowy mounds around it.

Maddie pointed. "That's where we're headed."

She squinted a bit. "It looks like a barn."

"It is a barn," Maddie said, laughing lightly.

She was stunned. Never in a thousand years would she have thought Stuart might consider something like this for his wedding venue. Sure, it was gorgeous out here, but they were so far outside of town, she couldn't fathom why anyone would want to get married here. Maddie had clearly seen her expression, and she laughed again.

"We don't actually have that many venues here in our little town, if you can believe it." She spoke with a slight hint of sarcasm.

"Ha, ha. I mean, I guess I realize that now, but…a barn?"

Maddie's eyebrows furrowed.

Ryann had the distinct impression that she'd upset her, somehow. Maybe insulted her. Perhaps this place was as good as it got out here in no-man's-land.

They pulled off the frontage road a few minutes later, drawing closer to the barn on a snowy side road, and soon they were in a surprisingly large parking lot. Two other cars were here—Stuart's and one other. Stuart and a much older, much shorter man appeared, coming from inside the barn as she and Maddie climbed out of the car. The older man stayed by the door, and Stuart walked directly over to meet them.

"So, what do you think?" he asked, waving at the barn.

She held her tongue, trying not to let her thoughts reflect on her face, but she obviously failed. Stuart laughed.

"I know, I know—it's not the Ritz, but wait until you see the inside."

"It's not just the inside I'm worried about," she said. "I mean, look at where we are." She gestured at the nothing around them.

"Don't be such a snob," Stuart said.

Both Maddie and Stuart were basically glaring at her now. She took a deep breath and pressed on. "I mean, don't get me wrong—it's gorgeous out here. Really very pretty. But we're so far outside of town. It took forever to get here from downtown. If you have the wedding at the festival, and the reception way the heck out here, how will people get back and forth?"

"I was planning to hire buses," Stuart said, still frowning. Maddie still seemed put out, and Ryann finally held up her hands.

"Okay, okay—I'm sorry. Let's see the inside."

Stuart brightened at once, dragging her forward, and Ryann threw a quick glance over her shoulder. Maddie had stayed where she was, still obviously upset, and she followed the two of them more slowly.

The inside was bright and spare, and the space had been insulated nicely so that it was very warm once they were inside. She and Maddie took a moment to hand the proprietor their coats and other winter wear. He excused himself to give them all some privacy, and Stuart walked to the middle of the wide-open floor, raising his hands.

"Look how open it is!" he said, his voice echoing.

"Yes." She agreed. "It's very open."

He laughed and gestured her forward. It seemed to take a long time to get to him. She walked through several bright spots of sunshine, and when she peered upward, she saw that several skylights had been installed above. The rafters were high and dark, a pretty contrast with the lighter wood of the ceiling. The floors were also made of polished pinewood, and she slid a little walking in wet shoes.

Stuart pulled her into a twirling dance step when she made it to him, and she barked a laugh before letting him lead her into a slow two-step, swaying softly, faces close. They'd taken dance lessons together a few years ago, and he'd clearly kept up. She was no slouch herself and had even followed their partner lessons with some of her own.

"What do you think?" he asked.

She paused, making both of them stumble before they found their footwork again.

"It's really pretty in here. Like you said—very open. And the floor is great for dancing."

"I hear a 'but' coming."

"But we're in the middle of nowhere. And also, it's open and lovely, but it's a little *too* open, if you ask me. Where is the bar? Where are the tables? Is there even a kitchen here? Toilets?"

He grimaced a little. "It has toilets and a kitchen, but you're right about the rest. We'd have to rent everything—tables, chairs, linens, a bar...the list goes on."

She could tell he was disappointed, and she stopped dancing, stepping away to consider him. His gaze was darting around the room, suggesting he was nervous and upset. She spun slowly, taking in the space again. Truthfully, it was very nice. It smelled like fresh wood and clean air, and it was bright and warm and inviting. It was a surprisingly large space—much larger than most event venues, in part because nothing was in here. That said, even with a bar set up on one side, it could likely fit a significant number of tables and still have room for a large dance floor in the center or on the side, depending on how he wanted it set up.

She turned back to him, and he was biting his lip, his face twisted with anxiety—a little like a kid that wanted something he thought he shouldn't have.

"You really like this place, don't you?" she asked him.

He hesitated before nodding. "It's my number-one pick."

"You've been here before?"

"Yes. At a reception for an artist I know. When Jai proposed, this was the first place I thought of."

She still didn't understand his enthusiasm for this barn, but she needed to get past her own misgivings. His eyes were already dancing with joy, and now he seemed excited rather than disappointed.

Maddie was leaning up against a wall some twenty feet away, and Ryann gestured at her to join them. When Maddie reached them, she still seemed a little reserved, a little angry even, and wouldn't meet Ryann's eyes.

Ryann clenched her hands, starting to lose patience. "Okay, Maddie, here's the deal. Stuart very clearly wants to rent this space. Now that I'm here, I can see the attraction, but the real question is: can it be done?"

Maddie immediately brightened and moved closer to her. She dropped her arms to her sides to give her more room, and Maddie stepped even closer, grabbing one of her hands. Maddie grabbed one of Stuart's too, squeezing both of them.

"Okay, listen," Maddie said. "I know you said you wanted to see a bunch of places, Stuart, but I also know how excited you were about this one. I mean, you spent half an hour talking about it the other day before even mentioning the others. I could tell you really wanted this space, so I called around. Basically, if you book today, Ryann and I can get everything else lined up tomorrow with a party-rental place. They do chairs and tables, linens, bars, the whole nine yards." Maddie smiled at her. "So—to answer your question, yes, it can be done."

Ryann gave Stuart her widest smile. "That settles it, then! Go pay the man and book it."

Stuart whooped, jumping into the air before pulling her and Maddie into a crushing hug. He gave her a quick kiss on the cheek and then dashed away, calling for the proprietor. He disappeared a moment later, and she and Maddie were left alone.

Maddie was smiling at her, and she had to look away, that tight, nervous heat rising in her chest again.

"Shall we?" Maddie asked, holding out a hand. "I have to try it out, too, you know."

She took Maddie's hand and let herself be pulled into Maddie's circle. They started dancing, slowly, as she'd done with Stuart, but of course it was different with Maddie. It shouldn't be, but it was. This closeness seemed intimate, and she was suddenly hot, awkward.

"You seem…happier now," she said, forcing herself to peer up into Maddie's eyes. "Why were you so upset earlier?"

Maddie lifted her shoulders, clearly at a loss for words. She opened her mouth, closed it, and opened it again before speaking.

"I…I was pissed, actually."

"Why?"

"Because you dismissed this place without seeing it. Because you seemed to have an idea of what Stuart wanted, like you knew better than either one of us."

"How could I know what he wanted? You didn't tell me anything before we got here."

Maddie met her eyes, that blue troubled, stormy. "Exactly. And I should have told you how much this place meant to him. But I didn't. Instead, I sort of let you flounder. No—that's not even it. I *made* you flounder by not saying anything. I wanted to see what you would do without any influence. Almost like I was trying to…I don't know, catch you out or something."

She made herself pause before replying, as calmly as she could. "Why?"

Maddie's brows knit a little. "I don't know." She shook her head, seeming almost angry. "No—that's not true at all. I had this idea that you wouldn't think anything was good enough, that you'd turn it down no matter what. You're from New York, and we're from here, and nothing would ever measure up."

She opened her mouth to protest, but Maddie cut her off.

"Wait. Let me finish." She took a deep breath. "And then we got here, and you saw it and said all those things outside, and I thought I was right. I was trying to make you wrong. But you weren't. You saw immediately how much it meant to him and backed off, like any good friend would do." She swallowed, her eyes a little red. "I'm sorry, Ryann. I underestimated you again."

She stayed quiet, absorbing this outburst as best she could through a haze of frustrated anger. Maddie was a fine dancer, taking her slowly around the wide-open room, smoothly enough, in fact, that she hadn't realized they'd moved much at all. They'd made it almost a full circle at this point, and her gaze wandered up to the piercing blue sky through the skylights above. A flock of geese was traveling far ahead, almost too distant to see. She swallowed against the strange tightness in her throat—a mix of dread and hurt. She made herself look into Maddie's eyes again but only found concern there, regret.

"I still don't understand why," she said, almost whispering. "Why did you want me to mess up?"

Maddie pulled her closer, and their bodies became flush. Maddie bent closer, face inches away. Her breath caught, and she waited for the kiss, her heartbeat leaping. Maddie's fingers were tight on her lower back and on her hand, both just shy of painful.

"It's because I don't want to like you," Maddie whispered. Her eyes were dark. "I don't want to like you, so I'm searching for reasons not to. But it's not easy. It's not easy at all."

She opened her mouth, lost for a reply, but the sound of a door opening saved her. The two of them sprang apart, and she walked away several steps, her face burning and her body shaking. She had her back to Maddie, and she clasped her hands together, trying to steady their trembles. She caught sight of the toilets and rushed over to the women's room, throwing the door open in her haste.

She had to take several deep breaths to calm down, now shuddering, but she finally calmed enough to go to the sink. She turned on the cold water, holding her hands under it before putting them on the back of her neck and dripping over the basin. She took several more deep breaths of the humid air, still thinking she might rattle apart. She clutched the edge of the sink with her fingers for support.

When she finally saw her reflection, she was ghostly pale, eyes circled in a dark purple. She still felt a little weak on her legs and continued to clutch the edges of the sink. She couldn't stay in here long—Stuart would send Maddie in after her any time now, and that idea was enough motivation to gather her wits. She met her own eyes again, startled at the fright she saw there.

"No, goddamn it," she told herself. "You don't get to fall apart right now. Go back out there, get back to the hotel, order yourself a nice stiff drink, and forget all of this."

The idea settled her enough that she was able to leave the restroom. Stuart was standing in the middle of the room, staring up at the skylights, and he turned toward her at the sound of the door. He was holding their coats and winter wear, and he handed hers to her. They took a moment to get wrapped up again, giving her longer to gather herself.

"Hey," Stuart finally said. "You okay?"

"Fine."

He moved closer, holding out his hands so she could take them. They stared at each other for a beat before he said, "You don't look fine. And neither did Maddie. You rushed to the bathroom when I came back in, and she was really flustered, which is totally unlike her. She even made an excuse to leave."

Her stomach dropped. "She left?"

He nodded, face hardening. "What's going on between you two? What happened?"

She met his eyes, desperately wanting to let him in on everything. Stuart was her best friend, but really, he was her only friend—the only friend she would ever talk about things like this with, anyway. She had some friends like Ted that she got drinks with occasionally, and a few friends from yoga and Pilates she brunched with sometimes, but truthfully, all of them were surface-level friends, at best. Still, she couldn't burden him with any of this stuff with Maddie—certainly not now, and maybe never. She tried to look reassuring.

"It's fine. It was a misunderstanding."

He raised an eyebrow. "Okay. If you're sure. I can always bring out a can of whoop-ass if she's giving you a hard time about something."

"Don't worry about it, Stuart. I'll see her tomorrow, and I'm sure we'll work it out together. Alone."

He looked unconvinced, and she made herself smile wider.

"So is everything sorted?" she asked. "Deposit paid and all that?"

He seemed to let it go, smiling back at her. "Yes. It is. I have the entire evening of the fourteenth and all of the fifteenth booked, so we don't have to rush out of here. That's actually another benefit of this place—no curfew. We can party all night."

"Sounds fun."

Stuart held out an elbow, and she took it, letting him lead her toward the door.

"I hope you don't mind, but Jai wants to cook for you tonight. He thought we could have dinner together, just the three of us. He wants to get to know you a little better."

"That sounds great," she said, meaning it. "As long as you have alcohol, I'm there."

"You know it."

They walked out into the late-afternoon sunshine, the air bracing. Stuart grabbed her hands, both of them squeezing more desperately than a simple sign of affection deserved.

"Can you believe I'm getting married?" he asked, his eyes sparkling with tears.

"I'm so happy for you."

"Thanks." He wiped his eyes. "It's starting to seem real now, I guess."

She squeezed again, and they turned toward his car. As they got inside, her gaze wandered to the tracks in the snow that marked where Maddie had driven away, leaving her here. Her stomach dropped again, and she pinched her eyes closed, trying not to cry.

CHAPTER TWELVE

After Stuart dropped her off at the hotel, Ryann spent the next few hours catching up on email. She also made several phone calls to her board members, all of whom had returned from London without contacting her. She could sound threatening when she wanted to, and she had the power to boot every single one of them, at least individually, out of the company. They knew that. She used her scary-boss tone and managed to get what she wanted: real answers. According to all of them, London wouldn't budge. The people there still insisted that nothing could happen sooner than the first week in March. Her company had spent a great deal of money to fly all these useless men to London, put them in a nice hotel for four nights, and they were no further than before they went. After an emergency phone call with Ted, they agreed—she had to go herself. But when? He was looking into it, but they couldn't plan much until Monday, when the London office opened again. The British actually took weekends off.

Work is always the solution, she told herself, closing her laptop. She hadn't thought about Maddie in hours. Stuart would be here any minute to pick her up for dinner, and she didn't even feel the need to overdress. Tonight was supposed to be casual, after all. She was calmer now than she'd been since she arrived in Loveland. Why she'd thought she could leave her work behind her for two weeks was a mystery. It was everything to her. Once this wedding was over, she would devote herself to it entirely. It was what she was good at, after all—no, more than good at. She was incredible at her job. And really, who needed more?

She had a nice, quiet dinner with Stuart and Jai. She'd been warned about the cats, but she found, once there, that they didn't bother her as much as she'd dreaded. Now that she'd had one cat on her lap at Jai's parents', another one didn't faze her. Jai was a good cook and prepared something he knew she'd like, thanks to Stuart—a fresh salad, some local cheese, and grilled fish. They drank some nice scotch afterward, and she and Stuart reminisced about their shared pasts. She'd brought the wedding journal Stuart made as a teenager, which Jai howled over, laughing so hard he strained a muscle in his side. Stuart was clearly pleased she'd kept it all these years, squeezing her hand and smiling at her while Jai laughed and laughed. Both men agreed they would have to display it at the reception for everyone else to chuckle over.

Jai told some of his own stories, and by the time she was getting in her Uber to return to the hotel, she knew him far better than before. Every moment she'd spent with him confirmed that he was a great person—the best, as Stuart had so frequently repeated (which was a lot when he had three glasses of scotch in him).

She slept well, deeply and late, waking up once again after the designated breakfast hours, blinking in the bright sunshine. She'd forgotten to close the blinds again. She had a slight hangover but seemed to have slept off most of it.

Her phone buzzed again on the side table—the sound that had woken her up—and she saw three missed messages from Maddie.

Appointment at the party-rental place is at 10:00 read the first, sent this morning quite early. *Are you up?* the second, from an hour ago. *OMW* the last, sent ten minutes ago.

"Shit," she said, sliding off the bed. It was nine thirty, and she was still in her PJs. She had no idea how far away Maddie lived or how long it would take her to get here, but no way could she get ready before she arrived. She could just get dressed and hope for the best.

She was opening her suitcase when she heard a knock at the door.

"Shit," she said again and then called out. "Yes? Hello?"

"It's me," Maddie said.

She approached the door, her hand hovering over the lock. "I'm not ready," she said. "Can you give me a couple of minutes?"

"Sure, but can I come in? I've got something for you."

She closed her eyes, cursing again silently. Naturally Maddie would see her like this after their conversation yesterday. Her PJs were rumpled, her hair was no doubt sticking out everywhere, her makeup was a mess. She sighed and unlocked and opened the door.

Maddie lips curled in amusement. "Wow, you're right. You're not ready at all."

"Slept in," she said.

"It's no problem—I'm sure you needed it. And I'm sorry. I should have told you yesterday what time to be ready."

Maddie was holding two cups of takeaway coffee, one of which she handed to her.

"Thanks," she said weakly. "Come in, then."

She closed the door after Maddie, who once again walked across the room and perched on the edge of the writing desk, watching her as she drank her coffee. The woman apparently never heard of chairs.

"How long do I have?" she asked.

"Ten, maybe fifteen minutes? I can call and tell them we'll be a little late if you need more than that."

"No. It's okay. I can be fast."

She grabbed her last clean outfit and dashed into the bathroom, closing the door behind her with relief. She took a quick rinse-off shower, used some makeup wipes to remove the last of the smeary gunk on her face and from her eyes, and yanked a comb through her hopelessly tangled curls. She didn't really like the way she looked without makeup, but she simply didn't have time to do anything about it, and the last thing she wanted was to put it on in the car in front of Maddie. She gave her lashes a quick brush of mascara, deciding that was enough. Plain Jane would have to do.

"That was quick," Maddie said when she emerged. She was now sitting on the foot of the bed, strangely, and Ryann averted her eyes, her heart leaping in her throat at the sight. Maddie's short, wavy hair was cute and tousled, likely from removing her hat. She was wearing a black-and-gray flannel today, which made her pretty blue eyes stand out. Seeing Maddie there on her bed made her think about things—things she shouldn't.

Get a grip, she told herself, knowing she was blushing wildly and unable to do anything about it.

"Shall we?" she asked as she pulled on her coat.

"Sure," Maddie said, springing up lightly. She hesitated at the door before turning back around to face her. "Look—about yesterday…"

She waved Maddie off. "It's okay. Don't worry about it"

Maddie stepped closer, her eyes troubled. "I shouldn't have said what I said, and I shouldn't have left you there. I acted like a child, and I'm sorry."

She made herself meet Maddie's eyes. "It's okay. Stuart had his car. Really, it was no problem." She paused, taking a deep breath. "And about what you said…let's just forget it, okay? I don't think either of us wants to complicate anything."

Maddie stood there silently, her expression somewhat cold. "Of course. No complications needed. We have a wedding to plan, after all."

"Exactly. Let's help our friends and try to keep things simple."

Maddie took another step closer, her eyes dark, hungry again like they'd been yesterday at the barn. She couldn't help the little gasp that escaped her lips. Maddie clearly heard it, the corners of her mouth turning up in a sly smile.

"Simple is good," Maddie said, her voice low and dark.

It took everything in her power not to reach out and touch Maddie then, kiss her, embrace her—anything to ease the impossible strain of her pounding heart rate. She finally wrenched her eyes away and took a significant step back and away, breathing heavily. Maddie was impossibly still, as if holding her breath, and when she risked a peek at her face, Maddie appeared troubled and full of regret. They stared at each other for another long pause before Maddie relaxed slightly.

"Let's get going or we'll be late," Maddie said.

She followed her out into the hall and downstairs. They ran into Ethel, who once again chastised her for missing breakfast, handing her a muffin before she could protest. The intrusion might normally have annoyed her, but the exchange acted as the final break in the tension between her and Maddie, and by the time they finally extricated themselves from Ethel and went outside, things were almost normal between them again. Maddie joked, as usual, about the heater in the Bronco.

"I think it's actually getting hotter," Maddie said as they pulled onto the road.

"Have you ever thought about getting it fixed?" she asked.

Maddie laughed. "I keep saying I'll get a new car, but it's been a decade since I said that the first time. I love this old thing, and it's hard to find something newer with so much space and not spend a fortune."

They drove in relative silence again for the rest of the trip, Maddie occasionally mentioning a point of interest—her former house, her high school again, a nice bar she recommended. Their companionship was easy again, comfortable. That moment they'd had seemed behind them for good.

Still, she occasionally thought of that look in Maddie's eyes, yesterday and earlier today—that dark hunger—and her heartbeat would pick up again. That was her own problem, however, and she'd get over it. Best to keep things completely innocent between them, and that started with her thoughts. She suddenly thought of Sunday school. Sister Margaret had told her something very similar once when she'd been caught kissing the other altar girl, something about pure thoughts leading to pure actions. She wasn't a believer by any means, but it was still good advice.

The party-rental business was housed in an enormous warehouse on the outskirts of town. Maddie drove into the lot and parked with a couple of minutes to spare. She pulled out a little sheet of paper from her coat pocket.

"Okay," she said. "Here are all the things we need to get."

"Do we have a guest count?" Ryann asked, scanning the list. They'd need numbers for all of this, especially this late.

"Jai and Stuart promised they'd keep it on the smaller side—seventy or eighty."

She laughed. "Yeah, right. Let's plan for an even hundred. I can always pay them back for extras, but better to be safe than sorry."

Maddie laughed, too. "Exactly what I was thinking."

They climbed out of the Bronco and went inside, Maddie's phone ringing almost the moment they were in the door. Maddie excused herself when she saw the name, disappearing outside again, and Ryann explained to the woman at the front desk that they had an appointment.

Like Joan's bakery, the reception area here was small—the rest of the warehouse and equipment behind walls and a closed door.

The woman indicated the fabric swatches and large plastic binders on the table, giving her an ordering sheet before leaving her there alone. As she was sitting down, taking off her coat, Maddie came back inside.

"Sorry about that. It was Erin—the brewer you met? Something came up on Monday, so she had to move the wine-and-cocktail tasting to today. I hope that's okay. We'll head over right after this."

"No problem. This rental place seems pretty straightforward. It's up to us what to pick, basically, and then we fill in this form. The woman that works here left me here alone."

Maddie rolled her eyes. "Nice customer service. Oh, well—can't expect people to leap over themselves during the busy season, I guess. We're actually really lucky they had an opening. I called all over the place, and this was the last one within an hour's drive."

"I thought everyone said it wouldn't be a problem booking things. That this 'isn't New York.'" She made air quotes.

Maddie chuckled. "That's complete bullshit. I told Stuart and Jai that because I didn't want them to panic. I've had to twist like a thousand arms to get any appointments at all. Jai was in charge of looking into venues, and let's just say it's lucky Stuart wanted that barn so badly. Most places have been booked for months. I mean, really—is there a single place in the US where Valentine's Day isn't a major wedding day, let alone in a town known for the holiday?"

She laughed, pleased with Maddie's deception. "You're a good friend."

Maddie smiled. "I try to be." She indicated the swatches. "Okay— so I assume we're doing red tablecloths with white napkins?"

"Or how about white tablecloths with red and pink napkins?"

"Both?"

"Great idea—let's do half and half. Which fabric do you like?"

Maddie shrugged. "I don't really care. You pick."

She fingered the different reds, deciding on a heavy satin finish for everything. The price was a little higher, but nice linens made everything classier. She deferred to Maddie's eye to choose the colors closest to the flowers.

They spent the rest of their time moving quickly through the list, occasionally debating on choices but compromising fairly quickly— she winning on the chairs (birch Chivari), Maddie on the tables, which, she rightly pointed out, would be covered with tablecloths, and no one would know they were cheap plastic. They chose relatively simple glassware and plates in midcentury, clean lines and spent a little more on nicer flatware. They found a nice bar that would suit the space, on the smaller side, but big enough for the somewhat limited beverages their friends would be serving.

Maddie generally deferred to her in terms of the quality of items, but Ryann let her make decisions in terms of style. They worked well and efficiently, finishing long before their hour-long appointment was up. Finished, she rang the little bell at the front, Maddie using Jai's credit card to put down a deposit. She called the florist before they went back into the cold to give her details about the number of table arrangements they would need.

Outside, the sun, for once, was hidden behind some low clouds, and Maddie stared up at it, shading her eyes.

"Uh-oh. That's not good. I haven't been paying attention to the weather, but that looks like snow, for sure."

"Should we try to move the appointment with Erin?"

Maddie eyed the sky a moment longer. "We'll be okay. Probably have another hour or two before it starts."

Back in the Bronco they drove back toward town—faster than usual, she noticed but didn't mention.

"I can't believe Stuart is letting us choose the drinks," she said instead.

"Right? Or Jai. That man likes liquor more than food, and that's saying something."

"Are they busy? Neither one of them mentioned anything they had going on today when I saw them last night. It's the weekend, after all."

Maddie paused before replying. "Well, I know Stuart is really swamped with his show, and Jai's trying to help as much as possible. Maybe they had to make up for whatever happened yesterday?"

There was likely more to it than what Maddie had said. Stuart's absence for a lot of this was already somewhat inexplicable, but missing cocktail-tasting went far beyond the strangeness of missing everything else. She couldn't help but think that the two of them were making themselves conspicuously absent for some reason, and she flashed back to her first conversation with Stuart at the brewery. Maybe he and Jai really were trying to set her up with Maddie.

She glanced at Maddie, glad now that she hadn't said anything to her at the time or since. Still, the idea that Maddie was in on it had crossed her mind. Maddie glanced over at her, flashing those dimples, and she was quick to return her joy. Whatever the situation, she just had to hope that she was wrong.

CHAPTER THIRTEEN

Erin had directed Maddie to come into the brewery through the back. The small beer garden back here was closed currently, and when they went inside, Ryann saw a smaller bar setup, with a short counter and two stools, Erin bustling around behind it. Maddie had explained on the way here that the beer garden was simply an extension of the brewery—open for special occasions and during the summer, but otherwise unused. Right now, she saw only empty taps. Erin had brought a couple boxes of liquor and mixers, as well as what looked like a case of wine.

"Oh, good," Erin said. "Right on time. I was just getting the first cocktail together. Grab a seat, get comfortable, and I'll pour it in a sec."

She and Maddie took off their coats and other winter wear, Maddie hanging it all nearby. Ryann took a seat on a tall stool at the bar and watched a master at work. Erin poured without measuring, with clear practice and assurance, throwing in a little flair here and there.

"So do you make liquor here, too?" she asked.

Erin was shaking the cocktail shaker very hard. She paused and shook her head before starting again.

"No. Darcy has been wanting us to try to make gin, but it's a much harder license to get. We're not allowed to sell any other alcohol here at the brewery—only beer." Ryann was confused, and Erin laughed. "You're probably wondering what the hell I'm doing then, right?"

"Something like that."

"Well, Jai and I worked together in a bar back in the day. A gay bar, actually—long closed. So long ago, it's not even funny, so don't even ask. Anyway, I also trained for a while in a winery in California, so I know wine, too. When Jai and Stuart approached me about the beer, I told them I could help with other alcohol. I know so many liquor distributors, I can get a discount."

"Ah," she said.

Erin gave the shaker a few more hard snaps of her wrist and then poured the cocktail into two small tasting glasses in front of them.

"So, Ryann—since Stuart and Maddie clearly left out some details here, the beer has already been chosen. The two of you are choosing the signature cocktail and most of the wine today. They've already decided they'll have strawberry margaritas in addition to the signature cocktail, and they've already chosen a red wine. You and Maddie need to select the white, the sparkling, and the cocktail."

"Why aren't they having an open bar again?" she asked. "Why do this signature-cocktail thing?"

"It's cost-saving," Erin replied. "If they only need to order booze for the margaritas and the cocktail you guys choose, they'll save a lot. It can also mean people will stick to the beer and wine, which is also cheaper. And it might mean fewer people get totally wasted."

"That's a stretch with the crowd that will be there—they'll get drunk no matter what you give them," Maddie said, laughing.

Ryann slid the little glass closer to herself. This one was tinged a slight red with orange overtones. It had the consistency of syrup, thick in the glass as she tilted it back and forth, the odor something like heady orange blossoms.

"How many cocktails are we trying?" Ryann asked.

Erin laughed and rubbed the back of her neck. "As many as you want? I have a whole library of choices in my brain. Stuart and Jai gave me some general ideas, and they want it to be red or pink, but I could still mix you as many as you want to try. I'll try to keep them small. I'm making halves and splitting each one between the two of you, so you're getting only a quarter of a usual drink."

"Still sounds like a lot," Maddie said.

"How about we put a limit on it?" Erin suggested. "Say, four quarter-sized cocktails? Three types of each of the wines? You don't have to drink everything—just taste."

She and Maddie made eye contact, Maddie widening her eyes slightly in alarm.

She laughed and held up the first trial in a toast. "To not getting too drunk."

Maddie laughed and clinked glasses with her. "I'll drink to that."

They both drained their drinks, Ryann sputtering slightly at the cloying sweetness, Maddie's mouth twisting with disgust.

Whoops, Ryann thought. They were only supposed to try it. Oh, well. Next time.

"Yuck," Maddie said. "Too sweet."

"It's not great," Ryann said. "Sorry, Erin."

Erin laughed. "Don't worry about it. That's what I used to make for party kids at the bar. Consider that one the control in our experiment here. So, considering what you know of the guys' tastes, what would the two of you suggest—more sour or bitter for the next one?"

"Both?" Maddie said, lips still peeled with disgust.

Erin nodded, turning around to the wide assortment of bottles and grabbing several things before starting to mix the next one.

"Yerg," Maddie said to her. "I don't know why Jai asked me to do this. I almost never drink cocktails or wine. I'm really a beer person."

"I'm wondering that myself. I'm a red wine and scotch girl, myself."

Maddie laughed. "Of course you are."

She raised an eyebrow. "And what's that supposed to mean?"

"Oh, you know, that's what fancy boss ladies drink. I can picture you in your office, high above Madison Avenue, staring down at the cabs below, amber liquid in a rocks glass, wearing a seriously tight pencil skirt, the sky darkening, long after everyone else has gone home."

She blushed. Her building's address was technically Madison Avenue, but her office looked out onto Fifth. She'd done exactly what Maddie had described a thousand times, at least.

Maddie put her hand on her arm. "Shit. I'm sorry. That was a mean thing to say."

She let out a weak laugh. "No—you're right. You even got the skirt down."

Maddie grimaced and leaned closer, dropping her voice. "Still, it's not my place to judge your life. I'm sorry."

She realized then that Erin was watching them, eyebrows up in her messy hairline. Maddie, seeing her expression, removed her hand from Ryann's arm and scooted slightly away.

"Okay," Erin said, drawing out the word. She poured the contents of the shaker into two small new taster glasses. "Uh, this next one is a little more sour and bitter, as per your request, Maddie."

Ryann held up the drink, pleased with its appearance. It was a dark red, sparkling, with a cherry in the bottom. It smelled better, too, lightly citrus, and when she took in a slightly biggish mouthful, she didn't immediately want to spit it out. She rolled it on her tongue before swallowing.

"This one is much better. I love the cherry—it's not sweet like a maraschino."

"They're gin cherries," Erin explained.

Maddie, reassured, drank hers, her eyebrows raising slightly as she swallowed.

"Not bad at all. In fact, I kind of like it. I like the bubbles a lot."

"Okay!" Erin said, clapping. "Do we have a winner, or do you want to try something totally different?"

She and Maddie shared a glance, one of Maddie's eyebrows raised. "What do you think, sea legs? Can you handle some more booze?"

She laughed and turned to Erin. "Let's try something different."

Erin seemed excited, turning around once again, and Ryann allowed herself to stare at Maddie fully and without fear, possibly for the first time all morning, maybe for the first time since they'd met. The last three days, she'd continually made herself look away, look elsewhere, any time she caught herself checking her out, even when Maddie didn't notice. This time, however, she let herself regard her at length. Maddie smiled at first, but as the moment dragged on, and she continued to stare, Maddie squinted, and her lips began working on themselves nervously.

"What?" Maddie finally asked.

"Just looking at you," she said.

"Why?"

"I want to."

Maddie's cheeks colored slightly, and she chuckled uncomfortably. "Maybe we should stop day drinking. I can tell you're getting a little…"

"Chummy?" Erin suggested, startling them both. She laughed, holding up her free hand. "I'm sorry. Didn't mean to interrupt." She gave Ryann a quick wink and poured the next cocktail.

This one was nearly clear, with only the palest hint of pink, a slight foam on the top, and a twist of some citrus rind inside. This too had bubbles, and it was sour and pleasant on Ryann's tongue as she drained the little glass.

"Oh, boy, I like this one, too," Maddie said, setting her glass down. She'd also drained hers.

"Me, too," Ryann said. "But I'm not sure if I like it better than the last one. I'd have to try that one again to be sure."

Erin raised an eyebrow at Maddie, who only shrugged.

"Okay," Erin said, "so you think it comes down to those two? Or I could make you another new one if you want."

Maddie answered before she could. "No—probably not, especially since we have to try the wines, still. I'm already pretty sure I'll have to call a cab."

"Okay," Erin said. "Here's what I'll do, then. I'll make a little of both of the ones you liked so you can try them together. How's that sound?"

"Perfect," Ryann said before Maddie could object.

"You're fun, Red," Erin said, laughing.

"And she's getting drunk," Maddie added.

Ryann laughed. "I'm okay, really. I feel a little silly, but I'll be okay if I have some water."

She was pretty sure she was telling the truth. She wasn't slurring, her vision wasn't cloudy, and she was perfectly capable of sitting upright on this high stool. After all, she hadn't even had a full cocktail yet. Oh, right, she suddenly realized. She hadn't eaten today. Still, it was no problem. Who got drunk on such a small amount of booze? And anyway, who cared if she flirted with Maddie. Maddie flirted with her, and it didn't mean anything.

Maddie was still watching her, appearing uncertain and a little worried, and Ryann, trying to reassure her, took her hand, squeezing it and hanging on to it.

"I'm fine. I swear."

Maddie stared down at their linked hands and raised an eyebrow. "If you say so."

She let go of Maddie's hand, and, needing to change the topic, she asked both of them, "So how long have the two of you known each other?"

Erin turned her head back over her shoulder, still mixing the cocktails. "Jesus. What's it been? Ten, fifteen years?"

Maddie let out a long breath. "Something like that. Might even be more if we could figure out the year."

"Nope," Erin said. "That's the last thing anyone needs to know. Anyway, it was in college. She started coming to the gay bar me and Jai worked at up in Fort Collins. She knew Jai already, he introduced us, and we all started hanging out."

"So you didn't know each other before that? Even though you both grew up here?"

"What? You think all lesbians know each other?" Maddie said, pouting with mock affront.

She laughed. "Well, I mean, I guess in a town this small, I assumed…"

"We went to different high schools, and Erin's older."

"Not *that* much older, mind you," Erin said, turning around with two cocktail shakers. She started shaking them. "I won't have you besmirch my image in front of a pretty girl, Maddie."

Maddie held up her hands. "Never. Though it might be worth reminding you that you're married now."

Erin laughed, pouring out the two cocktails into four new glasses. "That's right. I forgot. Someone's beauty made me dizzy."

Ryann couldn't help but laugh along and wasn't even self-conscious about the compliment. She might not be drunk, but she was certainly more at ease than normal with these two, who were still relative strangers. And who didn't like being called pretty and beautiful? She wished some of that were coming from Maddie again, too, joking or not. Still, Maddie hadn't objected to what Erin said, suggesting, maybe, that she agreed.

She clinked her next taster with Maddie's again, drinking about half before picking up the second one and drinking about the same. It really was hard to decide. They were both pleasant and easy to enjoy, strong but not boozy. She finished both before considering the empty glasses at length.

"Gosh, I don't know," she finally said.

"Me, either." Maddie agreed. "They're both really good."

"Should we flip for it? I even have a quarter from yesterday—I stole it from Jos."

Maddie grinned. "Sounds like a plan."

"Heads is the red one, tails is the pink."

"Agreed."

She immediately fumbled the quarter, nearly falling off her stool trying to grab it before it went rolling away. Maddie laughed, jumping up and off her seat lightly and with smooth agility. She found the quarter and walked it back, handing it to Erin.

"How about you do it? I think butterfingers here might need some help."

Erin flipped it easily, slapping it on the back of her hand before announcing, "Heads."

"Yeah!" Ryann said. "That was one of my favorites."

Maddie and Erin laughed and shared an amused glance.

"Hey! I saw that," she said. "You guys think I'm getting drunk."

"Getting, or…" Maddie said.

"Hey!"

"Maybe a glass of water for both of you wouldn't be a bad plan," Erin suggested. She tried one of the spouts behind her and cursed. "Oh, yeah—these are turned off when it's closed back here. I'll be right back." She disappeared through a door to the side.

When Ryann glanced her way, Maddie was smiling at her, the expression soft, still a little amused, and Ryann pushed her shoulder, lightly.

"I'm really not that drunk. I'm feeling a little…I don't know—relaxed?"

"You weren't before?"

She shook her head. "No. Not at all. This kind of thing," she gestured, vaguely, "makes me nervous. Meeting new people, joking around. It doesn't come naturally. I can do it for work, I guess because I have to, but socially, not so much."

Maddie's smirk widened. "That's kind of hard to believe."

"Why?"

"Well, you just seem so confident, so put together, you know? You live in New York, you have a really powerful job, and you're gorg—" She chuckled. "Anyway. Most people would be thrilled to be like you."

She'd heard her near slipup, and a wave of heat flashed through her. This time, however, she kept her eyes rooted on Maddie's, not looking away. Maddie's eyes widened slightly, and when she leaned toward her slightly, Maddie moved to meet her.

"And here we are," Erin said, backing into the room before turning with two glasses of water.

She and Maddie had jerked away at the sound, so that when Erin was facing them, it was as if nothing had happened. Her heart was still racing, however, and Maddie was fidgeting a little next to her on her stool.

"Say, Erin," Maddie said after setting her empty water glass down. "I know it's a pain in the ass, but could we do the wine some other time? I'd have a hard time choosing when I'm a little tipsy like this, and I think Ryann would agree."

She managed to nod, her heartbeat still pounding.

"Maybe we could even get the guys over here a little later today to choose themselves," Maddie said.

Erin checked her watch. "Yeah, sure, no problem. I can leave all this stuff here for a bit. If you can get the guys here today, I'm free until about four. Otherwise, we could do this Thursday. I should have no problem ordering it from the distributor that late."

Maddie stood to gather their things from the coatrack, and Ryann scooted off her stool, wobbly on her feet. She was a little tipsy, for sure, but nothing extreme. She could walk in a straight line, but when Maddie linked an arm around her waist, she still stumbled slightly until she steadied her.

"You okay?" Maddie whispered.

She could only nod, and Maddie made their good-byes for them. She waved briefly before they went outside.

It was snowing very lightly now, just a few flakes in the air, but it was strangely warm out here compared to earlier. She closed her eyes, tilting her chin up toward the sky and letting the flakes fall on her overheated face.

Maddie let go of her waist, and she opened her eyes. Maddie had taken a couple of steps away from her and was staring at the ground.

"What's wrong?" she asked.

Maddie met her eyes. "Well…you're drunk, and I don't know what to make of all that in there."

"All what?"

"All that flirting. That's what you were doing, right?"

She laughed. "Haven't we been flirting since we met?"

Maddie shook her head. "Not like that. I don't know how to read it."

"Why does it have to be so complicated? I like you, Maddie, if you hadn't already guessed. I'm attracted to you. And I think, no, I *know* you're attracted to me. It's all pretty straightforward, really."

Maddie closed the space between them in a heartbeat, pressing her into the door behind her. Maddie's eyes had that dark hunger in them again, and her breath caught in her throat. Maddie brought one hand up to her face, tracing the edge of her jawline with her fingertips. She shuddered, want and need flooding her so she could barely breathe.

"I want to kiss you now, Ryann. I've wanted to since the second I saw you. But that's the rub. You can't consent to more, and it wouldn't be right. I'm not even sure we should kiss, but—"

She kissed Maddie then, simply to appease her own hunger, and while Maddie didn't immediately react, freezing in place, in fact, her lips were warm and soft and everything she'd hoped they'd be. That scent of vanilla was nearly overwhelming this close to her, filling her nose and making her mouth water, and she opened her lips slightly against Maddie's to inhale fully. Maddie responded then, surging against her and pushing her back into the door even harder, her kiss so searing and hot, she groaned into it. Their tongues touched, and her whole body leapt forward to meet Maddie's. Maddie's hands were buried in her hair now, dragging her impossibly closer, and she pulled against the lapels of Maddie's coat.

Maddie leaned back first, breathing heavily, her hands on Ryann's shoulders. "Shit," Maddie said.

She laughed. "What?"

"I'm going to be thinking about that kiss every time I see you now."

The comment left her nearly breathless. "Is that a bad thing?"

"It is if we want to get any wedding stuff done."

"And if we're not busy?"

"Well, then, I guess we can do whatever we want in our free time."

They released each other, still breathing heavily and grinning stupidly. Maddie indicated with her head that they should start walking, and they began the route to the hotel, only a few blocks away. It was snowing heavily now, the flakes big and wet and starting to stick to the roads. Their hands were linked, and she slipped only a couple of times, despite her boneless-seeming legs. Maybe she was drunker than she thought, or maybe the kiss had undone her. She warmed again at the thought, throwing a quick glance up at Maddie, who immediately smiled down at her, squeezing her hand a little tighter.

Outside of the hotel, Maddie stopped in the parking lot.

"Do you want to come in?" she asked, tugging Maddie toward the front stairs.

"More than anything. But I'm not going to." Her chuckle sounded a little bitter. "I'm not sure you're going to even want to talk to me after what we did, let alone…"

"Hey!" she said, pulling her hand to get her attention. "You didn't do anything wrong. I promise I'm not that drunk. Tipsy, yes, but in complete control of myself. And anyway, I kissed you first. I won't be mad at you, I swear."

"Okay."

Maddie still seemed unsure, and she moved in front of her, standing on her tiptoes to plant a light, relatively chaste kiss on her lips. She took Maddie's hands in hers and met her eyes.

"Just so you know, I wanted to kiss you since the first time I saw you, too. You were seriously hot, even in that silly uniform you were wearing."

Maddie chuckled. "Really?"

"Yes. Now please get home safe. Call a cab."

"Okay. I will."

She reluctantly let go of Maddie's hands and started climbing the stairs to the front door of the hotel.

"Hey, Ryann?" Maddie called.

She spun back. "Yes?"

"Are you going to tell Stuart?" She seemed worried, face pinched.

"No. Are you going to tell Jai?"

Maddie's shoulders sagged, clearly relieved. "No."

"Okay, then. Good-bye."

"Bye."

She watched Maddie walk away through the falling snow. While Maddie was still visible, she would occasionally turn around, waving, and she would return the gesture. When Maddie finally disappeared due to distance and the storm, she was still strangely light and loose, as if something had been settled in her heart.

CHAPTER FOURTEEN

R yann ended up napping the rest of the afternoon and early evening, watching an old movie on the TV from bed, and eventually ordering a pizza. At eight, she decided to rest her eyes and slept the rest of the night. She woke somewhat late the next morning. Stuart had texted her that, with all the other venue appointments canceled, she had the day to herself.

It was Sunday, so she could do only so much on her computer. While some of her employees had weekend work, especially now, she never expected them to do it at the office, and she didn't expect them to be on call. Even Ted was MIA when she tried to reach him, so she answered some emails and went over the numbers again, playing with the projections and trying to think of a way to convince London to budge, if even by a few days. Even the last day of February was better than the first of March—that would settle basically everything. She spent the rest of the morning and afternoon glued to her laptop. The hours bled away without much notice.

Still, when she stopped to stretch, she would occasionally think back on the kiss with Maddie, flush with heat, try to shake it off, and then get back to work. This happened all day. When she started to get some real work done, she'd get distracted again and have to try harder to calm down. It helped to think about what Maddie had said, and how she'd reacted, and not just yesterday. She'd said something similar at the barn, after all. She was reluctant to start anything with Ryann, and with good cause. What on earth could the two of them offer each other?

Maddie's life was here—a good life, from what little she'd seen of it. Maddie had a great job, she was a talented, respected artist, and she had a wide range of different interests and friends. She was clearly happy with herself and everything she'd built here. She'd chosen to stay in this small town, after all.

And her own life was full, too, if only in other ways. Honestly, she rarely thought about being alone in her day-to-day life. She had challenging, fulfilling work, a great apartment in one of the best cities in the world, and she traveled widely and often. She was a very busy, successful person. Really, she wouldn't change much of anything about her life, given the choice. Being single rarely bothered her.

So, yes, she could understand Maddie's reluctance—she had the same misgivings, maybe more than Maddie. In fact, it had been pretty stupid to kiss her yesterday. But she didn't blame that on the booze at all. No, she'd wanted to, then and now, if she was being honest with herself. Maddie was an attractive, compelling woman. But her own misgivings and Maddie's reluctance were telling them both something. The fact that Maddie hadn't tried to contact her all day was also revealing—she probably felt the same way. They really shouldn't do anything more, even if part of her, more than part, wanted to indulge. They should remember that kiss and leave it at that.

Her phone buzzed next to her, and she jumped, reading Stuart's name before answering.

"Yes?"

"You snowed in over there?" he asked.

"Uh…" She stood up and looked out the window. When she'd glanced out this morning, she'd seen maybe three or four inches on the ground, and the roads had already been cleared. At least another foot of new snow had fallen over the course of the day, and it was snowing again in huge, fast-falling flakes. "Yes. I guess I am."

"Wanna come over to my place? Have that dinner I promised? I've got the groceries already. I've been waiting to cook it for you. I'm not that far away, so we could walk."

"How far is not far?"

"About four blocks."

"Really? You're that close?"

"Yep. I can come meet you and show you the way. It'll take me five minutes to walk over."

"Can you give me half an hour? I've been sitting here in my pjs all day."

"What? The fabulous Ms. Ryann Sands owns pajamas? The horror!"

She laughed. "Give me a bit, okay?"

"Sure. But remember—it's just us. No need to impress anyone."

She managed to tame her hair into a loose braid and put some clothes and makeup on before he showed up, his boots and jacket damp from the snow. He shivered dramatically when she opened the door.

"That bad?" she asked. ·

"It's pretty chilly. And harder to walk out there than I thought it'd be. A couple of places have been keeping up with the shoveling, but not everyone—less now that it's getting dark. But I blazed a path here, so it should be easier going to mine."

She grabbed her warmest cardigan, layering it over her sweater before pulling on her coat, hat, and gloves. Truthfully, she hadn't really walked around in snow like this before—not without skis and ski boots, at any rate. When they got outside, a blowing, wet wind, almost blinding, met them, and they both laughed.

"This might be a really bad idea," Stuart shouted.

"You think?"

"Maybe you should stay over at my place."

"Okay!"

"You need to grab anything?"

She always kept an extra toothbrush in her purse, and she could sleep in something of Stuart's, so she shook her head as vigorously as she could to be visible in the blowing snow.

"I'm good. Let's get going."

The walk to his place seemed interminable, though in reality, it took them all of ten minutes. With the snowy wind gusting in their faces, frigid and occasionally painfully sharp, she was nearly blind the entire way. She walked behind Stuart, hand on his shoulder, arctic style. By the time they stumbled into his little one-bedroom apartment, they were both soaking wet, red-nosed and shivering.

"Yikes!" he said. "I'm glad you're staying here."

"Me, too."

She let him take her wet jacket and hat and then removed her soaking socks and boots, feeling a little better with all the wet things gone. He handed her a crocheted blanket and steered her to the little loveseat under an enormous portrait window before disappearing into the bedroom. Beside the loveseat were an armchair and ottoman and a small coffee table, but little else in the room. Overall, the space was very small and sparely decorated, reminding her strongly of Stuart's many micro apartments in New York.

When he came back in a couple of minutes later, he'd changed his clothes entirely, and he held out a pair of wool socks for her. She took them gratefully, pulling them over her clammy feet. He cranked up the thermostat before sitting down next to her. A bottle of red wine was breathing on the table, which he pointed at. She nodded, and he gave them both a significant pour.

"Well, that was terrible," he finally said.

She laughed. "Basically."

"I'm sorry. I guess we should have done this another night."

She waved him off. "It's fine. I'm here now."

"What do you think of the place?" he asked, gesturing at the room.

She sipped her wine again before answering. "It's...cute."

He laughed. "I bet you're thinking—why the hell did he move halfway across the country only to live in another tiny apartment?"

"You said it, not me."

"It's an artist's residence. I get a discount on the place, actually— it's almost free."

"Oh?" She looked around with greater interest now. Actually, despite its size, the room was nicely appointed. It had lovely pinewood floors, exposed brick walls, and a recessed, tall ceiling. Judging from the window, it was likely very bright and inviting during the day. She stood up, walking closer to the far wall near the door, where Stuart had hung several framed photographs. She saw Jai, Maddie, and a series of her with Stuart throughout the decades. She looked back at him, and he lifted his glass in a toast.

"The place is lovely," she told him.

He got to his feet. "Thanks. I love it. I love being downtown near all the restaurants and breweries, and I can ride my bike to the foundry on nice days—it's only a couple of miles."

"You can ride a bike?"

He laughed. "Maddie taught me. But yeah—I like it. I'll be moving in with Jai after the wedding, of course, but it's been really nice living here. In fact, the only real drawback is the kitchen, which is the size of a postage stamp. I guess they think artists don't cook."

"So what are you making us in your tiny kitchen?"

"I've got fresh salad, and I'm cooking chicken tikka masala, with rice and naan."

"Mmmm—one of my favorites."

"I know. I'd invite you to chat while I cook, but we honestly couldn't fit in there together. But I prepped earlier—the chicken just needs simmering. Give me a few minutes to get it started, and I'll be back. Feel free to choose some music." He pointed at the record player.

She knelt in front of his vinyl collection, smiling at the memory of the two of them in high school scouring the stacks together in various music stores in their suburb and then later spending whole weekends at it in college in the city. She could tell that this selection was only part of his stash and wondered, idly, if he still had the rest somewhere.

She chose a Miles Davis and got it started, adjusting the volume so it would be easy to talk over. She retook her seat, pulling the blanket up over her legs, and leaned back on the surprisingly soft sofa, closing her eyes.

"Oh, gosh, sorry," Stuart said, startling her.

She blinked and rubbed her eyes, realizing then that she'd been dozing. "Wow. I didn't think I could sleep any more after last night. I guess I'm still catching up."

He sat down on the armchair and gave her a wry smile, apparently a little guilty. "Yeah. I'm sorry. I know it's been run, run, run since you got here."

She waved dismissively. "Not a problem. It's what I signed up for."

"No, not really. I've really thrown you to the wolves this last few days, and I'm truly sorry. I thought I'd be able to do a little more of the planning than I have, but a bunch of things came up for the show all at once. It should be better this upcoming week, though. Tomorrow should be my last busy day."

"It's fine, Stuart." She gave him a warm smile. "So tell me about your show."

He spent a long while regaling her with details. His show at the Denver Art Museum began in May and lasted through the summer, but he had it on some authority that it might be picked up for a traveling exhibition at some other museums around the country after that. Right now, he was in the middle of a major planning stage for moving the pieces from storage to the museum, and he and Jai were also working together with the museum's PR firm on promotions. He told all of this in high, gossipy spirits, making her laugh harder than she had in a long time about the various petty bureaucrats he'd run into in the museum, and the young intern that couldn't seem to stop flirting with Jai.

When he wrapped up, she leaned forward and squeezed his knee. "I'm so proud of you, Stuart."

"Oh, thanks. I mean, it was kind of inevitable once I got the position here. Almost everyone who works here gets a piece in the museum, at least temporarily, but I'm really happy about having an actual show."

He was doing that deflecting thing again, the same thing Maddie had done, the same thing she'd heard him do a hundred times before—dismissing his hard work and efforts. She squeezed his knee a little harder.

"Stop it. It's amazing, Stuart. I mean it."

His eyes teared up a little before he blinked them away. "Thank you."

"I hope I get to see some of your new work while I'm here."

He perked up. "Oh, totally—let's go tomorrow. And you should see Maddie's, too—her booth is right next to mine. She's doing these really cute dogs right now, and they're incredibly lifelike. Every time I see them, I keep expecting them to start barking."

"Sounds nice," she said, looking away. When Stuart didn't respond, she risked a glance his way to find him staring at her.

"What?" she asked.

"Uh, you went like ten shades of red when I mentioned Maddie's name. Seriously—what the hell is going on between you two?"

"Nothing!" she said, a little too quickly.

He narrowed his eyes. "It's not nothing, Ryann. You've been squirrely about her for a while now. Erin told me—"

Her temper flared. "What did she say?"

His eyebrows shot up. "Uh, just that you two seemed really... friendly. She said you guys were cute together yesterday."

"She has no right—"

"Hey, hey! It was totally off the cuff. She wasn't implying anything more than that. She said like one thing about it when Jai and I were picking the wine."

Her anger deflated, only to be replaced with shame. "Yes. Of course. I'm sorry."

He leaned forward onto his forearms. "You're getting really worked up about 'nothing,' honey. And something definitely happened at the barn the other day—I could tell. What's going on?"

She took a sip of her wine to give herself a moment to collect her thoughts. When she met his eyes again, she laughed, weakly. "It's nothing, really. We're…attracted to each other. That's all."

He perked up at once. "Oh, yeah?"

She smiled. "Of course, you doofus. She's hot, and you know she's totally my type."

He was beaming at her now. "And you're hers, for sure. I mean, you're anyone's type, really, but definitely hers."

She waved a dismissive hand. "But anyway, it doesn't matter."

"What do you mean?"

"It's not like, I mean, it isn't as if we could…she lives here, and I live in New York, and we have totally different, like completely opposite priorities. It's like she's this way, and I'm that, and if we tried—"

She might have kept rambling on like that for a while, but he burst out laughing. "Oh my God! You're totally into her."

"No. It's not like that at all. I mean, I think she's interesting and gorgeous and smart and nice, but I'm not 'into' her in any way. Any serious way, that is."

"Oh, for fuck's sake—you totally are. And I bet you're both being totally useless lesbians right now, denying what's right in front of you when you could take it and be happy with it. With each other."

"No—that's not true."

He set his wineglass down and grabbed her hands. "Listen to me, and listen to me well. She's one of the best people I know. You could be really happy with her if you let yourself."

She yanked her hands free and stood up, her temper back at once. "What are you talking about? How could we be happy? It's not as if she'd move to New York."

"You could move here," he said, shrugging.

She laughed. "You can't be serious."

"Why not?"

She laughed again. "What on earth would I do here? And anyway, my life is in New York. I have a business, a career that I love, a life—"

"That's totally empty."

"Fuck you."

They stared at each for a long beat after this. Both had tears in their eyes now, and her guilt was instant, crushing.

"I'm sorry," she whispered, sitting down again. She took one of his hands. "Really. I shouldn't have said that. But you have to understand,

Stuart, that it's not going to happen. I see where you're coming from. I really do. And it's a nice fantasy, but that's all it is—a fantasy. Maddie and I will never be more than friends."

He took a long, shuddering breath and blew it out. "Okay, Ryann. If that's the way you really feel."

"It is."

"I won't say anything more about it after this. I just want you to be happy—that's all. And I thought maybe Maddie could be the piece that's missing. Your person. The one you spend holidays with, the one that matters. I thought she could be your Jai."

"It's a nice idea, Stuart, and I won't lie to you—part of me really wants that. But not with Maddie, not when it would mean giving up everything else. That isn't realistic—it's not who I am."

His eyes welled up again, and she threw one arm over his shoulders. He kissed the side of her face, and when they both drew back, he had to wipe his eyes.

"You always were the practical one of us," he said. "I was always the one doing stupid, reckless things, while you focused on what was in front of you. That's probably why you make the big bucks, and I live here in a subsidized apartment." He sighed. "I guess I knew in my heart it was a long shot."

"Not even close. And I am happy."

"Okay," he said. "I'll drop it."

They drank their wine in silence for a while, the scents from the kitchen filling the little space with a heady, heavenly aroma. They both heard a timer go off, and he jumped to his feet.

"I'll go get the plates ready. I don't actually have a dining-room table, so we have to eat here. Hope that's okay."

They'd eaten every meal he'd ever cooked for her at various coffee tables in his tiny apartments over the years. The memory of this tradition made her warm and sentimental, and she grinned at him. "Of course it's fine."

He turned toward the kitchen and then paused, looking down at her. "I know I've said it a couple of times now, but I promise I won't say anything about you and Maddie again. I'm sorry I pushed. I've been a dick."

He didn't give her a chance to respond, disappearing behind the kitchen door, and she couldn't help the tears that suddenly filled her eyes. She was glad this whole thing was behind them now. Stuart's intentions had been good, but something about their conversation made everything with Maddie seem final to her, too. Whatever they'd started with the flirting and the kiss was absolutely over now. Talking with Stuart had clarified her own misgivings.

Still, she couldn't help a sharp pang of regret.

CHAPTER FIFTEEN

Ryann left Stuart's very early the next morning. He'd woken long enough to have coffee with her, and they made plans to meet in the afternoon to go to the studio together. He went back to his bedroom as she was leaving.

It had stopped snowing some time overnight, but the skies were uncharacteristically gray and dark, threatening more. The roads had been cleared, but the sidewalks were somewhat treacherous in places. Still, she made it back to the hotel in one piece, calling Ted the moment she walked into her room.

He let her know that the board wanted to force her to drop the deal—they had no confidence that she would pull this off without London in on it, and having been there, they were certain nothing could persuade the Brits to shift their dates. She asked Ted to call a virtual, emergency board meeting later that morning. In addition to getting her notes lined up, she spent extra time on her appearance. She had one dress suit with her for exactly something like this, and she was careful with her makeup—aiming for a femme fatale but professional look. She wanted to appear powerful but hot—something that always threw them off.

The meeting went poorly from the beginning. The board had apparently decided to band against her, even her closest allies, which left her as the only dissenting voice in the entire room. She couldn't ignore them—as a group they controlled the majority of the company—but the longer they argued with her and belittled her ideas, the more determined she became to prove them wrong.

Finally, Ted, who wasn't officially part of this discussion in any way, made a quiet suggestion: send her to London, let her try one more time to convince the London people to move their dates. After a lot of grandstanding and endless speeches, her board finally agreed. She had one week to get London to agree, or her company was backing out.

After the others logged out of the session, she and Ted were left alone, staring at each other silently.

"Well, that went terribly," she finally said.

He sighed. "I mean, I guess it could have been worse, but only if they'd made you back out now."

Her anger rose again. She'd managed to suppress it for the most part during the meeting, but only just. She hoped she came off as brusque and cold, not angry. Anger was read as weakness when it came from a woman.

She closed her eyes, squeezing the bridge of her nose, and took several deep breaths. She wasn't angry with Ted, after all. "They're so short-sighted! If we back out now, someone else will step in with a better position to renegotiate. All that money will go to another firm."

"Don't I know it. And the new terms will be even more enticing for whoever swoops in and takes over, since the others will be desperate to keep the deal afloat."

"And for us, it could mean the difference between staying a minor player for another year and bringing the company up to the next level. If we don't go seal this, we might never get another chance like it again."

"I hear ya."

She laughed. "At least I have one person on my side."

"Oh, don't worry. There are plenty of us. I could name like ten or fifteen right now. We were actually saying that if they…" He shook his head. "Never mind."

"If they what?"

He bit his lip, glancing to the side. "I don't know if I should tell you this since it's just rumors at this stage, but basically, some people have been muttering about the board forcing you out. Bill's heard them, and some of the other assistants have, too. A bunch of us agree that if they do that, we'll leave with you."

She'd been afraid of something like this. Sure, she'd started the company, but once she gave up majority control, she put herself in this exact position. She'd known going into this deal that it could end up this way if things went poorly, but that didn't make it any easier to hear now. She was paid to take risks, and this had been her biggest risk yet, but that didn't mean they would be happy with her if it fell apart. In fact, it would give them the precise opportunity they needed to force her out entirely, if that's what they wanted.

"I'm sorry, Ryann."

She waved at him dismissively. "It's fine, Ted. We both knew this was a possibility. And hey. We're not sunk yet. We have a week."

"How soon can you leave for London?"

She was suddenly struck by the thought of her other obligations. She was in a Valentine's themed hotel halfway across the country planning a wedding, of all things. The discrepancy between the two situations was stark. On the one side—her entire career. On the other— the best baker and caterer. The comparison was laughable.

"Well, I guess the sooner I can go, the better," she said.

"You don't have some crucial wedding task to accomplish or something?" He was grinning when he said this.

She laughed. "No. I mean, Stuart will be disappointed, but he'll understand. We've already taken care of a lot of it."

"Should I send the jet?"

"Only if you have to. I'd rather try to get on a business class tonight or tomorrow morning out of Denver. See what you can find, book it, and set up a meeting with London for as soon as you can after I land. I want to go right to them."

"Okay. I'll text you the details."

"Thanks, Ted."

"And Ryann? Don't worry about it, okay? Whatever happens, I support you. So do a lot of us. A bunch of us were really impressed that you took this risk. It was, no, *is* worth the gamble."

"Thanks."

They logged off, and she closed her laptop, too tired of it all to worry about her email or anything else. After all, this might be her last week of gainful employment. What difference did a few emails make?

She stood up and went to her minibar, opening it for the first time. She pulled out the mini bottle of Jameson and poured the entire thing into a little glass, draining it all at once. She caught sight of herself in one of the heart-shaped mirrors on the wall and almost laughed at the absurdity of it all. She should never have left New York.

Someone knocked on the door, and she flinched. "Yes."

"Hey, lady, it's me!" Stuart replied.

She checked her watch and then went to the door, opening it for him. "You're early."

He swept his gaze over her and whistled, long and low. "Wow! Look at you. Dressed up like the boss bitch you are." He handed her a coffee. "And I'm only twenty minutes early."

"I was going to change first."

"Uh-huh—no way," he said. "Keep that outfit on."

"Why?"

"Well, after the studio tour, you're going with Maddie to a caterer. One look at you dressed like that, and no one would give you two a hard time."

"Stuart, all of the vendors have been perfectly courteous to date. Everyone's been lovely, in fact, at all of the places we've been. I mean, the lady at the party rentals Saturday was a little brusque, but I don't think it had anything to do with us."

"Yeah, but who knows? Maybe you'll get a deal if they think you're rich and powerful. I mean, you are, but if they can see it when you walk in the door..."

She laughed. "Okay, okay. It's easier than changing, anyway."

She walked across the room and set her glass down. Stuart, seeing this and the empty bottle, raised his eyebrows.

"Tough morning?"

"The worst."

"Wanna talk about it?"

She shook her head, sipping her coffee. She didn't want to have to tell Stuart she was leaving. It had seemed simple ten minutes ago when she was talking to Ted. But now, faced with the idea of breaking the news to Stuart's face, she began to dread it. She was fairly certain she could be back in time for the wedding a week from tomorrow—after all, the board had given her only until Monday to settle things.

Still, that didn't negate the fact that she would miss everything between now and then. There was a big dinner coming up with Stuart and Jai's families, a joint bachelors' party, and all the other activities and meetings before and after those. She'd also be leaving the rest of the planning to Maddie. And maybe that was what she dreaded most, if she was honest. Leaving Maddie.

She sighed, trying to dismiss all of this, and indicated the door. "Shall we?"

He raised his eyebrows again and walked closer, holding out his arms. "Come here."

"What?"

"Just come here."

She hugged him, sighing into his chest. He was tall enough to put his chin on top of her head.

"I love you, kiddo."

"Hey," she said, pushing away from him. "I'm only two months younger than you."

"Yeah, and that makes you kiddo. Permanently."

She grabbed her winter wear and pulled on knee-high leather boots before she followed him downstairs. They greeted Ethel in the front room, and both ended up taking another German muffin with them on the way outside, Stuart immediately tucking in to both, eating, as usual, as if he'd never had food before.

The sun was peeking through the clouds again, but it was still much cloudier than usual. She'd been here only a few days and could already tell this was strange. Stuart was frowning up at the sky.

"It's weird," he said, before motioning them toward his car. "It's almost never cloudy like this."

"Is it supposed to snow again?"

"I don't know—I haven't been paying attention."

She wondered why she hadn't thought of this sooner. Missing another flight due to the weather would be a disaster. It might have been better to go right to the airport between storms—leaving now, in fact.

"Hey—you okay?" he asked when they got in the car.

She tried to smile. "Work stuff. Don't worry about it."

He still looked a little worried, but he started the car. Unlike the Bronco, his car's heater was very slow to start, and she wrapped her arms around herself, soon shivering hard.

"Sorry about the cold," he said. "Can't complain with a free vehicle, I guess."

"No. I guess not." Her teeth were actually clattering.

"Don't worry. It's not far. It'll probably be warming up when we get there."

He was right. She was relaxing into the rising heat as they pulled into the parking lot of an enormous warehouse. Several large bronze sculptures stood outside, as well as other metal works, many simply sitting here with little fanfare—perhaps on their way to somewhere else. After she got out, she paused before an abstract piece of swirling metal shards linked together and swooping from left to right in a way that suggested movement. The sign at the foot of the sculpture said "Rocky Mountain Wind," which was precisely what it reminded her of. Stuart joined her, smiling.

"My friend Jonathan's piece. It's beautiful, isn't it?"

"It really is. It's really incredible how many talented artists live in this little town."

He cocked an eyebrow. "Oh?"

She laughed. "I don't mean to sound like a snob—it's surprising, is all. I mean, who's heard of this city? You hear fine art, you think New York, Paris, not Loveland, Colorado. No offense."

He continued to stare at her, one eyebrow raised, and then he laughed. "I'm sorry. I'm just giving you a hard time. Of course it's surprising. That's part of the charm, I think. People in cities get so used to being the epicenter of the world. But actually, talented, lovely people exist everywhere you go. And small towns can really surprise you."

"I guess you're right."

She followed him inside, more surprised by what he'd said than she let on. They'd spent their teen years complaining about their small town almost endlessly, both desperate to escape. Then, once in the city, Stuart had really dived into gay New York life. He'd been more of a New Yorker than she was, really. He explored more, knew more cool hotspots to hang out, and had lived in various, hip places all over Manhattan and Brooklyn. She wouldn't know half the venues she frequented without his introduction to them.

When he'd lived there, he'd seemed to love it. And now here he was, waxing poetic about small-town life. It was a complete and entire reversal. She'd certainly known he thought this way now, at least to some extent, as he was clearly happy here, but hearing him say it was another thing entirely. It made her suddenly melancholy about losing him all over again. Some part of her had always hoped he'd come home, and she understood now that it would never happen.

Once inside, Stuart took her coat and ushered her into the studio spaces, pointing out the work of his fellow artists, all of which was in various stages of completion. Some of the artists were here, but many of the spaces were empty except for the partially finished work. She saw a wide array of different styles, ranging from a few artists who did people, another who did animals, like Maddie, and others, like Stuart, who did more abstract pieces. Altogether, fifteen artists were in residence, with several interns and students.

"This is really something, Stuart," she said. She was impressed despite early misgivings. She'd been afraid she'd have to fake enthusiasm. Instead, what she saw was like something out of the high Renaissance—a significant collective of talented artists working together in a shared space. She'd never heard of anything like it on this scale outside of a major city.

"Isn't it cool?" He was beaming, clearly excited. "Just wait until you see my new piece. It's back here."

He literally dragged her forward, her shorter legs struggling to keep up, his hand pulling hers with eager haste. They rounded a corner, and she knew his work at once, even though she'd never seen this piece before. It was enormous—larger than anything she'd seen him work on. It stretched nearly to the ceiling of this large warehouse, so twenty or more feet high. It was clearly incomplete, but she had a sense of the piece immediately. It was made of tall, thin pieces of metal, each overlapping another slightly taller piece. It looked, from this angle, like an enormous wildfire, with leaping, tall flames that almost seemed to crackle with heat. But when they circled to the front of the sculpture, the fire transformed into a forest of pine trees.

Stuart's expression had become deadly serious, troubled even, and he was watching her closely. She walked back to see the fire again, only to move a few feet to the right before the trees appeared once more. Tears welled up in her eyes, a strong pride sweeping through her and tightening her throat.

"I don't know what to say, Stuart." She could barely talk, and her words came out almost as a whisper.

"Do you like it?" he asked, his voice also quiet, pinched.

"It's one of the most remarkable things I've ever seen."

The smile that cracked his face then was like the sun breaking over the mountains. He leapt at her, pulling her into a fierce hug, and the two of them hopped up and down a couple of times, laughing. Pulling away, they both had to wipe at their eyes.

"Jeez," she said. "Warn me a little next time before you completely blow my mind, would you?"

He laughed again, throwing an arm over her shoulder and squeezing her. "Okay. The next time I make something half as good, I'll let you know."

"How does it work?"

He began explaining how he'd created the optical illusion, showing her from different angles how each piece of hammered steel could be two things at once. They climbed ladders to see the piece from higher up, so she could see the different side of the same piece of metal—one a part of a flame, the other, a part of a tree. He was clearly thrilled, and she continually caught herself remembering that uncertain, worried expression earlier. It was almost as if he hadn't believed in it himself until she'd told him how good it was. Now, permission given, he was genuinely elated, yammering away so quickly and boisterously that some of the other artists came by to listen to his lecture, clearly interested in hearing about the piece themselves. Eventually, they began asking him pointed questions about technique that she couldn't follow. She stood to the side, watching him gesture and speak, her heart swelling again. Someone touched her elbow, and she turned to see Maddie's smiling face.

"He's incredible, isn't he?" Maddie asked.

"He really is. I don't know when I've ever been so proud of someone."

Maddie's smile was almost as wide as Stuart's. "Me either. I think this will be the piece people will remember him for."

"Me, too." She licked her lips, her mouth suddenly dry, and returned her attention to Stuart to avoid Maddie's scrutiny.

"Are you here for your studio hours?" she asked, risking another glance at her.

"Nope," Maddie said. "Just came to pick you up. I finished my last class for the day. The college is right around the corner." She paused, her gaze dropping down and sweeping up Ryann's body. "Nice outfit, by the way. Picturing it and seeing it are really something else."

Ryann's heart hammered, and she almost reacted inappropriately. She kept silent, and eventually she managed to focus on Stuart's lecture. She wasn't surprised to see that more of the other artists and what she assumed were some of the students had joined the crowd. Stuart was obviously very happy to have people interested in his work. She glanced up at Maddie again and saw that she, too, was listening raptly. Ryann flushed with happy pride again. Whatever strange happenstance had brought him to this town, it was clearly the place he was meant to be.

He wrapped up, blushing a little when several people clapped and whistled. A few wanted to shake his hand, and she and Maddie shared an amused look, Maddie rolling her eyes. He joined them a few minutes later, a little sheepish and clearly embarrassed by the adulation, but she could tell he was proud of himself, too, and with good reason.

"That was really interesting," she told him.

He waved a hand dismissively. "Okay, thanks. I'm sorry I kind of went off on a tangent there."

"No, it was really cool—what I could follow *and* what I couldn't. You should be a professor or a teacher."

"Ha!" Maddie said, pointing at him. "That's what I keep saying.

I've been telling him to adjunct a class or two over at the college, just to see if he likes it. He'd be great."

"You would," she said.

He rolled his eyes. "Okay—maybe I'll think about it. Nothing could happen 'til next fall, of course."

"Of course," Maddie said, smiling. "Anytime you want, let me know, and I'll introduce you to my chair."

"I'll do that." He was deep in thought before shaking his head. "Never thought I'd actually want to teach, but maybe I'd be good at it. I think you're right, Maddie."

"I know I am."

"Okay, know-it-all. Let's go see your new piece. I want Ryann to see it before you guys leave."

Maddie's expression clouded. "Boy, I don't know, Stuart. It's going to be a letdown after seeing yours."

Ryann laughed and took Maddie's hand. "Oh my God! You artists are all the same. Take me to it, would you? I'm sure it's lovely."

Maddie still seemed a little uncertain, but she led Ryann to the art space just beyond Stuart's. A wall stood between each artist's area, but they were otherwise open. Ryann saw the dogs Maddie had described, and her heart lifted with wonder. Each of the animals had a distinct personality. The larger one on the right was that kind of messy mutt used in Disney films—no real distinct breed, just wild hair and crazy, lopsided ears. It was standing up, alert, his tongue lolling out, his expression open and friendly. The other dog was sitting in that funny way dogs do sometimes, one hind leg extended forward from its haunches. It had a funny, squishy face with bug eyes—a pug, she remembered.

"Wow," she said, smiling at Maddie. "They're amazing."

Maddie colored slightly and gave her an uncertain smile. "Thank you."

She walked closer, realizing now that the dogs were made of clay. From farther away, it had seemed like stone. Having seen Maddie's other piece, she realized now that she must work in bronze almost exclusively. This clay would eventually be covered in a kind of rubber or silicone to make a mold for the metal. Stuart had done a few pieces like this before his transition to hammered metal, but some of his current works were done this way, too.

Up close, she could see individual tufts and strands of fur on the dogs—the detail so lifelike, it seemed almost soft, pettable. The dogs' expressions were the real magic, however. Both had eyes that seemed alive, mouths ready to lick or bark. She turned to Maddie again.

"They're incredible. I can barely believe they're not actual dogs, even standing right next to them."

Maddie's face underwent a series of expressions from shock to pleasure to uncertainty and back to pleasure again, and she and Stuart couldn't help but laugh.

"You're ridiculous," he said, pushing her lightly.

"You both are," Ryann added. "You're both absurdly talented, and you would think you'd know that about yourself. You should both be proud of your work. I am."

They looked embarrassed then, and she chuckled again before giving them both a quick embrace. Maddie seemed surprised when she turned her way but, after a moment's hesitation, hugged her back.

"Shit," Stuart said, glancing at his watch. "If you two don't leave now, you're going to be late."

"Oh, crap," Maddie said, glancing at hers. "I think we are. It's clear on the other side of town."

"The caterer?" she asked, only now remembering the plan. The others nodded. "You're not coming with, Stuart?"

"No. I'm already seriously behind for the day. But like I said— today's the last of my obligations for a while except for some phone calls later this week. I'm open after today through to the wedding."

She remembered that she would miss most of his free time because of her trip to London. She also realized that she hadn't gotten the chance to tell him about it. I'll do it later, she thought.

"Okay. Let's get going then," Maddie said, taking her hand.

They picked up her coat on the way out, and she thought little of the fact that they joined hands again until they were outside and Maddie was letting go to get inside the Bronco. She might not have even thought of it at all, except that her hand felt strangely empty now, incomplete, without Maddie's warm one in hers. She squeezed it into a fist, cursing herself and her weakness.

Damn it, she thought.

CHAPTER SIXTEEN

They drove in silence, which seemed comfortable on Maddie's end, to judge from her placid expression. Ryann, on the other hand, was tortured with nerves. Once or twice, she thought to ask Maddie why she hadn't called or contacted her since the kiss two days ago. She wondered if Maddie, like her, had realized they'd gotten carried away, made a mistake. After all, Maddie had been reluctant to kiss her even then. But then, they'd held hands in the studio, and Maddie had complimented her clothes. It was all so confusing and contradictory.

She watched the town pass without speaking, not willing to risk an awkward conversation or, possibly, a fight. In the end, she didn't want to know what the woman thought about it all. It was too painful to imagine the kiss or the flirting had meant nothing to her, but on the other hand, that was the best option. If it had meant something more, then where were they now?

They were running about ten minutes behind when they finally made it to the catering company, another anonymous building in the middle of nowhere north of town. She was starting to get the impression that everything here in Colorado was known by word of mouth only. How anyone would see this building and know it housed anything but boxes and crates was beyond her. It didn't even have a sign.

"Is this the only caterer they're considering?" Ryann asked as they climbed out of the car.

"Yep."

She stopped, holding up a hand. "So let me get this straight. They're considering *five* bakeries, but only one caterer?"

Maddie laughed. "Not exactly. They actually wanted a choice of caterers, but it was the same problem as most of the other businesses—

everyone was booked up. Still, this place is really good. I've been to some events that used them."

"So what are we doing here?"

"Deciding on the main courses, hors d'oeuvres, and sides."

She rolled her eyes. "That's all?"

Maddie laughed again and then stepped toward her, brushing a curl of hair off her face. She realized, perhaps for the first time in her life, that it was actually possible for her heart to skip a beat. She held her breath, waiting, her lips unconsciously parting. Maddie stepped forward, almost flush, and then pulled her even closer with her hands on Ryann's lower back before kissing her. Maddie's kiss began light, almost ghost-like on her lips, before deepening. She heard herself whimper slightly and tried to move closer, meeting Maddie's passion with her own. Finally, Maddie drew back, her eyes dark, her grin almost smug.

"I've been wanting to do that for the last hour."

"Me, too," she admitted.

"So why didn't you call me yesterday?"

She laughed. "Why didn't you call *me*?"

"I guess I thought you were angry with me. You were kind of drunk. I shouldn't have—"

She kissed Maddie again to quiet her, and they stood there in the parking lot exploring each other's lips for an immeasurable beat of time. They might have stayed there longer, but for the sound of someone clearing their throat. They jumped back slightly, embarrassed, seeing a slight, young, blond man standing in the doorway to the building.

"Uh, sorry to interrupt, but are you my two thirty?" he asked.

"Yes," Maddie said, her face scarlet. "Sorry about that. And sorry we're late."

He waved a hand in the air. "Don't worry—I've seen it all before out here. There's something about this parking lot and soon-to-be newlyweds. It, uh," he cleared his throat and raised his eyebrows, "it has an effect on people."

All three laughed, and before she could even think to correct him for the misunderstanding, he was gesturing them inside and disappearing behind the door.

"Do you want me to tell him who we are?" Maddie asked as they made their way inside to meet him.

She shrugged. "I guess it doesn't matter. This is the last one, so we might as well keep up the charade."

Maddie's brow furrowed. "What do you mean 'the last one'? We still have all sorts of places to go tomorrow and later this week."

She opened her mouth to explain, then shut it, shaking her head. "Never mind. My mistake." She didn't want to get into the fact that she was leaving soon.

Maddie frowned, but she seemed to have let it go by the time they got inside. A long, narrow table was set up in this small front room, the young man they'd seen on the far side. He gestured to the two seats across from him, and before they sat down, Maddie took their coats and hats to the rack. She was always doing that for her, Ryann realized, smiling at the idea of being cared for in that way—silently and without explanation or motive. The young man caught this secret smile and winked at her before Maddie joined them again, and her face reddened at being caught.

"Okay," he said, bowing dramatically. "I'm Giorgio, and welcome to Love Bites."

She snorted at the name, and Maddie squeezed her hand a little roughly under the edge of the table to silence her.

"I understand the two of you are under a bit of a time constraint, which means we have to do all of this today. Any dietary restrictions?"

"I don't eat a lot of pork, but I will today if it makes things easier," Ryann said. "Otherwise, no."

"I'm wide open," Maddie added.

"I hate to say it, but good!" Giorgio laughed. "And I hope you both came hungry. We're going to begin with the hors d'oeuvres."

He clapped twice, and several catering staff appeared from two doors behind him, all carrying small silver trays of food. Eventually ten trays were set on Giorgio's side of the table, each with two of everything on it—one for each of them to try. The last staff member dropped off a pile of tiny plastic forks, and soon the three of them were alone again.

"How many do we choose for a wedding?" she asked him.

"As many as you like," he replied.

She and Maddie shared a glance, and Maddie looked a little lost. She tried to think back to the last event she'd thrown with hors d'oeuvres, but that had been a lavish, over-the-top affair, and it hadn't been a dinner, which meant the appetizers had been the only real food besides the charcuterie and crudité table. With a wedding, these were usually served during the cocktail hour before dinner while the wedding party took pictures.

"Shall we choose four?" she suggested.

"Sounds good to me," Maddie said.

Giorgio made a note and moved the first tray directly in front of them. He handed each a plastic fork. "Feta watermelon," he explained.

"Mmmm," Maddie said, after she swallowed. "That's nice."

"It's fresh and light," she said.

Next they tried fruit skewers, lamb meatballs, bacon dates, seared scallops, mozzarella-and tomato skewers, vegan mushroom pastries, mini lobster rolls, duck summer rolls, and vegan spring-pea spread on vegan bruschetta. By the last one of these, Ryann was so full, she was almost struggling to choke it down. How on earth would they get through the mains and the sides?

"Wow," Maddie said, finally done with her last bite. Her expression was slightly disgusted, her lips peeled back, and she was leaning away from the table.

"That good, huh?" Ryann said.

Maddie grimaced. "Not a fan of peas. And I'm really, really full."

"Any ideas which ones we should choose?"

Maddie shook her head and took a glass of water from Giorgio, sipping with a content sigh. "No idea. I liked all of them but that last one."

They both looked at him for help.

"How many vegetarians do you think you'll have?" he asked.

Maddie paused. "I can think of at least ten or so off the top of my head, but that probably means there's more of them. I know a lot of people are pescatarian, and there's at least a couple of vegans."

"You're probably right," he said. "I usually suggest half and half for most weddings—that is half vegetarian—one vegan, one cheese—and half meat or fish. Meat eaters will eat the vegetarian ones, too, after all."

Maddie opened her palms toward Ryann. "You choose, oh wise one."

She laughed. "Okay, but you can veto anything, all right? And you have to choose the next thing."

Maddie grimaced again, probably dreading more food and more choices, but she nodded.

She thought and said, "Feta watermelon, vegan mushroom pastries, lamb meatballs, and the seared scallops."

Maddie grinned. "I was hoping you would pick those."

Giorgio chuckled. "Oh, you two are *cute*!"

They exchanged an amused glance, and Maddie grabbed her hand again, squeezing it. She squeezed back, a warm, quiet peace rising from within. She liked holding Maddie's hand. In fact, the longer they did it, the more it seemed like they should keep doing it.

"We like to think we're cute," she said.

He clapped. "Okay. Shall I give you a little while before the next course? Normally I'll serve the sides now, but since we have some time before the next clients, we can wait a bit and serve the rest together. Some of the mains won't be ready for a little bit yet—maybe ten or fifteen minutes."

"That would be great," she said.

"The longer the better." Maddie nodded.

He excused himself, and she stood up to move around a little, hoping that would help her feel a little less like her entire body was ready to burst. Maddie joined her a moment later, and the two of them bent back and forth at the waist, chuckling slightly when they realized they were doing the same thing.

"You'd think we'd run a race, not eaten five pounds of food," Maddie said.

"It felt like a marathon. I can tell you that. I'm literally sweating meatballs."

"And after today, we have to turn around and do it again tomorrow," Maddie said.

"What do you mean? I thought you said we were only trying the one caterer."

Maddie curled her lips. "We have two bakeries lined up tomorrow."

"Oh, I see." She remembered, once again, that she wouldn't be here. It was easy to forget that fact when the two of them were kissing or holding hands. Whether she flew out tonight or tomorrow, it didn't matter. She should say something now, as the longer she waited, the worse her omission would seem. Of course, she could always lie and pretend she hadn't known until the last minute, which, in a way, was true, as she wasn't quite sure when she was flying, but that was a quibble. Lying by omission was one thing. Outright lying was another.

"Is something wrong?" Maddie asked, stepping closer, brow creased with concern. She held her hands out, and Ryann took them, sighing. Maddie pulled her closer.

"I have to tell you something," she said into Maddie's chest. She felt a little braver now, near to her and yet hidden, in a way.

"Hmm?" Maddie asked, her chin on top of her head. Her voice rumbled slightly, ticklish on her scalp.

"I don't know how…that is, I don't want to…"

"Let me guess," Maddie said, the two of them still tucked together. "You're married."

"Ha! No."

"You're part of a crime family."

She laughed again "No."

"You're wanted by the FBI for bank fraud."

"Ha! No, again. Why do you think I'm a criminal?"

"You hate dogs and cats."

This time Ryann stepped back and batted at her lightly. "No, and no. I don't hate animals. I just…don't get them."

"What's to get?"

She made a cutting gesture with both hands. "All of this is beside the point."

Maddie shrugged. "I know. I did it on purpose. I wanted to lessen the tension. I think you're going to tell me something that's going to make both of us sad."

Ryann's eyes were suddenly welling. Maddie's eyebrows shot up, and when she spoke, her voice was low, tight with worry.

"Is it about us? Do you regret—"

"No, Maddie. It's not about us. I don't regret any of it."

"Well, that's good."

She didn't say that it was about her, too, knowing that if they started down that road, she'd never get to what she had to say now. In fact, the idea of telling her that they needed to stop, to end whatever was happening between them, was almost horrifying. Regardless of what she'd told Stuart yesterday, and regardless of what they'd eventually have to talk about, she couldn't fathom doing it now, especially here in Maddie's arms.

Maddie suddenly stiffened and grabbed her hands. "Wait…is this about what you said earlier?"

"What?"

"Before we came inside. You said something about this being the last place. What did you mean?"

She opened her mouth, but the words wouldn't come out. Once again, tears sprang to her eyes, and when they started to fall, Maddie let go of her hands, her face hardening. When Maddie spoke, her tone was cold, stern.

"Just tell me, Ryann."

She took a deep breath. "I-I have to leave. Tonight or tomorrow morning. For work." Once the words were out, she winced, expecting Maddie to erupt at her. Instead, Maddie remained calm, but her expression and tone were still cold.

"For how long?"

"At least a couple, maybe a few days."

"Did you tell Stuart?"

"No. Not yet. I was going to tell him tonight."

"Before you leave, I hope."

Her temper flashed. "Of course I'll tell him before I leave."

Maddie seemed ready to fight back, but that coldness suddenly wavered, and she turned away, her back to her and her arms crossed tightly. Ryann desperately wanted to stop this scene, wanted to make this better, and she took a step toward her, reaching out. Maddie flinched away, stepping out of the range of her hand, as if she'd sensed it coming for her.

"You're going to break his heart," Maddie finally said. She no longer sounded angry and stern, only defeated.

"Don't you think I know that? Don't you think I'd do just about anything to avoid this?"

Maddie turned back, confused. "Then why don't you?"

"I tried! I should have gone last week, but I sent my board members in my place. It didn't work, and now I have to go myself."

"What would happen if you didn't go?"

"What do you mean?"

"What if you blew it off? What if you stayed?"

She scoffed. "I already told you—I can't. A lot of money is on the line—"

"Oh. I see."

She continued as if she hadn't been interrupted, raising her voice and angry now. "A lot of money and a lot of people's jobs are on the line, including my own. I run a business, Maddie. I can't do whatever I want."

"Why not? Aren't you the boss?"

She laughed. "I wish! Not with my board breathing down my neck. They're just waiting for the chance to get rid of me."

"Then why don't you quit?"

"What?"

"It sounds like a nightmare. You own a company, and you don't seem to control anything. What's the point?"

"It's not that simple."

"Then explain it to me!" Maddie said, nearly shouting. "I thought you cared about Stuart."

"I do!"

"Then how could this be more important?"

"It's not more important, but it is *as* important. To me, anyway. I've spent my entire adult life building this business. I'm not going to lose it. Not like this, and not without a fight."

Maddie opened her mouth, and she knew what she was going to say. After all, she had just admitted that her job was her main priority. The implications for the two of them were clear. Almost as if reading her thoughts, Maddie's mouth snapped closed. "I see."

"Maddie, it's not like I wanted to hurt you, or Stuart—"

Maddie held up a hand. "Look—let's not argue about it. You're right. Jobs are important. I get it."

"You do?"

Maddie started to nod but stopped. "No. I mean, not really. I would never put a job before my friends or people I care about. But you're not me, and I'm not you."

"I'll be back for the wedding!" She couldn't keep the note of pleading out of her voice.

"Yeah? And then what?"

She didn't respond, and the two of them stared at each other in silence. Finally, Maddie said, "That's what I thought."

Her eyes were red, and Ryann had a similar emotion trying to choke her. She turned and moved away, willing herself not to cry. After all, they would have had this conversation next week, anyway. Maybe it was better that they had it now, before things got even more complicated, and the feelings she already had for this woman deepened. Better to make a clean break of it now—exactly as she'd promised herself and Stuart yesterday.

Giorgio entered then, making them both jump.

"I'm so sorry, ladies," he said. "Something in the back took longer than anticipated. Ready for the entrées and sides?"

"Yes."

"Fine."

If Giorgio noticed the chill between them, he didn't remark on it. He did a very good job of hiding whatever he thought of the sudden change for the rest of the tasting. He's probably used to high emotions in here, Ryann thought. Weddings make everyone crazy.

The two of them tried several dishes, and she had a hard time swallowing any of the food. She was still full from earlier, but she also had what seemed like a permanent lump in her throat. Maddie ate quickly and with very little comment, never once glancing at her. It was possibly the worst meal in Ryann's life, and she would never know how Maddie managed to make any kind of informed decision when they were done. Everything tasted like ash.

CHAPTER SEVENTEEN

Maddie drove Ryann back to her hotel without saying a word, and this time it was a distinctly uncomfortable silence. Ryann would occasionally comment on the weather or something they passed, but Maddie did little but grunt or raise her eyebrows, offering one or two words beyond this, but little else. The longer this treatment went on, the more and more she regretted getting herself in this mess. While it was true they didn't have anything to talk about in terms of why she was leaving, it was immature and childish of Maddie to act this way. After all, they would see each other at the wedding, and possibly once or twice before that later this week, if Ryann could get back sooner. Being angry and upset would only ruin any of those events. At least Maddie could be civil, like an actual adult.

When they pulled into the hotel parking lot, she continued to sit there, chewing her bottom lip. She wanted to say something, wanted to make all of this between them at least a little better before she left for London, but she couldn't think of how to begin.

Maddie sighed next to her and took her hand, squeezing it lightly before letting go. Her expression was softer now, sad instead of hard.

"Ryann—I'm sorry. I said I get it, and I do. I'm not very good at dealing with disappointment. I shouldn't have acted like that just now."

Her eyes welled up, and she looked away and out the front window, blinking quickly. "Thank you. And I'm sorry, too. About everything. Really, I am."

"Are you sure…?" Maddie said.

"What?"

Maddie hesitated. "Are you sure you have to go? I know it's stupid to ask, but I'm going to regret it if I don't at least try one more time."

She moved forward, leaning across the gap between the bucket seats. Maddie met her halfway, and they hugged, awkwardly, before moving back a little, their foreheads pressed together, arms braced on the other's knees. The tears that had threatened earlier were back, and she watched as they dripped off her face to fall on the dusty, carpeted floor.

"I have to go," she finally whispered.

"I know."

She had nothing more to say, nothing to make this any better, and the longer she stayed here, the harder it was to leave. She wanted to stay in this old car forever if it meant staying here with Maddie, but the idea was ridiculous. They both knew that. She made herself move away first, sitting back fully in her seat before flashing Maddie a quick, weak smile.

"Okay then. I'll see you later this week or early next."

Maddie's eyes were red too, and she returned a similar, strained smile. "Okay. Have a safe trip."

She got out of the car as fast as she could, a sob escaping her lips almost the second she closed the heavy door behind her. The ground out here was slick with melting snow and ice, and she had to blink through her tears again to see where she was walking, her progress far slower than her haste and heartbreak warranted. She wanted to run inside, hide in her room, and cry.

She heard the other car door open behind her and spun quickly, almost losing her footing. Maddie was there in seconds, steadying her, and they were clinging to each other moments later. She nestled into Maddie's chest and sobbed into her jacket, her fingers twisted into the heavy wool fabric, and soon Maddie was rubbing her strong hands up and down her back, her voice soothing and quiet as she murmured reassurances.

"Let me help you to the door," Maddie finally said.

She took Maddie's arm, the two of them using each other as anchors to stay upright. The stairs into the hotel had been salted and cleared, and she felt steadier when she finally stood on one. She turned to Maddie, their eyes even with Maddie on the ground a step below.

"Look," Maddie said, licking her lips. "We'll see each other later this week, and then maybe—"

"No. Let's not…I don't want to get our hopes up. It's really better this way—now instead of later. I think we both know that."

"But it really sucks. I like you."

"And I like you. More than I thought I could like anyone in such a short time. But we hardly know each other, and we live thousands of miles apart."

"I could move to New York."

She laughed before finally kissing her one last time. The kiss was sweet and soft, and it felt like a better good-bye than they'd had in the Bronco. When she drew back, she could see Maddie had decided something like this, too. Her smile was more genuine now, and her eyes weren't as red.

"Can you make it back to the car okay?" she asked.

Maddie lifted one sensible boot. "I'll be fine. So, I'll see you soon?"

"Yes. Soon."

She didn't stay there watching her leave. If she did, she'd be tempted to call her back. She made her way directly into the lobby, blinking in the dim light as the glass door closed behind her. As her eyes adjusted to the relative darkness, she saw Stuart standing there with two takeaway cups of coffee in his hands, his mouth hanging open. Ethel stood nearby holding two plastic-wrapped muffins, her mouth also gaping wide.

"Did you see all of that?" she asked them.

They both nodded.

She tried to shrug, pretending nonchalance, and then burst into tears. Soon Stuart was pulling her into his arms and leading her upstairs. He took the key from her to save her from fumbling with it, directing her into the hotel room and steering her to the armchair. He left her there to retrieve the coffees and muffins, which gave her enough time to gain control of herself again. She was wiping her face with her hands when he returned, his expression a mixture of worry and sorrow.

"I'm okay now," she said.

"Really? Cause you didn't seem okay. I don't remember the last time I saw you cry like that. I think it nearly killed Ethel on the spot."

She laughed and patted the other chair. "She'll be okay. She's seen me cry before actually."

Stuart looked as if he wanted to follow up on that comment, but instead he sat, handing her the muffin and the coffee. She set the muffin down next to the others she hadn't eaten and drank the coffee gratefully. She felt worn paper-thin again, and it was only late afternoon. She glanced at her phone as they sat there quietly, Stuart munching away, loose bits spilling out of his mouth. Ted hadn't contacted her yet about her flight.

Stuart swallowed hard after his last enormous mouthful. He had crumbs dusting the corners of his mouth, and she handed him a napkin without comment. He grinned and wiped his mouth.

"So, are you going to explain what I just saw?" he finally asked.

"Did you hear any of it?"

He shook his head, and she rubbed her eyes again. Her makeup was likely a real mess, but she couldn't care about that now. She made herself meet Stuart's eyes.

"We got a little carried away, I guess."

"Carried away! Maddie practically chased you out of her car, and then the two of you were clinging to each other like a lifeline. It was obvious you were trying not to cry and still hold on to each other all the way to the door, and then you kissed and she left. Carried away is underselling things a bit, I think."

She took a deep breath, knowing she had to tell him now. "I got some news this morning."

"What?"

"I have to fly to London for work. Tonight or tomorrow morning. I was going to tell you when I saw you this morning, but I chickened out. Anyway, I ended up telling Maddie, and we had…a sort of fight, I guess you could say. You saw us making up. But also saying good-bye."

"If that's how you say good-bye…"

She laughed again. "No, not just good-bye. That was us ending it, too. We both knew it couldn't work out. Long distance, I mean."

He was squinting at her, his lips puckered in a tight grimace. "Are you sure? Cause what I saw would suggest otherwise. I think you really care about each other, Ryann."

She swallowed, that lump back in her throat. "Maybe we do. Or maybe we're starting to, anyway. But it could never work. Better we realize that now."

He let out a long breath, his lips flapping a bit. "Boy. And they say gay men are dramatic."

She pushed his knee. "Asshole."

He winked and leaned back in his chair, peering at her closely. "When were you going to tell me about London? From the plane?"

"No. Before I left. After all, I'll probably need a ride to the airport."

He stood up all at once, shaking his head. "Uh-huh. No fucking way. I draw the line at that. You can get your own damn self to the airport."

He started walking away, and she threw her most recent muffin at him, smacking the center of his back. He flinched, laughing, and came back toward her, holding out his arms. She stood, and he stepped closer before giving her a quick peck on the cheek.

"You'll be back for the wedding, though, right?"

"Yes. No matter what."

"But you're going to miss everything else?"

"Some of it, anyway. Tell me the days again?"

"Friday is the family dinner. It'll just be my parents, his parents and sisters and their husbands, and at a restaurant so Jim doesn't invite half the town again. Then Saturday is the bachelors' party. His sisters are in charge, so it's probably going to be crazy. There's going to be a party bus, and I think we're going dancing somewhere. Then a bunch of us are going to meet up a couple of times over the weekend at the festival. We decided to skip a rehearsal dinner since we're having the family thing Friday, so Monday is basically open. We might take some out-of-towners up to Estes, something like that."

She sighed. "I'll probably miss some of that, at least. If I get to London tomorrow, I might make it back by Friday. If not, I'll try to make it back for the bachelors' party, but I'm not sure, especially with the time difference. I might miss it."

He pouted before lifting his shoulders, letting it go. "It's okay. A boss bitch has to be a boss bitch sometimes. And I know you're married to your work."

"I'm not—"

He raised his eyebrows, and she had to laugh. After all, they hadn't broken up per se, but she had broken it off with Maddie because of work. She *was* married to it in a way.

"Okay. You're right. And I am sorry. I really wanted to be here for you this week."

"You are, honey. You did a lot of the work already."

"But I'll miss so much of your time off. And I might miss some of the fun stuff."

"Not your fault."

"Thanks for understanding. I don't know why I didn't tell you this morning."

"It's okay. What about dinner later? With me and Jai before you leave?"

"Yes, of course, if there's time."

"Do you want me to invite Maddie?"

She froze, eyes wide, and he laughed.

"Oh, man! You should see your face," he said. "I was fucking with you. Just let me know your flight times. We can always do something fast if we have to."

"Are you leaving now?"

"Yes, unfortunately. I'm already late for my last meeting. I thought you and Maddie would be back earlier. But after this, I'm free and clear."

"Oh, okay. So did you drop by to say hi, or did you need something?"

He checked his watch. "Oh, fuck it. What's five more minutes? I did want to ask your opinion about something."

"Shoot."

He reached into the inside pocket of his coat, holding out four rings a moment later. She leaned forward and picked them up one at a time, examining each in turn. All four were polished metal—the design work on them reminiscent of the sculpture she'd seen earlier this afternoon. As she looked at them, she realized they were actually two matching sets, not four different rings. One set seemed to have little metal flames flowing through the metal, and the other had a design reminiscent of a forest of pine trees.

"Oh, wow, Stuart. They're beautiful."

"Thank you."

"These are your wedding rings?"

"Yes. Jai put me in charge of getting them, and I thought, 'Hey. I work with metal. Why not make them?' Of course it was harder than I thought, and I only finished today, with a lot of help from my friend who does jewelry. But now I can't decide. Which ones do you like better—the fire or the trees?"

"Gosh. I don't know. They're both gorgeous."

He laughed. "That's not what I want to hear. I want you to tell me which ones my husband and I should wear for the rest of our lives."

"Oh, is that all?" she said with a laugh.

"Yes."

She considered the options for a solid minute, the fire bands in her left hand, the pine trees in her right. Both had their merits, and both were, as she'd said, stunning. Still, as she considered what they'd represent, and why they mattered, it was suddenly no question. While what she'd seen of Stuart and Jai's love was a quiet affair, comfortable, demonstrative without being over the top, at least on the outside, she knew Stuart, and she knew what she herself wanted in a relationship, and that kind of passion always had heat.

"Do one of each," she said holding them out. "I think you should be the fire, though."

He took them. "Yeah? Why?"

"Now you're questioning my choice?"

He held up his hands and laughed. "Nope, nope! You're right. I asked, you told, and that's the end of it."

They stood there staring at the rings in his palm, and her eyes teared up when she saw his lip quivering. She put her hand over his and the rings, and he squeezed it into a fist.

"I'm getting married," he said.

"You are."

"I'm going to marry the man I love."

"That's right."

"I never thought—"

She pulled him toward her, and they hugged, both of them crying now.

He finally moved back, wiping his face. "I don't know why I'm crying. I'm so happy."

"I'm happy for you, too."

They sat there smiling at each other, her heart swelling again. Suddenly all of the day's drama with Maddie seemed petty, silly in comparison. Everything she ever wanted for Stuart was happening for him. She didn't think she could be happier for anyone.

"Fuck," he said, checking his watch. "If I don't get to this meeting, I'll have to reschedule, and that's the last damn thing I want."

"Go, go," she said, shooing him. "I have to pack, anyway."

She followed him to the door.

"I sure hope we're doing this for you sometime soon," he said. "I can't *wait* to plan your bachelorette."

She laughed. "I bet. Okay. Call me when you're done, okay?"

He waved, and she locked the door after him, sighing again. She wanted to lie down for a nap but made herself go through her clothes, realizing as she did that she didn't have nearly enough of her work clothing with her here in Colorado. Ted, however, planned to meet her in London, and he had a key to her apartment. She took out a pad of paper and made a list of what he needed to pick up for her and packed what she could in her smaller carry-on. She wasn't checking out of the hotel, so she decided to leave her casual clothing in this room's dresser. Stuart was right. She needed to look like the boss bitch she was, or this whole deal would fall apart. She got her laptop squared away and double-checked that she had her passport with her. Except for the extra clothes she needed, she was as ready as she could be.

Ted finally texted her the flight time—tonight at eight thirty, which would get her into London a little after noon tomorrow. The first meeting was at three p.m. His plane would get there right before hers, and they would take a car into the city together, stopping at the hotel first if they had time. She responded, telling him what she needed from her apartment and realized then just how little time she had to get to the airport. Denver International was about an hour away, which meant she needed to be leaving here by five thirty for an international flight, which was less than forty-five minutes from now. She texted Stuart, waited five minutes, texted again, and then called him five minutes later. No response.

"Shit," she said, now starting to panic. Ethel might be able to suggest a means of getting to the airport on her own, but she decided to try Jai. He picked up on the first ring.

"Hey there, pretty lady."

"Hi, Jai. I'm sorry to rush, but I'm kind of freaking out here. I need a ride to the airport, and Stuart said he'd take me. Do you know where he is?"

"I think he's in a meeting."

"Do you know when it's over?"

"Pretty sure he said six, but since they had such a late start, it might be later."

"Shit. I guess I need to get a cab. Do you think I can get one this late?"

"I'm sure you could, but hey, don't sweat it. I can give you a ride."

"Are you sure?"

"Yeah. No problem. What time do you want to leave?"

"Is thirty minutes too soon?"

"Not at all. I'll pick you up then."

She let out a long sigh of relief. "Thanks, Jai. You're a lifesaver."

Twenty minutes later, she was heading downstairs. She rang the bell and explained the situation to Ethel, leaving the key with her so she wouldn't lose it. Ethel insisted on giving her a muffin for the trip, and while she hadn't eaten a single one since she got here, she still didn't have it in her to turn her down.

By the time she made it outside, Jai was already there, waiting in an oversized orange pickup truck, nearly an antique. He jumped out at once to help her with her bags, giving her an arm to lean on over the now-icy ground. It took some effort to climb into the high cab, and by the time she was finally seated, she could hardly believe she was inside this hideous vehicle.

The truck did, however, seem to handle the icy roads very well. Once or twice as they drove out of town to the interstate, she spotted an icy patch, but the wheels sailed over them as if the ice wasn't there at all.

Jai wasn't talking, but he was humming along with the radio—classic rock. Still, it wasn't an awkward or uncomfortable silence. The sun was nearly set now, with only the palest line of light glowing behind the mountains, their black outlines nearly fading into the horizon to their right. The traffic, luckily, was light in this direction, all the commuters on the northbound side, and they were making good time. At some point he turned onto a secondary toll road, and Ryann saw the symbol for the airport on the road sign. Her heart dropped slightly, and she fought against her own rising sense of dread. Leaving now meant returning to her old life, which was seeming less and less appealing.

"So," he suddenly said, turning down the radio. He glanced over at her and winced a little. "I wasn't going to say anything, but I can't help myself."

"What?"

"Did you think to wonder how I knew you were leaving?"

"I guess I thought Stuart must have told you."

"It wasn't Stuart."

"Oh."

"Yep."

She took a deep breath and let it out. "So she must have told you—"

"She told me everything, Ryann. She and I talk every day. No secrets."

"I see."

She was glad for the dark interior of the cab. It was one thing to cry in front of Maddie and Stuart (and even Ethel), but she didn't need another person she cared about seeing her in tears today. When she didn't continue, he finally spoke again.

"Look—I don't want to tell you how to live your life. And I know you're successful and you run an important business, but Maddie's the best person I know."

"I care about her, Jai."

"I know you do, and she knows you do. And she cares about you, too. So what's the problem?"

"It would never work. We're from two different worlds—"

He laughed. "Do you think she's worried about that? She told me the other day she was pricing apartments in New York."

"What?"

"You heard me."

She squeezed her eyes shut, fighting back more tears. Eventually, Jai's enormous hand covered hers, and she put her other on top of his. He glanced her way, the light from a passing car illuminating his warm, soft eyes.

"Just think about it, okay?" he asked. "You've got some long international flights ahead of you. Maybe think about what you could have if you let yourself accept it."

She managed a quiet assent, and they stayed like that, holding hands all the way to the airport. He gave her a rough hug outside on the curb in the drop-off zone, and she stood there waving at him until his ugly truck disappeared. When it did, she turned toward the airport door, suddenly desperate to get through security and put this whole mess behind her.

CHAPTER EIGHTEEN

Ryann managed to get drunk in the airline lounge. She'd planned to do that, and it took very little time to cross that line. Maybe the elevation was still working in her favor, or the fact that she'd barely eaten all day, but it was a quick transition. She was alone at the bar for a while, and the bartender seemed to know she was ready for a next one even before she asked, replacing her last glass of wine with a full one. Midway through her fourth, a handsome, middle-aged guy tried to buy her fifth, and she laughed so hard, he sat down as far away as possible, clearly unnerved. She guessed she looked like she was on the verge of a breakdown. She hadn't even had a chance to clean her face from crying earlier.

The flight was remarkably quiet. She had a fully reclining seat in the back of the business section, but the one next to her was empty. After she downed her sixth? seventh? drink of the evening, her first on the plane, her eyes closed as if of their own accord, and she drifted off. She'd planned to stay up long enough to get another little bottle but didn't fight her fatigue. An old flying pro, she'd already buckled her belt over her blanket, so no one disturbed her the entire time she slept—nearly eight hours.

She woke when the breakfast trays were being passed out, confused and hung over. She ordered a mimosa, a little hair of the dog, to go with her bacon rasher sandwich and vanilla yogurt. She managed a couple of bites of each before she felt like she might actually throw up, covered the tray, and closed her eyes for the rest of the flight, dozing slightly and fighting a migraine.

She always found sunlight after a long international flight strange, unexpected, even when, logically, she knew it would be daytime when she landed. Still, as she exited the plane, she found the very idea that she was many thousands of miles away from where she'd fallen asleep unsettling in a way that didn't usually bother her quite to this degree. She pulled on some sunglasses, lifting them only as she went through customs. For once, the customs official basically waved her through, and no wonder. She'd avoided glancing at the mirror in the toilets, but she likely looked as wrecked as she felt.

This was confirmed when she walked past the last part of security and saw Ted milling with the small crowd waiting for people to show up. He was staring at his phone, grinning slightly, clearly wrapped up in whatever he was reading. He was fresh and smart in one of his usual dapper suits—the gray pinstripe, she saw, as she approached—with a purple floral silk shirt and white tie. He didn't react as she approached, clearly not recognizing her. When she finally stopped two feet in front of him, he glanced at her, obviously annoyed, and then reacted as if he'd been slapped, actually taking a step away from her.

"Oh my God, Ryann..."

"I know."

"You look like—"

"I know."

He seemed almost frightened. She'd never once appeared at anything less than a hundred percent in front of any employee in her entire life, and certainly never anything like this. She could smell her own wine breath and sweaty hair.

He glanced at his watch, and his shoulders relaxed a little. "Thank God. We have plenty of time to stop at the hotel before the meeting."

"Did you get the things from my apartment?"

He patted a garment bag draped over his carry-on. "Gloria did."

She sighed. "I hope she didn't fuck it up. I'm going to need a miracle."

He held out his elbow and she took it, the two of them walking slowly through the bustling airport. Even now, on a Tuesday afternoon, it was surprisingly crowded, and the loud, boisterous screams of people being reunited and laughing together, coupled with the quick movements of the crowd, did nothing to help her aching head. Thank God for sunglasses, she thought, closing her eyes and letting Ted lead her.

"Do you want to talk about it?" he suddenly asked.

She paused, trying to make her expression neutral. "About what?"

He gestured up and down her wrinkled, reeking body. "About this."

"It's not worth discussing. Not now, anyway. Not when I can't laugh about it yet."

She realized then, though not for the first time, that she actually liked Ted a lot, and not just as a colleague. And yet, while he told her everything, every detail about his life outside of work, she'd kept him somewhat at arm's length their entire career together. Still, she trusted him a lot. She was relieved to see him now, put together and ready to help her do whatever needed to be done. It was reassuring to know she could always count on him like this.

They continued walking, making their way toward the car stands, and she glanced over at him, suddenly wanting to tell him everything after all. But no. It wasn't the time or place. Maybe later, after the meeting this afternoon. London offered a hundred lovely pubs to drown her sorrows in, after all, and Ted was usually up for a pint when they were here together, as they'd been many times before.

As they stepped outside into the blinding sunlight, she wished she had a second layer of eye protection. Ted peered up and down the line of dark sedans. Then he pulled slightly on her arm and pointed at a car, holding up his phone to show her that the plate matched what was on his phone. The chauffer helped them with their bags, and then they were inside in the blissfully darkened back seat. He sat facing her, and a privacy screen separated them and the driver.

"Should only be about forty-five minutes to an hour to the hotel," Ted said, checking his phone. "Once we're there, that'll give you about an hour to get ready before we have to leave for the meeting."

She nodded. "Okay. And don't worry, Ted. It will be enough. I know I look like hell, but it won't take more than an hour to be myself again."

He relaxed a little, rubbing his palms on his slacks.

She felt bad, then, realizing how worked up he was. After all, if this didn't pan out, he might soon be out of a job. It was one thing for her to be blasé about losing her position, given the hefty severance package she would get, but another thing entirely for him. Of course, she would hire him, if he wanted to work for her, at whatever came next, but that wouldn't necessarily help him in the interim. She leaned forward and patted his knee.

"Have I ever let you down?"

He smiled and relaxed a little more, sinking back into his luxurious leather seat. "No. Of course not. You always know how to bring old men to their knees."

She laughed. "I do, at that. And I'll do it today."

"I know you will."

"Good. Now be a pal and find us something to drink that will knock out this headache."

He dug around in the little leather-topped icebox and handed her a bottle of water. She glared at him—ineffectively with the sunglasses—and he pretended not to notice. Still, he was right, of course. She needed to be running at full capacity. If she meant to really try to win this thing, more alcohol wouldn't help. The "if" gave her pause, the bottle of water stopping halfway to her lips. Of course I'm going to try, she told herself. Why wouldn't I?

She watched the cars driving on the other side of the highway, a sight always disconcerting and incredibly strange the first few days here in the UK, more so now as she was so exhausted.

She glanced at Ted, who was staring at his phone and grinning again, texting like mad. Probably a new boyfriend, she thought. He'd been dating Rick from the art department somewhat recently, but she'd been led to believe that was over a while ago. Must be someone new.

Ted had told her about every boyfriend he'd ever had, and so had Stuart, for that matter. Yet she couldn't remember the last time she'd even mentioned a girlfriend to either of them. Not because she hadn't dated—she did, on occasion—but because each and every one of those women wasn't worth talking about. How pathetic was that? And now here she was, wanting to talk about Maddie, desperate to talk about Maddie, and she couldn't, or at least wouldn't.

Ted seemed to realize he was being rude and put his phone away.

"Sorry. It's Bill," he explained. "I was telling him we made it."

Ryann let the little white lie pass. They'd clearly had more to talk about than that. Maybe they'd only recently started dating. He was being awfully coy.

"Bill?" she asked. "The CFO's assistant?"

He nodded, his cheeks reddening slightly. She tried to picture the man but could remember him only vaguely—cute, slight, youthful, a little like Ted himself. Bill wasn't the kind of guy Ted usually dated, but he was clearly smitten. She stared at him longer, and he blushed harder.

"Okay," he said. "We're dating. You always seem to tease these things out of me. We just didn't want it getting out at work until we had a chance to talk to HR."

She pretended to button her lip.

"He's really great. I mean like a *real* nerd, but he's fun, too."

As he launched into an everything-Bill story, their car was leaving the highway, finally heading into London proper. She was surprised to see the sunny skies had followed them all the way here. The last time she'd been in London this time of year, it had been a week of solid rain. Now it seemed almost springlike, despite the date on the calendar. Her spirits lifted a little as they passed the Tower, wishing, suddenly, that she and Maddie were here together. Maddie would love all of the art and the really incredible museums. She shook her head, squeezing her eyes shut, suddenly, once again, ready to cry.

Get it together, she told herself. She could absolutely not fuck this up.

Ted was still talking, having clearly missed her internal crisis, and she managed to give him a weak smile once or twice as he prattled on. She didn't blame him for not noticing her absent-mindedness. She was, after all, still wearing her sunglasses, and he was clearly over the moon about this guy. She felt bad, however, that she couldn't pay attention. That wasn't fair to him, but she also didn't want to bring him down. All of this crap was her own fault.

They finally pulled up in front of the hotel, and she tried to leave her crisis behind as she climbed out of the car, pretending, as the chauffer closed the door, that her problems were still inside there on the seat, ready to drive away for good. She needed to get through today and possibly tomorrow. If she did that, then she could go back to Colorado and...

And what?

Ted was pulling her inside the lobby, still talking and letting the bellboys take care of their luggage. He didn't stop talking all through check-in, or in the elevator, and not even when they made it inside her room. She made Ted overtip the bellboy, the kid's face going a dark shade of red at the sight of the £50 note Ted handed him. Finally, the young man bowed himself out of the room, near tears. She and Ted shared an amused glance, and she made her way to the luggage rack, unzipping her garment bag. She hoped that would be obvious enough for Ted to realize she wanted him to leave, but he didn't.

He had fallen silent, and when she turned back, he was staring at her critically, brows bunched with seeming concern.

"Just so you know, I was totally testing you."

"Oh?"

He laughed. "That's all you have to say? Normally, if I admitted something like that, you'd be halfway down my throat and yelling at my spleen. I kept wondering how long you were going to let me talk about Bill. After five minutes, I knew something was up, so I decided to keep talking as long as I could. I told you every goddamn detail I know about the man and then had to make some stuff up so I could keep going."

"Did you really?"

He bit his lip, his face crinkling with worry. "Jesus, Ryann. What's gotten into you? You're like a ghost."

She opened her mouth to reply and then closed it, tears welling up in her eyes again, and choking on a lump in her throat. She was glad for the sunglasses still perched on her nose even here inside, but he seemed to have seen through them anyway. He walked closer and pulled her into his arms. She let him, knowing it would make him feel better. It was only the second time they'd ever been this close, physically. Their first and last time had been a couple of weeks ago in her office, right after she'd told her board about this deal. Another stab of guilt followed this thought. She'd known this man for years now—almost a decade—and this was how she behaved? She really was a cold bitch.

Finally, she gently pushed him away. "I'll be fine."

"But—"

"Maybe later. Let's get through this goddamn meeting. I need a shower, and I need some very strong coffee, I need some aspirin, and I need these fucking idiots to see how much money they're going to lose if they don't get their goddamn heads out of their asses."

His shoulders sagged with relief. "That's the woman I work for. Okay," he checked his watch, "you have exactly forty minutes before we have to leave."

"I'll meet you in the lobby in thirty."

❖

If someone had been filming her earlier today, they would have captured a master class in negotiation. She'd shown up to the meeting with a face and style like someone out of a movie—she knew that without a touch of vanity. People had stopped and stared at her on the street on the walk there and in the lobby of the hideous office building. All the men she'd interacted with (and a few of the women) had been visibly dumbstruck, gaping at her stupidly. One of them had even spilled coffee all over himself. She'd asked Ted (via Gloria) to get her this outfit from her apartment on purpose, and despite her hangover, she'd looked her absolute best.

Beyond that, she'd laid everything out for the London people in a clear, precise way without losing her cool or raising her voice a single time. Usually, at best, she could do cold and simmering. Instead, she'd managed firm and friendly. She'd explained the stakes in easy-to-understand terms for even the dullest (or possibly most dazzled) of those listening. When she'd shown them the charts of the money they stood to lose simply by not shifting their timeline seven measly days—from the 6th of March to the 27th of February—that had finally convinced them. Why her board members, who had been here for several days last week, hadn't managed to do this was completely beyond her. She was reminded, not for the first time, of what Maddie had asked yesterday: why even have a board as useless as they were?

She and Ted were now in a lovely historic pub outside their hotel, ostensibly celebrating. Unlike her board members last week, she'd outright refused to go out to dinner with the people she'd met with in the London office, managing, however, to make it seem like an outcome of exhaustion. She didn't like that kind of glad-handing crap on her best days, let alone now. So she and Ted had made their excuses and snuck away for a celebratory pint. But Ted had been on his phone almost the entire time, and she'd barely started her first bitter in the hour they'd been here. They were in a little closed snug nestled at the bar, so they had privacy, but she might as well have been alone. She'd been watching cricket on the tiny television behind the bar, simply to have somewhere to train her eyes. She wasn't really watching or following, not the least because she had no frigging clue how the game was played. It was just something to look at.

"Oh, Jesus, Ryann," he said, finally flipping his phone facedown on the bar. "I'm being such a millennial. I'm sorry for phone-snubbing you."

"It's okay. New love and all that."

"Well, it was also more than that. I was also letting him know that you completely and utterly killed it today. He's telling the CFO now."

She smiled. "Thanks."

He touched her hand. "No, Ryann—you're not hearing me. I've never seen anything like that. You'll have the board kissing your ass now. Twelve men couldn't do what you did in five hours, and they had days."

She laughed. "Of course they couldn't. Who the hell wants to listen to them? Even I don't, and we work together."

He laughed and motioned to the bartender for another round. He frowned at her still-full glass but didn't comment.

"And you look like dynamite, by the way," he added.

"So you've said."

"No. I mean it. I've never seen you look better. The hair, the clothes, the makeup, everything. You're like a fashion plate."

She raised her eyebrows and turned back to her glass, taking a small sip and pushing it away. It was starting to turn her stomach.

"So what's wrong?"

She glanced at him and away. "What do you mean?"

"You just made the most important deal of your career. The entire New York office was beginning to doubt you. I mean, I never did, but almost everyone else was starting to wonder if you could pull it off. Especially when you flew halfway across the country in the middle of it for a wedding, of all things. Then you're here, you have one meeting, and it's all fixed."

She lifted her eyebrows.

He touched the back of her hand, this time leaving his there, and waited until she made eye contact.

"So why aren't you excited? I mean, Christ, Ryann—it's the biggest deal you've ever pulled off, and you made it seem effortless. You're sitting here like your dog died."

She laughed, a little thrill of triumph racing through her. He was right, after all. She'd made her company, potentially anyway, tens of millions of dollars—and possibly much more long term. And she had shown her board who was boss. And she did look the best she ever had while doing it, too.

"I'm sorry. You're right. I'm just a little hungover and tired. And there have been some...complications in Colorado."

"Oh?" He raised his eyebrows and once again motioned for the bartender. Ted waited when the man stopped in front of them, staring at her, and she sighed.

"Fine. Gin and tonic, please. A double."

"That's my girl," Ted said. "Okay. Tell me about these complications."

"There's a woman there. Maddie."

He was staring at her, clearly surprised, and he stayed quiet while they waited for her drink. Once she'd taken her first sip, and the bartender had left them alone again, he leaned forward.

"Spill it."

She gave a much-shortened version of the story, trying to keep her tone light and the details vague. He listened raptly, his lips bunched together, clearly to stop himself from interrupting, his eyes twinkling.

Finished, she shrugged. "Anyway, it's over now. And I'm a little sad about it. That's all."

He immediately stood up. "Uh-huh, Ryann. That's not all. Come on. Grab your coat."

"Where are we going?"

"I'm staying here and wrapping things up. You're going back to Colorado on the next flight."

"What?"

He stamped his foot, his hands going to his waist. "Are you kidding me right now? Jesus. No wonder Stuart kept pushing you. You're obviously in love with this woman."

She laughed. "No, I'm not."

He stared at her, hard. "You are. And you're going to get on a goddamn plane and win her back—do you hear me?"

"But why? What good would it do? Next week, after the wedding, I'll be coming back to New York—"

"Fuck that, Ryann. You don't turn away from something like this. Not ever. Details come later."

He was clearly serious, and despite her scoffs and eye rolls, he wasn't backing down.

"You really mean to drag me to the airport right now?" she asked.

"You're damn right, I do. Like I said, get your coat."

She checked her watch. "There's no way a flight is leaving for Denver this late. I wouldn't even get to the airport before ten or eleven."

He pouted. "Fine. But first thing tomorrow."

"Okay."

This promise seemed to satisfy him, and he sat back down on his stool, finishing his beer in one long chug. For such a small, slight guy, he could really drink. She was watching him, and he raised an eyebrow when he noticed.

"What?" he asked.

"You were really going to drag me to the airport?"

His lips twitched, fighting a smile. "Hell yes, I was."

"You really think—"

"I do. Now shut up and finish your drink. Then have another. Let's at least get a little tipsy. This is a celebration, after all."

As much as she wasn't in the mood for it, she decided not to argue, draining her first glass but nursing her next as he continued to finish pint after pint. She was glad for the early hours most pubs had, as he was definitely a little more than tipsy by the time they left just before ten. This time she helped him to his room.

Back in hers, she almost didn't follow through on what she'd told him, but then, as she lay there in the dark, the time difference was so jarring to her internal clock that she was wide-awake. She finally got up and booked a flight back to Colorado on the plane leaving Heathrow tomorrow at noon. Once done, she fell asleep almost at once.

CHAPTER NINETEEN

She landed in Denver in the late afternoon, the brilliant blue of the sky so startling and stark and stupidly unexpected, she felt, once again, disconnected from reality. She wanted to surprise Stuart with her return and had planned to rent a car and simply show up at his place. But when she walked off the plane and found herself literally stumbling from jet lag, she realized it might not be the best idea to get behind the wheel of a car. Jai, however, was happy to pick her up and keep it from his soon-to-be-husband, knowing how much it would please him. He was at the airport in what seemed like record time, and they made it back to the hotel by five. Ethel immediately plied both of them with a plate full of her awful muffins, which Jai was nice enough to gush over and begin eating in front of her.

Jai followed Ryann into her room, setting the extra muffins on the desk. She flopped backward onto the bed while he sat in an armchair, continually checking his phone and dismissing calls and messages.

"Stuart thinks I've died," he announced, reading a message on his phone.

She laughed. "How long have you been gone?"

He glanced at the clock. "Less than three hours."

She sat up again, rubbing her face. "Do you two normally check in this often?"

He nodded. "We text and chat all day unless we're working, and he knows I'm not working. I was helping Maddie with the cake earlier today, but that was hours ago, and he knows that, too."

She didn't react to Maddie's name, instead asking, "Do you need to call him?"

"Yes—if only to divert suspicion. What should I tell him?"

Her mind was still fuzzy. She wanted to surprise Stuart but hadn't really thought it through in any way beyond her original plan.

"Maybe tell him to meet you somewhere in a little while?"

He pointed at her. "Good idea. We were supposed to have dinner and drinks with Erin and Darcy in a few. I'll say I got caught up, and I'll meet them all over there in a little bit. Then you can show up with me."

"How long do I have?"

He tilted his head back and forth. "Thirty, forty minutes? I could push it a little, but you know how Stuart gets if you make him wait for food."

She laughed and made herself get up, her whole body protesting. It was strange. After all, she'd slept well on the plane going to London, had slept solidly in her hotel last night in London, and had gotten a decent nap on the flight and on the drive here. She'd probably slept more the last two days than she had any night the last two weeks, but she was still terribly tired.

"Are you sure you're up for this?" he asked, squinting critically. "We could always do this tomorrow. You look like you need some rest."

She shook her head rapidly. "Thanks, but I'll be fine. Just need some coffee."

"I'll go ask Ethel—no, better yet, I'll pop over to a little café down the street. I'll call Stuart and come back for you in half an hour. What do you want to drink?"

"Double espresso. Thanks, Jai."

A quick, scorching shower made things better. It already seemed strange to wear her casual clothing again, and with the limited time she'd been given, she once again had to settle for very light makeup. She could hardly remember the last time she'd gone out in public like this before recently, and she'd done so more than once here in Colorado. It helped, perhaps, that so few people she'd seen here seemed to wear much makeup themselves. And Maddie had seemed to like her this way, too.

She frowned at her reflection. She'd studiously kept her mind away from Maddie ever since her conversation with Ted in the pub. She didn't want to think about the implications of her actions yet. They were too overwhelming. After all, she'd basically flown back here for her. Sure, she was here for Stuart, too, but she'd come back early for her primarily—there was no denying that. And she didn't know what to make of it, even now, standing in this silly hotel room half a world away from that decision. It was too much to absorb, and much better to ignore, at least for now. She made herself dismiss that whole train of thought. She'd worry about Maddie tomorrow and try to enjoy Stuart's surprise.

Jai knocked soon after, and she chugged her espresso after he handed it to her. He raised his eyebrows and did the same with his hot cocoa, sending both of them into pealing shrieks of giggles and laughter. Eventually he took her arm, leading her downstairs past the exuberant Ethel, who insisted each of them take Stuart a muffin.

"Shall we walk?" he asked her when they were outside. "It's just a few blocks."

"Sure. I could use the fresh air."

It was strangely warm out for a February evening, and the sunset was brilliantly pink, almost hard to look at. She'd never seen anything like the skies here.

"Supposed to snow again tomorrow," Jai said.

"Really?"

"You can always tell. When it gets weirdly warm, it's often a sign a storm's coming—at least this time of year."

"Hard to believe."

She felt, in fact, overdressed in her warm winter wear, and she was sweating lightly by the time they reached Henry's—the restaurant where Stuart and the others were already waiting. She'd been outside this place before on her first night, when she'd run away from Maddie's weird behavior. As it had been that night, the restaurant was incredibly busy despite the relatively early hour. She managed to hide herself behind Jai's enormous back and shoulders, and the crowd helped conceal her. She heard Stuart call Jai's name and stayed as hidden as she could, hoping that if she couldn't see Stuart, he couldn't see her. Jai finally stopped, and she almost collided into his back.

"Where the hell have you been?" Stuart asked.

"I had to pick someone up at the airport," Jai said.

"What? Who? I thought everyone was getting here Friday or this weekend."

Jai stepped out of the way, revealing her, and Stuart and the others he was with were also revealed to her—Erin, Darcy, and, of course, Maddie. Ryann realized then that she should have anticipated seeing her tonight, but it was clearly a shock to them both. Her eyes locked with Maddie's, who didn't look happy to see her. No, if anything, her surprise seemed to border on anger. Her eyes were smoldering, dark, her brow and lips creased.

But Stuart shrieked and leapt forward, pulling her into a dancing, jumping hug. She laughed along with him, grateful, suddenly, to have someone else to focus on.

"You came back!" he finally said, almost screaming. Several people nearby glanced their way, but their curiosity seemed friendly, not annoyed.

"Of course I did, you ninny," she said. They'd spun in circles so many times her back was now to Erin, Darcy, Jai, and Maddie at the little corner table they were sitting at, and she could almost sense Maddie's dark-blue eyes burning holes in the back of her cashmere coat.

"I can't believe it!" he said. "I'd convinced myself I wouldn't see you until next Tuesday—that you'd show up just as we said 'I do.'"

She grinned. "I told you I'd get back as soon as I could, and here I am."

"Yeah, but gosh! It's like you just left. Did you really go to London and back since I saw you ?"

"I sure did. And I made a multi-million-dollar deal while I was at it."

He shrieked in triumph again and jumped up and down. With any other person, she might have thought he'd had a few too many, but she'd seen him excited and overjoyed like this a few times before. The feeling was catching. She was suddenly thrilled to be here again with him, happy tears prickling the corners of her eyes, like his.

But then she turned around and caught Maddie glaring at her again. She looked away as quickly as she could, but her stomach dropped with dread. She greeted Erin and Darcy instead. Both were very happy to see her, Erin nearly fawning over her and jumping up to get her a drink. Darcy stood and motioned for her to take her seat. There was only enough space for four behind the little corner table.

"Oh, I couldn't," she said, laughing.

"Oh, but I insist," said Darcy.

Sitting, of course, meant seating herself next to Maddie, who didn't greet her at all. Luckily, with Maddie on her left and farther back into the corner, she could only sense her there—they didn't have to talk or interact in any way. Erin was soon back with a dark beer—Cupid's Kiss, which was on tap in local restaurants and bars now. She took a grateful sip, smiling at Erin's expectant face, and gave her a thumbs-up.

"Even better than I remember."

Erin hooted with glee, pumping her fist in the air, and everyone laughed. The men insisted on having the four women sit at the little table, both still standing as they waited for one of the nearby tables to clear.

"You really are going to give her a big head," Stuart said, winking at her.

"She deserves it," she said, smiling at Erin. Erin went five shades of red, and Darcy rolled her eyes.

"You truly shouldn't compliment her like that. Now she'll never stop talking about you. She was already half in love with you before the praise."

Erin glared at her wife, sticking out her tongue, and the two of them laughed, leaning close for a quick kiss. Ryann turned to her beer to stop from watching them, once again very aware that not a single other patron in this room seemed to give one iota that two women were having a little PDA here. No one nearby even gave them a second glance.

"How was your trip?" Maddie said next to her, startling her so badly she choked on her beer. Maddie slapped her gently on the back a couple of times. "Are you all right?"

She took another sip to clear her throat and gave her a quick smile. "I'm okay. Wrong pipe. And London was great. Very successful."

"Glad to hear it."

She looked at Maddie more fully then, trying to read her expression, but Maddie seemed genuinely pleased for her. The recognition of this response made Ryann's stomach flop a little with nerves, and she sipped at her beer some more to cover her confusion. Moments ago, Maddie had seemed upset at seeing her again. Now she was acting like nothing had changed. She was her usual charming self. It was hard to keep up with Maddie's mood, and if her mind had been clearer, this behavior might have even upset her. As it was, she was simply very confused.

Luckily, Stuart saved her from trying to continue a conversation by knocking on the table in front of them. He waited until he had everyone's attention and held up his beer.

"A toast! To Ryann's success and her triumphant return."

"Hear, hear!" everyone said, clinking glasses.

They ordered dinner, the little two-person table right next to theirs opening up for the guys by the time the food arrived. Maddie was mostly quiet, directing most of the conversation to Erin and Darcy.

Ryann decided she must have picked up on her awkwardness, as Maddie barely glanced her way beyond a couple of polite inquiries about the food and drink. Maddie seemed, at least to Ryann, on her best behavior.

At one point, Erin was describing the other beers that had been submitted for the Valentine's Day beer competition at the festival. She and the other local brewers were all friends, and all had already tried each other's beers. Erin, however, seemed confident that hers would win this year. She eventually left for the bar to get everyone a sample of the other breweries' entries, all of which were on tap here. Darcy watched her leave and then leaned forward a little when Erin was out of earshot.

"She's really nervous about the competition," Darcy explained.

"What happens if she wins?" Ryann asked.

Darcy smiled. "Nothing really—no money's involved, anyway. The winning beer, brewery, and brewer will be featured in the local newspaper, which can help sales, I suppose, but she's never had a problem selling out before. And a couple of bars like Henry's here and some others in town will have some specials with it, but there's no real reward beyond bragging rights."

"She's never won," Maddie added.

"She's been second and third every year, but never first," Darcy added.

"Ah," Ryann said, understanding quite well. That was almost harder than losing, in some ways. Second best was a hard spot to be in—close but not good enough.

"When does this festival start again?" she asked.

"Friday afternoon, and it lasts through the holiday Tuesday," Darcy said.

"There are different activities every day through Valentine's," Maddie said. "I know Stuart and Jai want to hit up some of them this Saturday and Sunday between wedding stuff, so you should get to see a bit of it. The festival ends with the group wedding and closing ceremonies on Tuesday."

Ryann was still a little baffled. Stuart had explained the group wedding, but it was hard to wrap her mind around it. Something like forty or fifty couples would be getting married or renewing their vows at the same time as he and Jai—maybe more. Indeed, for the actual wedding part of it, she wasn't involved at all—none of the party was— beyond standing nearby. Later, at the reception, they would do group photos together, and Jai and Stuart would exchange their vows there, but bringing the rings was the extent of her responsibilities as maid of honor on the day itself.

The whole thing was bizarre. But he and Jai had watched the group wedding together last year on their first date, which was what had given Stuart the idea to begin with. She'd never envisioned anything so corny for his wedding, but apparently Stuart was a cornball at heart.

Erin returned with two flights of beer, a waitress carrying a third. Erin set one in front of her spot and Darcy's, one in front of Jai and Stuart, and one in front of Maddie and her. As Erin explained each beer, Ryann was forced to watch and interact with Maddie, their hands brushing more often than was probably necessary as they exchanged samples. As they continued the tasting, her face flushed with heat and alcohol, and Maddie's steady gaze on her wasn't helping. Erin was explaining why her beer was superior to all of the others, but Ryann was only half-listening. She finally met Maddie's eyes, and the outside world seemed to disappear in a hazy fog of relief. It was so nice simply to see her.

Finally, she held the second half of the last little glass out for Maddie, her fingers trembling slightly. Maddie took it, pausing briefly to squeeze her fingers and grinning somewhat wickedly at her blush. She looked away, suddenly embarrassed, and realized then that their friends had fallen silent. Even Erin was quiet, watching the two of them with a smirk.

"What?" she asked.

"Uh, nothing," Erin said. "Just that you two are ridiculous."

"What do you mean?"

Erin laughed. "Oh, I don't know—maybe that you're flirting over a glass of beer?"

Ryann colored, Maddie's eyes catching hers for a minute. Her grin seemed smug, and Ryann was suddenly overwhelmed. She stood up, scooting out of the little booth. Everyone stared at her.

"Toilet?" she asked. Erin pointed, and she had to force herself not to run away.

Safely locked in the little stall, she splashed some cold water on her overheated face, realizing as she did that this was one of several times she'd done exactly this in the last week—hidden in the bathroom to cool off. She was being ridiculous and wasn't angry per se, but she also didn't like the direct interference from Erin and Stuart, or the passive version from Jai and Darcy. Everyone had been watching her and Maddie like they knew exactly what was happening between them. And Maddie's behavior hadn't helped. She too seemed to think that whatever was going on between them was obvious and sure. And while Ryann had, in fact, come back early for her, she didn't like the assumption, especially as they hadn't had a chance to talk about anything yet.

She took a deep breath and frowned at her reflection. She was overreacting. Her friends were excited, that's all. Maddie was another thing, but she shouldn't be upset by her, either. After all, she seemed happy to have her back, and that's all that really mattered.

When she came out of the bathroom, Maddie was waiting in the hallway, presumably to use the toilet, and Ryann gave her a quick smile before starting back to the restaurant. Maddie stopped her, grabbing her hand, and when Ryann turned her way, Maddie stepped closer and pulled her into a searing kiss. Ryann relaxed into it before recognizing what was happening. It wasn't that she minded—no, in fact, she wanted to go on kissing Maddie for the rest of the night. But they were in a public place. Anyone could show up at any moment. She pushed back and away, both of them breathing heavily.

"I wanted to do that the second I saw you," Maddie finally said, gasping.

"It didn't seem that way to me. You were upset when you saw me."

"I was upset. I'd convinced myself I'd never see you again—or maybe only at the wedding. I told myself it didn't matter, that you were right—that it would never work out between us. Then I saw you and knew I'd been fooling myself. I was angry at myself, not you."

"Why?"

Maddie stepped closer again, tilting Ryann's chin up with the tips of her fingers. "Because you said you'd be back as soon as you could, and here you are. I should have trusted you."

Ryann raised her eyebrows. "You should have."

Maddie kissed the tip of her nose, her eyebrows, her chin, and then, lightly, her lips. Ryann's eyes fluttered open, and Maddie's smile was open, warm, and happy. She seemed perfectly content, comfortable and pleased.

"We should get back to the others," Ryann said, reluctant.

Maddie laughed. "It's already going to be very obvious what we were doing back here."

She grimaced. "They're never going to let it alone, are they?"

"Nope."

"Okay then. Fine. How about we give them what they want?"

Maddie hesitated. "What do you mean?"

Ryann grabbed her hand and Maddie laughed, linking their fingers together. "Do you think we should stop hiding this?"

"Like you said, it's perfectly obvious to everyone else. Why bother?"

Maddie's expression faltered.

"What?" Ryann asked.

She met Ryann's eyes, her face slightly pinched. "I really missed you. I know it's stupid, but—"

She stopped Maddie with a kiss. "It's not. We can figure it out later, okay?"

Maddie held back, seeming uncertain, but she smiled when Ryann started walking again. When the two of them rejoined their friends, still holding hands, the others pretended not to notice, or at least didn't mention it, their eyes only occasionally straying to their linked hands. Jai caught her eye and winked, and she knew from that he must have put the kibosh on further teasing, at least for now, as even Stuart restrained himself beyond a few absurdly happy glances their way. And when she and Maddie left together a while later, no one said a word.

CHAPTER TWENTY

It was still warm outside, the air heavy with moisture as if it were about to rain. She and Maddie walked quickly, hands clasped tight enough that Ryann's fingers were starting to go numb. She hardly noticed in her haste to get inside. She was breathing heavily from both the exertion of the walk as well as her rising excitement and desperate desire.

Two blocks from the hotel, Maddie stopped, peered around them intently, and pulled her into an alley. Moments later, Maddie's hands were in her hair, her lips on hers, the kisses breathless and frantic. Ryann's already racing heart seemed to seize and start again, pounding to catch up to the little pause, her body liquid fire in Maddie's hands.

"Couldn't"—Maddie kissed her several times on her lips, her cheeks, her forehead, and then her neck—"wait," she finally breathed out, reattaching her lips to Ryann's neck a second later.

A little moan escaped her lips, and Maddie increased her attentions to her pulse point, nibbling slightly as she kissed and sucked.

"Jesus," Ryann gasped, her breath ragged.

Maddie's hands explored her body next, wandering over and squeezing her backside before traveling up and under the back of her shirt. They were almost hot on her skin. She shuddered all over, sinking into the strength of Maddie's arms, and Maddie pulled her closer, moving her lips from Ryann's neck to her lips and back again.

Maddie slotted her thigh between Ryann's legs, and she ground down into it. Her desire, already making her feel like something feral, exploded, and the moan that followed the pleasure spiking through her was loud and unhinged.

On the brink of falling to pieces, a tiny part of her brain that had been quiet—taking in all these sensations as if too surprised to protest—

suddenly woke up, and her common sense returned. She pushed Maddie away, none too gently, gasping for breath when she was free.

Maddie looked still dazed, her lips still pursed, her hands held out as if to pull her in again, but Ryann shook her head.

"No."

Maddie seemed to shake herself awake, her expression guarded, confused. "No?"

"Not here, anyway. I don't want our first time," she gestured, "to be outside in a dirty alley."

They were a few feet away from a series of open trash containers. Ryann was currently leaning against the side wall of a restaurant, and the dumpsters reeked. A black stray cat, who had apparently been watching them, darted away when they looked its way.

"Fair enough," Maddie said. She grabbed Ryann's hand and started striding back into the street, nearly dragging her along as she stumbled along on semi-numb legs.

They could see the hotel now, the pink shiny and gleaming from the sunset as if lit from within, and they sped up, suddenly giggly and silly. Ryann was caught with a wild, vast joy and had to fight the urge to stop and scream about it to the world.

As they approached the door to the hotel, Ryann put a finger up to her lips, wanting, for once, to sneak into her room without being noticed. Maddie, clearly catching on, pointed upward at the bells above the door on the inside, and Ryann sighed, realizing her plan wasn't likely to work.

"Let's be as quick as we can," she told Maddie. "Say hi and keep walking."

As predicted, Ethel popped out of the dining room and into the lobby the moment they were inside, and while she and Maddie greeted her briefly, they kept moving forward and up the stairs to her room, almost as if they had somewhere they had to hurry off to, which was, in a way, true.

Once inside her room, that quiet, calming voice in her mind turned off, and she launched herself at Maddie, pushing her back and onto the silly heart-shaped bed. Maddie gasped and barked a laugh of delighted surprise before sitting up again to pull Ryann down and on top of her. Maddie flipped her a moment later, pushing her legs out and to the sides around her hips. Maddie's lips were back on her pulse point soon after, and then Ryann was pulling at her clothes, urgently trying to wrestle her shirt over her head. Maddie laughed, sitting up a little to help her before unbuttoning and tossing her own shirt to the side. Their pants followed, and then they were back in each other's arms, only their underwear and bras dividing their naked bodies.

Maddie's shoulders were a revelation, broad and strong, with rippling, sinewy muscle. She had washboard abs, and Ryann was too dazzled by both her shoulders and her stomach to explore while she had the chance. Almost as soon as she recognized what she was seeing, Maddie was moving back down onto her, her lips traveling down from her neck to her collarbone. Ryann threw one arm over her eyes and bit her lower lip, so overwhelmed by the pleasurable sensations she almost cried out. She clenched her other hand into a fist at her side, terrified of what she might do if she let herself touch Maddie. She was already close to the brink of something overwhelming, almost terrifying in its power rising up from within.

Maddie lifted her slightly before moving to the clasp of her bra, releasing her breasts. Still, Ryann kept her eyes covered, breathing lightly between clenched teeth, waiting.

"Holy shit, Ryann," Maddie said, almost whispering. Ryann moved her arm slightly to see Maddie staring down at her, her eyes and hair wild. "You're even more beautiful than I could have imagined."

Ryann sighed, the last of her restraint abandoning her, and with both hands she pulled Maddie down into a heated kiss. Maddie's lips started moving downward again soon after, latching onto her pulse point. Then she grasped Ryann's breasts, squeezing, lightly, at first, and then with more force. The fingertips of her right hand pinched Ryann's nipple, and she shrieked with delight.

"Touch me, Maddie, please," she said. "I don't know how much longer I can take it."

Maddie nodded, her face against Ryann's neck, and then, finally, her fingers slid down and under Ryann's underwear.

"Jesus, Ryann," Maddie said, lifting slightly to make eye contact with her.

Ryann groaned, her hips already undulating under Maddie's hand.

"Please, Maddie," she murmured, breathing hard.

"Okay," Maddie said, and sank into her.

❖

Ryann stretched languidly, reaching out, but her arm met an empty, wrinkly sheet. She sat up, startled by the bright sunshine, and blinked against it until her eyes adjusted. The room was overly hot, almost sultry, and she flipped away the bit of cover twisted around her naked body and fanned herself with a hand. The bathroom door was wide open, the bathroom empty, and she didn't see Maddie there in the room. Her stomach twisted a bit, anxiety rising, and she made herself take a long, deep breath.

She's probably getting us coffee, she told herself. Don't freak out.

She scooted over to the edge of the bed and stood up, stupidly embarrassed to be standing here naked despite being totally alone. She grabbed her robe and went into the bathroom, coming out a few minutes later, still robed but with a clean mouth, at least. She wasn't ready to get dressed and wasn't in the mood for a shower, so she grabbed her laptop and settled into an armchair to check her email.

When half an hour passed without a sign of Maddie, her earlier anxieties returned. Beyond this, she was also starting to get angry. How dare she leave, as if this were some kind of one-night stand? She could have at least left a note, just to be polite.

Almost as if the anger had summoned her, Ryann heard a muffled knock, and when she peeked outside, Maddie was standing there with bags of food and a coffee carrier. Ryann opened the door, and Maddie gave her a guilty smile as she entered. She looked ridiculously good for being unwashed and ruffled like she was, and the cold air outside had given her cheeks a rosy glow.

Maddie set the food down on the little table and quickly hugged and kissed her. "I'm so sorry I was gone so long. I didn't want to wake you when I left. I was going to text from the café, but when I finally got there, I realized I didn't have my phone."

Ryann was still a little miffed but tried to let it go. Maddie, perhaps seeing some of this reaction, gave her a worried smile. "I'm really sorry."

She waved a hand. "It's nothing. I got…anxious, I guess."

"I know. I would have been, too. I thought I'd get back before you were up. I also thought it would be faster, but the line and the snow slowed me down."

"Snow?"

Maddie indicated the window. Ryann pulled the light scrim out of the way and revealed a winter wonderland. The heavier snow from last week had a new layer—perhaps three more inches. Everything was soft and white, pretty and clean. And, as the snow had been light, the roads, at least, looked to be in good shape, which was a relief with all the wedding guests arriving over the next few days.

"It's beautiful," Ryann said.

"I think so, too. Maybe we could take a walk later this morning?"

"I'd love to."

Maddie motioned toward the little table. They sat and Maddie opened the bags, pulling out two warm, paper-wrapped sandwiches and some doughnuts.

"I wasn't sure if you were a savory or sweet breakfast person, so I got both."

"I'm not a breakfast person at all," she said. "I'm usually a coffee-and-go type."

Maddie rolled her eyes. "Of course you are."

She pushed her lightly. "But I'll make an exception since you braved the elements for us."

She ate the whole of her egg sandwich and most of two doughnuts, surprised at her hunger. But then she remembered that, despite the dinner at Henry's last night, she'd barely eaten in the last couple of days—too busy and too discombobulated by the back-to-back international flights. And, of course, last night had built up an appetite. A blush heated her cheeks, and Maddie, who had been watching her, barked a laugh.

"What?"

"I was thinking about last night. And I assume you were, too."

She grabbed the little back pillow behind her and swatted Maddie. "You perv."

Maddie laughed and grabbed the pillow, yanking it out of her hands and hitting her knees with it. "I know you are, but what am I?"

She giggled and tried to get the pillow back, the two of them soon wrestling for it, both shrieking with laughter. Eventually, as both had probably secretly wanted, Maddie had pinned Ryann to the floor, hands above her head, and was kissing her neck and along her collarbone, the laughter entirely forgotten. Soon Maddie opened Ryann's robe, and Ryann ripped off every bit of Maddie's heavy clothing with trembling hands.

Later, after they had moved to the bed to nap, Ryann woke again, this time snuggled under Maddie's arm—a much better awakening than before. Maddie was still asleep, and when Ryann moved to prop herself up, she still didn't stir. Her face was turned her way, and Ryann was tempted to run her fingertips along her strong jaw and soft lips. She made herself bunch her fingers into a fist to stop herself, wanting to examine her beautiful, peaceful face while she had the chance. Maddie's tan, which Ryann imagined was quite striking in the spring and summer, was faded but visible. She had a slight smattering of freckles across her nose and two faint but long scars—one through her left eyebrow and one on the tip of her chin in an angle that suggested that whatever had done the one had continued and done the other—slashing through both parts of her face. Did it come from something reckless when she was younger, or something daring? She once again itched to touch it. When she leaned forward a little, inhaling deeply, that hint of vanilla, though faint, was still present. That same nostalgia that had overwhelmed her before tugged at her, and this time she smiled with the new memories it evoked.

"Are you smelling my hair?" Maddie suddenly asked, one eye slitting open, cat-like.

She beamed and leaned in for a kiss. "No. I was smelling you."

"Good. Though I could use a shower."

"Mmm. Me, too," Ryann said, lying down again under her arm, cheek on Maddie's shoulder. She closed her eyes and snuggled a little closer.

Maddie laughed. "Well, I can't really shower from here, can I?"

She laughed but didn't move for a long time. Eventually, she sat straight up and checked the clock.

"Oh, shit! Maddie, I think we're missing one of our appointments. I know I had something in my calendar for today."

"Nope. We're good. I canceled everything else. I told Jai earlier this week that it was stupid to keep going to bakeries when Joan's cakes are so good. He pouted a bit but agreed."

Ryann knew she'd missed a couple of things on Tuesday and yesterday when she was in London and coming back—the photographer and some bakeries, she was pretty sure—but aside from the appointment today, she couldn't remember what else was left.

"So, wait…does that mean we're done?" she asked.

"We are. The wedding is planned."

She sighed with relief and lay back down, pulling Maddie's arm over her again. Maddie laughed and let her, eventually playing with a lock of her hair. It was soothing, and soon the two of them were dozing again. Ryann eventually fell asleep entirely.

She woke when Maddie attempted to wriggle her way out from under her.

"Sorry. I need the bathroom."

"Fine," she said. "You may go."

"Thank you, almighty ruler."

She laughed and flopped onto her back, deliciously sore and sated. She closed her eyes but realized once again that she was overwhelmingly hot. Despite the wintery day outside, this room was like midsummer. She kicked the sheets off her, still too lazy to sit up and do anything else, and when Maddie came back from the bathroom, she stopped entirely to stare at Ryann. Maddie had pulled on Ryann's robe, which looked ridiculous on her, and Ryann almost laughed at the sight, but Maddie was so serious, so stern, almost, the teasing jibe died on her lips. They were silent for a long spell, Maddie staring, and Ryann let her. She was exhilarated, excited at the hungry look in Maddie's eyes.

"Like something you see?" she finally asked, trying, but failing, to sound coy.

It took Maddie a moment to reply, and she just nodded.

Ryann stood up and walked to meet Maddie, holding out a hand.

"Then come on. Let's take a shower."

Maddie grasped her hand and followed her silently into the bathroom. They stayed in the water long enough for it to go cold, neither of them noticing, and then went back to bed, repeating this process several times throughout the day. Eventually, they gave up on the notion of leaving for that walk, both happy to stay inside in the warmth, together.

CHAPTER TWENTY-ONE

It was Friday, and the restaurant was bustling by the time Ryann got there with Stuart and his parents. Crowds of people were milling around outside as they waited for tables to open up. Stuart let his father Dick part the crowd for them, his grumpy expression and grumbling enough to get people out of their way without complaining.

Dick and Kathy Aldridge had arrived in Colorado earlier this afternoon. Stuart had asked Ryann to join him when he picked them up at the airport, too anxious to go on his own. She could understand this reaction. While Stuart's folks had been far more understanding than her own when he came out, he wasn't particularly close with them. He saw them once or twice a year for holidays and similar occasions, but that was, as far as she knew, the extent of their contact outside of a monthly phone call. He rarely mentioned them.

She had seen them on and off over the years since they were kids, at graduations and the occasional run-in visit in the city, but they weren't what anyone would call warm. The airport reunion and the drive up here had been a perfect example. Both of them had given brief handshakes and exhibited typical self-centered behavior. Dick had groaned and moaned about the flight, the weather, and the taxi ride to the airport in New York and hadn't mentioned the wedding at all. Kathy had spent most of the drive talking to her about her gardening club, never asking a single question about her or Stuart or the wedding.

Maddie was waiting just inside the restaurant by the hostess stand, and her face broke into a stunning, wide smile when she spotted Ryann. Maddie was dressed, for once, in something other than flannel, spruced up a bit for the occasion. She wore a nice, blue, light-wool suit. The jacket was open over a gray silk shirt, and Ryann was pleased to note she had three unfastened buttons at her neck, showing off her delicious collarbones and her muscular, tan throat. Her ankles were bare above smart, shiny oxfords that matched her shirt. Her hair had been styled into a smart pompadour of swirling golden locks.

Maddie scanned up and down her dress. It was a tasteful and somewhat casual blue-and-gray affair in wool—a bit stodgy for a celebration, but not as formal as most of her business wear. Maddie stepped forward and pulled her into a long, very sweet kiss.

"I missed you," Maddie said, her voice low, almost inaudible in the din of the crowd.

She swallowed, hard, against the rising heat in her chest and nodded eagerly. "Me, too."

Maddie leant closer, her lips brushing Ryann's ear. "I can't wait to get you out of this dress." She spoke so low and stood so close she tickled her, making her shiver. Her face, ever the betrayer, was hot and likely red. Maddie gave her a wolfish grin, her eyes sparkling.

"A-hem," Dick said, a little louder than necessary.

She and Maddie sprang apart, she realizing then that she'd entirely forgotten the people she came here with.

Stuart's expression was playful and wicked when he caught her eye, and she had to force herself not to stick her tongue out at him.

"Mom, Dad," Stuart said, "this is my friend Maddie. She's also Jai's maid of honor. Maddie, these are my parents, Dick and Kathy Aldridge."

Both of his parents seemed confused by this introduction, throwing her baffled looks. They'd clearly assumed that Maddie was here for her, but all of this was too complicated to explain in the press of the crowd.

"Pleasure to meet you," Maddie said, shaking their hands.

"Mmmm," Dick managed, still obviously thrown off.

"The pleasure's mine," Kathy said, her warmth more genuine. She flashed Ryann a wink and continued to hold on to Maddie's hand, tucking it under her own arm.

"Are you here to escort us to the table, dear?"

Maddie laughed and squeezed the woman's arm under hers. "Absolutely, Mrs. Aldridge. Right this way."

Dick followed, clearly dumbfounded. Stuart didn't let the opportunity pass, immediately snatching Ryann's arm under his like his mother had done.

"Oh my God!" he mouthed, not actually saying anything. "What the fuck was that?"

She lowered her voice as much as possible. "We got carried away."

"You call that getting carried away?" He spoke loud enough that his father glanced back at him. Quieter, to her, he said, "You looked ready to eat each other…" He paused, clearing his throat. "Sorry. I mean that you looked ready to jump each other in front of me, my parents, and half the City of Loveland."

She elbowed him as Dick turned his face their way again, and Stuart gave his father a wide, fake smile.

Eventually they reached the back of the restaurant, where an open doorway led into a smaller, more intimate dining room reserved for their party, clearly designed for occasions such as this. One long table was set up here in the center of the room, and Ryann realized at a glance that they were the last people to arrive. Jai, his parents, and all his sisters and their husbands were already here, still standing, drinks in hand. Everyone stopped what they were doing or stopped talking to swarm Dick and Kathy, which meant Stuart was forced to let Ryann go to make introductions. Maddie freed herself from the throng and escaped to her side, pulling her away from the bustle of Jai's boisterous family.

"There's a nice scotch with your name on it," Maddie said, steering her from behind. They paused to put Ryann's heavy coat on the back of a chair before continuing to the far side of the room that featured a bar cart with a couple of open bottles of liquor and wine. It was quieter here, though only just.

"We can serve ourselves?" Ryann asked, picking up the scotch. It was, she was pleased to see, one of her favorites.

"They have a bottle service for the night. You can order beer, too, from the bar out front."

"Nice." She poured herself more than her usual draught of scotch and took a long pull, eyes closed.

"So how was the airport?" Maddie asked when she opened her eyes.

When they'd parted late this morning, they'd planned to come here together after Maddie spent a few hours in the studio and picked up a change of clothes. But Stuart had called Ryann and asked her to go with him to get his folks. It had taken so long that she'd lost her afternoon with Maddie, and the wedding tension had returned, tenfold, with Stuart's folks here.

"Terrible," she said, pulling Maddie closer by her lapels, and Maddie obliged her by leaning down into a solid kiss. She lost herself in Maddie's lips, their torsos suddenly flush, her mind staticky and hazy with the sensation of sinking, drifting away.

"Well, well, well," a voice said, and once again she and Maddie sprang apart. Jos stood there, one hand on her hip, every ounce the high-powered lawyer in her severe black designer clothing. Julia stood behind her, a little smug too.

"Oh, shut it, Jos," Maddie said. She was still smiling slightly, and Ryann was pleased to see a little color in her cheeks, too.

"You two together are not even slightly a surprise," Jos said.

Maddie frowned at her. "Can it."

"Don't be a jerk, Jos," Julia added.

She held her hands up in defeat. "Okay, okay. I'll let it go. But this," she motioned between them, "was inevitable."

Ryann and Maddie shared a look, and Ryann smiled to show that she wasn't offended. Maddie grinned back at Jos.

"Yeah. Maybe you're right. It feels like that—meant to be."

Jos pouted. "Still—it's a little sad. I wanted to flirt with you guys at the wedding."

"Oh?" Julia asked. "And what would your husband think of that?"

Jos snorted. "I don't care."

Ryann laughed without meaning to, and Jos winked at her. Moments later, Maddie was called for, and she left after a quick parting kiss.

"You really have a catch there," Julia said, watching her watch Maddie walk away.

"I know."

"Good. Oh, say, before I forget," Julia said, "I need you to come by this weekend for the final dress fitting."

"Okay. I can do tomorrow, but can it be in the morning? I have a ton of work to do all day."

"No problem. I'm an early riser. Just text when you're up, and we'll take care of it first thing." Her eyes darted behind Ryann's shoulder. "Sorry—will you excuse me? I think I see my husband doing shots."

"No problem," she said.

She and Jos were left alone, both holding a glass of the same nice scotch. Jos was eying her, critically, and she took a nervous sip of her drink, not sure what to say.

"You better treat Maddie right, you hear me?" Jos asked, her tone aggressive and clearly serious. "She doesn't have any siblings here to give you the shovel talk, so consider it done."

"Of course."

"I mean it. If I hear anything bad, I'm coming for you, girlie."

Jos was well on her way toward being drunk, so rather than attempt to have any kind of conversation with her while she grew more antagonistic, Ryann saluted her and left her there at the little bar cart.

She hoped, briefly, that she might be able to sit somewhere and quietly finish her drink, but then Jai was calling her over, one arm thrown over Maddie's shoulders. She approached, realizing at once that Jai was more than tipsy by the slight tilt to his posture and his red cheeks and nose.

"Ah, and here she is—the lady of the hour," he said, much too loudly.

"Oh?" she asked. Stuart met her gaze and lifted his shoulders. He didn't know either.

"Oh, nothing," Jai said. "We were just talking about you."

"Good things, I hope?"

Jai's smirk was slightly wolfish, and he jerked a thumb at Maddie. "That's what she said, anyway."

Maddie stepped out from under Jai's arm, her expression darkening, and Jai seemed to realize a beat too late what he'd said. Ryann, Stuart, and Maddie glared at him, and he paled.

"Damn it. I'm sorry, Ryann, Maddie. I don't know why I said that."

"I know why you did, you lout. You're soused," Stuart said, quiet enough that only the three of them could hear him.

"I am," he said, almost sobbing. "I'm so sorry. I got really nervous about meeting your parents. I had a few too many before you guys got here."

All of them looked over at Stuart's parents. Dick and Kathy were deep in conversation with Jai's parents, Jim and Jackie. Jim was squeezing Dick's shoulder, laughing loudly, and Dick seemed distinctly uncomfortable. He was trying to smile, but it was more a grimace than anything. Kathy was staring at Jackie in wide shock, and Ryann wondered what Jackie had said or done to elicit that response. Two different sets of people could hardly be imagined.

Stuart stepped closer to Jai and gently took his arm. "What say you and I go see if the bartender can whip us up a cup of coffee, okay?" He kissed the side of his cheek. "And you don't have to be nervous. They're not that impressive."

Ryann and Maddie were once again alone. Maddie seemed to take this as another opportunity to get closer to her, and she welcomed it, stepping into her arms and sighing against her chest. Though she wasn't tall—slightly above average—it was still a rare thing that another woman was this much taller than her, and she'd certainly never dated someone this tall. She decided then, wrapped in her arms, that she liked Maddie's height a lot. Here, tucked into her like this, she relaxed again, warm and comfortable.

Hearing a funny sort of squeaking sound, she opened her eyes. Janet was standing in front of them, hands over her mouth, eyes wide.

"Ohmygoshyoutwoaretogether!" she said, speaking so quickly the words ran together.

Maddie laughed. "What was that?"

"Yes. We are," Ryann replied, grabbing Maddie's hand.

Janet laughed and clapped her hands. "I'm so happy for you two! I was hoping you'd start dating." She grimaced slightly. "I'm sorry. That makes me sound like I was fantasizing about you. No—that sounds even worse. I mean, when I saw you together last week—"

Maddie held up a hand. "We know what you mean. And thanks. We're happy about it, too."

Janet seemed relieved, her shoulders relaxing. "You also look great together, especially tonight. Did you plan these outfits? They're amazing."

"No," Ryann said. "Happy accident. This one cleans up nice."

Maddie pulled her a step closer. "And this one is always gorgeous."

Janet batted her eyelashes, making both of them laugh.

"You two are seriously dreamy." She put her hands together in a mock prayer. "So which one of you is moving?"

Ryann's stomach dropped, the blood draining from her face. One glance up at Maddie was enough to see that she'd reacted similarly, that easy smile no longer on her lips.

Janet whitened, too. "Oh, gosh, guys. I'm sorry. I shouldn't have—"

"You couldn't know," Maddie said, subdued. She met Ryann's eyes and shrugged. "We…just haven't really talked about it."

Maddie's expression was bleak, and Ryann's stomach clenched. The scotch soured in her stomach, and she was suddenly hot all over— whether from dread or anxiety or nausea or all three, it was hard to tell. She had to look away from Maddie's sad expression, suddenly afraid she might start crying.

"Oh, man, guys," Janet said. "I really stepped in it, didn't I?"

"It's okay," Maddie said, a little quickly. "Don't worry about it. But you'll have to excuse us. Ryann and I are going outside for some air before dinner."

Janet nodded, still clearly upset, but Ryann couldn't think of a thing to say to make her feel better. She let Maddie steer her out of the room, and they walked back through the crowds they'd only recently come through before, passing Jai and Stuart at the bar, neither of whom noticed them.

Outside, the air was now distinctly chilly, the earlier warmth dying with the setting sun. Maddie was wearing her blazer, but as it was lightweight, neither of them was really dressed for a February evening. Maddie, seeing her shiver, pulled her closer under one arm and then led her around the edge of the restaurant to the alley. Ryann had a flash of their earlier encounter in an alley just like this one right before their first time and warmed slightly at the memory. Maddie, however, was still all sad eyes and bleak grimaces when she stepped in front of her, taking her hands. Maddie chewed on her lip before finally speaking.

"Sorry to strong-arm you. I just had to get out of there for a minute. And I wanted to say that…I'm sorry. About that whole conversation with Janet."

"What? Why are you sorry?"

Maddie sighed. "I guess I hadn't really thought about what we would say. When people asked about us, I mean. I should have anticipated it, especially tonight, since most of these people didn't know yet. I was surprised and didn't react well."

She was still confused, and Maddie, apparently thinking she was upset, stared at the ground and squeezed her hands. "Anyway, I'm sorry."

She let her hands go and stepped closer and waited until Maddie met her eyes. "You don't have to apologize. I clammed up, too. People were bound to ask, and I couldn't think of anything to say."

Maddie was working at her lip with her teeth again. Hating to see her so anxious, she ran her fingers along the edge of Maddie's jaw. Maddie shuddered, closing her eyes, and leaned her face into Ryann's palm. When Maddie opened her eyes, heat filled them, a low ember anyway, smoldering. She pulled Ryann into a rough kiss that sent fire racing through her veins. They might have stayed there in that freezing alley groping each other and making out, but someone wolf-whistled at them, and they jumped apart. Whoever had done it was gone by the time she looked, but then, seeing Maddie's guilty expression, she couldn't help but laugh, which sent both of them into a fit of giggles.

"Hope it wasn't anyone we know," Maddie finally said.

"Same."

Maddie's smile died a little again, her eyes sad again. "So are we okay?"

"Of course we are, Maddie."

"I just don't want you to feel any pressure about any of this—"

She cut her off with another quick kiss. "I don't feel any pressure. I want this. You want this. That's enough, okay? We can talk about details later. After the wedding. Let's enjoy our time together until then."

Maddie was clearly still a bit reluctant to let it go. "And what if someone asks? I mean like Janet did?"

"We tell them we just started dating. If they push, we change the subject."

Maddie finally sagged with relief, that sadness fading from her eyes. She glanced up and down the alley each direction and smirked.

"Think we have a minute to warm up before we head inside?"

"What do you mean?"

Maddie's kiss was answer enough. The cold chill of the dying day was certainly the last thing she was worried about after that.

CHAPTER TWENTY-TWO

R yann finished her fitting with Julia very early Saturday morning. The dress for the wedding fit very well, and while she couldn't really ignore the fact that it seemed like she'd walked off the set of *Masterpiece Theater* when she was wearing it, even she had to admit that it suited her figure. Maddie drove her, but she insisted on waiting until the wedding to see her in the dress, staying in the car when she went inside.

Almost as if we're getting married, too, she thought. A stab of real remorse and pain followed this idea, and she made herself dismiss the thought before rejoining Maddie in the Bronco.

Maddie drove her back to the hotel, and she spent the rest of the morning, afternoon, and early evening on the computer, videoconferencing and working. Maddie was there with her in the hotel room through lunch, reading a book and puttering around just out of the line of sight from her colleagues. She would catch herself watching Maddie while Ted or one of her board members was talking about something important, crucial even. It was a miracle no one noticed or mentioned her absentmindedness, though she caught Ted giving her a couple of smirking grins. He probably knew exactly who she was watching. Finally, in one of the quick breaks between meetings, she had to ask Maddie to leave.

"Too distracting?" Maddie asked, voice low.

She didn't bother playing coy. "Yes. All I want is to close my laptop, throw you on that ridiculous bed, and take advantage of you all afternoon."

Maddie's eyebrows shot up, and Ryann pulled her into a hot kiss before swatting her butt. "Now get out of here before I have to explain to my coworkers why my clothes are suddenly a mess."

Maddie saluted and grabbed her coat, giving her a quick kiss before leaving. She was meeting some of the others related to the wedding at the festival, something Ryann had wanted to do herself, but it was out of the question today. Anyway, they'd see each other later that night for the bachelors' party. Still, she resented the interim more than she cared to admit. Luckily, she lost herself in the work again, and she and her board managed to cover a lot of ground together. She didn't like making anyone else work on a Saturday, but as most of the new paperwork had been delayed a couple of days, they hadn't been able to do anything sooner. It was going to be like this for a while now—solid, all-day work every day of the week, including Saturdays, and likely for at least another month or two until the deal was firmly underway and running smoothly. Already, she had to plan how to make up the missing day for the wedding on Tuesday, as well as the time she'd lose on her trip home Wednesday.

The very thought of going back, of leaving Maddie behind, was enough to distract her again, so she forced her mind elsewhere whenever she discussed dates and meetings with her colleagues. She couldn't worry about that now.

By the time the final meeting was wrapping up, she was nearly spent. The moment the last of her board members logged out, she immediately loosened the tight bun she'd had her hair in all day, scrubbing at her scalp with her fingertips, hard.

Ted laughed. He was the only person left in the virtual conference room, clearly holding back to talk to her one-on-one.

"I thought that went well," she said.

"Yes. And you didn't even see what I saw here in New York."

While she'd been virtual, and some of the others had as well, many of the older board members had been together in person in the Manhattan office all day, which meant Ted had to be there, too.

"What did you see?"

"The overwhelming jealousy and spite some of these guys have for you and this deal. Not a single one of them had the vision for it, and not one of them could do a damn thing in London. Yet there you are, half a country away, handling it like a pro. You'd be eating it up if you could see their pinched little faces. They hate you more than ever."

She laughed, but their jealousy didn't give her nearly as much pleasure as it might have even two weeks ago. The thought of gloating or holding this over them now didn't appeal in the slightest. She was proud of herself—she'd always been good at her job, and this coup proved it once again. But now that the deal was in the works, she simply wanted it done. If she could take care of this one last thing—get the whole thing running smoothly—she might actually enjoy having pulled it off. For now, her pleasure was ruined a bit with the mountain of work in front of everyone and the likely tens of meetings, short and long, between now and then. Further, she simply couldn't give a damn what any of those men thought of her. Here, removed from them in space and time, they simply didn't matter to her.

"There you go again," Ted said.

She snapped back into reality, shaking her head to clear it. "What?"

He rolled his eyes. "You've been zoning out off and on all day today. I'm pretty sure I even saw a shadow of a certain someone earlier today, but I thought she left."

Heat crept into her cheeks. "You're right. I'm supposed to meet her and everyone else in a little while—shit. Make that a little less than two hours from now." She sighed and rubbed her face. "I'm never going to make it that long."

"Oh? What's going on tonight?"

"Bachelors' party," she said, sighing again.

He laughed. "You don't sound very excited about it."

She shrugged. "After a ten-hour day, the only thing I want to do is soak in the bathtub, drink a scotch, and go to bed."

"Well, you better get your shit together if you want to have any kind of fun. Get an espresso or something."

She didn't bother explaining how difficult that would be this late at night in a small town. Still, he was right. She needed something to pep herself up a bit.

"What are you wearing tonight?" he asked. "Something fun, I hope."

"Jos, that's one of Jai's sisters, is supposed to bring something any minute. We're going to get ready together before we're picked up."

"Good. I didn't think you took any club wear with you."

She laughed. "I don't own any."

After a knock on the door, he insisted on staying logged on while she went to let Jos inside. Jos blew into the room without saying anything, holding an armful of clothing with boxes of shoes balanced on top.

"Jesus, look at this place," Jos said after she'd set the pile down on the bed. She spotted the open laptop and stepped closer. "Oh! And who is this?"

"Ted," he said. "I want to see what you're planning to dress her in."

Jos laughed, clearly delighted. "Awesome. I'm Jos, and you're in for a treat, Ted. I'm going to make her a thousand percent hotter tonight. Maddie's not going to know what hit her."

He clapped and hooted, and Ryann rolled her eyes, making both of them laugh.

"Okay, Ted," Jos said. "I brought several options. Ryann here, as you can see, is a bit smaller in the chestal area than I am—"

"Chestal?" Ryann asked.

Jos continued, her attention still on Ted. "But I think I have some things that will fit her, anyway. I can't wait to see her in something that doesn't scream business wonk."

"Me, too," he said.

"Hello? I am hearing this," she said.

Ted and Jos both gave her an identical, pitying frown.

"She's right, Ryann," he said. "Your clothes for work are hot as hell, but they're still work clothes. I don't know that I've ever seen you in anything fun before. Sexy, maybe, in an elegant, ballroomy way, but not a fun, hip way."

"Jeesh," she said, but didn't argue further.

Jos had her try on several outfits, each more ridiculous than the last. Ryann insisted on changing in the bathroom, for which both Ted and Jos gave her grief for her modesty. Still, each time she stepped out of the bathroom, there was a bigger and bigger reveal, and both of them were getting more and more excited with each progressively wilder outfit.

"That's the one," he said as she stepped out of the bathroom for the seventh time.

"Agree," Jos said.

"You've got to be kidding me."

She was wearing a skin-tight, black lace dress and open-toed black kitten heels. The dress had no sleeves, plunged daringly over her breasts, and barely hit mid-thigh. Altogether, it revealed far more skin than she was comfortable with, and that didn't even begin to describe her other issues with it. For one thing, it was very tight, making it hard to walk normally, and for another, it was almost see-through. Only the fabric over her breasts was slightly opaque, covering her actual nipples. Otherwise, her skin peeked through everywhere between the patterns of the lace.

"Incredible," Ted said.

"Amazing," Jos said.

"It's like wearing lingerie!" Ryann said.

"Exactly," Jos and Ted said together.

"No friggin' way I'm walking out the door like this." Shaking her head, she turned back toward the bathroom.

"Wait! Just wait a second, Ryann," Jos said.

She turned back to her. "What?"

Jos walked closer and took her hands, leading her to the bed. Ryann sat down, peering up at her expectantly. Jos turned the laptop to face them and pulled up one of the room's chairs, sitting down on it backward.

"You look amazing right now," Jos said. "I know you don't believe me, but you really do."

"And what's more, it's fun, carefree," Ted added. "It's really different and appealing because of that."

She sighed. "I know you both think that, and I guess I can see it a little, but this isn't me. I would be uncomfortable all night."

"So?" Ted asked.

"Maddie will love it," Jos added. "And Ted's right—comfort is not what we're going for. We're going for mad sexy, and this outfit nails it."

"Think of it like a costume," he said. "You could wear a costume for a night, right?"

"I guess." She held back a groan.

Jos, recognizing a win, clapped. "Good. Next, we do your makeup and hair. You want to be here for this, Ted?"

"You know it!"

Later, as they waited in the chilly lobby of the hotel for the party bus, Ryann still hadn't adjusted to the ridiculous getup, but on the other hand, having worn the dress for a while now, she had started, at least physically, to adapt a bit, recognizing now how far she could move her legs without pulling on the fabric too much. That was something, at least. Her makeup was much heavier on her skin than she was used to wearing, but with that element, at least, she'd been pleased with the final product—even if she looked nothing like herself. Why dressing up as someone else was supposed to be appealing to Maddie was beyond her, but both Jos and Ted were so confident that she'd like it, she'd finally simply let them do whatever they wanted with her.

She had insisted on black nylons to help with the chill, but every other thing on her body right now belonged to Jos. Even the leather jacket was one of Jos's sisters' jackets (she couldn't remember whom she'd stolen it from). Her hair had been done in a surprisingly interesting updo, clenched loosely behind her head, stray curls allowed to hang willy-nilly. Of all the weirdness, she didn't mind the hair and makeup that much. Still, she couldn't see how she'd possibly keep it up and on all night.

They heard the music and saw the lights long before their ride pulled into the parking lot. It was red and the size of a small school bus, decked out in bright-pink and red neon lights along every edge and around the rims of the wheels. There were also neon hearts and cupids, and all of the lights would pulse and then race along each side, as if chasing themselves, then pulse again. It was bright enough that she could hardly see the people inside, all of whom were apparently standing up.

Once she and Jos were outside the hotel, the music, which had already been quite loud from the lobby, nearly made her take a step back with the volume blasting out the open bus door. With a mix of amusement and dismay, Ryann realized that the lights were programmed, in a sense, to dance along with the music. Pulsing flashes of light followed the beat of the tune.

Jos, seeing her hesitate, grabbed her arm and nearly yanked her off her heels and toward the accordion bus door and up the little stairs.

"Jos!" Several people shouted when they saw her. Then, "Ryann!" when she appeared behind her. The crowd inside was surprisingly dense, and she wondered if there would be room for the two of them. She recognized Jai's other sisters, of course, and Erin and Darcy, but no one else. Then, almost as if the crowd heard her thoughts, they parted for her and Jos, scooting to the edges of the bus. The mass of bodies had been an optical illusion. Maybe twenty people were in here, total, and despite this, the bus still had quite a lot of room once they moved out of her way.

Stuart jostled several people and pulled her into his arms just as the bus started moving again. She couldn't help the little squeak that escaped her lips, startled, and he brayed with laughter, right into her ear. The music drowned out much of what he said to her, but she heard, "Hot!" and "Maddie!" and "Soon!" and she decided that meant that she looked hot and that they were picking up Maddie soon. She let him help direct her toward the middle of the swaying crowd, but she was still occasionally obliged to grab one of the looping hand straps dangling from the ceiling to stop herself from going down.

"This is insane!" she screamed over the music.

Stuart laughed, giving her a big thumbs-up. Whether that meant he heard her and agreed or was responding to her tone, she couldn't tell. They finally made it to the back of the bus, and he bent down in front of an open cooler. When he stood up, he turned around with a bright-pink plastic champagne flute. She took it, grateful, draining it at once. He laughed again, though she could barely hear him, and handed her a second. This one she sipped and tried, unsuccessfully, to dance along to the music as the bus crept along the street. It was driving at a ridiculously slow pace, but it was still hard to stand in her heels with the swaying movement. She wished then that she'd been firm in insisting on her boots back at the hotel room, but it was too late to worry about that now. Hopefully, this bus was only the transportation to wherever they were headed, not the destination.

Jai appeared on her right just as she almost fell again, his huge arm snaking around and holding her upright with very little effort. She saw his mouth open and close, talking, and imagined he said something like "I got you," but she didn't hear a word. He was much too soft-spoken to register over the blaring cacophony.

They were soon turning into another parking lot, and she took the moment the bus stopped to get her legs more firmly in place and her hand more securely looped into one of the dangling straps directly above her. As they waited, she bent down to peer out the window but could see nothing but the flashing lights outside and the silhouette of a dark building. Suddenly she heard shouts of "Maddie!" from the front, and a moment later, Maddie appeared as the crowd parted for her.

The moment Maddie saw her was something she would remember for the rest of her life. Maddie was scanning the crowd around her, clearly looking for her, and her gaze skated past, not recognizing her at first, before it returned to her, and her eyes widened comically. Then her mouth dropped open, as if in a cartoon, before snapping closed. Her eyes narrowed, darkened, and Ryann's stomach dropped as Maddie marched toward her, surefooted despite the now-moving bus. Maddie's kiss was like none before it—desperate, eager, starving, and passionate. It was overwhelming. She felt alternately hot, cold, and almost electrified as the sensation of that kiss raced through her heart and soul. When

Maddie finally pulled away, she felt almost drunk, certainly dazed, boneless in Maddie's arms.

I guess she likes the dress, she thought, grateful now for Jos and Ted's assistance.

It was too loud to talk, so they simply stared at each other, she up into Maddie's eyes, Maddie down at her the entire trip, which seemed both interminable and too short. When the bus finally stopped, in yet another parking lot, she didn't notice until the music abruptly cut off. Several people booed and shouted, but the bus driver quickly announced that they were at the first stop for the night. He also announced the name of a business she didn't recognize, but nearly everyone around her hooted with glee, clapping and cheering in drunken excitement. She had to shake her head to come back to reality, finally stepping out of Maddie's arms. Maddie took her hand and led her toward the door, the last ones out.

A low, single-story building stood in the middle of a wide, open field, and maybe forty or fifty cars and trucks were parked there in addition to the party bus. A large, circular wooden sign had been mounted to the roof with a spotlight beaming on a red drawing of a cowboy hat sitting atop a pile of rope. She couldn't quite make out the wording there and had already forgotten what the bus driver had said.

"What is this place?" she asked as they hurried to catch up with the others.

"Howdy. It's a gay cowboy bar," Maddie said.

"Really?"

"Really."

She was delighted, excited to see the inside. She could already hear country music blasting now and again as the doors at the front of the building opened and closed. While she'd seen the occasional person wearing a cowboy hat around town—men and women—she hadn't expected something this niche for a gay bar in a small town. She and Maddie joined the others, all of whom were waiting in a bunch as Jos went inside. She'd made some kind of reservation, so they needed to go in as a group.

"There are a couple of these here in the state," Maddie explained. "Charlie's, in Denver, is much bigger, of course, but we're close enough to Wyoming to get some of the Cheyenne and Laramie queers down here, so it's actually pretty popular, at least on the weekends."

"Incredible," she said. Maddie laughed at her excitement and kissed her, and only now did she realize that Maddie was, in fact, a little dressed up herself. She wore another silk shirt, this one a red-and-white swirling paisley. She'd paired it with a dark and smart brown leather jacket, and very tight, very dark jeans. And, she saw, fastening her gaze on them—brown cowboy boots that matched the coat.

Maddie, seeing her spot them, held one foot up for her and then the other. "Nice, right?"

She didn't reply in words. Instead, she grabbed the lapels of Maddie's coat and kissed her, her enthusiasm making the kiss a bit messy and hasty.

Maddie leaned back, laughing. "Gee. I guess you like them. I guess I should have brought my hat."

Again, she couldn't reply right away with words, showing, instead, what she thought of the idea with another kiss—a little gentler this time, but with some more heat in it.

Maddie's eyes darkened into that hungry shadow again, and her lips were curled into an impish grin.

"You should stay at my place tonight," Maddie suggested. "I can show you the hat."

She nodded, lips pinched tight, afraid, suddenly, that she might do something incredibly inappropriate here in the middle of all of Jai and Stuart's friends and family.

"I'd like that," she managed to say.

CHAPTER TWENTY-THREE

Ryann woke, as usual, at six the next morning, confused for several seconds by her surroundings. Unlike the hotel, Maddie's bedroom was pitch-dark, with heavy blackout curtains over the windows. Maddie's soft sleeping sighs didn't change at all as she got up to use the restroom and rinse her mouth.

She'd been in this room last night, of course, before and after, but hadn't paid much attention, too excited to get back to Maddie to examine it in any depth. The bathroom was small but nicely appointed, recently remodeled. The tiles on the walls and over the tub were a cerulean blue with a subtle but gorgeous mosaic of waves done in lighter blues and whites around the room. The linens were a light gray, which matched the paint and floor tiles. It was also very clean in here—far cleaner than her own bathroom would have been with no notice.

She vaguely remembered Maddie mentioning that she'd been restoring her historic home since she bought it, and she was pleased that this was all her work. She herself had avoided buying a place in New York for exactly this reason—she hated the thought of fixing things herself or of having people in her place to do it for her. Maddie, on the other hand, had purposefully bought a place she could make her own. She didn't remember a lot about the outside of the house when the cab had dropped them off last night, except that it was quite small. Room enough for one. Her heart sank a bit. She turned the light off before rejoining Maddie in the warmth of the bed, hoping to doze a little longer.

She hadn't meant to fall so deeply asleep and was startled awake when Maddie opened the curtains.

"Rise and shine, sleepyhead! We're meeting everyone at the festival in a little while."

She sat up, rubbing her face, and Maddie helpfully put some pillows behind her back as she stretched. "Hmm? What time is it?"

"Almost eleven."

"What?"

Maddie laughed. "You must have been exhausted. I've been up a couple hours, just puttering. I was quiet at first, but I was less and less subtle as the time passed. I played some music and dropped a pan like half an hour ago—sort of on purpose—but you didn't even move when I checked on you."

"I'm sorry. I guess I was wiped after all that last night."

Maddie leaned down and kissed her. "I bet you were."

"You perv!" She swatted at her with one of the other pillows.

Maddie laughed and jumped back. "What is it with you and pillow fights?"

She shrugged. "No one gets hurt?"

"Says you. Now get up and come to the kitchen for breakfast. You can use my robe if you want."

"No breakfast in bed?"

Maddie gave her a level stare and, not replying, left the room. After a few more seconds of warm covers, she climbed out, grabbing Maddie's enormous green flannel robe. It smelled vaguely of her—vanilla and warmth—and she inhaled deeply before tying it on. She glanced around the tidy, tiny room, wondering if there were any slippers she could use. Maddie's cowboy hat had been set on top of her dresser, and a sliver of delight ran through her at the sight. Last night, briefly, Maddie had worn that hat and nothing else.

She walked out of the bedroom and into a long but narrow midcentury-style living room with a loveseat, a recliner, a very small TV, a fireplace, and walls packed with bookshelves. An orange cat lay curled up on the recliner. It lifted its head, blinked at her a few times, and then lay down again, as if dismissing her, apparently to sleep some more. Small models of sculptures sat on the side tables and between some of the books—Maddie's working models, she realized.

She paused, taking in the room, a funny, squeezing pressure in her chest. She could picture herself here quite easily in some distant future, the morning sunlight filtering in just as it was doing now, a book in one hand, coffee in the other, that little cat in her lap, Maddie coming in with a refill so they could plan their Sunday afternoon together. The fantasy was so vivid, she could almost feel the texture of warm fur on her bare legs, the pages of the book in her hand.

"Do you want to eat out there?" Maddie called. "I usually do."

"Sure!"

She followed Maddie's voice, coming from the right, into a gorgeous, petite kitchen. This room clearly had its original, early twentieth-century layout, but the cabinets, countertops, and appliances had been replaced. The wood floor was a little worn, but everything else was pristine. To her right was a small countertop with two stools pushed under it—a kind of mini eating space. A set of copper pans hung near the oven.

Maddie had her back to her, standing in front of the stove, her broad shoulders flexing under a tight red T-shirt as she flipped pancakes. Stuart had given everyone specific shirts to wear today, and when Maddie turned, Ryann read "Maid of Honor" in bold text across the chest.

"Like what you see?" Maddie asked.

She nodded, unable to speak. Maddie grinned wider, turned to shut off the burner, and then walked across the room to kiss her gently several times before hugging her into the warmth of her chest.

"How do you like my place?" Maddie asked, moving back to the food.

"It's lovely."

"Not too small?"

"Not at all. I like smaller places. And it's really gorgeous. You've clearly done a lot of work on it."

"It's getting there. I'm kind of learning how to renovate as I go. I've worked on some of my friends' projects, and a little with my dad, but nothing like this. I kind of bit off more than I could chew, but it's kind of fun, too. I still have to do the floors, which I should have done first, but that's okay."

Maddie walked back to the stove and started plating her food. Ryann crossed the room and grabbed her own plate. There were scrambled eggs and pancakes, a basket of raspberries, slices of kiwi, coffee, and fresh orange juice. Her plate was heaping by the time she joined Maddie in the living room, her stomach rumbling loud enough to hear. The cat watched them eat briefly before once again settling down to sleep. Maddie, seeing her watching it, laughed.

"That's Jinx," she said.

"Cute name."

"Thanks. He's an old man now—just turned sixteen. He's basically there or in his little bed by the oven all day."

She could deal with a cat like that more easily than the more forward and aggressive ones she'd met at Jai's and his parents' place. She opened her mouth to say just that but realized in time what that might imply. She smiled instead and turned back to her breakfast.

The food was delicious, and both simply sat there when they were finished, smiling at each other across the loveseat. Her heart began tripping around in her chest again, that rising, funny euphoria back once again. Maddie, as if sensing her feelings, put her mug down and scooted closer, kissing her deeply before standing up. She held out a hand and helped her up.

"We really better get going. You still need to change, and we're supposed to meet the others in less than an hour."

She pouted. "Do we have to?"

Maddie laughed and bussed her lips. "Stop that. You're going to make me take you back to the bedroom, and then we'll never get out of here."

That wouldn't be a bad thing, but she sighed and went to gather her clothes. She'd gone to sleep with them scattered all over the bedroom floor, but at some point, Maddie had folded them neatly for her and put them on top of her dresser next to her cowboy hat. As she struggled into Jos's ridiculous dress again, she realized she would be doing a walk of shame this morning in front of Ethel. In this dress, it was obvious that she hadn't come back last night. The idea made her giggle several times on the way to the hotel, and sure enough, Ethel turned pink when she and Maddie entered the lobby, excusing herself so quickly she almost ran away from them.

Thirty minutes later, Ryann was freshly showered. She wore her own red "Maid of Honor" T-shirt, Jos's leather jacket, a warm black hat and scarf, black leggings, and knee-high boots. She and Maddie walked down the block from the hotel to the festival, the sun so bright and gorgeous, she was squinting even behind her sunglasses.

The entire downtown, it seemed, had been fenced off, and they had to wait in line to be carded for a wristband as they entered. It was warmer today, but still chilly, and the crowds inside the festival grounds were surprisingly dense for a Sunday afternoon. Already, nearly everyone in here seemed already on their first beer of the day. She and Maddie began searching for the others right away. She hadn't thought this would be difficult, but it took them nearly half an hour and several phone calls to link up with Jai and Stuart next to one of the ice-cream carts. Both were wearing red "Groom to Be" T-shirts under their open white flannel shirts, and both seemed a little subdued after the wild shenanigans last night at the bachelors' party. Stuart was pale and his eyes were a little red around the corners, and Jai was a bit green and pinched. Both were holding dark beers and sharing a corndog.

"Hey, ladies!" Stuart crowed, waving wildly when he spotted them.

"You just missed my sisters," Jai said, pointing vaguely into the crowd, "but I'm sure we'll bump into them again. My parents, Stuart's parents, some of my cousins, and some of our other friends are supposedly here, too, but we keep missing each other."

"I'm amazed how crowded it is," Ryann said.

"It's really the only thing happening this time of year like anywhere," Stuart explained. "We get people from all over for it. We met a gay couple from Boston a few minutes ago."

"Stuart invited them to the wedding," Jai said, rolling his eyes. Everyone laughed.

"They were nice," he said.

"And I thought my parents were bad," Jai said, low but loud enough for all of them to hear.

Stuart briefly glared at him, and then his eyes went wide. "Oh! Maddie! We already saw it, and yours is definitely the best," Stuart said. "You're going to win for sure."

"Totally," Jai said.

"Win what?" Ryann asked.

"First prize. For her ice sculpture," Stuart said.

"Really?"

Maddie nodded, a little sheepish.

Stuart rolled his eyes. "Hers is really the best one. There's a competition. Sometimes it lasts the whole festival, but on a warm year like this, they put them out only for a single afternoon, and that's today. You can vote and everything."

"When did you have time to do it?" she asked.

"Last week. I had to carve it in a walk-in freezer." Maddie shuddered.

"You've done one before?"

Maddie hesitated, appearing embarrassed. "No. This was the first one."

"Oh, jeez," Stuart said, rolling his eyes again. "It's only the most beautiful thing in the world, so of course it's your first one ever. You're so talented, it makes me sick. Anyway—you two should go over now before it melts too much. Oh! And make sure you vote for Erin's beer, too. The beer tent is that way." He pointed.

Maddie led the way, weaving expertly among the various groups of people. Everyone was laughing and talking very loud, and no one gave their linked hands a second glance. She and Maddie bumped into Julia and Jos a few minutes later. Jos recognized her leather jacket and tried to take it from Ryann's shoulders.

"That's mine!"

"Hey, hey," Maddie said, playfully pushing her away. "Don't undress my girlfriend."

"But she's so hot in it. Even wearing that stupid T-shirt. She's going to ruin it for me forever."

Both Julia and Jos were wearing red T-shirts with "Bridesmaid" on the chest under their jackets.

"You'll get it back later," Ryann said. "And I won't ruin it. I promise. You'll be just as hot the next time *you* wear it."

"Fine, fine," Jos said. "Oh, and Maddie—that ice sculpture is really something."

"Holy crap," Julia said. "It's incredible."

Maddie tried to look like she agreed, but Ryann could tell she was more uncertain than she let on, a slight nervousness pinching her lips.

A loud beep came from Jos's pocket, and she checked her phone. "Shit! My mom is looking for us, and she's pissed because she lost Dad. Now we have to find both of them." She rolled her eyes. "Anyway— see you guys later."

Maddie took her hand again, leading her toward a large canvas tent. They had to show their over-21 wristbands to enter, and it was even more crowded inside than out.

"Damn," Maddie said, standing on her tiptoes and peering toward the front of the lines. "I don't know how we'll ever get a drink in here."

"I might be able to help you with that," someone said behind them. She and Maddie turned to see Erin's wife Darcy standing behind them. Ryann realized now that she hadn't actually stood near the woman before and was only now aware of how tall she was. She had several inches on Maddie, even. Her platinum hair brushed the shoulders of her stylish gray peacoat, and her cool, icy-blue eyes were twinkling. She had high, aristocratic cheekbones and lush lips, and that bright-white smile was like something out of a toothpaste commercial. She was breathtaking—a Nordic supermodel trolling a beer tent.

"Would you? That'd be great," Maddie said, seeming unfazed.

"Follow me," Darcy said.

She led them around the edge of the tent, behind every line, to a small alcove in the corner behind a rack stacked with beer kegs. The alcove was roped off with a sign that said "Employees Only." Darcy unclipped the rope and led them to a little high-top table. They were completely hidden from the crowds.

"Wait here. I'll be right back," Darcy said.

Once out of sight, Ryann waved a hand in front of her face dramatically. "Jesus."

"What?"

Ryann stared at Maddie. "Are you kidding me? That woman is ridiculously gorgeous. I mean, I knew she was before, but damn. Something about seeing her dressed down makes it more obvious."

Maddie frowned in obvious confusion, her eyes trained in the direction Darcy had gone. She shrugged. "I mean, yeah, I guess."

"Are you kidding me right now?"

Maddie pulled her into a long kiss. "I only have eyes for you, babe."

She was still laughing when Erin and Darcy returned. Erin carried a flight board, and Darcy had two plastic pint cups full to the brim. Erin's mousy short curls were ruffled and messy, as if she'd been running her hands through her hair all day, which, based on this crowd, was likely. She was struck once again by the fact that Erin and Darcy made a strikingly contrasting pair—Erin smaller altogether, almost elfin next to the tall blonde.

"These are the lineup for the competition," Erin explained, indicating the flight of tasters. "And these are the voting cards." She set down a golf pencil and two small pieces of cardstock. Each beer in the flight was numbered one through six, and the cardstock had boxes next to the same numbers. "Choose your favorite, and then drop this off on your way out in the box by the entryway."

"It's a blind test this year?" Maddie sounded surprised.

Erin sighed. "Yes, and no one's happy about it. Still, I guess it's fair. No one can say I bribed anyone when we win."

Darcy set the two pints down on the table near the flight. "Two pints of Cupid's Kiss. For after. It's only sort of cheating." She winked.

"Oh, and Maddie, your ice sculpture is amazing," Erin said. "We voted just before we came here."

Darcy nodded. "It's lovely."

She watched Maddie receive this praise, noted her awkwardness at accepting it, and squeezed her hand. Oh, artists! she thought.

"Sorry we can't stay," Erin said. "I'd love to catch up with you both, but I'm swamped, and Darcy's going to help the rest of the afternoon. But we'll see you at the wedding Tuesday."

"See you there," Maddie said.

There were two light beers and four dark in the flight, and she and Maddie decided that they would judge only the dark beers before voting. Even if, by chance, the lighter beers were better, both of them knew Erin's was one of the darker ones. She was tempted to taste her pint so she could pick the right one, but she and Maddie decided to play it fair. They both ended up choosing number five, hoping it was Erin's.

They were happy to get outside despite their semi-private hiding spot and waited until they were there, the voting cards submitted, to taste their pints.

"Oh, that's definitely number five," she said.

"For sure. I'm so glad you like it."

She was confused. "Why?"

Maddie's cheeks colored a little, and she laughed, awkwardly. "No reason. I mean, I guess I'm glad you like my friend's beer."

Maddie refused to meet her eyes, but she didn't say anything, letting Maddie lead her through the crowds again without further comment. Still, she guessed it was, perhaps, in line with everything else they hadn't talked about. Sometime soon they would have to talk, really talk, about all of this between them. But now wasn't the time.

She saw the line of ice sculptures appear in front of them, her heart leaping crazily with excitement. She'd seen these things off and on over the years at various functions—usually as a centerpiece at a party—but all the sculptures out here were much, much larger than those—some far taller than her. Maddie stopped walking, looking suddenly embarrassed again, and Ryann laughed, dragging her forward. The sculptures were set up in a long line about five feet apart, behind low ropes. She took one of the voting cards, but Maddie refused, and she became even quieter as they walked down the line of ice sculptures, pausing at each one. On the whole, none of them moved her. A few were cute, some were actually quite bad, and others had little depth or detail. There were several hearts, several vague cupids, some dog-type creatures, and a swan, but nothing really stood out.

She had seen the crowd standing in front of the sculpture near the end of the row long before they got there, and even before she saw it, she understood that it must be Maddie's. Everyone they'd run into today had mentioned it, and she could tell from their expressions and admiration that they hadn't been flattering her. Maddie stopped and waved her forward, seeming to want to stand back away from the crowd, but she was just being bashful. Ryann didn't argue, however, elbowing through everyone in the best New York fashion to get to the front and see this thing finally.

At first, she couldn't accept what she was seeing. Venus de Milo stood before her. Ryann had seen the original at the Louvre, and if she had to guess, she imagined this was precisely the same size as the marble version—a little smaller than you expect having seen so many pictures of it. Even beyond that, however, the similarity was more than striking. It was almost impossible to believe that what she was seeing wasn't stone of some kind. The ice was creamy white with light-blue veins, like actual marble, not the clear ice of many of the other sculptures here. It was, in a word, an incredible piece of artwork, made all the more breathtaking by its medium.

She craned her neck around, trying to spot Maddie, and she saw her, hunched up on herself, arms crossed tightly, biting her lip, and once again, she fought her way back through the crowd to her. Maddie still seemed nervous as she approached, and she had to force down a gale of wild laughter.

"It's incredible!" she said.

"Yeah?" Maddie said, smiling a little.

"Maddie, are you kidding me right now? It looks like an actual Greek statue, for God's sake."

"It's only a re-creation. It's Valentine's, so I thought the goddess of love made sense. No one said it had to be ice water, so I used—"

She didn't let her continue, leaping forward and kissing her, trying to put every ounce of her feelings into it. Maddie reacted with surprise at first, freezing, before she returned the kiss fully. For perhaps the first time in her adult life, Ryann didn't care who saw the two of them like this. She let the kiss go on and on, the noise of the crowd dying away as she lost herself in Maddie's lips. Finally, they drew apart for air, their arms still linked around each other.

"It's one of the most incredible things I've ever seen," she said, holding her gaze. "It's beautiful."

Maddie finally smiled, a slight redness warming in her cheeks. "I'm glad you like it."

"Now take me home," she said.

"What? Now?"

"Now."

One of Maddie's eyebrows shot up, but she didn't argue.

CHAPTER TWENTY-FOUR

Ryann's feet were soaking in a warm bath of bubbling Epsom-salt water. Her chair was reclined almost entirely, and she was wearing nothing but a thick terry-cloth robe, an avocado face mask, and cucumber slices on her eyes. Soft instrumental music was coming from a nearby speaker, and the attendants and massage therapists quietly bustled about the room, while she, Stuart, two of Jai's sisters, and Stuart's mom were pampered before their final wedding styling at the salon. Jai's other sisters and his mom were at a different spa, both men having decided to keep up the tradition of not seeing each other the day of until the wedding. Maddie had laughed when Ryann had asked her if she was going to be there with him today, but Ryann really thought she'd missed out. This was great.

She hadn't realized she needed this, but she did. After Maddie dropped her off at the hotel early yesterday morning, she'd had to work all day—on the phone, on videoconferences, on her computer—until late last night. Maddie had driven over from campus for a quick lunch between classes, but otherwise they hadn't really seen each other since she spent the night at her place Sunday. She had never longed for anyone like this, and certainly not after just a day apart. They still hadn't talked about the fact that she was leaving tomorrow, but she kept telling herself they had time enough for that tonight after the reception.

This morning she and Stuart had argued, part of which included whether she should get her hair blown out for today. But now, lying here almost comatose, she didn't care one bit. Maybe having her hair wild, like he wanted, wasn't such a bad thing. The straightening process was hardly fun, and after her massage and the mimosas, she didn't want to put herself through anything unpleasant. In fact, if she could keep feeling like this the rest of the day, it might be the most pleasurable wedding experience she'd ever had.

She heard someone clear their throat near her, and then her chair began to gently rise on its silent hydraulics. She pulled the cucumbers off her eyes and blinked, somewhat dazed and blind despite the soft, candle-like lighting. Jos was on her left, Stuart on her right, his mother in the chair to his right. All three were in similar states of confused wakefulness. Janet, also here with them, was in another room getting a massage.

Ryann leaned over to squeeze Stuart's hand. "How you doing?"

He smiled. "Better than this morning." When he'd shown up at her hotel, he'd been a wreck, pale and rumpled, having had a poor night's sleep. That, more than anything, had likely caused his snappishness with her earlier.

He grimaced. "I'm sorry I said you were being stupid about your hair."

She squeezed his hand again. "It's okay. I knew it was wedding jitters. I shouldn't have gotten upset, and I shouldn't have called you a groom-zilla."

"I was being one. I shouldn't have pushed you. Your body, your choice."

She waved at him, dismissing the situation. "No, no, really. It's not a big ask, and you're right. Having it straightened will ruin the effect of the dress. And anyway, I'm starting to like it curly like this."

"It's gorgeous," Jos piped in, clearly eavesdropping. "You should leave it curly forever."

She had gotten used to Jos stating her opinion any time she felt like it, brashly and without invitation. She'd worked with women like her and gone to college with more, and this kind of behavior didn't faze her. Despite being the eldest sister, Jos had ended up in Stuart's side of the party, entirely by chance. The men hadn't been able to decide how to split the sisters up, so they'd essentially drawn lots. Joan and Julia were with Jai, but they'd see the other sisters when they all went to get their dresses after the salon.

"How's your mom doing?" Jos asked, peering that direction. Stuart and Ryann glanced over, and Ryann was amused to see that Kathy appeared to be relaxed and dazed, blinking owlishly. Judging by her goofy expression, she was also a little drunk. She was already holding another mimosa.

"Having a good time, Mom?" Stuart asked. She raised her glass and giggled, and the three of them laughed. "That's good. I'm glad. You're really going to like your hairdresser, too."

"Oh?" Kathy seemed a little intimidated, her face now twisted with anxiety. Her hair, while clearly expertly cut, was still styled in a classic over-fifty-mother way, in this case a Hillary Clinton bob.

"That's right! What do you think of having pink hair, Mom?"

She paled, and the three of them laughed again before she realized the joke and smiled. "Oh, Stuart. Please don't tease me. You know I'm not good at it."

"I'll try not to."

Janet came out then, looking boneless and willowy, her long hair down for the first time in Ryann's memory. It reached past her waist. She rolled her head around on her shoulders and stretched, languid and catlike. She'd had to schedule a substitute teacher for the day, but from what she'd said about it this morning, she seemed absolutely thrilled. Kids on holidays sounded like lunatics. A morning at the spa had loosened her up.

"Oh, gosh, that was something," she said, collapsing on a little divan in the middle of the room.

"Would anyone care for another drink?" one of the employees asked.

"Love one, but better not. Long day ahead of us," Stuart said.

Ryann and the others agreed, and after chatting and lounging for another ten minutes, they all went to the changing rooms, washed their faces, dressed, and left for the salon. It was a short walk, but the day was so brisk and the wind so biting, all five of them were doing a funny near-jog the last block to get out of the cold. Ryann dreaded the idea that she'd be standing outside in this chill in a sleeveless dress later this afternoon.

The salon was surprisingly busy for a Tuesday morning, but, given the way this town hyped Valentine's Day, she realized she shouldn't be surprised. They were immediately handed mugs of cocoa and directed to wait on a pair of couches in a cozy nook by a gas fireplace. It had started flurrying outside, and everything was pretty, charming. They might have been at a ski lodge.

She and Jos were sharing a stylist, as were Kathy and Janet, while Stuart had his own. The three stylists appeared, calling back the first three.

"Ooh, stay back with me," Janet said, grabbing Ryann's hand. "I wanted to talk to you at least once today before the hoopla starts."

"Okay."

Janet scooted closer on the seat next to hers, covering her hands with her own. "I'm so glad we've gotten to know each other."

"Me, too."

"No—really. I mean it. Stuart's been like this enigma since we met him. He seemed so alone in the world, so independent. Our family is so big, and so…in-your-face, I guess, and we all have a million cousins and friends around all the time. You're never alone in our family, even when you want to be. And we love Stuart so much. It was hard to think of him by himself like that all the time."

Her face heated with shame, and she stared down at their hands. "Yes. I suppose he was pretty alone."

"Oh, gosh, Ryann—it's not like that was your fault. You live so far away, and he's not that close to his folks, either. No. I just meant that it's so nice to meet some of his people, you know? And you're so great, and you get along with everyone so well, even Jos, and she doesn't like anyone. It's nice to meet you and spend time with you is all."

"Thanks. I feel the same about all of you, too. And I'm so glad he has you. He was so lonely when he first moved out here. I thought for sure—" Her mouth snapped closed over what she'd almost said.

Janet, however, smiled. "You thought for sure he'd move back to New York. Right?"

She nodded.

Janet laughed. "That's what we all thought. That's what Stuart kept saying when he and my brother were first dating. You know they broke up for a while, right?"

"I'd heard, yes."

"It was because of that. Those first few months they were together, Stuart kept saying how much he missed New York and how much he was looking forward to moving home when his residency was over. It was New York this and New York that every time you saw him. Jai sort of went along with it for a while, but then, when they started getting serious last summer, spending like every second together, Jai started calling him on it. They fought about it a lot and broke up a couple of days before he left for a trip. With you, I think."

"Yes. We met up in California."

She thought back to that trip, remembering it differently now in hindsight. At the time, he'd seemed like his old self. Bitter, cynical. He drank a lot that weekend, but they always had when they were together. He'd been interested, as always, in happenings and gossip in New York, and, except for that one conversation when he'd mentioned Jai, he hadn't spoken a bit about his life in Colorado the whole weekend.

"So what changed, do you think?" Ryann asked.

"Isn't it obvious? Stuart stopped being stupid—that's what."

She laughed. "I guess that's true. Took him a little while, though, right?"

"Yes. He didn't come crawling back, quite literally, until October. Me and Julia were there when it happened, actually, over at Verboten—the brewery? Anyway. He and Jai arranged to see each other—well, Stuart called him like a thousand times that week before Jai caved. Me and Julia were there for like moral support, kind of hiding and waiting in a back booth, just in case. Stuart came inside, got down on his knees in front of Jai, and burst into tears. It was a real scene. By the end, people in there were clapping and crying, like us, when they kissed and made up."

She let her gaze wander over to Stuart, who was laughing with his stylist, a cute little punky goth woman. She could not, even at the very stretches of her imagination, imagine the old Stuart, the Stuart she'd grown up with, the Stuart in California last summer, the cynical, bitter Stuart she thought she knew *ever* doing something like Janet had described. This Stuart, on the other hand, this lovely, well-adjusted man who was both her oldest and newest friend, was exactly the kind of person to cause that kind of scene. At first, she'd been a little shaken by all his changes—no, not just shaken, also saddened. He seemed to have grown up, somehow, all on his own, and seemingly all at once. It had happened without her, and that made her sad for both of them, almost as if she'd been holding him back. But she realized now that was never true. He'd simply done it on his own, and love had helped him get here. She loved this new version of her friend as much as the old one. No—she loved him even more.

"What about you?" Janet asked, startling her.

"What about me?"

"Are you going to make the same mistake?"

"What do you mean?"

Janet rolled her eyes. "Oh, come on. Don't play dumb. I mean with Maddie. Are you going to make the same mistake with her?"

She frowned. "I wouldn't put it that way, but I have to go back. My life, my career, everything is in New York. I can't just give that up."

"Not everything. Stuart and Maddie are here. They matter, too. Your job means that much to you?"

She sighed. "It's not only my own job. A lot of people depend on me for their livelihoods. I would be putting more than my career in jeopardy."

Janet squinted at her, pouting. "Well, that sucks."

She couldn't help but laugh. "Yeah. It does."

"So you'll leave her behind? Leave us behind?"

Her gaze traveled over to Stuart again, who was laughing at something Jos had said. She'd missed him terribly and knew she would again. Then she looked outside, at the brightly decorated downtown street now dappled with fresh snow—the town she liked more than she would ever have believed. She already had a favorite coffee shop, brewery, and restaurant here—more than she could say of New York, actually, where it seemed like the moment she started liking something, it closed.

She met Janet's eyes, realizing, then, that she liked this woman a lot. She didn't have many close female friends, but Janet already seemed like one. This conversation, for example, was like something between friends, sisters even, not someone she'd just met. In fact, though she liked all Jai's sisters, the two here today were her favorites. She could easily picture herself hanging out with them without their brother or Stuart. They'd met only a few times, but she wanted to continue seeing them regularly.

Then, of course, there was Maddie. Any time she allowed herself to think about leaving tomorrow—tomorrow!—her brain immediately revolted at the implications. She'd fallen for her, entirely. They made sense together. Anytime she was around Maddie, it was as if she'd come home. And after today, she'd be alone again.

When she answered, her voice was nearly a whisper. "I have to."

Janet looked troubled, but she didn't push her further. Ryann was grateful. Already, the effects of the mimosas and the massage were fading, her shoulders stiff with anxiety and dread. Janet kept talking, now about herself and her students, and she followed most of her comments, responding appropriately as needed, but by the time she was getting up to have her hair and makeup done, she still felt like crying.

"Oh my good God," her stylist Zane said as she sat down.

"What?" she said, blinking away a few tears.

"You have got to be fucking *kidding me*!" he said, almost squealing.

"Tone down the flames a bit there, Zane," Stuart said. His hair and beard had been trimmed and styled already, but he was still sitting at the station next to her finishing a glass of wine.

"Oh, you!" Zane said, waving a brush at him. "I'm just shocked. You didn't tell me your friend's hair is like the most gorgeous thing in the whole world. Or that I'd be doing makeup on a movie star."

"Right?" Janet said on her right. "Can you frickin believe her?"

Ryann watched her face redden in the mirror, and everyone laughed.

"You must have the entire city of New York at your fingertips, honey," Zane said.

"And Loveland," Stuart added, winking at her.

"Your boyfriend going to be at this shindig today?" Zane asked her.

"My girlfriend is, yes."

All three of them let out a long, wavering "Oooooh!"

"She hasn't called her a girlfriend before," Stuart explained.

Zane grinned. "Ah, I see. A new lady friend, huh? You're so beautiful, this is going to be really easy, Ryann, but I'm still going to make you so hot, she won't know what hit her."

She smiled at him and sat up straighter, her earlier upset already waning. If what he said was accurate, this was going to be fun.

CHAPTER TWENTY-FIVE

It was bitterly cold by the time they were waiting for the wedding ceremony to begin. It was so crowded near the officiant, it was difficult for the entire wedding party to stand together. Fifty couples were getting married today, which meant everyone's guests were scattered and mixed together in the tiered seating above and behind them. The man performing the ceremony was a local judge. He was dressed somewhat somberly in his robe, but he wore a bright-red tie with white hearts. He'd invited the marrying couples to join him as close as possible to the podium in front of the frozen lagoon. It took all the couples some time to complete the paperwork before he began, so by the time he started the ceremony officially, Ryann could hardly feel her frigid toes or fingers.

Jai and Stuart had crowns of red, pink, and white flowers and stark-red-rose boutonnieres that contrasted with their suits. They wore white jackets and red breeches, with silver waistcoats like Maddie's. Everyone in the party looked incredible—better than *Masterpiece Theater*, after all.

As the officiant talked, Jai and Stuart clasped hands, hunched up so close they could have kissed. Ryann was holding their bouquets, and the rest of their wedding party was crammed on either side of them to allow the photographer to see the two men between the crowds of couples and wedding parties around them. Jos and Janet were behind her on either side, pressed against her back, one hand on each of her arms. Both began tearing up even before the ceremony started, their sniffles catching her ear.

Maddie was just behind Jai with Julia and Joan, her eyes sparkling, too. Ryann had hardly been able to tear her eyes away from her since the moment she'd arrived. She had already seen her in her regency outfit, but out here, under the bright Colorado sky, the red of her suit was a deep, almost burgundy red, a match to her dress. The silver of her breeches and waistcoat shone in this light, and she occasionally caught a flashing gleam off her highly shined buckle shoes. Her loose, wavy curls were styled back and away from her face, which made the blue of her eyes stand out that much more. Maddie was staring at her, too, both of them missing most of the ceremony. Ryann would wrench her eyes away, listen to Stuart and Jai repeat the judge's words, only to find her gaze drifting back, always finding Maddie's eyes on her.

She only realized that she was called on for her one task today when Jos pinched her arm. She had to shake herself into awareness, and, seeing Maddie reaching into a little watch pocket under her suit jacket, she handed Jos the bouquets briefly before digging around in her own hidden pocket. She found the ring for Jai and handed it to Stuart. Tears were coursing down his cheeks as the ring exchange began. Once he had it on his finger, Jai held up the pretty platinum band to admire it, his eyes now also swimming with tears. Stuart had managed to keep the design a secret, after all.

The ring ceremony complete, the judge intoned the finale in a booming, sonorous voice. "I now pronounce you married at last! You may kiss your new spouse."

A roar of clapping and screaming came from the tiered seating, some three or four hundred people here to watch the group wedding— strangers and friends and family. The loudest batch of cheers, of course, came from Jai's family, and when she located them, she saw and heard Jim and Jackie screaming and cheering the loudest, along with fifty or sixty people that resembled Jai and his family in some way. Stuart's parents, Kathy and Dick, were clearly pleased, too, but in their quieter way, they were almost lost in the group of jumping and hollering locals.

Jai and Stuart were still kissing when she finally looked back at them, ready to offer her congratulations, and Maddie and Jos were laughing at something she'd missed. The men pulled apart with an audible pop, and she and the others laughed. Everyone in the party took turns hugging them, she staying a little longer in Stuart's arms than anyone else.

"I love you. Congratulations," she whispered.

He pulled back a little, his face still wet with tears. "I love you, too. Thank you for being here. It means so much to me."

"Okay, okay, you're married now," Jos said, clapping his shoulder. "Can we *please* go to the limo now? I'm freezing!"

Jai and Stuart took their bouquets back from her and followed the rest of the crowd up the stairs to the street, she and the others behind them. People were still shouting their congratulations as they passed, and Jai and Stuart seemed to revel in the experience, stopping to wave far too many times. She could see Jos, who was next to her on the stairs, starting to lose patience and grabbed her arm before she could push her brother from behind.

"It's just a few more minutes, Jos. Relax."

Jos fumed for a moment longer and then took a deep breath. Before long, they were at the top of the stairs at street level. The wedding party had their own limo, the parents were sharing a luxury sedan, and while some people would drive themselves, Jai and Stuart had arranged for two shuttle buses to take most of their guests out to the reception and back to various hotels all over town. As the maid of honor, she should stay out here in this frigid chill and help direct the guests to the right buses, but she could hardly focus on any of that right now, as she, like Jos, was far too cold to do anything but shuffle as fast as she could to the limo on her frozen legs and feet. She had to hope the parents would take charge of the logistics before leaving.

The limo was white and new, with heart and cupid decals splashed everywhere across the side panels and windows. She waited by the door a moment until Maddie caught up to her, the two of them kissing briefly before climbing inside at last. Maddie's hands were warm, and she covered hers with them, rubbing them lightly. Jai and Stuart finally climbed in, and everyone in the cabin cheered and clapped again, especially when the door was shut behind them. More cheering erupted as Jai and Stuart popped two bottles of champagne, and everyone passed the glasses down the line until they were all holding one.

"Uh," Jai said, clearing his throat. He held up his glass. "We're doing our vows after dinner, but I wanted to say thank you to all of you wonderful ladies for being part of this today."

Stuart held his glass a little higher, too. "It was so nice to have all of you together for this, and I wanted to add a special thank you to our maids of honor, who did most of the footwork with very little time. Thank you, Ryann and Maddie!"

After more cheering, and everyone took a long sip. She could hardly stomach more of the cold drink right now, and Maddie, seeing her expression, took her glass from her, setting it in a little cup holder to her right. Maddie put an arm around her shoulders and pulled her closer, and eventually, finally, she began to warm up. Everyone was chatting around them, but she and Maddie stayed like that, she quiet and happy simply to be here with her. A little tremor of misgiving continued to try to intrude. Tomorrow, she thought, and then pushed it away from her mind. She needed to enjoy this moment.

"You look incredible," Maddie said, low enough that only she could hear.

"Thanks. So do you."

Maddie lowered her voice, bending closer to her ear. "I hope you've saved a dance for me, Ms. Sands."

Her voice tickled her ear a little, and a flush of excitement raced over her. She tried to mimic her flirtatious tone. "My dance card is yours for the evening, Ms. Walker."

Maddie stilled for a moment, then shook her head. "No—I'm afraid not. I've already promised myself to some of the other women here. And to both the grooms, of course."

She pretended to pout. "Well, then, I'll have to find someone to dance with myself, then, too. I want to drive you crazy with jealousy."

Maddie kissed her then, their pretending over, and she let herself sink into the sensation. Like their kiss at the festival, and many kisses before that, the world seemed to fade away. They might have been the only people in here.

When she opened her eyes and they drew apart, she saw Stuart watching them. He appeared troubled, almost upset, but then he gave her a weak smile. She glanced up at Maddie, who'd also seen this exchange, and saw a similar worry pinch her lips and eyes. That earlier misgiving tried to steal into her heart, but Maddie's expression cleared, and she gave her another quick kiss.

Maddie had done all the work regarding decorations for the reception, and no one had seen any of it. She'd explained last weekend that because no other events had been scheduled recently, she'd been allowed to spend a great deal of time setting up. Already, as the limo pulled into the parking lot, Ryann could see that the outside of the barn had been festooned in thousands of red and white twinkle lights. The sun was still up, but the lights were visible, especially on this side of the barn. Above the door, the names Jai and Stuart had been spelled out inside a heart of lights that flashed on and off in strobing rainbow colors. Jai and Stuart positively squealed at the sight of it, Stuart leaning forward to slap Maddie's knee.

"I knew we could count on you to knock our socks off," he said.

"Wait 'til you see it inside," Maddie said.

A red carpet had been rolled out in front of the door, and the limo dropped them off there. After the men got out, Maddie climbed out and helped Ryann upright, her hand still much warmer than Ryann's. They continued to hold hands all the way inside.

The barn had been transformed. It had already been a lovely space, wide and open, but now, with Maddie's attention, it had become a magical, Valentine's Day fairyland. White and pink twinkle lights were wrapped around every single exposed wooden beam, up above and on the pillars throughout the barn. The tables were in contrasting colors, red and white, with beautiful white-and-pink flower arrangements on the red tables, and red and pink on the white. A smaller table was set up on a small platform opposite the others across the dance floor, where Jai and Stuart would sit, decorated with what appeared to be a linked chain of red, pink, and white roses. Heart-shaped balloons had been tied in enormous bunches to various places, flying high enough not to impede anyone's line of sight, but bobbing merrily in the moving air of the crowd and warm air blowing out of the heaters.

Guests followed almost directly behind them. Many in the crowd had taken the opportunity to wear somewhat outrageously colored suits and dresses, nearly everyone in Valentine's Day reds, pinks, and whites. People were arriving in large batches, almost entirely from the buses, and almost everyone paused and gasped as they came inside, obviously blown away, like her, by what Maddie had done with the place. Jai and Stuart had kept their guest list on the smaller side, about eighty-five people and the wedding party, but it seemed like a sizable crowd.

Three photographers swirled around the wedding party where they waited in the far corner of the barn. She felt a little like she was under the watch of the paparazzi with all the flashing lights. Some formal photos would be taken in here now as the guests enjoyed the hors d'oeuvres and cocktails, but Jai and Stuart had already told her that the process would be as brief as possible.

She and Maddie held hands between each set of photos—grooms with the full party, grooms with the maids of honor, Jai and his sisters, Jai and Stuart with the sisters, then both sets of parents and individual photos with each set of parents. All of this was over very fast, and she was excused to join the festivities. She and Maddie wandered over to the bar.

Erin and Darcy were there talking to the bartender, an employee of Erin, it so happened. The women were wearing matching red suits and white silk shirts. After exclaiming very loudly about the outfits she and Maddie were wearing, Erin pointed at the bartender.

"I was telling Phil here that this is the only place allowed to have our Valentine's Day beer for a wedding. Jai and Stuart don't know how lucky they are. We're almost sold out."

"Already?" Ryann said.

Erin laughed. "Don't worry. I gave the fellas a full keg. You can have as much of it as you want tonight."

"Don't be so sure," Maddie said. "I've seen the way Jai's family drinks."

"In that case, give this lady a beer, Phil," Erin said.

Soon all four of them were sipping Cupid's Kiss, Ryann now warm enough to enjoy it. Erin looked anxious, and she patted her arm. "It's wonderful, Erin, just like last time."

Erin's shoulders slumped, and she swiped at her brow dramatically. "Sorry. I always worry people will change their minds."

"When will you find out about the contest?" Maddie asked.

Erin frowned. "Not until tomorrow." She bit her lip. "I sure hope it's as good as you two say it is."

Darcy rolled her eyes. "Hon—you have to let people like the things you make, and you have to learn to accept their opinions. You make the best beer in the whole state, maybe the whole world."

Erin grinned and they kissed, and she and Maddie took the opportunity to sneak a quick smooch, too.

"Oh my God, you two are too, too cute," Darcy said.

"Who knew those retro outfits could look so hot?" Erin added. "I think you could walk onto the set of a BBC miniseries and replace any of the actors. Seriously."

A microphone squealed, making everyone flinch, and they all turned toward the sound. Jai's sister Janet was the MC tonight, and she waved apologetically.

"Sorry, everyone! I think we have it working now. Anyway, I'd like to introduce you all to the newest married couple in the room: Mr. and Mr. Jai and Stuart Aldridge!"

Everyone clapped and shouted in happiness.

"Jai's changing his last name?" Ryann whispered.

"Yes, he is."

She was surprised. Jai came from such a close-knit family, she'd imagined if either one was changing his name, it would be Stuart.

Still, she could appreciate the symbolism, too. As so many people had pointed out to her, Stuart was all alone out here. By changing his name, Jai wasn't necessarily leaving his family behind. They were making something new—a party of two. She started to tear up for the first time since the ceremony began and clasped Maddie's hand all the tighter, blinking hard and swallowing the lump in her throat.

Janet continued once the cheering had died down a little. "Dinner will be served shortly, so please take your seats."

The wedding party and the sisters' significant others were seated together. Their table was next to the parents', which also included the one attending grandparent and some of Jai's aunts and uncles. Nearby, Erin and Darcy sat with a group of other women, all of whom set off Ryann's gaydar, and she recognized a few of Jai's cousins here and there throughout the room. Otherwise, this was a room full of happy strangers. She was proud of Stuart for making so many new friends. Once again, she was struck by how much better things were for him here than in New York.

Everyone was given a glass of champagne or sparkling juice for the toasts later, and she decided to stick with her beer for the meal, as it went well with the steak medallions she'd chosen for her main course. Before the meal was set in front of her, she flashed back to the moment she and Maddie had chosen the food. They'd fought that day. She'd had to leave for London, and it had been difficult to tell Maddie about it. She glanced over at her, wondering if she was remembering that afternoon, too, but Maddie was talking to Jos's husband, on her right. The two of them were laughing so hard they weren't even making any noise—all squeezed up on themselves, mouths wide open, eyes pinched shut. Jos was staring at them, unamused, and when she spotted Ryann watching them, she shrugged.

"It wasn't that funny."

Jos's husband—Bill? Bob?—clapped a hand on his wife's shoulder and laughed even harder, sucking in great breaths, only to laugh some more.

"Lawyer joke?" she asked Jos.

Jos laughed. "Basically. I was just telling them about a client. He's suing a lightbulb company for getting one stuck in his ass."

She couldn't help her own bark of laughter, and soon the three of them were in near hysterics, Jos watching them with one eyebrow raised. Others at the table and the tables around them turned their way, which only set one or more of them off again.

"Ooooh," Maddie said, wiping her eyes. "Damn, that's funny."

"If you like ass jokes," Jos said, and Ryann nearly choked on her beer.

"Sorry, sorry." Jos continued. "I won't say ass again."

"Thank you." Maddie picked up her silverware. "I'd like to actually eat something."

They ate in relative silence, Ryann occasionally eavesdropping on one of the other sister's conversations but not really joining in. Despite her continued attempts to push the intrusive thoughts away, her heart dropped every time she thought about tomorrow. She could hardly glance Maddie's way, afraid, suddenly, that she would start crying.

You got yourself into this, she told herself. Suck it up.

Janet eventually excused herself to take one of the microphones up to Jai and Stuart. Since the wedding ceremony had been so impersonal, they'd saved their vows for now, and gradually the room quieted as the newlyweds stood up and moved to the front of their table, still up on the little platform so everyone could see. They were still wearing their flower crowns, and with the warm spotlight on them both, Ryann thought they looked marvelous together. Jai spoke first.

"I want to begin by thanking everyone who took a workday off for our celebration today, and especially those of you who came from far away last minute to join us in our happiness. Thanks also to our families and our wedding party for supporting us throughout this adventure."

After a smattering of applause, he turned to face his new husband.

"Stuart. When we met, exactly one year ago, I never imagined the kind of happiness I'd have here with you today. Growing up gay here wasn't easy, and that was our first connection, since you came from a similar background. Then, as I spent more time with you, I realized there was more to us than that, and more to you than your handsome face."

Stuart broke into a wide smile, and they joined hands. Jai cleared his throat and swallowed a few times before continuing.

"You are, to begin with, an amazing artist. Your work is breathtaking, and I'm proud to know that I'll be the first person to see what you create next. You're also incredibly loyal, and you're fierce in that loyalty. I pledge to you my heart, my life, and my own fierce loyalty. And I know with you that I'll be the happiest man alive."

After more wild clapping and shouting, it took a little longer for everyone to fall silent for Stuart's speech. She could tell, however, that this was a good thing, as it took a couple of minutes for him to compose himself.

During the pause, she and Maddie shared a long, piercing exchange, eyes locked. Both had tears streaming down their cheeks. Maddie grabbed her hand, squeezing it ostensibly to reassure her, but Ryann's heart sank once again despite herself. As they stared at each other, she wondered how she could have allowed herself to think that she could accept what was about to happen to them. Still, they had tonight, and she wanted to enjoy it.

Stuart cleared his throat. Even so, when he spoke, his voice was choked with emotion.

"Jai. Oh, Jai. How can I even begin to tell you what you mean to me? A year ago, when I met you, I was so alone and so…afraid. I'd moved my life here, to this funny little town, but I was still outside of it, still removed. Meeting you last Valentine's Day was like opening a window. The light came in, and I could see again."

He had to pause to wipe his face and clear his throat a few times, and Ryann heard several people around her sniffling, too.

"You are, without a doubt, the kindest, gentlest person I've ever met. In fact, when I first met you, I couldn't even believe that what I saw in you—your actions, the way you treated others and animals, and a host of other things—was the real you. I couldn't allow myself to hope there was someone like you in the world that truly liked me, too. I tried pushing you away, but that honesty—that character—that allows you to walk around in the world *actually* caring about everyone and everything, finally drew me back. Jai, I love you. I pledge to you my heart, my life, and my own attempts at honest caring. And I know with you that *I'll* be the happiest man alive."

People rocketed to their feet with applause, most everyone crying as the newlyweds kissed and embraced. A sob broke loose from her lips, and Maddie, hearing it, pulled her close under one arm. Their eyes met again, and Maddie was clearly just as overwhelmed as she was. Ryann had never been this happy about anything, possibly ever.

Some brief speeches followed. Jos spoke for Jai's side of the family, Dick for Stuart's. Jos was funny, of course, Dick touching— more than Ryann could have imagined. Once again came a chorus of sniffles and a flutter of tissues passed around, and Stuart and his father embraced for a very long time.

Finally, it was time for the first dance. Jai and Stuart had told the wedding party, their spouses and dates, and their parents to join them halfway through their song. Ryann and Maddie had been shown the signal, and they waited through the first half of an extended version of Etta James's "At Last" until Stuart made eye contact with them and touched his nose, very obviously. Maddie grabbed her hand and pulled her into a spin, and soon enough, several couples were twirling around the dance floor.

Maddie danced beautifully, of course, and Ryann's previous lessons kicked in with muscle memory, so she could keep up and occasionally flourish. The song shifted seamlessly into Elvis's "Can't Help Falling in Love," and she and Maddie stayed on the dance floor, clenched together and swaying now, not really dancing. She wanted to stay here, forever, in Maddie's arms, and the idea sent a spike of terror through her heart. She was leaving tomorrow, and they'd likely never dance again. She squeezed her harder, pinching her eyes shut against the rising tears.

"Oh, Maddie," she said, whispering into her chest.

"Hmm?"

"What are we going to do?"

Maddie stumbled slightly before finding her rhythm again. "Do? We're not going to do anything. We're going to have a perfectly lovely evening. The limo will take us to my place, and we'll have an even better time when we're alone."

She couldn't help but laugh, and when she moved back a little and looked up into Maddie's eyes, they were twinkling merrily.

"And then?"

"And then is later. We don't have to worry about that tonight. Okay?"

"Okay," she said, and she didn't.

CHAPTER TWENTY-SIX

It was one of those gray New York days that always brought Ryann down. Rain in the country could be pretty, relaxing, but in the city, it just made everything uglier, dirtier. Even here, several stories above the street, she could hear splashing water as the cars drove by, likely drenching any poor pedestrian stuck out in this downpour.

She stared out the rain-splashed window, her mind as dark and cloudy as the sky. She rarely let herself think about Maddie, which meant when she did something like this—staring out the window, sitting in an armchair at home—she was at constant war with her thoughts. Right now, she had her eyes trained on the sliver of Central Park she could see to the right. She still hadn't been there in months. Was the nut stand open in this weather? Someday soon, on a day with actual sunshine, she would get out there again, buy her honey-roasted pecans, and sit somewhere green and quiet. She'd be alone, like she always was, but at least she'd have that quiet green.

Some part of her heard the door open behind her, but she didn't turn that way, still immersed in that little glimmer of the park. The last time she'd stared outside like this, it had been snowy and white, and the loss of time was temporarily disorienting. How many weeks ago had that been? It had been before Maddie, anyway. Her life was divided now—before and after Maddie—and she wondered, without letting herself think about details, how long she would view time that way. The question was academic, anyway. It would always be after, now.

Someone cleared their throat, and she turned to find Ted standing in the doorway. He met her questioning gaze briefly and came in, closing off the sound of the bullpen as the door latched behind him.

"Sorry to interrupt," he said. He and everyone else in the office had recently begun apologizing to her all the time. She didn't think she'd treated anyone in a way that merited such a response, but on the other hand, she was well aware that she wasn't herself lately either. Not like she was before Maddie, anyway.

She waved a hand dismissively and sat down at her desk, indicating the open chair across from her. He sat, a tablet in his hands, and simply gaped at her. She saw the questions in his eyes, saw the urge there to ask them out loud, but he smiled again—that fake, boardroom smile she was so practiced with herself—and launched into the end-of-quarter update. She listened, half aware of the good news he was sharing, but not particularly affected by any of it. She should be thrilled with this news, at the very least, because everyone here stood to make a great deal of money, but she couldn't will herself to care much of anything about his report. She only realized he'd stopped talking after what must have been a very long pause, as he was fidgeting and twisting his hands together.

"Sounds good," she said. "Is that all?"

His expression went through many changes in quick succession— shock, sorrow, fright, before settling on outrage. He leapt to his feet.

"Are you kidding me right now? Jesus, Ryann. You can fire me if you have to for saying it, but it can't go on like this. What's happening right now," he gestured broadly with his hands, seeming to suggest her, the building itself, possibly the world, "it's not all right. Not by a long shot."

A flash of heated temper washed through her, and she narrowed her eyes. "Are we not making a shitload of money? Are we not doing better than we've ever done before?"

"Well, yes, but—"

"But nothing. The deal, no, *my* deal, is working flawlessly. Do you have complaints about my work beyond that?"

"No, but—"

"Good. I'm your boss, and your complaints would be baseless. My work, as always, is exemplary. We're making lots of money, we'll continue to make lots of money, and I'm already starting to formulate the next steps to make even more money. So again—I don't see the problem." She stood up and turned around to her window again. "You can leave, if you have nothing else to discuss."

She heard him huff and the stomping of feet as he made his way to the door, but she didn't hear it open. She knew without turning around that he was standing there staring at her back. She didn't look his way when she heard him approach again. He appeared in her peripheral vision as he joined her at the window. He stood next to her for a long, silent pause, his arms crossed, near enough that she could touch him. Finally, she turned his way, meeting his stern expression with her own. His anger soon softened, but her own emotions were at war once more.

"Damn, Ryann," he said, nearly whispering. "You really did a number on yourself, didn't you?"

She looked away, suddenly sure she would start crying. "I don't know what you mean."

Finally, as if he couldn't help himself, he touched her arm. She tried to keep her expression neutral, almost stern, but a rising panic, horror struck her as he peered into her eyes.

"Was it worth it, Ryann?" He asked. "Was she worth this? You're like a shadow of yourself."

She had to pinch her lips together against a sob. Apparently seeing something of this in her eyes, he pulled her closer. She collapsed against him, still managing to hold in her tears but welcoming his embrace nonetheless. He froze, momentarily, most likely with surprise, before he squeezed her against him, rubbing her back. Finally, he moved away, steering both of them to her small couch.

She sat down, still pushing her emotions away and down into herself. She squeezed her eyes closed, counting backward from ten.

You can feel like this for ten seconds, and then you have to stop, she told herself.

"I won't tell you what to do," he said when she looked at him again. "And you can be as mad at me as you like, but you can't keep on like this. You're functioning, yes. I think you could go on like this forever and still make this company money. You're good at it—you could do it in your sleep, which is basically what you're doing now. But you won't be living, not like this. You're barely here right now."

She opened her mouth to protest and then closed it, thinking about her life these last few weeks. The day after the wedding, Stuart had driven her to the airport. She and Maddie had decided that was best. In fact, she hadn't even let herself look back as she and Stuart left the hotel. She and Maddie had said good-bye as if it were something temporary, as if she were going on a trip, not leaving forever. This had happened by unspoken agreement. They hadn't had that deep talk, not at the wedding, and not after during the long, passionate night they'd shared. They both knew nothing they said would make any of it better than before. So they had one last fantastic night together, and she'd come home. They hadn't talked or contacted each other since.

She'd known she was acting different after she came back, and she'd known Ted was likely to call her on it eventually if she didn't get her life together, exactly as he was doing right now. But the enormous divide between wanting to be back to normal, back to herself before Maddie, and the way she felt right now was currently unbridgeable. She had no idea how to cross it, or even attempt to beyond what she'd been doing, trying not to think about it.

She finally met Ted's eyes, which were sympathetic and warm— perhaps the only comfort she'd gotten from anyone since she'd come home. Stuart had stopped calling, too, after she dodged his attempts for weeks. She'd left for New York and essentially left that part of her life behind forever.

She licked her lips, her mouth suddenly parched, and when she spoke, her words were hardly audible. "I don't know what to do."

He grabbed her hands and squeezed them. "Like I said, I won't tell you what to do. I know what *I* would do, but I won't even tell you that. You have to figure it out for yourself. And I know you, Ryann. Maybe not as well as Stuart or any of your close friends, but we spend a lot of time together here at the office, and I know you've been suppressing all of this. You're trying not to think about it, which means you're not really thinking at all." He let go of her hands. "So I want you to do something for me."

"What?"

"I want you to go home, right now, and let yourself think. Let yourself have your feelings and think your thoughts, just for the day."

She was tensing up, which must have been visible, as he squeezed one of her hands again. "It's only one day, Ryann."

She stared at him for a long time, seeing the honesty and genuine concern there. He was upset—far more than she could ever have expected of him. She thought back to their moment together in that beautiful pub in London all those weeks ago, recognizing an echo between that moment and this. Ted cared for her, and not only as his employer. He cared about her as a person. Whatever he'd suggested, he meant it for her good.

Finally, she agreed. "Okay. I'll do it."

She stood up, ready to start gathering her things, and he stood with her, grabbing her arm and squeezing it, almost roughly.

"I mean it, Ryann. Think about things. Really think about them— don't deflect, no matter how upsetting you find it. Promise me you'll try."

She hesitated. "I promise, Ted."

Half an hour later, she greeted the doorman at her apartment building and got into the elevator. She stood there, brain fogged and dazed, staring at the buttons for a long time before remembering to push the one for her floor. The doors shut, closing off the view of the curious doorman, who had apparently watched her stand there as she did nothing. She saw his head whip forward again when she noticed him watching.

Her apartment was incredibly dark for this time of day, and it was on a high enough floor that the fog was starting to close off the world outside the windows. She stood by the door for a while, wondering what to do with herself, before finally remembering her dripping coat. She hung it in the closet, dropped her purse and keys onto the little seat by the door, and kicked off her heels, not caring, for once, if she ruined her stockings. She changed into a tracksuit, some of her only nonwork clothes, and made herself an espresso in her dark kitchen.

Like in her office building, she could usually see a little patch of the park from her floor-to-ceiling windows, but the fog made that impossible today. She sat down on her loveseat, looking around the darkened room, at a loss with what to do with herself. She remembered Ted's edict—to let herself think about things with Maddie—but she was having a hard time letting herself do exactly that. She shied away from any thoughts of her, or Stuart, or Colorado, almost as if her mind had its own plans and agenda. She'd been training herself, after all, not to indulge during all these lonely weeks.

Ever since she'd been back in the city, she'd simply gone to work and come home, staying as late as she could and putting in weekend hours with some of her colleagues. It had been necessary at first—she simply had so much to do. But now, not so much. She could go into the office, certainly, and she found it easier to void her mind of worries with all the silly minutiae of running a business, but her work, and the deal she'd brokered, was now running itself. The last time she'd been in a holding pattern like this between big projects, she'd taken a vacation, but the idea of going anywhere right now held no appeal. After all, if she could choose to go anywhere, she knew exactly where she'd choose.

She frowned. She was being stupid. She could fly to Colorado at the end of this summer, or maybe at the holidays, but certainly not sooner than that. She needed more time to allow some of these feelings to fade.

A chime sounded somewhere in her apartment, and after a moment, she recognized the tone—a text message on her phone. She so rarely checked her messages, it took her a moment to remember that she'd left the phone in her nightstand.

Her bedroom was even darker than the living room, and she almost tripped on a stray nylon, cursing it and herself for her earlier carelessness. She opened the nightstand to see a preview of the text pop up on her screen. She opened the message fully.

Delta Flight 2555, JFK to DIA
Departs 5:25 pm April 3
Arrives 8:05 pm April 3

Below this were her passenger details in a business-class seat. The sender seemed to be anonymous—no phone number attached—as if it had been sent by a machine. As she read the message, over and over, trying to make sense of it, she saw the little ellipses appear at the bottom of the screen, indicating another message was incoming.

Your driver, BILL, *will arrive at 3:00 pm to transport you from* YOUR ADDRESS *to the* DELTA TERM. JFK.

A few seconds later, her address appeared with a phone number for her driver, Bill. Once again she puzzled over this message, struggling to make sense of it all.

Only one person knew she was home right now, which meant only one person could have arranged the flight and driver. She closed her message app and called Ted, but the line continued to ring long enough that his answering message played. She called again, but the same thing happened. After trying a third time, she sat down heavily on her bed, her phone lying loosely in her lap, her legs liquid and weak.

As she sat there, a powerful emotion was mounting inside her—something she didn't recognize for several seconds. Her heart was racing, and she was hot, overheated, and shaken. A sob escaped her lips, and she clapped her hands over her mouth to hold it in. Tears sprang from the corners of her eyes, and she made herself stand up, stomping one foot theatrically.

"No, goddamn it! I will not let myself be railroaded into—"

Into what, exactly? she wondered, her mouth snapping closed. Into doing exactly what I want to do? Going exactly where I want to go?

She was breathing heavily, still shaking all over, but she finally recognized the feelings cascading through her: exultation, happiness, relief, and hope—all in equal measure, and all so entirely overwhelming, she almost collapsed on the bed again. She laughed, a brief hysterical chirp, and then made herself stop, slapping her hands over her mouth, suddenly afraid that if she started laughing, she'd never be able to stop.

She checked her watch, realizing that her driver would be here in less than half an hour, and started toward her armoire, pausing only when she remembered that most of her clothes were in storage in the basement. She kept her work clothes here in her bedroom, and a couple of tracksuits for her workouts, but even in her big-for-New York apartment, she simply didn't have space enough to keep everything in her bedroom. She laughed and dismissed this problem, grabbed her coat, a hat, and a bigger purse for her makeup and toothbrush before leaving and heading for the lobby, hoping, for once, that her driver would show up early. Now that she'd decided to leave, she didn't want to wait a moment more.

❖

"Welcome to Denver!" the voice on the train said, followed by a funny, country-western-style guitar riff.

Ryann checked her phone and the time again, her anxiety rising. When she'd first landed, she'd hoped that, like he'd done in New York, Ted would have arranged a car service for her, but she saw no new messages when she'd turned on her phone. Her flight had been delayed, of course, and it was now closer to ten in the evening. She had no idea if the car-rental agencies were on site or off, but she was worried that if she got there too late, they'd either be closed or out of cars. Her flight here had been packed—lots of tourists heading here for spring break, she supposed, if they were anything like her boisterous seatmates. Both had spent the majority of the five-hour flight discussing the best place to buy pot. She'd be battling it out with the new-age hippies for the last car on the lot. Still, she decided, just in case, to check the Delta baggage claim for a driver with one of those paper placards, as the message might have been lost when her phone was off.

Finally, the train pulled into the terminal, and she once again used her New York skills to push her way through to the front, not one person fighting back or even complaining. She ran to the escalator, walking up it as quickly as she could. Then, spotting the signs for the Delta baggage area, she raced that way, power walking through the milling friends and families reuniting by the roped-off security checkpoint.

"Ryann!" someone called.

She didn't immediately react. The name was common enough, but the next time someone called her name, she turned.

Maddie stood there some ten feet away, clutching an enormous bouquet of red roses. Her hair had grown longer in the last few weeks— no longer a neat pompadour, but messy and clearly in need of a trim. She looked a little wan, too, perhaps a little thinner, and her tan was even more faded than it had been in February.

They stood there, simply staring at each other in the midst of a few hundred people bustling around them. Ryann's heart was pounding so hard and fast, she felt a little light-headed.

"What—what are you doing here?" she asked, moving one step forward.

Maddie laughed. "I'm here for you, of course. Someone named Ted texted me, and so I bought the ticket—"

"You did?"

Maddie nodded, finally stepping forward, too. Like Ryann, she stopped, as if uncertain whether to come closer. "I didn't know if you were going to come. I've been waiting here for hours just hoping, I guess. I just...I had to try, you know?"

She ran then, launching herself at Maddie just as she dropped the bouquet and held out her arms. Maddie caught her, twirling her around and laughing. She had never doubted that she would catch her. Maddie's sweet vanilla scent flooded her nose, and then they were kissing. They kissed as if it were the only thing keeping them alive, as if the very act were keeping them breathing, their hearts beating. In many ways, it was. She felt herself come back to life, her spirits lifting with her racing heart rate.

They finally pulled away, if only to breathe, Maddie setting her gently back on the ground. Then both of them were laughing at the other's expression.

"God, I missed you," Maddie said, running her fingers along her jawline.

"Me, too. I love you, Maddie. I never wanted—"

Maddie kissed her again, gripping the sides of her face with strong fingers. She drew back, her eyes wild and dark.

"I love you, too, Ryann. And I know you didn't want to hurt me. I didn't want to hurt you, either. I promise I'll never do that to you again."

"I promise, too. If you'll have me—"

Maddie laughed before kissing her forehead, cheeks, nose, and then lips again. "You have *me*, Ryann—anyway, anytime, anywhere."

They stood there, foreheads together, breathing each other in, eyes closed, the world swirling around them without notice.

"Fucking finally," Stuart said, startling them both. He and Jai stood a few feet away, their faces tear-streaked and joyous.

"No shit," Jai said, choking back a sob. "It's about damn time."

"We did this on purpose, you know," Stuart added, motioning between them.

Jai bobbed his head up and down, grinning. "Yep. We set you up."

"And it worked."

"Though it took you long enough," Jai said. "We wanted a double wedding."

Maddie and Ryann laughed before wiping their wet cheeks, neither of them in the least bit angered by this claim.

"Then I guess I owe you one, Jai," Maddie said.

"Me, too, Stuart," Ryann said. "I owe you my whole life."

Jai and Stuart left them alone for a few minutes after that, but Ryann hardly noticed their departure. She was too lost in Maddie's lips.

EPILOGUE

R yann twitched in her seat again, her stomach bubbling with nerves. "My God, would you calm down? We'll get there when we get there," Stuart said.

She stared at the side of his face, evenly, long enough for him to glance over at her in the passenger's seat. "What? Why are you staring at me?"

"'We'll get there when we get there'?" she repeated. "We're already ten minutes late!"

"Oh, pish," he said, flapping a hand briefly at her like at a fly. "It doesn't matter."

"Of course it matters! We paid for two hours. We're losing time and money while you drive," she leaned forward to peer at the dashboard, "exactly the speed limit."

"You sound like Jai," he said. Jai was the scheduler of the two of them, and she had learned he hated being late even more than she did. "But they can wait. Safety is always the priority."

She snorted. "Okay, Grandma. Listen, if you're not up for driving on the highway, just pull over and let me. Look at all the cars passing us!"

He didn't look her way, but the car picked up speed a little, the old engine chugging a bit louder.

"Thanks," she muttered. She leaned back into her seat a little, trying to force herself to relax.

"It's okay, Ryann. I promise. You should chill out a little. Nicole is Maddie's friend. She won't mind staying a little longer, and we're almost there now—ten, fifteen minutes tops."

Maddie had hired Nicole to take the photos today, but the fact that she was a friend made their lateness more awkward, in her opinion. She hated being late mostly because she hated making anyone wait for her, especially a friend, even if she was Maddie's friend, not hers.

She finally saw their exit for Loveland and made herself let out a long, deep breath. Stuart glanced her way again, grinning, and grabbed her hand when they had to wait at the light off the exit.

"Are you ready for this?"

She shook her head without hesitating, and he laughed.

"Well, you should be," he said. "Maddie's crazy about you. She'd wait a thousand years for you if you asked."

She knew this intellectually, but she was still crawling with nerves, her heart hammering, her fingers trembling. Something about today made all of this more real. Maddie had proposed a little over a week ago, on Groundhog Day, of all times. Last summer, when she moved to Colorado full time, she'd admitted to Maddie that she didn't grow up celebrating any holidays. Both of her parents traveled a lot for work, so they usually had an excuse, but, in retrospect, they either didn't care or bother to keep anyone but themselves in mind. Maddie had taken her history as a personal challenge, and ever since, they'd celebrated every holiday, major and minor, lavishly and without irony. Groundhog Day had been a surprise, however, as she hadn't even realized it was a thing outside of, perhaps, Punxsutawney. However, Maddie's family celebrated by baking a groundhog-shaped cake and watching the Bill Murray film, and she had been there with them to celebrate. The credits were rolling when Maddie got down on one knee.

Today was Valentine's Day, and she and Maddie were doing their engagement photos at Erin's brewery—exactly a year from the day they planned to get married. Her new office was in Denver, which was an awful commute, but workable in the short term. Ted was splitting his time between Denver and New York, but she was fairly certain he would be joining her here full time, soon. All in all, at least on the work front, she felt pretty set. She planned to open a branch of her new business in Fort Collins or Boulder and transition herself there in the next couple of years, but Denver was functioning for now.

Or at least it was until her car broke down this morning. Maddie couldn't cancel her classes, so Stuart volunteered to pick her up.

"Hey," he said, squeezing her hand again. "You really don't have to be nervous. Try to have fun, okay? You look gorgeous, by the way. Only you could make that shirt look designer. I'm sure the camera will love you, as always. I honestly think you're the most attractive person in our wedding album. You make the rest of us look like extras in a rom-com—cute, but a little uglier than the star."

"Thanks," she said, smiling down at her shirt. It was a red flannel, a match to what Maddie would be wearing. She hadn't lasted long before the flannel bug caught her, too. Two months living here in Colorado, and she'd given away most of her old clothes.

"I'm so glad I set the two of you up," he said. He said this only to get a rise out of her, and she swatted his arm. "Hey! It's true, you know."

"Sure, sure." She rolled her eyes. "And you'll never let it down."

"I'm going to be telling your grandkids about setting up you two."

"Asshole."

They both laughed, the last of her nervousness lifting. The light changed, and he had to drive again, but as she watched the side of his face, she was struck once again by how much she loved him. Her own family hadn't replied when she'd sent them the news about her engagement, but that hurt less than she'd feared. This man was the only family she needed. She and Maddie had already decided they would have only their two best friends—Stuart and Jai—as their wedding party next year. They were enough.

"So what did you get Maddie for Valentine's Day?" he asked.

She flinched. It hadn't even occurred to her to buy something. Stuart, evidently confused by her silence, looked her way and frowned.

"You didn't get her anything?"

"I, no, I didn't know I should—"

He laughed. "Oh, come on. Even you would know you should give something to your sweetie on Valentine's. I mean, my God, they call it Valentine's Day. You should have at least gotten her a valentine."

"What did you get Jai?"

"Well, that's more complicated. Since it's also our anniversary, I had to go a bit bigger than I might normally. My friend Rita does these really beautiful paper cutouts. First-anniversary presents are traditionally paper, so I commissioned a piece from her. I went back and forth with the subject but decided on cats, since he's such a cat nut. The cats are at Pemberley—you know, Mr. Darcy's place?—having tea. He's going to love it."

She was struck by his confidence. She'd bought Maddie two major presents so far—one for her birthday and one for Christmas—and both times she'd triple-guessed herself to the point that the entire experience of giving the gifts to her had been ruined. Maddie had claimed to like both, but she hadn't and still didn't believe her. Apparently gift-giving wasn't one of Ryann's strong suits.

"What can I buy last-minute?" she asked.

He laughed. "You mean, like now? Here, in the car, five minutes from seeing her?"

"I have my phone. I could have something overnighted and show her a picture now."

He tapped the steering wheel. "Uh, you could book a romantic getaway. You know her schedule pretty well, so being spontaneous shouldn't be a problem. Or you could—"

"No, no—I don't need more choices. That's a good one. Where and how long?"

"She really loves Glenwood Springs and Estes Park. Either would be easy, since the two of you could just leave after work sometime. Drive there on a Friday after her studio hours and come back on a Sunday. That way, no one needs to take any time off."

"Done," she said, two minutes later, just as they pulled into a parking spot.

He laughed. "You're ridiculous. You know that?"

Her stomach dropped, and she stared out the window, fighting tears. They sat there in silence for a long time before he touched the back of her hand, appearing a little guilty.

"I'm sorry," he said. "I didn't mean to make you feel inadequate."

She laughed, weakly, brushing at her eyes. "No—you're right. I am ridiculous. I don't even know how to buy a present for the woman I love."

He squeezed her hand. "Hey. Stop that. She knows you love her even without a present. I mean, Jesus, you basically gave your former life away to be with her. She damn well better appreciate that, if nothing else. You have a few years to get better at gift-giving with that sacrifice in your pocket."

She laughed and squeezed his arm. "Thanks. I needed that."

"Good. Don't you dare forget that woman loves you no matter what. Now let's get inside before Jai kills both of us."

The brewery was packed, partly because Erin had roped off a little area for the photos, thereby lessening the usual space for customers, but it was like this in here nearly every night of the week, every day of the year. She and Maddie had visited almost every brewery within an hour's drive, and even without the bias of knowing the owner, she could claim this was the absolute best beer she'd had, and clearly the regulars agreed.

The Valentine's decorations in here were a little more over the top than she remembered from last year, with heart-shaped red, pink, and white streamers draped from corner to corner and the walls festooned with giant red wooden conversation hearts and paper cutouts of cupids. A large canvas banner hung over the bar announcing that they had last year's award-winning Cupid's Kiss on tap for a limited time. Everyone would learn sometime tomorrow if this year's entry, Sweetheart Stout, would net Erin's brewery a second Fire and Ice Festival win.

"There they are!" Erin shouted, spotting them and waving wildly.

"About damn time," Jai called their way, a hand cupped around his mouth.

The crowd was nice enough to let them through, several people smiling and greeting them as they made their way to the far corner. Ryann finally saw Maddie, seated at one of the little tables there—exactly the same table where they'd first met. She was relieved she didn't look at all put out by her lateness. Why she'd ever worried was another question entirely, but she couldn't think about that now when Maddie was moving toward her, warm and inviting with her strong arms ready to pull her in. The kiss was sweet and went on a little too long, several of their friends and some strangers in the bar hooting and whistling at them.

"You made it," Maddie said when they drew back. She still held her in her arms, her warm hands sending little trilling shivers up her back.

"I know. I'm sorry. Stuart drives like a—"

"A grandma—I know. Anyway, it's no problem. Nicole and I were just catching up." She pointed at a woman with a camera bag standing next to Darcy. She waved briefly. "She's not in any hurry."

She sagged with relief. "Oh, thank God. I thought for sure we'd run out of time."

"Again, not a problem. That's why it's nice to work with friends."

She moved forward to join their friends, but Maddie pulled her into a tight embrace again. Their friends were all gathered several feet away, all of them wrapped up in their own conversations.

"Hey, wait a minute," Maddie said. "I haven't had my fill of you yet, and this might be our only moment alone tonight."

She sighed and nestled in closer to her chest, breathing in that sweet scent of vanilla Maddie used on her clothes. The scent was hers now, and nothing and no one else's. Now when she caught a whiff of vanilla out in the world, it recalled only Maddie and warmth and love.

"And also," Maddie said, grinning down at her, "I want my present."

She swatted Maddie's arm. "Hey! What about mine?"

Maddie leaned closer, her lips brushing her ear. "It's at home. I'll show you tonight."

She shivered, flushing with heat. Maddie, catching this response, grinned more broadly, more wickedly, but she couldn't find it in herself to reply offhandedly. Maddie still managed to unsettle her like this nearly every day.

She licked her lips. "Okay. I can wait. But only if we leave right after this."

"Deal," Maddie said, beaming. "Now give me mine." She opened and closed her hands like a greedy child.

She pretended to delay, watching Maddie's face fall, before laughing and swatting her arm.

"You thought I forgot, didn't you?"

Maddie hesitated before nodding. "I guess I did. I'm sorry. I shouldn't have doubted you."

"Well, Stuart was nice enough to remind me, so you're half right. Anyway, we're staying at the Hotel Colorado the first weekend in March, and we're taking the train through the mountains to Glenwood Springs from Denver."

"Wow!" Maddie said. "That's amazing! What a good idea."

Maddie kissed her then, and she finally knew what it meant to give the right gift, as Maddie's enthusiasm on her birthday and Christmas had been nothing like this. She would always book trips as presents if it meant this kind of response.

"Okay," Maddie said. "Thanks again. I can't wait to go."

"Me, too."

"I guess we need to finally take some engagement photos," Maddie said. "Shall we?"

Maddie was holding her hand with one of hers, the other indicating Nicole and her cameras, but she was caught for a moment at what all this meant. Moving forward, moving into the circle of their friends and starting this whole wedding process meant moving forward with her life with Maddie. Engagement photos were just the beginning. Soon they'd be booking their wedding venues and services, and, as they'd already planned, looking for a bigger place to live. Moving forward meant that all of this was finally real. Her future was finally here.

"Let's get started," she said.

About the Author

Charlotte was born in a tiny mountain town and spent most of her childhood and young adulthood in a small city in Northern Colorado. While she is usually what one might generously call "indoorsy," early exposure to the Rocky Mountains led to a lifelong love of nature, hiking, and camping.

After a lengthy education in Denver, New Orleans, Washington, DC, and New York, she earned a doctorate in literature and women and gender studies. She currently lives with her wife, son, and their cat in a small city in Wisconsin.

Charlotte is a two-time Golden Crown Literary Society "Goldie" Winner for *Gnarled Hollow* and *Legacy*, and a finalist for a Lambda Literary Award for *Gnarled Hollow*.

Books Available From Bold Strokes Books

Always by Kris Bryant. When a pushy American private investigator shows up demanding to meet the woman in Camila's artwork, instead of introducing her to her great-grandmother, Camila decides to lead her on a wild goose chase all over Italy. (978-1-63679-027-5)

Exes and O's by Joy Argento. Ali and Madison really only have one thing in common. The girl who broke their heart may be the only one who can put it back together. (978-1-63679-017-6)

Paris Rules by Jaime Maddox. Carly Becker has been searching for the perfect woman all her life, but no one ever seems to be just right until Paige Waterford checks all her boxes, except the most important one—she's married. (978-1-63679-077-0)

Shadow Dancers by Suzie Clarke. In this third and final book in the Moon Shadow series, Rachel must find a way to become the hunter and not the hunted, and this time she will meet Ehsee Yumiko head-on. (978-1-63555-829-6)

The Kiss by C.A. Popovich. When her wife refuses their divorce and begins to stalk her, threatening her life, Kate realizes to protect her new love, Leslie, she has to let her go, even if it breaks her heart. (978-1-63679-079-4)

The Wedding Setup by Charlotte Greene. When Ryann, a big-time New York executive, goes to Colorado to help out with her best friend's wedding, she never expects to fall for the maid of honor. (978-1-63679-033-6)

Velocity by Gun Brooke. Holly and Claire work toward an uncertain future preparing for an alien space mission, and only one thing is certain—they will have to risk their lives, and their hearts, to discover the truth. (978-1-63555-983-5)

Wildflower Words by Sam Ledel. Lida Jones treks west with her father in search of a better life on the rapidly developing American frontier, but finds home when she meets Hazel Thompson. (978-1-63679-055-8)

A Fairer Tomorrow by Kathleen Knowles. For Maddie Weeks and Gerry Stern, the Second World War brought them together, but the end of the war might rip them apart. (978-1-63555-874-6)

Changing Majors by Ana Hartnett Reichardt. Beyond a love, beyond a coming-out, Bailey Sullivan discovers what lies beyond the shame and self-doubt imposed on her by traditional Southern ideals. (978-1-63679-081-7)

Highland Whirl by Anna Larner. Opposites attract in the Scottish Highlands, when feisty Alice Campbell falls for city girl about town Roxanne Barns. (978-1-63555-892-0)

Holiday Hearts by Diana Day-Admire and Lyn Cole. Opposites attract during Christmastime chaos in Kansas City. (978-1-63679-128-9)

Humbug by Amanda Radley. With the corporate Christmas party in jeopardy, CEO Rosalind Caldwell hires Christmas Girl Ellie Pearce as her personal assistant. The only problem is, Ellie isn't a PA, has never planned a party, and develops a ridiculous crush on her totally intimidating new boss. (978-1-63555-965-1)

On the Rocks by Georgia Beers. Schoolteacher Vanessa Martini makes no apologies for her dating checklist, and newly single mom Grace Chapman ticks all Vanessa's Do Not Date boxes. Of course, they're never going to fall in love. (978-1-63555-989-7)

Song of Serenity by Brey Willows. Arguing with the Muse of music and justice is complicated, falling in love with her even more so. (978-1-63679-015-2)

The Christmas Proposal by Lisa Moreau. Stranded together in a Christmas village on a snowy mountain, Grace and Bridget face their past and question their dreams for the future. (978-1-63555-648-3)

The Infinite Summer by Morgan Lee Miller. While spending the summer with her dad in a small beach town, Remi Brenner falls for Harper Hebert and accidentally finds herself tangled up in an intense restaurant rivalry between her famous stepmom and her first love. (978-1-63555-969-9)

Wisdom by Jesse J. Thoma. When Sophia and Reggie are chosen for the governor's new community design team and tasked with tackling substance abuse and mental health issues, battle lines are drawn even as sparks fly. (978-1-63555-886-9)

A Convenient Arrangement by Aurora Rey and Jaime Clevenger. Cuffing season has come for lesbians, and for Jess Archer and Cody Dawson, their convenient arrangement becomes anything but. (978-1-63555-818-0)

An Alaskan Wedding by Nance Sparks. The last thing either Andrea or Riley expects is to bump into the one who broke her heart fifteen years ago, but when they meet at the welcome party, their feelings come rushing back. (978-1-63679-053-4)

Beulah Lodge by Cathy Dunnell. It's 1874, and newly betrothed Ruth Mallowes is set on marriage and life as a missionary...until she falls in love with the housemaid at Beulah Lodge. (978-1-63679-007-7)

Gia's Gems by Toni Logan. When Lindsey Speyer discovers that popular travel columnist Gia Williams is a complete fake and threatens to expose her, blackmail has never been so sexy. (978-1-63555-917-0)

Holiday Wishes & Mistletoe Kisses by M. Ullrich. Four holidays, four couples, four chances to make their wishes come true. (978-1-63555-760-2)

Love By Proxy by Dena Blake. Tess has a secret crush on her best friend, Sophie, so the last thing she wants is to help Sophie fall in love with someone else, but how can she stand in the way of her happiness? (978-1-63555-973-6)

Marry Me by Melissa Brayden. Allison Hale attempts to plan the wedding of the century to a man who could save her family's business, if only she wasn't falling for her wedding planner, Megan Kinkaid. (978-1-63555-932-3)

Pathway to Love by Radclyffe. Courtney Valentine is looking for a woman exactly like Ben—smart, sexy, and not in the market for anything serious. All she has to do is convince Ben that sex-without-strings is the perfect pathway to pleasure. (978-1-63679-110-4)